Heathcliff
The Lost Years

A Novel

DAVID DRUM

Burning Books Press
Los Angeles

First print edition ISBN # 978-0-9911857-7-1.
Library of Congress Control Number:2019905374

Cover design by Karrie Ross, KarrieRoss.com
Cover illustration of Heathcliff and Catherine courtesy
toby guerre

WWW.HEATHCLIFFTHELOSTYEARS.COM

Burning Books Press
Los Angeles

For You

ILLUSTRATIONS

1. Heathcliff and Catherine, a drawing by toby guerre.

2. William Green, "A View of the Old Docks of Liverpool," 1799. Courtesy Liverpool Record Office, Liverpool Libraries.

3. "Negroland and Guinea with the European Settlements," map, 1736. Wikimedia Commons.

4. "A group of men and women being taken to a slave market." Courtesy Wellcome Libraries, London, England. Wellcome Images. Creative Commons Attribution 4.0 International licence.

5. "A View of the Sea on the Morning after the Storm, with the distressed situation of the Centaur, Ville de Paris and the Glorieux as seen from the Lady Juliana, the Ville de Paris passing to Windward under close reef'd Topsails," February 17, 1783, John Harris; Robert Dodd; Robert Sayer and John Bennett. Wikimedia Commons.

6. "King Street, Kingston", illustration of article "Cast-away in Jamaica" by W.E. Sewell, in *Harper's Monthly Magazine,* January 1861. Wikimedia Commons.

7. "Gin Lane," from *Beer Street and Gin Lane.*" 1750-1751. By William Hogarth, etching and line engraving, Wikimedia Commons.

Heathcliff's Lost Years

In Emily Bronte's classic English novel, an adopted gypsy child named Heathcliff must flee his home in Wuthering Heights penniless, and with a broken heart.

Heathcliff returns in three years, a ferociously changed man.

How Heathcliff changed from stable boy to gentleman is one of literature's unsolved mysteries.

This is the story of those lost three years.

Wuthering Heights

Chapter 1

As the house-master's cane sailed down, the boy felt a movement in the air, as if from the wing of a small bird. Then Mr. Hatchett struck him. A wave of pain rang through his skull like a loud brass bell ringing.

"Head down," snapped the house-master. "Keep working."

To be hit again shocked and infuriated the boy. He didn't deserve it. He scowled. He looked down. Only the weak lads cried, and he refused to do it. He took a deep breath, lifted up a section of rope, and began picking it apart with his small, calloused fingers.

"Dirty gypsy," hissed a pale-skinned lad. "Serves you right."

"Go to the Devil," the boy replied.

Mr. Hatchett slapped the work-bench with his rattan cane.

"Attend to your work," he said. "All of you."

The room fell silent.

The pale-skinned lads had long ago taken a dislike to the boy's dark skin and black, wavy hair. When the house-master was gone, they skittered about him like yapping dogs, taunting him, calling him a dirty gypsy, and claiming his gypsy parents sold him away.

HEATHCLIFF: THE LOST YEARS

For a long time, the boy could imagine no end to life in the work-house. But as he grew older, he noticed boys sold into service on ships, and boys running away.

Every morning, Mr. Hatchett unlocked the dormitory and herded the orphans into the kitchen for breakfast. After the morning meal, their tall, thin-lipped caretaker marched them into the work-room. They all took their places at the work-bench and spent the day pulling apart stiff dry ropes to make oakum. After evening prayers, the house-master marched them back into the dormitory, watched them unroll their pallets on the floor, and locked the door for the night.

The dormitory was infested with rats. Each night, the boy dreaded the sight of them multiplying out of the walls like a stream of dark, dirty water. The afternoon he dared complain about the rats, the house-master caned him so severely his shoulders rang with pain.

That night, as he tried to sleep, a rat skittered onto his pallet. He slapped it with the back of his hand. The rodent clung to his fingers. It sunk its claws into his flesh and wouldn't let go. Terrified and frantic, the boy finally shook the hideous creature off and sent it sailing across the room.

"Mr. Hatchett!" someone wailed, but nobody came.

The boy lay awake in the crowded, foul-smelling dormitory, licking blood from the back of his hand and despising them all.

A soft rain began falling. Raindrops pattered against the window-panes like angelic voices, calling him away.

Droplets of rain kissed his face when he pushed up a small window, squeezed through, and dropped into the alley. A horse and carriage splashed past on the streets.

Without looking back, the boy scurried away from the work-house, the welts on his body drenched and soothed by the gently-falling rain.

He found no shelter on the cold, wet streets of the little seaport. At last, he saw a flash of light through an open carriage-house door.

He stepped into the doorway, dripping wet. He listened warily to the stamping and snorting of the carriage horses. When he was certain he was alone, he pulled together a pile of straw, and lay down. He fell asleep listening to water trickle down the cobblestone streets of Liverpool on its way to the sea.

For days, he scurried about the city like a homeless animal. He found scraps of food behind bakeries, butcher-shops, and inns. He stole from push-carts. When he could find no food, he begged.

One morning he put out his hand to a kindly country gentleman in a greatcoat and top hat, the sort of gentleman who sometimes threw him a penny. Old Earnshaw bent at the waist and looked him squarely in the eye. When he asked the boy a series of kindly questions, the boy blurted out all he knew of his life.

Old Earnshaw's face visibly softened. He took the boy's hand.

"Come with me, lad," he said. "I shall take you home."

The voice of Old Earnshaw quieting the dogs stirred him awake in the darkness. The boy remembered setting off for a walk in Liverpool. When he could walk no farther, Old Earnshaw wrapped him in his greatcoat and carried him until, finally, he fell asleep.

"I'll not hear any criticism of this," came Old Earnshaw's voice, as they apparently entered a house. "I've walked much too far and I am tired. I would not have another walk like that for the three kingdoms."

Before he sat down, Old Earnshaw opened up his greatcoat and set the boy on his feet before the hearth.

The boy rubbed his eyes and looked into the faces dancing before him in the firelight.

"I knocked on doors all over Liverpool but I could not find who owned this child," Old Earnshaw said. "I had little time. I thought it best to bring him home."

He then turned to his wife with a kind, knowing expression. "We shall call him Heathcliff," he said.

"The name of our lost child," said Mrs. Earnshaw, with quavering voice. "The infant God snatched away from us the day he was born."

HEATHCLIFF: THE LOST YEARS

"Attend to the lad, Nelly," Old Earnshaw said.

A female servant bustled forward to take the boy's hand.

"Heathcliff," she said. "Come along."

As Nelly led him away, the boy saw the Earnshaw children going through the pockets of their father's greatcoat, looking for presents. Nelly took him into the kitchen, washed him up with soap and water, and dressed him for bed. But when she tried to put him into bed with the two Earnshaw children, both vigorously protested.

"No!" cried young Catherine. "He shall not sleep in my bed!"

"Father should not bring that terrible creature into our house," said her older brother, Hindley. "He has no place here, Nelly."

"I shan't permit it!" Catherine cried, standing up on the bed in her night-gown. "No! Take him away!"

Muttering to herself, Nelly fixed the boy a place to sleep on the landing of the stairs, made him comfortable, and bid him good-night.

The boy could not sleep. He watched the fire die in the hearth. Wind whistled ominously down the chimney. The creaky old house seemed alive with frightful, popping sounds.

In the middle of the night, he heard the comforting voice of Old Earnshaw.

The sound of it drew the boy crawling quickly up the stairway, pulling his bedding behind him. He lay down outside Old Earnshaw's bedroom door, wrapped himself in a blanket, and waited to hear his benefactor's voice again.

Chapter 2

The next morning, Nelly took Heathcliff into the parlor. Old Earnshaw placed him between Catherine and Hindley on one of the curved wooden benches he'd arranged in a half-circle around the hearth. When he taught their lessons, the master of Wuthering Heights made something of a game out of educating his children.

Old Earnshaw ended his lessons by reading aloud from one of his leather-bound books. While he read, he paused to show the children illustrations of strange animals and plants, tall sailing ships, and exotic peoples who inhabited distant lands.

When he closed the book, Old Earnshaw delighted in asking the children to tell him what they had learned. Heathcliff quickly caught on. After a few lessons, he eagerly began to respond.

"What did you learn to-day?" Old Earnshaw asked.

"You read us a tale of darkest Africa," Heathcliff cried. "The land of crocodiles and cannibals."

"And lions!" Cathy immediately added. "Lions, too."

"Heathcliff is even quicker to respond than you, Cathy," said Old Earnshaw. "To-day, I believe the lad might answer any question I could pose."

HEATHCLIFF: THE LOST YEARS

During lessons, and when he sat down for meals with the family, Heathcliff felt he had been spirited away to a safe, enchanted land.

But for much of the day, neither of the Earnshaw children would play with him. He had not been around many girls, and Catherine seemed as cold and distant as the winter hills. Her brother Hindley was disdainful and aloof, and he could be mean. When they were alone, and he tried to approach Hindley, the older lad shoved Heathcliff away. Even the self-righteous old male servant Joseph looked down his nose at young Heathcliff from time to time.

One evening at dinner, Heathcliff noticed Catherine repeatedly glancing at him, as if trying not to stare at a dangerous but fascinating animal in a zoo. Bravely, the boy ventured a smile. Young Catherine smirked; he caught her staring; she quickly turned away. Her pretty face turned bright red.

A moment later, Catherine kicked him under the table. He knew it was her. Something leapt alive inside him; joy swept through him like a gust of warm wind. Heathcliff smiled at her again. Catherine kicked him under the table a second time, looked away, and they both burst into spontaneous, uninhibited laughter.

"Spare us your foolishness, Catherine," Hindley said. "Father, we really must allow no more of this."

Old Earnshaw and his wife said nothing. When Heathcliff excused himself from the table, Catherine's older brother watched him leave the room with glowering disdain.

In the parlor, Heathcliff took one of Old Earnshaw's books down from the shelf and opened it, as he had been given permission to do. He sat before the hearth and began trying to read.

He did not hear Catherine slip into the room. When he looked up, she could have been a disembodied spirit, her face and hands sparkling and shimmering in the light of the golden flames. Catherine rubbed her hands together for a long time without looking at Heathcliff. At last, she showed her small white teeth in an enigmatic smile.

"Hindley told me I must never have anything to do with you, Heathcliff," young Catherine confided to him, her eyes twinkling. "But I don't care what my brother wants. I shall do exactly as I please."

Chapter 3

When spring finally arrived at Wuthering Heights, Catherine drew Heathcliff outside. Out past the fields, when they could no longer see the house, she led him on wild scampers across the heath. Somewhat timidly, Heathcliff followed her up and down low, grass-covered hills, through brooks and becks, and out to the bogs and marshes. His wild-eyed new friend was nimble as a goat. At first, Heathcliff could not keep up with her but before the end of the summer, he could run as quickly as she.

One summer afternoon, exhilarated by his new strength, Heathcliff sprinted toward the top of a high, heather-covered hill. Halfway up, he heard Catherine scream. He stopped. He looked behind him.

Catherine dramatically clutched her chest.

"Heathcliff, stop!" she wailed. "My heart will break!"

Fearful and worried, he stumbled back down the hill. When he reached her, Catherine sat down on the ground, flung out her arms, and then laughed like an imp because she had tricked him.

"Heathcliff, you must never, ever run away from me," Catherine said. "I shall not allow it."

Catherine bounced to her feet, broke into a run, and scampered away.

Catherine was more than a friend. Instinctively and completely, he trusted her. They were inseparable. He felt he had known her forever.

Old Earnshaw sometimes took Heathcliff out with the dogs to hunt and trap game, times that he relished. And Catherine was always awaiting his return, ready to greet him with a hug and girlish kisses.

His pretty new companion lectured him incessantly, tickled him, laughed at him, and let him laugh at her. Twice she led him into a graveyard, where they tried to call up spirits. When winter confined them to the house, she could throw a length of cloth over a piece of furniture, turn it into a castle, christen him a king, and declare herself a queen. As they scampered about the hills, he thought her a whimsical sprite, as wild as the moor itself. She was the wind and the stars to him.

One summer afternoon, Catherine took him to her Fairy Cave. She had told him stories, and he supposed it quite a magical place.

They walked into the hills and followed a path below Penistone Crags. As Catherine pulled away brambles from the entrance to the cave, the sun ducked behind a cloud. Crawling inside, Heathcliff saw long dark roots dangling down over his head ominously as icicles. The cave smelled of moldering earth and hardly seemed enchanted at all.

"I don't see any Fairies," he said.

"The Fairies are sleeping to-day," Catherine said. "They only come out at night, but they hear us."

Heathcliff said nothing. They sat together quietly. He heard the breeze brush through the vegetation outside.

Catherine nuzzled closer. As she did so, he noticed the entrance to the cave light up in a sudden splash of sunlight.

"Heathcliff, some day I will marry you," Catherine announced.

Heathcliff blushed. He felt something raw open up inside him. He wasn't sure he heard Catherine correctly at all.

"You would marry a man such as me, Cathy?" he asked.

"You must love me with all your heart and soul," she said. "And you must stay with me always and forever and ever."

HEATHCLIFF: THE LOST YEARS

Catherine giggled. Of course, she was playing. But when he crawled outside, Heathcliff did think the cave rather enchanted.

After Heathcliff's second summer at Wuthering Heights, Old Earnshaw's wife became seriously ill. On an autumn afternoon, Old Earnshaw called the children to the parlor.

"I'm afraid your mother has gone to see the angels," he said.

Catherine immediately began to cry.

After the funeral, Heathcliff felt a terrible gloom descend upon the house. One cold winter afternoon, he came upon Catherine by the parlor window, holding a locket he knew contained a snippet of her mother's hair. When he asked if she was all right, Catherine clasped the locket to her chest. Tears formed in her eyes. Catherine shook her head and stared sadly out the window at the quietly falling snow.

Winter seemed to last forever. When Heatchliff noticed a sudden break in the weather, he tried to cheer up his melancholy friend.

"Come outside, Cathy. You must help me check my trap," he said.

Nelly bundled them up in boots and wool cloaks. Heathcliff led his friend down the drive past the fir trees, then kicked a path through the snow to where he had set his trap more than a month before.

On that autumn day, he and Catherine had been strolling home from the heath when Catherine noticed a lapwing circling over their heads, as if to lure them away.

"A mother bird," Catherine said. "Perhaps her nest is nearby."

Catherine soon found a pretty black and white lapwing feather. It delighted her so much she took it home and added it to her collection.

Later that afternoon, Heathcliff returned and found the nest. It contained four warm, speckled eggs. He set a trap over the nest but he hadn't checked it since the snows began.

Now he kicked snow off the trap and pulled it off the nest in the sunlight.

"Bah! Empty!" he announced, not attempting to hide his disgust.

Catherine bent over to look inside. Inside a circle of twigs and sticks she saw the corpses of four dead lapwing chicks. The little birds had frozen to death with their beaks wide open, crying out to their mother for food.

"Heathcliff!" Catherine shrieked. "You have murdered the chicks!"

"The old one wouldn't come into my trap," Heathcliff snarled.

"Murderer!" Catherine cried. "Heathcliff, you are cruel!"

She struck his chest with her fists and wept. He tried to calm his friend, to put his arms around her until she stopped crying, but she continued to back away, fitfully sobbing. It took her a long time to calm herself and finally talk to him.

It pained Heathcliff to hurt her. He felt her disappointment, her anguish, and her grief. He couldn't cry as freely as she, but when he saw her crying that afternoon, he truly wished he could. He longed to make his friend happy.

On the way back to Wuthering Heights, he solemnly swore to Catherine that he would never, ever trap or shoot a lapwing again.

Dark winter clouds returned. Snow piled up beneath the fir trees and against the brambles that lined the walkway outside the house. Clouds of blowing snow rolled ominously across the hills.

Chapter 4

One summer evening, Catherine snapped back to life. After dinner, she pulled Heathcliff aside. "To-night we must go to Gimmerton Kirk," she whispered. "Nelly says we might see a ghost."

They set off at twilight. By the time they arrived, a full moon had risen over the hills. Catherine led him behind the old stone church to a dilapidated rock wall that enclosed the ancient burial ground.

Catherine turned to Heathcliff, her face glowing in the moonlight. She pointed to the moon, which was encircled by a lavender ring of eerie light.

"When there is a nimbus around the moon, as there is to-night, Nelly says a ghost will rise up from her grave," she whispered.

"Bah," Heathcliff snorted.

"A nimbus is the spirits' wedding ring," Catherine said. "When a maiden dies before she marries her true love, her ghost rises from the grave and roams the hills until she finds him."

"You won't make me believe in ghosts, Cathy."

"You must believe, Heathcliff," Catherine whispered "If you don't believe in them, Nelly says spirits will haunt you. *I* will haunt you."

The old cemetery became deathly quiet. Catherine jumped at the whoot of a distant owl, which startled Heathcliff, too.

"There's your spirit," he scoffed. "Your spirit is an owl."

"The spirits are here!" she said.

"Then call for your spirits to appear!" Heathcliff scoffed. "Right now! Call up the spirits, Cathy! We've tried it before."

Catherine turned her back on him and stared at the moon.

The nimbus around the moon seemed to grow larger and brighter. Inside the graveyard before them, the tombstones began to shimmer in the moonlight. This unsettled Heathcliff. His fear made him so angry at himself that he stepped boldly through the gate and extended one hand.

"I will walk through this graveyard to-night; and you must come with me," he said.

"We must not walk into the graveyard on such a night," Catherine blurted. "We will disturb the spirits."

Heathcliff took Catherine's hand and yanked her through the gate. She staggered sideways against it: the gate squealed like a wounded rat on its rusty hinges.

A dark river of flying creatures erupted from the church belfry and poured down low. They circled the graveyard in a flurry of palpitating wings. Heathcliff felt a terrible quickening in the air. The squeaking, shrieking creatures began swirling up into an ominous gyre, flapping toward the nimbus around the moon.

"Heathcliff!" Catherine cried.

He felt her cold fingernails sink into his arm. *He had called up the spirits.* It was up to him to save them.

"*Run*, Cathy!" Heathcliff cried, seizing her hand.

For a moment, Catherine froze. As if in a dream, he struggled to pull his frightened, gasping friend away.

Chapter 5

Hindley Earnshaw was a few years Heathcliff's senior. Perhaps a foot taller than Heathcliff, the future master of Wuthering Heights towered over Heathcliff like a giant. But Hindley's face was incapable of concealing the slightest emotion. Across the young country gentleman's lightly freckled face, with its dull eyes and large fishlike mouth, Heathcliff often glimpsed flashes of anger, resentment, jealousy, and fear.

Hindley did not approve of Old Earnshaw's taking Heathcliff in. Hindley objected to buying Heathcliff decent garments or taking Heathcliff on to Sunday services at Gimmerton Kirk. When Hindley's father bought a colt for each of the boys at a country fair, and gave Heathcliff the better horse, Hindley told anyone who would listen that Heathcliff should never have been given a horse at all.

Hindley was not fond of Catherine, and frequently said so, but it disturbed him enormously when his sister leapt to Heathcliff's defense and kept Heathcliff from being punished.

When Old Earnshaw was away, Hindley sometimes jumped on Heathcliff from behind, held him down, and called him vile names. Heathcliff was not as strong as Hindley but he was quicker, and too proud to call for help. It infuriated the older lad when he could not make Heathcliff cry, or Heathcliff waited him out and slipped away.

One afternoon, Old Earnshaw returned home early and found Hindley holding Heathcliff to the ground outside the stables.

"Hindley!" Old Earnshaw cried, pulling both boys to their feet. "How dare you persecute this poor, fatherless child! You shame me. Go to your room!"

Trembling with emotion, Old Earnshaw led Heathcliff away and brushed off his clothes.

"There you are, as good as new," Old Earnshaw smiled, slapping Heathcliff on the rear. "You mustn't always look so sullen, Heathcliff. And please, do tell me if Hindley ever does this again."

Heathcliff knew that Old Earnshaw favored him, since he was not punished for anything. But Old Earnshaw did expect a great deal of Hindley, Heathcliff noticed, and he was often disappointed. Heathcliff sometimes even pitied Hindley, who couldn't stand to hear his father compliment Heathcliff at all. Even a small compliment could send Hindley into sputtering paroxysms of resentment and bile.

"The lad is clever. I believe he may make something of himself," Old Earnshaw predicted one day after a lesson. "Hindley, would you not agree?"

"A person of his ilk could make a decent plough-boy," Hindley snorted. "Perhaps he could become a blacksmith or a groom, although he would need a good bit of instruction from his betters to master a trade."

"Hindley!" Catherine cried. "You are jealous!"

"What foolish, feminine fancy is *this*?" Hindley bolted to his feet. "You have the gall to call me jealous? *I*? Jealous of him? *Him*? What you say is absurd!"

"Hindley—" Old Earnshaw began.

The three of them observed the spectacle of Hindley slinking away, vaulting up the stairs, and slamming the bedroom door behind him.

"Let me apologize for my son's behavior," said old Earnshaw to Heathcliff. "Hindley may someday realize that generosity and civility are the hallmarks of the gentleman I would dearly wish him to be."

HEATHCLIFF: THE LOST YEARS

The next time Old Earnshaw went away for several days, Hindley caught Heathcliff unawares several times and brutally thrashed him.

The afternoon Old Earnshaw returned, Heathcliff learned his new horse was lame. The horse's weakness infuriated him. Heathcliff was still sore from Hindley's beatings, and the younger lad felt something harden inside his chest when Hindley blithely sauntered into the stables.

"You must exchange horses with me," Heathcliff said. "I don't like mine. If you won't, I shall tell your father of the three thrashings you've given me this week, and show him my arm, which is black to the shoulder."

Hindley cuffed Heathcliff on the ears. Heathcliff ran onto the porch with the older lad on his heels, then whirled to face him.

"You'd better do it at once," Heathcliff said. "You will have to. And if I speak of these blows, you'll get them again with interest."

Hindley whirled and picked up an iron weight used for weighing potatoes and hay. He lifted the weight over his head.

"Throw it!" Heathcliff boldly defied him. "I'll tell your father how you boasted that you would turn me out of doors as soon as he died, and we'll see if he does not turn *you* out directly."

"Off, dog!" Hindley cried.

Hindley flung the weight into Heathcliff's chest and knocked him over backwards. Heathcliff stood up, clutching his chest and gasping for breath. He staggered toward the back door to tell Old Earnshaw but Nelly opened the door and blocked his way.

"You lads must not upset Mr. Earnshaw!" she said, as Heathcliff tried to get around her. "He is not well to-day."

"Take the horse and be damned, you beggarly interloper!" Hindley hissed. "Wheedle my father out of everything he has, then show him afterwards what you are—imp of Satan! Take my horse! I hope he'll kick out your brains!"

With Hindley and Nelly following, Heathcliff slowly walked to the stables to claim his new horse. When he backed it out of Hindley's stall to move it, the older lad shoved Heathcliff down beneath the animal's legs, and quickly ran away.

Heathcliff scurried out from beneath the horse and picked himself up. As Nelly watched, he maneuvered Hindley's horse into his stall and calmly switched out the saddles and tack.

"You mustn't bother Mr. Earnshaw to-day, Heathcliff," Nelly said. "I'll tell him those bruises came from your horse. You got what you wanted, and that's enough. You must not be vindictive, lad."

Heathcliff sat down on a bale of hay. He scowled at Nelly, shook his head, and cradled his head in his hands.

Chapter 6

After Hindley went away to agricultural college in Manchester, Heathcliff's bond with Catherine grew much stronger. One grey morning they scurried up into the hills together. Suddenly, spontaneously, under a billowing drapery of fat grey clouds, they broke into a long punishing run to the very top of Penistone Crags, a run that left them both exhausted.

On the edge of the cliff, under an overcast sky, they both stopped, sweating, exhausted, breathing hard. Gasping, laughing, clutching each other's shoulders, they danced together like exhausted marionettes.

Without thinking, Heathcliff's hands slipped down Catherine's back and caught her slender waist. Catherine moved closer. A wave of tenderness surged through him. The way her body felt in his hands took his breath away.

Catherine looked into his eyes. With one hand, Heathcliff brushed a lock of hair from her face.

"Dear Cathy," he said.

Heathcliff kissed her forehead gently and with great tenderness, in a way in which he had never kissed her before.

He felt a rush of emotion that shocked him. For a moment, he thought he might well faint.

Like a wave of water that began at her knees, Catherine's body slipped against his own. For an instant, she leaned back, her hands lightly touching his chest, her hips pressing against his.

Her lips parted. Roughly, Heathcliff pulled her toward him. He met her soft wet mouth in a long, slow, anxious, sweat-drenched kiss.

She placed her hands on his shoulders, not quite pushing him away, then impetuously threw both arms around him. She was heat and light, her hot breath in his mouth, the two of them melting together like one hopelessly entangled, ravished animal.

Finally, with apparent difficulty, blushing, blinking, shaking her head, Catherine pushed Heathcliff away. Her face was white as death. She looked stunned, confused, and frightened. Heathcliff's heart beat madly in his chest when she turned away from him, a gesture he found almost impossible to bear.

Walking back to Wuthering Heights under a cloudy sky, Heathcliff felt he and Catherine had somehow become one indivisible being. All the way home, holding her hand, he believed they would remain united forever.

Chapter 7

One October evening, an autumn wind blustered down the chimney and whistled through the old house. The Earnshaw family relaxed around the hearth. Joseph read his Bible. Nelly attended to her knitting.

Old Earnshaw fell asleep in his chair next to the fire, one hand stroking Catherine's hair. Seated on the floor next to him, with her head on her father's knee, Catherine sang a pretty little song for her ailing father. Heathcliff lay on the floor beside Catherine, half asleep, with his head nestled comfortably in her lap.

Joseph picked up a candle. In a gruff voice, he called his master to prayers and bed. Old Earnshaw didn't move.

Joseph shook Old Earnshaw's shoulder. Joseph's eyes widened. He set down the candle. He snatched Catherine and Heathcliff by their arms and tried to hurry them off to bed.

"Frame upstairs, and make little din," Joseph said. "You may pray alone this evening. I have something to do."

"I shall bid father good-night before I go," Catherine announced, squirming away.

She threw her arms around her father's neck and pressed her lips to his cold cheek. Then she backed up, shrieking.

"Oh, he's dead, Heathcliff!" she cried. "He's dead!"

Catherine threw herself into Heathcliff's arms/When she burst into tears, Heathcliff began crying. Before long, Nelly was holding them both and weeping with them, too.

The next morning, Heathcliff awoke to the sight of cold October rain drizzling over the moor. He had lived at Wuthering Heights for more than six years.

Heathcliff saddled his horse and rode to Manchester to tell Hindley the terrible news. Hindley thanked Heathcliff for coming, then sent him back to Wuthering Heights in the rain without inviting him in.

The carriage that brought Hindley back to the moor also contained his frail new wife, Frances. No one in the family knew Hindley had married. It was an additional surprise when Hindley informed them at the dinner table that his new wife was heavy with child.

That first evening, Hindley stepped firmly into his role as master of the house, a role granted him by birth.

"Heathcliff, you will stay away from Gimmerton Kirk to-morrow. You are not family. I don't want you at my father's funeral," Hindley told him after dinner.

Although Heathcliff adored old Earnshaw, and was shattered with grief at his passing, he did as he was instructed by the new master of Wuthering Heights.

On that dismal afternoon, the Gimmerton Kirk bell pealed out its grim funeral message over the cold wet hills. Bundled up in a wool cloak, his fingers so cold he could barely hold the reins of his horse, Heathcliff viewed the proceedings from the crest of a nearby hill. He watched the neighbors follow Old Earnshaw's wooden coffin out of the church and down into the little country graveyard, where all the tombstones were slick with rain.

It was dusk when the grave-digger departed. Heathcliff rode down the hill, tied up his horse at the gate, and walked into the graveyard. He fell to his knees, pressed his forehead to the mound of dark wet earth, and wept bitter tears over Old Earnshaw's grave.

HEATHCLIFF: THE LOST YEARS

Heathcliff's body ached with grief. He had never felt so abandoned and alone.

The following Sunday, the rains intensified. Since the family could not attend church, Hindley instructed Joseph get up a Bible lesson for Catherine and Heathcliff, and to include the plough-boy. Joseph set them all down on a sack of corn in the garret and hectored them all morning, reading Bible verses and warning them of the wages of disobedience and sin while rain spattered loudly against the skylight.

Finally, Nelly called them downstairs to lunch.

Sunday afternoons, Old Earnshaw had always allowed the children to play. But when Catherine set up their castle in the arch of the dresser, Joseph self-righteously yanked away the pinafore Catherine employed for a curtain. The old Pharisee pulled Heathcliff and Catherine out of their castle, sat them both down, and shoved Biblical tracts into their hands. Heathcliff received *The Broad Way to Destruction*, Catherine *The Helmet of Salvation*.

"I can't stand any more of this!" Catherine quickly cried, and hurled her book into the dog-kennel. Heathcliff threw down his tract and kicked it away.

After a few words with Hindley, Joseph grabbed both children by the collar and walked them into the back kitchen.

"The Devil will fetch you here," growled the old Pharisee, his eyes glimmering. He slammed the door. They remained in the cold room until bedtime.

Early the next morning, Hindley Earnshaw summoned Heathcliff to the stables. He quietly handed him a pitchfork.

"You must work for your keep now, Heathcliff," Hindley began. "From now on, you will attend to the stables and manage our livestock. And I promise you, I shall find additional work for you around the estate."

"I don't fear honest work," Heathcliff said.

"Nelly will move your things up to the garret to-day," Hindley added. "Frances will have your room as a nursery for our child."

That night, Heathcliff slept in the garret for the first time. The squat, musty little room had a perilously slanted ceiling and contained only some moldering cast-off things, a rickety old dresser, and a small rope bed. It was hardly fit quarters for a servant.

When he went to bed, Heathcliff noticed the overhead skylight was dirty. Although it was a clear night, he could not even see the stars.

Chapter 8

One cool December evening, Catherine made an unfortunate joke at the dinner table. Hindley did not understand the joke, but his face clouded up when Catherine and Heathcliff began snickering. Their laughter drew a sniveling complaint from Hindley's wife Frances, who had a notoriously weak stomach and no visible sense of humor.

"Joseph!" Hindley called in the servant. "Lock this ill-mannered pair in the wash-house. Let them laugh at me in there."

Joseph very righteously walked the guilty pair to the wash-house, saw them both inside, and bolted the door.

The rear window of the wash-house was easily dislodged. As soon as Joseph left, Heathcliff pried the window open with a stick, snickering quietly as he did so.

"Let's have a scamper on the moor," he said.

Heathcliff helped Catherine crawl out the window. Clouds drifted in clumps beneath the harsh blue light of a winter's moon. When they sprinted to the heights, Catherine noticed the distant lights of Thrushcross Grange.

"Heathcliff, we must spy on the Lintons," she said. "It's Sunday night. Whatever do you think they do?"

Behind the sprawling façade of the Linton estate, a low brick wall surrounded the family's rose-garden. Heathcliff quietly opened the rear gate, and left it ajar.

The mansion seemed to slumber in the moonlight as they picked their way toward it. Heathcliff found a spot beneath the drawing-room window. He stood on a flower pot, stepped up on the basement, and peeked inside.

Under a crystal chandelier shimmering with tapers lay an ornate, crimson-carpeted room. Isabella Linton stood on the far side of the large room, shrieking at her brother. Her older brother Edgar Linton stood near the hearth, weeping and arguing with his sister. Between them sat a small dog, yelping and lifting its right front paw.

Catherine peered over the windowsill.

"Those weaklings are going mad over that little dog," Heathcliff whispered. "They've pulled it apart between them and made it cry, now they're quarreling over who might hold it first. Have you ever seen such fools?"

Catherine snickered. Heathcliff began laughing, too.

"Let's make noise and frighten them," Heathcliff said.

He and Catherine banged on the windowpane with their hands. Heathcliff howled like a wolf. Catherine shrieked and then began to hoot like an owl.

Heathcliff noticed the Lintons moving towards the window. He heard someone draw the bars over the back door.

"Let's go!" he whispered.

Heathcliff grabbed Catherine's hand. He tried to pull her away. But she fell down, and she pulled him down, too.

"Run, Heathcliff, run!" she said. "They have let the bull-dog loose, and he holds me!"

The Lintons' fat little bull-dog had already fastened its teeth onto Catherine's bare ankle. Heathcliff ran back and kicked the dog. It shook its thick, fat head, snorting and growling and it wouldn't let go.

HEATHCLIFF: THE LOST YEARS

Heathcliff found a stone, crammed it between the dog's jaws, and tried to push the stone down its throat. The bull-dog only growled and shook its head.

The back door opened with a flash of yellow light. A husky male servant ran down the steps. He snatched Cathy up while Heathcliff tried to pry her from his hands.

"What prey, Skulker?" came the voice of Mr. Linton.

"Skulker has caught a little girl, sir," said the servant. "And there's a lad here making a clutch at me, who looks like an out-and-outer!"

"Come in, I'll furnish them a reception."

The servant pulled them both inside the mansion. Heathcliff's eyes widened. Mr. Linton held a fowling-piece at the ready.

"To beard a magistrate in his stronghold, and on the Sabbath, too! Where will their insolence stop?" he asked.

The servant pulled Heathcliff into the drawing room. Mr. Linton sat Heathcliff down on the crimson sofa and interrogated him beneath the chandelier while the family and servants looked on. Heathcliff cursed and snarled at them all.

"Frightful thing! Put him in the cellar, Papa," said Isabella. "He's exactly like the son of the fortune-teller that stole my tame pheasant, isn't he, Edgar?"

Edgar Linton gawked while Catherine limped into the room. She hurried toward Heathcliff, her ankle bleeding. When she clasped hands with Heathcliff, she defiantly laughed.

"That's Miss Earnshaw!" Edgar Linton told his mother, "Look how Skulker has bitten her—how her foot bleeds!"

"Miss Earnshaw scouring the country with a gypsy? The child is in mourning—surely it is—and she may be maimed for life!" Madam Linton said.

"What culpable carelessness in her brother!" said Mr. Linton. "He lets her grow up in absolute heathenism. But who is this? Where did she pick up this companion?"

"A wicked boy, at all events, and quite unfit for a decent house," said Mrs. Linton, peering down at Heathcliff through her spectacles.

"*Let us go!*" Heathcliff shouted, and cursed them again.

Mr. Linton ordered Heathcliff out of the house immediately; Heathcliff refused to go without Catherine. Linton's man servant turned Heathcliff out, gave him a lantern, and sent him away.

Heathcliff returned the drawing-room window, prepared to break the glass into a million pieces with his bare hands if they didn't let Catherine go. Instead, he watched a female servant bring a basin of warm water and wash Catherine's feet. Isabella Linton dumped a plate of sweet cakes into Catherine's lap. Edgar Linton stood gaping at her from a distance while the servants combed and dried her long brown hair, then gave her a pair of slippers and wheeled her to the fire.

It had begun to sprinkle rain by the time Heathcliff returned to Wuthering Heights. When Heathcliff told the servants what happened, Joseph led Heathcliff by the ear to Hindley, who sat dumbly before the hearth. Hindley was in his cups and in a foul mood.

"How did you get out of the wash-house, you foul little bastard?" Hindley demanded.

"He went sneaking over to the Lintons," hissed the old Pharisee. "This one and Miss Catherine."

"You dare disturb the Lintons? With my sister? Like a thief in the night? Do you seek to humiliate me?"

"No, of course not," Heathcliff said. "I do not seek that at all."

"Where is my sister?"

"The little devil left her there," Joseph cawed. "Abandoned her. Left her with the Lintons."

"Good God, Heathcliff. How you humiliate my family."

Hindley rose from his chair and slapped Heathcliff in the face.

"You despicable little vagabond! Sleep in the stables! You will not return to this house until I permit you to return," Hindley snarled, squeezing Heathcliff's arm so hard it frightened him.

HEATHCLIFF: THE LOST YEARS

"And I swear to you, if you ever dare lead my sister astray again, I give you my word I'll turn you out of this house and you'll be gone for good."

Before long, the elder Linton paid a call on Wuthering Heights. He had summoned Doctor Kenneth. The doctor insisted Catherine remain at the Linton estate until her wound completely healed.

Catherine remained at Thrushcross Grange for five weeks. A few days before Christmas, she returned to Wuthering Heights astride a handsome black pony. She had covered the ringlets of her thick brown hair with an artfully-feathered beaver, Heathcliff noticed. She wore a handsome cloth habit so long she had to hold it up with both hands as she sailed gracefully through the front door.

Looking on, Heathcliff did not dare speak to her until Hindley approved.

"Heathcliff, you may come forward," Hindley eventually cried, rather obviously enjoying Heathcliff's discomfort. "You may come and wish Miss Catherine welcome, like the other servants."

Catherine threw out her arms and embraced him heartily. She kissed Heathcliff again and again on the face and cheek until he pulled away, confused and embarrassed. His dear friend had never looked so beautiful. Around her, he had never felt so low.

"Heathcliff," she whispered. "How very black and cross you look—and how funny and grim. But that's because I'm used to Edgar and Isabella Linton. Well, Heathcliff, have you forgotten me?"

He could not manage a reply.

"Shake hands, Heathcliff," said Hindley, using the condescending tone of voice he used to address the servants. "Once in a while, that is permitted."

"I shall not," Heathcliff replied. "I shall not stand to be laughed at. I shall not bear it!"

Blushing and humiliated, Heathcliff backed away. But Catherine grabbed his hand.

"Heathcliff, I did not mean to laugh at you. What are you so sulky for? It was only that you looked odd. If you wash your face and brush your hair it will be all right: but you are so dirty!"

As Catherine spoke, she glanced at his hand and made a face. This shocked him. Hindley and Frances laughed.

"You needn't have touched me!" Heathcliff replied, snatching away his hand. "I shall be as dirty as I please."

Heathcliff heard laughter as he hurried from the room. He took a lantern to the barn and brushed down every horse in the stables. In his mind, he still heard them laughing.

Nelly came to the stables and begged him to return for dinner. Heathcliff proudly refused. He stayed with the animals until late into the night, and then crept up to the garret to sleep.

The next day was Sunday. Heathcliff awoke early and took a long silent walk across the heath with two of the dogs. When he returned to the house, the family had left for church and Nelly was busy in the kitchen.

"It's high time, Heathcliff. You have grieved Catherine," Nelly said. "She's sorry she ever came home."

Heathcliff feared he had hurt his friend. "Did you say she was grieved?"

"She cried when I told her you were off again this morning," Nelly said.

"Well, I cried last night," he said. "I had more reason to cry than she."

"You had the reason of going to bed with a proud heart and an empty stomach, but if you be ashamed of your touchiness, you must ask pardon, mind, when she comes in. Greet her heartily, and not as if she has been converted into a stranger by her grand dress," Nelly said. "I have dinner to get ready, but I'll steal time to arrange you so that Edgar Linton shall look quite a doll beside you when they come for dinner."

While she worked, Nelly washed him up in the kitchen. After that, she untangled and combed his black, curly hair.

"I wish I had light hair and a fair skin, and was dressed and behaved as well, and had a chance of being as rich as Edgar Linton will be," Heathcliff said.

"You could knock him down in a twinkling," Nelly replied.

"But, Nelly, if I knocked him down twenty times, that wouldn't make him less handsome or me more so," Heathcliff replied.

Nelly snorted. She led Heathcliff to a glass and bade him look at his own reflection.

"Tell me whether you don't think yourself rather handsome? I'll tell you, I do," Nelly said. "You're fit for a prince in disguise. Who knows but your father was Emperor of China, and your mother an Indian queen, each of them able to buy up, with one week's income, Wuthering Heights and Thrushcross Grange together?"

Nelly's attention cheered him up. Heathcliff determined to make himself cheerful when the family returned from church.

Edgar and Isabella Linton arrived for a visit in the family carriage, wearing their cloaks and furs. Waiting in the kitchen, Heathcliff heard Catherine lead the Lintons into the house and seat them before the fire.

"Go into the parlor now," Nelly urged Heathcliff. "Be amiable."

Heathcliff pushed open the kitchen door to make his entrance. At the same moment, Hindley pushed on the door from the other side.

The master of the house was not pleased to meet Heathcliff in the doorway. He immediately shoved him away.

"Joseph, keep the fellow out—send him into the garret till dinner is over. He'll be cramming his fingers in the tarts and stealing the fruit."

"Nay sir," Nelly stepped between them. "He'll touch nothing. I suppose he must have his share of the dainties as well as we."

"He shall have his share of my hand, if I catch him downstairs till dark," Hindley sneered, and stepped forward.

"Begone, you vagabond! What! You are attempting the coxcomb, are you? Wait till I get hold of those elegant locks—see if I won't pull them a bit longer."

Edgar Linton stood in the doorway, languidly peeping in.

"They are long enough already," Edgar Linton said. "I wonder they don't make his head ache. It's like a colt's mane over his eyes!"

This infuriated Heathcliff. He picked up a tureen of hot apple sauce and flung it toward Linton. Edgar threw up both hands, and shrieked like a girl.

"Joseph!" Hindley snapped. "Help me discipline this little ruffian."

The two of them grabbed Heathcliff and pulled him through the back door and out to the barn. Hindley barred the door and fetched his riding crop while Joseph threw his arms around Heathcliff, and cried out admonitions.

"Get down, flaysome divil of a gypsy!" the old Pharisee shouted. "Fall down on your knees before the Master!"

Hindley tried to whip Heathcliff in the face, but Heathcliff could move so adroitly that the riding crop often struck Joseph.

"Fall to your knees!" Joseph cried, struggling to push Heathcliff to the ground. "Apologize to Master! Repentance stops the lash!"

Joseph grabbed Heathcliff by the hair and tried to pull him down. Hindley flailed at him with his crop. Somehow, Heathcliff remained on his feet, staggering but stubbornly refusing to kneel. He told himself he would die before he would bow down to Hindley.

Finally, the blows ceased. Joseph pulled Heathcliff up to the garret and locked him inside.

That evening, Heathcliff woke up to the sounds of the Gimmerton band, which made the rounds of the respectable houses at Christmas. A blast of trumpet awakened him with a headache, followed by the sounds of a trombone, clarinets, and a good many festive singing voices.

"Heathcliff!" Catherine knocked at the door to the garret.

HEATHCLIFF: THE LOST YEARS

"What?" he groaned.

"Unlock the skylight," Catherine whispered. "I must come to see you."

He heard Catherine skitter across the dark roof. Heathcliff's arms and shoulders ached. He found it difficult to reach up and open the skylight, but he helped Catherine down into his small, dark room.

She lit a candle. As the music continued, Catherine sat down on the bed next to him, put both arms around his aching shoulders, and took him under her wing like a mother bird.

After the music stopped, Nelly unlocked the garret door. She stood silhouetted in the doorway.

"Miss Cathy, you must come down for dinner," Nelly said.

"Heathcliff must come too. He must never be beaten again, Nelly. Where is my brother?"

"Mr. Hindley has gone to bed and the Devil's music long ago drove Joseph away. Come now. You must both eat something."

Taking Heathcliff's hand, Catherine led him limping down the stairs and onto the bench by the fire. She presented Heathcliff a pretty enameled music-box for Christmas. Nelly offered him a quantity of good things, but his stomach revolted so much he could not eat.

Heathcliff only put his elbows onto his knees and stared pensively into the fire.

"Heathcliff, what are you thinking?" Nelly finally asked.

"I'm trying to settle how I shall pay Hindley back. I don't care how long I wait, if I can only do it at last. I hope he will not die before I do," Heathcliff said.

"For shame, Heathcliff!" Nelly said. "It is for God to punish wicked people: we should learn to forgive."

"God won't have the satisfaction that I shall," Heathcliff said. "I only wish I knew the best way! Let me alone, Nelly, and I'll plan it out. While I'm thinking of that, I don't feel pain."

Chapter 9

Not long after, Hindley forbade Heathcliff from eating dinner with the family. Heathcliff was to take meals in the kitchen with the servants, and Hindley admonished him to not bother Catherine. Hindley forbade Heathcliff from attending church with the family. He ordered Heathcliff to stop looking at Old Earnshaw's books, or taking them to the garret as he had begun to do.

Still stunned by Old Earnshaw's death, and feeling unmoored and abandoned, Heathcliff did as he was told. If a pig was to be killed for dinner, Heathcliff was given the bloody task of killing and butchering the poor animal. And when it was time for planting and harvesting, Hindley sent Heathcliff from the house at daybreak to work with the yeomen in the fields.

Heathcliff's better garments soon fell apart or grew too small for his frame. Hindley gave him coarse cotton and flax field garments, and in the summer presented him with a fustian smock. That winter, he was given a shabby wool cloak, Hindley's hand-me-down boots, and one of Joseph's old hats as befitted his lower station at the estate.

For some time, Heathcliff stubbornly worked hard to show his merit. He threw himself into the tending of the animals and labored as long and hard as any yeoman in the fields. Without being asked, he helped the cottagers harvest the small plots they kept on the commons.

HEATHCLIFF: THE LOST YEARS

Outdoors, in the fresh air, Heathcliff felt entirely clean and free. It was only when he returned home in soiled garments, his hands chapped and raw from working around the estate, that he felt shame. The way Catherine looked away from him when he entered the room made him ashamed of his low station, and gave him the full measure of his fall. Hindley noticed this, and seemed to delight in Catherine's efforts to keep Heathcliff at bay.

One June morning, Frances bore Hindley Earnshaw a son. The master of Wuthering Heights named the fat little cherub Hareton. The day Hindley became a father, he took Heathcliff's old stallion, visited the Rainbow, and spent the entire day and much of the night gambling and celebrating his paternity.

Hindley's wife became increasingly frail. Doctor Kenneth forbade Frances to rise from bed immediately after childbirth, and he kept her in bed for many weeks after that. Over time, as Frances languished away from consumption, it became obvious to everyone but Hindley that his wife was seriously ill.

On a dreary September evening, Hindley's wife slipped into the shadowy netherworld of death, leaving Hindley a widower and Little Hareton a motherless child.

The day his wife was buried, Hindley so disabled himself with strong drink that he could hardly get into the mourning coach after the funeral. All evening, Hindley slouched in his chair before the fire, unable to stop weeping.

Hindley's black moods grew darker. His drinking bouts became more frequent. More than once, the cottagers whispered, the innkeeper at the Rainbow had lashed Hindley onto his horse in the early morning hours, and sent the horse plodding home. Nelly cautioned Heathcliff to keep to his room on the nights when the tyrant drank, or when he staggered into the house after a disappointing night of cards. The master of Wuthering Heights took little notice of his infant son, unless little Hareton was unfortunate enough to get in his way.

With a bitterness as palpable as black bile, the master of the house seemed to search for cruel ways to press Heathcliff down.

Hindley faulted Heathcliff for everything that went wrong on the estate. If an animal fell ill or a horse lost a horseshoe, if a shed lay in poor repair, or if crops were planted late or the harvest short, Hindley affixed the entire blame to Heathcliff.

In his foulest moods, the drunken tyrant stalked into the barn with Joseph at his side to punish Heathcliff for his misdeeds. Heathcliff bore these thrashings silently and proudly until the blundering master of Wuthering Heights, weakened from drink and dissipation, exhausted all the venom he could muster and staggered away.

Heathcliff despised the depths to which he had fallen. Sometimes he dreamed of fleeing Wuthering Heights, and testing himself among other men. But when he thought about it, he could not abandon Catherine. In some unexplainable way, he felt, Catherine needed him near her, and he also needed her.

Chapter 10

As the seasons changed, Heathcliff filled out and grew taller. His black hair curled to his shoulders. His skin darkened in the sun. His shoulders became muscular from heavy work in the fields, and his hands became calloused and coarse. When he looked into a glass, beneath his heavy black eyebrows his dark eyes glared back at him with an angry intelligence.

Catherine, too, was changing. She had become a proud young woman. She no longer ventured outdoors. She seemed determined to perfect her manners. Worse, she began to criticize Heathcliff's manners, too. One afternoon, she actually called him uncouth, an insult which pricked his devoted heart.

Catherine had Nelly spend long hours combing and powdering and padding her long brown hair. She primped before a mirror. She bought many new garments, and she would not let Heathcliff touch her clothes. She passed through the house and out the door as regally as the wind and climbed into a carriage with Isabella Linton to attend gatherings to which he was not invited.

Heathcliff thought Isabella Linton a frail, pretentious girl who labored to put on the airs of a fine, high-born lady. Isabella's older brother Edgar was a fair-haired young gentleman a few years older than he, and

Edgar worked quite diligently at playing the gentleman. Edgar Linton did have the finest clothes Heathcliff had ever seen; the effete young gentleman had impeccable manners. Although Heathcliff did not like the young Lintons, he had to admit both were handsome, well-dressed, and unimpeachably genteel.

Catherine strove to emulate her new friends, but Heathcliff felt she was being false to herself. He tried to warn her of this, but to his horror Catherine often chose to ignore him. Several times, he struggled to find words to tell her exactly how he felt. By betraying her own wild, animal nature, he wanted to tell her, a nature he believed identical to his own, he feared Catherine would somehow betray him, too.

Every night a storm raged in his heart while he lay in the garret, thinking of her. It infuriated him to feel like a eunuch, kept at arm's length by his distant and untouchable mistress.

"Cathy," he blurted out one evening. "Do you remember all those times we spent together, scampering across the moor?"

"Do you dream I could forget?" Catherine laughed, rising to her feet. "We are *still* together, Heathcliff. We shall *always* be together. Trust me, I shall see to it."

Always together. The words sent a thrill through his body. Without thinking, Heathcliff bounded to his feet and clutched Catherine's shoulders. He stared into her face. There were the eyes he remembered, the woman he would die for. When Catherine smiled impishly back at him, as she did when they were young, Heathcliff's heart surged out to his beautiful friend and once again, they were as one.

But Catherine's pretty face darkened. She glanced at his garments, removed his hands from her shoulders, and hurried away.

At dinner, from his bench at the servants' table, Heathcliff strained to hear Catherine's easy laughter, or just the sound of her voice. His eyes kissed her the moment she entered a room.

He sat with her in the parlor at every opportunity, on the evenings when Hindley was away. Being near her delighted him, but he could find little to say to her, and she to him. On a few occasions Catherine teasingly approached him with words and baby kisses, as she had done when they were young, but he thought this false and condescending, and for this he brushed her away.

One night, Heathcliff dreamt he heard the sound of ghostly finger-nails scratching on his skylight. Catherine's face and hands appeared in the glass; she opened her mouth and soundlessly cried out. When he reached the skylight to let her in, Catherine's face became a skull and her fingers became bones that scratched away across the glass. He awoke with a start, gasping for breath, fearing his only love was dead.

L ate that summer, Heathcliff noticed Edgar Linton begin-ning to call. He dreaded the visits of the fair-haired young gentleman from Thrushcross Grange. Heathcliff would have ripped Linton's heart from his chest with his bare hands and eaten it had Catherine asked it of him, but she did not ask him anything of the kind.

Only once, on a Sunday afternoon, did Heathcliff dare confront her about these visits. He stopped Catherine on her way through the parlor.

"Why must you entertain these visits from Edgar Linton? He is not worthy of you," Heathcliff blurted.

"Edgar amuses me, Heathcliff," Catherine retorted, with a toss of her hair. "Unlike most men I see, Edgar is very much a gentleman."

"But Edgar is *weak*," Heathcliff said, daring to clasp her arm. "He has a weak spirit, Cathy. He cannot care for you as I do. I think he is beneath you."

"*Beneath* me? Edgar Linton was born into the finest family on the moor," she said, and dismissed him with a wave of her hand.

Bursting to say more, but realizing he could not, Heathcliff obedi-ently bowed his head and walked outside. It was almost harvest-time. He had to meet with the cottagers to plan their work in the fields.

Chapter 11

A **low sound caught Heathcliff's attention.** It could have been the growl of distant thunder. Black clouds massed over the hills to the north, a harbinger of autumn storms. A gust of cool wind swept over the field as Heathcliff turned to see the master of Wuthering Heights, riding away.

Heathcliff lay down his scythe, took leave of the cottagers, and sauntered toward the house. With Hindley gone, he would give himself a holiday and spend a pleasant afternoon with Catherine.

He found Catherine in the parlor wearing a very pretty silk frock and Nelly smoothing down the folds of her dress.

"Cathy, are you busy, this afternoon?" Heathcliff asked.

"You should be in the field now, Heathcliff," she said. " It is an hour past dinner time: I thought you were gone."

Heathcliff sprawled out on the couch before them.

"Hindley does not often free us from his accursed presence," he said. "I'll not work any more to-day: I'll stay with you."

"Isabella and Edgar Linton talked of calling this afternoon," she said. "You run the risk of being scolded for no good."

"Order Ellen to say you are engaged, Cathy," he said.

"Don't turn me out for those silly, pitiful friends of yours! I'm on the point, sometimes, of complaining that they—but I'll not—"

"That they *what?* What are you on the point of complaining about, Heathcliff?" she snapped.

"Look at that calendar on the wall," he said, annoyed and hurt that she should speak to him so sharply. "The crosses are for the evenings you have spent with the Lintons, the dots for those spent with me. Do you see? I've marked every day."

"Yes—very foolish: as if I took notice!" Catherine peevishly replied. "And where is the sense of that?"

"To show that I do take notice."

"And I should always be sitting with *you*?" she demanded. "You might be dumb, or a baby, for anything you say to amuse me, or for anything you do, either!" she replied.

"You never told me before that I talked too little, or you disliked my company, Cathy!" Heathcliff replied, crestfallen.

"It's no company at all when people know nothing and say nothing," Catherine sniffed.

Before Heathcliff could reply, he heard a horse clatter up onto the flagstones outside. Edgar Linton knocked and entered with a silly smile on his face. Edgar removed his high-crowned green hat and revealed a head of blonde hair which had been quite recently powdered.

"I am not come too soon, am I?" Edgar asked Catherine.

Heathcliff noticed that Edgar was alone. He fumed out the back door and returned to the fields, but he could not keep his mind on his work. Heathcliff watched the house. He noticed that Edgar Linton remained until Hindley returned and then left quickly, looking dapper and smug as he trotted past.

When Heathcliff entered the house, Hindley was already shouting.

Hindley stood above him on the landing, holding little Hareton out over the bannister and drunkenly bellowing at the infant at the top of his lungs.

"Kiss me, Hareton!" cried Hindley, as the child kicked at his arms. "Damn thee, kiss me! By God, as if I would rear such a monster. As sure as I'm living, I'll break the brat's neck."

The screaming infant squirmed out of his hands. Heathcliff jumped forward and managed to catch little Hareton before he hit the floor. The master of Wuthering Heights staggered down the stairs as Nelly snatched up the child.

"It is your fault, Ellen. You should have taken him from me. Is he injured anywhere?" Hindley snorted, making for his bottle of brandy.

"Injured!" Nelly wiped a spot of blood from her lip. "I wonder his mother does not rise from her grave to see how you use him. You're worse than a heathen—treating your own flesh and blood in that manner! He hates you—they all hate you—that's the truth!"

"Convey yourself and him away," Hindley snarled, with a wave of his hand. "And hark you, Heathcliff, clear you too, quite from my reach and hearing. I wouldn't murder you to-night."

As Hindley poured himself a glass, Heathcliff headed for the barn. He stopped inside the house and sat down on the settle, whose high wooden back concealed him from view. He heard Nelly carry Hareton into the kitchen behind him, sit down, and begin singing the child to sleep with a pretty lullaby. Catherine's voice startled him awake.

"Are you alone, Nelly?" Catherine asked. "Where's Heathcliff?"

"At his work in the stable," Nelly replied.

Heathcliff sat still as a stone, listening hard, his back pressed against the bench. A drop of rain spattered against the window-pane.

"Nelly," Catherine said. "Will you keep a secret for me?"

"Is your secret worth keeping?"

"Yes, and it worries me, and I must let it out! I want to know what I should do. To-day, Edgar Linton has asked me to marry him, and I've given him an answer. Now, before I tell whether it was a consent or a denial, you tell me which it ought to have been."

"To be sure, considering the exhibition you performed in his presence this afternoon, I might say it would be wise to refuse him."

"If you talk so, I won't tell you any more," she sniffed. "I accepted him, Nelly. Be quick, and say whether I was wrong."

"Do you love Mr. Edgar?"

"Who can help it? Of course I do," Catherine replied.

Heathcliff put his knuckles into his mouth and bit them. He could have torn Edgar Linton apart with his bare hands.

"Why do you love him, Miss Cathy?" Nelly asked.

"Nonsense, I do—that's sufficient," Catherine snapped. "You're making a jest of it."

"By no means. You must say why."

"He's handsome, he's rich, he's young, he's cheerful…and he loves me," Catherine said. "And he will be rich, and I shall like to be the greatest woman of the neighourhood, and I shall be proud of having such a husband."

"But there are several other handsome rich young men in the world: handsomer, possibly, and richer than he is. What should hinder you from loving them?" Nelly asked.

"If there are any, they are out of my way. I've seen none like Edgar," Catherine snapped.

Heathcliff felt the wind rising. A dead branch screeched across the kitchen window-pane. From under the door of the kitchen came the first cold breath of a storm.

Heathcliff pressed back against the settle, his heart hammering. He didn't dare speak. The certainty of what was happening hit him like a slap in the face. Yet he could not stir from the bench where he sat as if shell-shocked, and silent and numb as a stone.

"If I were in heaven, Nelly, I should be extremely miserable," said Catherine.

"Because you are not fit to go there," Nelly replied. "All sinners would be miserable in heaven."

"I dreamt once I was in heaven but it did not seem to be my home. I broke my heart with weeping to come back to earth; and the angels were so angry that they flung me out into the middle of the heath on the top of Wuthering Heights; where I woke up sobbing for joy," she said.

"I tell you I won't hearken to your dreams, Miss Catherine," Nelly said. "I'm superstitious regarding dreams."

"I've no more business to marry Edgar Linton than I have to be in heaven, Nelly. If that wicked man in there had not brought Heathcliff so low, I shouldn't have thought of marrying Edgar Linton," Catherine said. "Heathcliff is more myself than I am. But it would degrade me to marry Heathcliff now—"

Degrade her? *Degrade* her, he thought, quietly rising to his feet.

He slipped out of the kitchen and staggered up the stairs, flushing and gasping for breath. He was drowning in a roiling sea of anger, grief, and pain.

In the musty desolation of his garret, and still gasping for breath, Heathcliff experienced an overwhelming urge to flee. Nothing on earth could hold him at Wuthering Heights. As he picked through his things, he felt utterly and totally betrayed.

He plucked up the enameled music-box Catherine had given him, the most beautiful thing he owned in the world. He hurled it against the wall. The music-box broke to pieces. The prickly metal heart of the mechanism dropped onto his pillow and released a few melancholy notes into the stuffy air.

Anger and pride welled up in him like a storm. He gathered what little money he had, pulled on a cloak, and hurried to the stables.

His old stallion stood in its stall, its back coated with sweat. The master of Wuthering Heights had not bothered to remove its saddle.

Wind whistled through the barn. Shutters banged against the side of the house. Joseph would be outside, he knew, pulling the shutters closed against the wind.

Heathcliff backed the horse out of its stall. Joseph burst through the door in a gust of wind, his eyes blazing with anger.

"Lowly flaysome Divil!" Joseph hissed. "What are you doing?"

HEATHCLIFF: THE LOST YEARS

"I'm leaving, and I'm taking this horse. A horse is little payment for all my labor!"

"You *steal* Master's horse?" Joseph cawed. "Thief!"

Joseph pulled a hatchet from a wooden stump near the barn door. Heathcliff picked up a pitchfork. When Joseph stalked forward, his blue eyes blazing, Heathcliff lifted the pitchfork and backed the sputtering old Pharisee flush against a wall.

Joseph lifted both hands. He dropped the hatchet. A clap of thunder shook the timbers of the barn.

"Demon from Hell!" Joseph hissed. "Master will take the hide off you!"

"You can all go to Hell," Heathcliff said. "I'll endure no more foul treatment here."

Heathcliff took a step back, tossed aside the pitchfork, and vaulted onto the stallion.

"Evil gypsy demon!" Joseph shouted. "You have nothing, you are nothing! You'll crawl back here on your knees and beg for mercy! Master will tie you to a post and whip you until you die!"

Alongside the driveway, a shape-shifting wind stirred the tops of the fir trees. A few fat drops of rain struck the packed earth.

Heathcliff pulled up before the porch of the old house. He tugged his cloak tight around his shoulders and took a final look at Wuthering Heights. He thought he saw two female figures framed in the golden light of the parlor window, staring out into the maw of the gathering storm.

"Heathcliff!"

For a moment, he heard Catherine's haunting voice cry out across the moor.

He kicked the stallion in the ribs and turned the horse away.

Liverpool

Chapter 12

Heathcliff bent low over the neck of the horse. He pulled Joseph's old hat over his eyes and kicked the stallion forward into the darkening storm.

Heathcliff fled all that held him and hurt him and broke his heart at Wuthering Heights. In the punishing rain, kicking the beast forward, he could not stop riding. He wished only that he might be immediately struck dead, or allowed to die.

Wind came in cold stiff gusts from the north. Icy pellets of rain began to sting his face and hands but the stallion held fast to the road. From time to time, lightning lit up the distant hills, trailed by ringing claps of thunder.

Finally, when he could kick the stallion no more, the animal slowed to a walk. It snorted and shook its head in the swiftly-blowing rain, its chest heaving, unable to run farther. Blinking back rain, Heathcliff rolled off the stallion and collapsed onto the wet grass.

He struggled to his feet, gasping for breath. Rain slapped at his face. He grabbed the bridle. He tied the reins to a bush.

In a flash of lightning, Heathcliff glimpsed a flimsy structure perched on the side of a low hill not far away. He staggered up the slope toward it, his boots slipping on the wet grass and mud.

HEATHCLIFF: THE LOST YEARS

It was a crude lean-to, an empty sheepherder's hut. Inside, he felt straw on the earthen floor. He removed his hat, stooped low, and wormed his way into the hovel. He stripped off his wet cloak. With a great effort, Heathcliff pulled off his wet, mud-caked boots and fell back onto a bed of straw.

Raindrops spattered against the roof. Droplets of cold rain leaked between the planks, dripping onto his face. Covering himself with his wet cloak, he positioned his hat over one ear to keep out the rain.

The makeshift cocoon soon warmed from the heat of his body. To the sound of hammering rain, Heathcliff fell asleep like an exhausted babe in his gypsy mother's arms.

Chapter 13

Awakened by the trilling of a skylark, Heathcliff crawled out of the lean-to into the moist early morning air. The storm passed in the night. A few white clouds remained in the sky. The sun rose over wet, glistening hills.

The wet grass glittered with diamonds. On the slope of a distant hill, Heathcliff noticed a herd of sheep making their way down the hill on a carpet of thick green grass.

Heathcliff squeezed the water out of his garments, put them on, and slipped into his cold, tight boots. The morning sunlight warmed his body. On the far side of the road, the stallion grazed quietly next to a small still pond.

Heathcliff cupped his hands and drank from the pond. He caught the horse, stroked its soft muzzle, pulled himself up onto its back, and kicked the stallion into a canter. As the stallion carried him down the narrow road, it splashed through long silver puddles that quivered with rain.

Heathcliff's swore to himself he would never return to Wuthering Heights. He experienced a surge of righteous anger at the thought of Catherine's betrothal, followed by a trembling pang of regret that broke his heart and made him want to cry.

HEATHCLIFF: THE LOST YEARS

He grimaced as his horse approached a slow-moving wagon. He kicked the stallion into a gallop and guided the horse through the tall grass on the right side of the road to pass.

The stallion suddenly buckled, flinging him forward into grass and mud.

Heathcliff bounded to his feet, shocked and gasping for breath. He saw mud on his hands. He barely heard the stallion squeal with pain.

"Whoa, Lilly!" The driver of the wagon pulled up his mule. The man leaned sideways to squint at Heathcliff.

"Are ye hurt, lad?" he asked.

"I don't think so," Heathcliff replied.

He glanced at the stallion. It drew up its right front hoof and whinnied with pain.

"I'm afraid my horse is hurt," Heathcliff said.

"Let's have a look at the animal."

The stranger removed his broad-brimmed hat and climbed from the wagon. He was a tall bear of a man with a ruddy complexion. Heathcliff followed behind as the man approached the stallion, calmed the horse with his big hands, and carefully lifted its right front knee.

The man showed Heathcliff a stub of cannon bone protruding like a bloody yellow knife through the skin of the animal's leg. Heathcliff's heart sunk. The stranger put one arm over Heathcliff's shoulder and led him away from the horse.

"Your beast is finished, lad. He'll not stand on four legs again."

The stallion whinnied with pain.

"I've a knife in me wagon. Do you want I put the beast out of its misery?

"Give me the knife," Heathcliff snapped. "I'll lay him down myself."

Holding the knife, Heathcliff slipped up next to the little stallion. He grimaced and stroked its neck for the last time. He felt a great stab of regret as he put one arm lightly across the animal's shoulders. He clenched his teeth, and slashed the upturned blade across the horse's muscular neck, then immediately backed away.

The stallion squealed and tried to rear up on its hind legs, its jugular veins spraying blood.

Heathcliff felt faint when the horse thudded to the ground. The stranger gently removed the knife from his hand, wiped the blade clean on his pants, and tossed the knife into the back of the wagon. Then he climbed aboard and put on his wide-brimmed hat.

"Where you be going, laddie?"

When Heathcliff looked up at the big man, he did not know how to reply. He shook his head.

"You'd best ride a bit with me." The stranger stuck out a beefy hand. He pulled Heathcliff onto the wagon seat, took up the reins, and clicked at the mule.

"My name is Heathcliff," Heathcliff said.

"I am called Nathanael, Nathanael Jones."

Nathanael's mule plodded west. All morning long, the sun broke in and out of swiftly-moving clouds. When Nathanael pulled up beside a stream to feed and rest the mule, he shared a tin of cooked potatoes with Heathcliff.

"I'm worried, lad," Nathanael Jones said.

"Why?"

"I fear for our cottages."

"You're a cottager, then?"

"We're but four families at Crosston commons. We've lived in Crosston for years, but Lord Margrave would enclose our land. Twice he has told us we must leave our homes."

"Can he force you to leave?"

"I hope not, laddie. Anyway, we've a bit of grain to harvest, and it's a big job for all of us this year. Could you lend a hand? We might feed you, at least, for a few days."

"If you need a hand, I'll help you."

HEATHCLIFF: THE LOST YEARS

Heathcliff felt grateful for the company of Nathanael Jones, a solid man who said nothing more. For much of the day Heathcliff stared out over the rolling hills, trying not to think of all he left behind, and wondering what might lie ahead.

Chapter 14

Under the light of a half moon, Nathanael pulled up the mule. Heathcliff made out four small cottages lined up in the moonlight, with a wooden barn behind.

Nathanael Jones whistled. The front door of the nearest cottage opened in a burst of light. A very small boy limped out to meet them, carrying a small lantern.

"Hello, Robert," Nathanael said.

Nathanael's son shyly nuzzled up to his father. Nathanael hugged the boy and bid him lead away the mule.

Under the thatch roof of their cottage, Nathanael's wife bade them sit down. Nathanael's two young daughters, shyly competing to serve their unexpected guest, brought Heathcliff a spoon, a bowl of warm soup, and a good chunk of bread.

"No man in Crosston will work to-morrow," Nathanael said. "We'll begin our harvest on Monday."

"We must put you in the barn, to-night, but we'll try to make you comfortable," said Nathanael's wife.

Picking up a lantern, Nathanael led Heathcliff through a moonlit vegetable garden behind the cottage and into the wooden barn which already housed the mule. Nathanael's wife brought a sleeping pallet stuffed with straw. The oldest Jones girl, Matilda, carried out a blanket and bed linen from the house and Heathcliff was soon asleep.

He awoke to the sound of male and female voices rising to the heavens. Heathcliff walked outside to find Nathanael conducting a Sunday morning prayer service behind the barn. Standing atop an empty wagon, Nathanael preached a sermon on the Good Samaritan, and the cottagers sang again.

After the service, Nathanael's wife caught two chickens, chopped off their heads, and took them inside to cook them. One cottager dug potatoes, another baked bread. At Nathanael's insistence, Heathcliff joined the cottagers in their communal meal.

That afternoon, Nathanael walked Heathcliff to the common area behind the barn. Nathanael paused at the edge of the field. A thick stand of golden wheat grew almost to Heathcliff's waist, with visibly fat kernels weighing down the heads.

"You've a fine crop," Heathcliff said.

"We drained the lower commons and last year seeded the ground with clover. This year we dunged the entire field and planted by the moon, all of it in two days, every family working together," he said. "It's my hope we'll make enough to buy our village a cow, to give our little children some good milk and cheese."

On Monday morning, Heathcliff awoke to a cacophony of whinnying horses, whistles, and bleating sheep. It was not yet light when he stumbled outside.

Near the wheat field, Heathcliff saw several figures on horseback, herding a flock of sheep. Using whistles and herd dogs, the mounted men drove the sheep directly into the wheat and held them there. Men and women hurried out of their cottages, shouting and waving their arms.

"Hey! Not in our field!"

"Take off the sheep, man!"

One of the women threw rocks at the sheep but the animals tramped dumb circles through the field, bleating and stamping down the grain.

"What is this?" Heathcliff asked Nathanael Jones.

"Lord Margrave," Nathanael said. "Over there. On the grey. Come with me."

Heathcliff followed Nathanael around the edge of the field. They approached a rotund gentleman sneering at them from the back of a fat grey horse. Nathanael Jones approached the man and diffidently pulled off his hat.

"Lord Margrave," he said. "This is surely a mistake, sir. You must take off your sheep. You'll have a fair share of our crop."

"I don't want a share of your bloody crop. You commoners plant on my land, again and again, and you don't have my permission. You know very well this land belongs to me."

"Crosston farms the commons, Lord Margrave," Nathanael said. "It's our family's right to do as we have always done. You help us, we help you. Your own father understood this well."

A small group of excited cottagers circled the horse. Lord Margrave clutched his riding crop in one hand and scowled at them from atop the grey. The animal snorted and took a step to one side.

"Please take off your sheep, Lord Margrave," came a woman's plaintive voice. "Please, sir, now move them off."

"I've told you all, Mary, all of you," Lord Margrave said, his voice rising. "You cannot work this land. It's my land, all of it. Those cottages sit on my land."

Across the field, Heathcliff saw children with sticks try to chase away the herd-dogs. He recognized Nathanael's son limping along behind the other boys.

As the sheep bleated anxiously, and turned about in the field, a horseman charged at the children to chase them away.

"You've no claim here, Nathanael, none of you," Lord Margrave said. "You have no claim from a legal authority."

HEATHCLIFF: THE LOST YEARS

"We've our history in Crosston, Lord Margrave, and our fathers' history, and their fathers' fathers," Nathanael Jones replied. "Our four families farm the commons since any of us can remember."

"Yesterday morning I went before a magistrate, Nathanael," Lord Margrave said. "And I tell you again, you have no claim. My patience is gone."

Pulling up the reins with one hand, Lord Margrave backed his horse out of the group, causing the cottagers to back away.

"All of you—for the last time—get off my land!"

Lord Margrave wheeled his horse around and galloped away but his sheep remained. A few hours later, his men whistled off the dogs and moved away the flock, leaving the wheat trampled into the ground.

At dusk, Nathanael called the cottagers together outside the barn.

"Lord Margrave would make Crosston his paddock. We must stand together, all of us," Nathanael Jones began.

"My William wants to pack up and leave," a woman cried. "Lord Margrave will have us out."

"No, William! You must stay. We are only strong if we stand up together," Nathanael said. "Now, all of you, what shall we do?"

Heathcliff leaned against the wagon and listened to cottagers argue into the night. One determined woman wanted to walk to the estate of Lord Margrave the very next morning, and throw herself before Lord Margrave's ageing mother, who knew many of the women well. The woman's husband disagreed; the man thought they should take Lord Margrave to court.

Others swore they had not money to oppose such a well-connected gentleman. Jeremiah Evans, the oldest of the cottagers, believed the cottagers needn't do anything at all.

"Lord Margrave is a Christian man. He'll regret the evil he's done us to-day. To-morrow, he'll return to apologize, and he'll reimburse us for our lost crop," the old commoner said. "In my opinion, we need only to stand and wait."

At the end of the evening, William and his wife still insisted to the group they had no choice but to pack up and move away.

"This does not bode well," Nathanael Jones told Heathcliff. "Our little village is divided. If we cannot act together, how can we possibly save ourselves?"

Chapter 15

Heathcliff **woke up** the next morning in a mad whirl of smoke and flame. For a brief moment, coughing and blinking, he believed he had awakened in the crackling fires of Hell. Smoke burned his eyes. Over his head, the timbers of the wooden barn sputtered and flamed. The mule brayed loudly, kicking at the timbers of its stall.

Heathcliff rose from his pallet, gasping and coughing. He stumbled toward the mule, opened the stall, and pulled the animal out of the barn into the smoky, eerily illuminated darkness.

"Fire!" he cried. "Fire!"

The frightened mule jerked away, braying and kicking up its heels. Heathcliff saw one of Lord Margrave's men toss a burning torch onto the roof of a cottage, and spur his horse away into the dark. The thatch roofs of all four cottages broke out in flames.

"Fire! Everybody outside!"

Men and women staggered out of the cottages in their night-clothes, pulling and carrying children. Nathanael Jones burst out the door of his cottage, followed by his wife and daughters.

"To the well, men. Let's have our bucket line!" Nathanael cried, making for the well.

"Where is my Robert?" Nathanael's wife shouted at Heathcliff, looking about. "Where is my son?"

Without thinking, Heathcliff plunged through the open door of Nathanael's cottage. The air was thick with smoke. Bits of burning thatch fell around him like orange rain.

Heathcliff found young Robert curled into a ball in a far corner of the cottage, whimpering quietly, holding both hands over his head. Heathcliff snatched up the lad, carried him outside, and placed him in his mother's arms.

The air was bright as daylight when Heathcliff joined the bucket line. Despite their efforts, the barn collapsed into a heap of orange flames. Amidst the shouts and screaming of women and children, Heathcliff heard a lone horse galloping away.

Chapter 16

Lord Margrave came to Crosston early the next morning in a fine carriage, followed by three mounted man. Heathcliff heard the carriage approaching. Confused, he stood up. He had barely slept. Around him, exhausted cottagers rose up in disarray, their faces smeared with soot.

"Lord Margrave brings old Smee," said Nathanael Jones.

"Men of Crosston, listen to me," Lord Margrave began, without getting out of his carriage. "I will pay for your lost crop. You will take what I give you and leave right away, all of you. If you don't get out, Constable Smee has orders to take you to jail."

"You burned our homes!" a woman cried.

"Constable Smee will settle with you," shouted Lord Margrave, with a nod to the Constable. "I'm sorry, Mary. The fact is you must go, to-day. Good-bye."

With a wave at the coachman, the lord of the manor hurried away.

Old Constable Smee slowly and grimly dismounted. He tied up his horse and looked about, a leather pouch over his arm. He shook his head and walked forward to where Nathanael Jones stood flanked by his wife and daughters.

"Nathanael, I'm sorry," the Constable began.

"Lord Margrave is rich as a king. To take a bit more land he hardly needs, he would send us all to the poor-house! We worked all our lives here, George, all of us. Our parents and their parents, too."

"Lord Margrave chooses to enclose his land, Nathanael. He will plant hedgerows and such. He has a legal right. So line up now, you men, all of you!" Smee said, raising his voice. "Come get your money. You have no choice but to move along."

Heathcliff watched the Constable count out a few bank-notes into Nathanael's hand.

"Lord Margrave's greed severs us from our land, and our very lives. This bit of money is nothing for my cottage, and my family's life," said Nathanael Jones, examining the bank-notes.

"Call it progress, Nathanael," the Constable replied. "Villages all over England are being enclosed. Things are changing everywhere. You will surely find work in the city."

Nathanael turned to his wife. "We'll go to Liverpool, Meg. Your older brother will surely put us up, until I get work."

His wife hugged the girls. "I'm afraid, Nathanael," she said.

"I say we'll get along, every one of us," Nathanael stood up on a rock and shouted to the cottagers. "God will provide for the righteous! Let Lord Margrave have his bloody land. I say, let the greedy bastard rot in Hell!"

Chapter 17

Nathanael's mule-drawn wagon teetered slowly through the green hills. The narrow country road wound past meadows, hills, a few cottages, and fields of grain.

Heathcliff sat in back with the children. In the far corner of the wagon, surrounded by the few possessions they salvaged from the fire, Nathanael's son clutched his knees and stared up at the clouds, trying hard not to weep. Wrapped in charred blankets that still smelled of the fire, the girls huddled on either side of Heathcliff. For much of the afternoon, Heathcliff kept his arms around the girls and let them cry.

That night, the men slept by the side of the road, while Nathanael's wife and daughters slept in the wagon.

The narrow road ended at a toll-house. Nathanael sent Heathcliff inside with money to pay the six-penny toll. When the gate-keeper lifted the toll-gate, their cart joined a caravan of wagons, carriages, and pack-horses on the wide, hard-surfaced turnpike that led to Liverpool.

Not far from the collieries, Heathcliff watched barges loaded high with coal being pulled along a narrow channel of water by plodding draft horses. Closer to the city, the turnpike began to parallel the dark, sediment-laden water of the River Mersey flowing toward Liverpool and the sea.

At twilight, just outside the darkening city, the tall brick chimneys of the Liverpool Salt Works emitted smoke that smelled of burnt brine and burning coal.

Nathanael Jones pulled up his mule before a modest, comfortable-looking inn on Duck Lane.

"Come inside, laddie," Nathanael called to Heathcliff. "You can stay the night. I know the place. I've had dealings here."

Nathanael put down a week's rent and handed Heathcliff a room key. Heathcliff suddenly realized Nathanael meant it as a gift.

"I cannot accept this, Nathanael," he said. "Please. You must save your money."

"You pulled my Robert from the fire, lad. My wife says without you we surely lost him."

"You've your family to care for, Nathanael."

"Laddie, I will take care of my own. My father did it and his father before him. Don't fret about me," Nathanael said. "But I have learned one thing. We must work together, lad, here on this earth, all of us. If the good people don't help one another, all the goodness we create on this earth will die."

Heathcliff followed Nathanael outside. He shook Nathanael's big hand in the twilight. When the wagon rolled away, he saw all three of Nathanel's children in the back, solemnly waving goodbye.

Chapter 18

Heathcliff woke up the next morning, delighted to find a fine breakfast served at the inn. The innkeeper was an ebullient gentleman with a small moustache who kept a close eye on the servant-girls. He told Heathcliff Liverpool was peopled by fifty thousand souls, and rapidly growing. Ships arrived daily from all over the world, he proudly added, and goods moved through the seaport at an unprecedented rate of more than thirty thousand tons a year.

"As many vessels make landfall in Liverpool as London or Bristol. We've wet docks to speed unloading even in in ten-meter tides, and we're building more," the innkeeper boasted. "The sea trade is the life's blood of this city. Take a stroll around this morning. You will see prosperity everywhere you look."

In the commercial heart of the city, hanging signs of blacksmiths, rope-makers, and coopers advertised their affiliation with the sea trade. New buildings were springing up everywhere. The windows of Liverpool's shops displayed more goods and exotic items than Heathcliff imagined could exist in the world.

Along Liverpool's wooden sidewalks, sharp-eyed men in silver-buckled shoes, long coats and three-cornered hats went about their business with their heads down.

A gentleman relieved himself on a pissing post. Mysterious ladies sailed past in carriages. Unseen church bells rang out the hour while sad-looking beggars extended their hands.

In shipyards along the River Mersey the hulls of half-finished ships lay sprawled across the earth like the skeletons of huge wooden fish. Heathcliff watched in awe as hardwood logs hewn and bent into shape with hand-tools were fitted together by huge cranes. A virtual army of carpenters, fitters, and sail-makers swarmed over half-finished vessels like industrious insects.

Along Water Street, vendors with push-carts hawked trinkets and scarves, fresh oysters, chunks of cooked fish, fried potatoes, meat pies, and more. The sea air mingled with the odors of frying fish and meat, horse manure, sweat, tobacco, wood smoke, and burning coal. Groups of mariners strutted into town from the docks, their clothes marking them as sailors.

Along Liverpool's great docks lay an astounding number of tall-masted ships. Rows of ships and masts extended as far down the wet docks as he could see, and beyond them Heathcliff saw more ships at anchor in the pool.

The seaport's rough and tumble energy filled Heathcliff with hope, but it also frightened and overwhelmed him as he made his way back down Hanover Street to sleep at the inn on Duck Lane.

The next morning, Heathcliff told the innkeeper, "To-day, I intend to search for work."

"There's gainful employment to be found," the inkeeper replied.

At an unmarked two-story warehouse on Bank Street, a gang of older boys pulled boxes from a huge wooden wagon with no sides. When Heathcliff asked a boy about work, the lad pointed out a large, pock-marked man observing the crew with folded arms.

"You must speak to Mr. Willits," he said.

Henry Willits stared at Heathcliff with a sour, suspicious face as he approached.

"I am looking for work," Heathcliff began.

"I will have no one who loafs or complains or talks back. My men all work hard."

"I do not fear honest work," Heathcliff said.

"Come back to-morrow morning," Henry Willits said, turning to spit on the ground. "Maybe you will do."

Chapter 19

Early the next morning, Henry Willits pulled up the dray near a tall, three-masted ship named the *Commerce* and set the brake. While Willits attended to the horse, Heathcliff hurried off the dray and scurried up the gangplank with the crew.

Willits had the boys gather around the hatch, pick it up, and move the hatch aside.

"All of you, below," Willits snapped.

Heathcliff followed the boys down a ladder into the ship's dimly-lit upper hold and watched Willits maneuver the cargo net down into the hold. The others showed him how to pick up wooden boxes of sugar and stack them on the net. When the net was full, Willits hauled it up.

"Get up here, all of you," Willits said.

Heathcliff scrambled up in time to see Willits maneuver the loaded net over the side and lower it next to the dray, using block and tackle. Following the other boys, Heathcliff hurried down the gangplank and began stacking boxes onto the dray.

Willits drove the back to the warehouse with the crew running along behind. They ran the boxes into the warehouse, stacked them in place, then jumped onto the dray to ride back to the ship.

The hold became warm as they worked. When the boys were all freely sweating, a trembling young boy said to the others, "I believe I shall faint." Other boys cautioned him against it, but he climbed up the ladder to speak with Henry Willits.

"It is rather warm down here, sir," Heathcliff heard the boy say. "I am afraid I will faint."

"Get out! Get off this ship and faint!" Henry Willits shouted and shooed him off the boat. "Get away now and don't come back."

Henry Willits bent down to point at the boys down in the hold. "No complaining, you. If another complains, I'll fire the lot of you."

The crew finished work at dusk.

"Come back in the morning," Willits told Heathcliff. "You may do for a while. We pay in cash on Friday."

The next morning, the crew finished unloading the upper hold. They slipped down the manhole into the lower hold where quarters were much closer. The lower hold contained barrels stacked on and between double wooden racks and the air was hot and foul. Heathcliff thought it smelled of dead or rotting farm animals.

"It stinks terribly down here," Heathcliff whispered to another boy, as they strained to pull a barrel from a rack.

"The *Commerce* is a slaver," the boy whispered. "The slavers all smell like death."

By the light of a single lamp, perspiring boys pulled hogsheads of rum and molasses from wooden racks and pushed them up through the manhole where other boys loaded the barrels into the net.

That second day in the lower hold, Heathcliff heard a peculiar sound. It sounded like a hand slapping the wooden timbers somewhere beneath them.

"What is that?" Heathcliff asked an older boy who seemed to be directing the crew.

"The owner's likely pressed some hands. They lock pressed men in the bilge until they're on the sea. Don't speak of this to Mr. Willits. He'll fire you."

After they unloaded the *Commerce,* the flow of containers changed directions. Under the eye of Henry Willits, the crew began moving goods from the warehouse onto the dray and hurriedly loading boxes onto the ship.

Down into the hold came the net containing wooden boxes and barrels that sloshed, rattled, and clanked. Several containers were quite heavy, while others seemed to weigh nothing at all. All morning, the crew handled crates and hogsheads that smelled of tobacco, oil, salt, new fabric, and sweet perfume.

Late in the day, Heathcliff heard the heavily-loaded cargo net over their heads began to rip open.

"Heads up!" Willits shouted.

Heathcliff jumped back. Wooden crates and barrels rained into the hold and broke open against the timbers. Necklaces and glass beads erupted from broken boxes. A heavy wooden crate broke cleanly in half, scattering an array of iron manacles and leg-irons all across the floor.

Chapter 20

Those first few nights in Liverpool, Heathcliff left the Inn on Duck Lane to walk after his evening meal. He sometimes saw tired-looking men and women sleeping in doorways or huddled together beneath streetlamps. One night, in an alley, he watched a cockfight beneath a hanging lantern. Gangs of sailors seemed to be everywhere, roaming the streets of the seaport at night in search of excitement.

On his walks, Heathcliff could not stop thinking of Wuthering Heights. He despised Hindley, but he sorely missed Catherine Earnshaw. The more he tried to forget her, the more he longed to see her again. She had crushed him, but in leaving her, he realized he had left some vital part of himself behind. The idea that he was neither rich nor gentleman enough to contend for Catherine's hand infuriated him, and punctured his heart like a poisoned thorn.

Walking beneath the streetlamps of Liverpool, material wealth seemed to be everywhere he looked: the desire to rise in the world seized him by the throat. If he was ever to see Catherine again, and to settle with Hindley, Heathcliff knew he must put iron in his heart. He swore to himself he would find a way to make himself a rich and proper gentleman. It was only as a rich gentleman, he believed, that could he even dream of returning to Wuthering Heights.

On Friday night, the crew finished loading up the *Commerce*. Heathcliff waited in line with the crew for his pay envelope, which Henry Willits distributed under the lantern by the warehouse door. Willits held Heathcliff's pay envelope until last.

"We have no more work for you here, Heathcliff. But attend to what is written down here," Henry Willits said.

On the back of Heathcliff's pay envelope someone had printed an unfamiliar name, Joshua Bullin, and an address on Paradise Street. Heathcliff stared at the grizzled face of Henry Willits. He understood he was being let go, but he had no idea why. This perplexed him.

"Did I not work hard enough?" Heathcliff asked.

"You're a sturdy enough lad but there's other work for sturdy lads. Go visit the gentleman Sunday morning."

Heathcliff looked at the unfamiliar name and address and struggled to understand. "Who is Joshua Bullin?" he asked.

"Master Joshua Bullin, a very upstanding gentlemens of Liverpool," Henry Willits said. "Mr. Joshua Bullin what owns this warehouse. Mr. Joshua Bullin what invests in ships and things of that sort. The same Mr. Joshua Bullin whose brother is mayor of this very city."

"Sorry," Heathcliff shook his head, still trying to understand. "What do you wish me to do?"

"Pay a call on the gentleman, I said," Willits snorted, slapping the envelope. "If I were a dumb lout such as you, I'd thank my lucky stars a rich gentlemans like Mr. Bullin invited me to call."

Chapter 21

On Saturday morning, Heathcliff walked up Paradise Street into a neighborhood of large grey-stone mansions. These were the homes of Liverpool's wealthy aristocrats and merchants, he sensed, but to his eye the huge houses seemed austere and intimidating despite the formal beauty of their design, the orderly gardens, and their great spreading trees.

Set back from the street, behind four imposing marble columns and an elaborate stone facade, Number 55 Paradise Street looked to be among the very greatest of the great houses. Heathcliff looked at his pay envelope to double-check the address, then crept diffidently up the sidewalk toward the mansion. He paused under the portico to catch his breath, dwarfed by the sheer magnificence of it all.

In the center of a tall, hand-carved wooden door lay a gleaming brass door-knocker shaped like the head of a roaring lion with a ring through its nose. Heathcliff thought the door-knocker made of solid gold, and for a time he hesitated to touch it. But he took a deep breath, lifted the golden ring, and rapped twice.

The door opened a crack. A dark brown eye and bloodshot eyeball peered at him.

"Your business, sir?" came a high-pitched voice.

"My name is Heathcliff," he said, holding up his pay envelope. "I was told to call on Mr. Joshua Bullin here this morning."

The first Negro Heathcliff had ever seen opened the door. The little man's skin was blacker than coal but he wore a pressed white shirt and loose-fitting midnight blue velvet livery. The Negro's wiry hair was heavily powdered and his features so perfectly cut they could have hewn from black marble.

"Are you Joshua Bullin?" Heathcliff asked.

"My master is Mr. Bullin. Master Bullin call me Pompey. Have you calling card?" the Negro sniffed.

Heathcliff shook his head no. The Negro pointed out a chair in the hallway.

"Wait here," he said.

Heathcliff sat down. The little Negro walked away.

On the marble-topped table before him stood two large Dresden figurines that seemed to welcome visitors to the house. A bewigged porcelain gentleman in a black suit looked at him with an amused smile, one hand on a walking-stick and the other extended in a fey, courtly bow. Next to him, a white-skinned porcelain lady in a pale blue gown stood frozen in a ladylike curtsey. On the wall above them was a large oil painting in a gilt-edged frame: pink-skinned angels stroked harps of gold above an ominous white castle on the shore of a distant sea.

Joshua Bullin's mansion smelled of cooking spices, rose petals, and smoking tobacco, Heathcliff noticed. He began to think the mansion a somewhat welcoming place.

Pompey opened the door to a nearby drawing room.

"Come in, young mariner," came a thin voice from within the room. "I believe I have something of interest to you."

In a high-backed chair behind a desk sat a pink-faced gentleman perhaps fifty years of age. The blue-eyed gentleman was casual in his appearance. He wore only a bathrobe, and no periwig atop his stringy grey hair. On his desk, a pewter teapot steamed beside an open ledger.

HEATHCLIFF: THE LOST YEARS

Joshua Bullin lit a white, long-stemmed ceramic pipe and exhaled a plume of smoke before motioning for Heathcliff to sit down. As the smell of American tobacco spread through the air like dusky perfume, Joshua Bullin fixed Heathcliff in his cool blue eyes.

"You're a young man who must think of his future. I offer you an opportunity to make a handsome sum of money. Are you interested, sir?"

"I certainly may be," Heathcliff said, leaning forward.

"It's hard physical work, in exotic climes. I know a captain who needs but one additional hand to complete his crew."

"I am no sailor, sir. If that's what you suggest."

"To-morrow, a ship will sail on the most lucrative voyage to riches in all of Christendom," Joshua Bullin said. "It carries English goods to Africa, black ivory to the New World, and returns with sugar and rum to England. The triangle trade, sir. Every man in Liverpool with money to invest wants in on it. Excuse me, but I am pressed for time. Will you avail yourself of this opportunity?"

"But sir. I have no experience at sea."

"Every seaman alive has learnt, sir! My good-hearted captain will teach you all you need to know. Do look over this document, and give me your decision right away."

Joshua Bullin's eyes seemed cold and blue as the sea as he pushed some papers across the desk, and looked away.

When Heathcliff saw the amount of money being offered, he blinked, and looked again. He looked up at the merchant, not quite believing his eyes. Joshua Bullin quickly handed him a pen.

"You are very generous, sir," Heathcliff said, and quickly signed his name.

Joshua Bullin waved off the compliment, then signed and double-checked the documents. "My word is my bond, sir. Of course, you must have a copy."

"Thank you," Heathcliff said, and accepted his copy of the articles.

"Keep your papers in hand, lad. To put matters in writing is good business," the merchant said. "Now, listen up, you must get to the docks first thing in the morning. The *Commerce* sails with the tide."

Joshua Bullin pulled a hanging velvet cord. Pompey hurried into the room and held the door. Heathcliff stood up and happily extended his right hand to the merchant.

"I am grateful for the opportunity you have proffered me, sir," he began.

Puffing vigorously on his pipe, Joshua Bullin made a note in his ledger and closed it. Without looking up, he waved Heathcliff away.

Chapter 22

The seaport was overcast when Heathcliff arrived at the docks the next morning, carrying a satchel containing what little he owned in the world. The *Commerce* floated in the wet dock, tied up, and shifting like a cat on its haunches. A line of wooden barrels blocked off the gangplank. Heathcliff walked the length of the ship and for the first time looked her over.

The *Commerce* was almost two hundred feet long, and thirty feet wide at the beam. Near the front of her newly-painted crimson hull was the ship's name painted in black letters outlined in gold.

Beneath the long needle of the bowsprit was the ship's figurehead—a painted wooden figure labelled *Mercury, the god of Commerce*. Below the figurehead's pink painted wooden face and flowing hair, golden wings and white hands burst out of its sky-blue robe as if to embrace the world.

"Are you the c-c-captain?" came a deep, rich voice.

Heathcliff felt a hand on his shoulder.

He turned to see a gangly young man named Peter, struggling to introduce himself. Peter was a homely lad with protruding ears. He had an unusually deep resonant voice and a pronounced stammer. As he blurted out his name, Peter looked to be about sixteen years old.

"The house-master sent us here for s-s-service," Peter explained. "A gentleman s-s-stopped by the work-house. Tom saw money change hands but I suppose we must s-serve to acquire what's due us."

"We're to become mariners!" cried Peter's younger companion, a short, enthusiastic towhead.

"That's young Tom," Peter told Heathcliff. "We're t-t-together."

Tom was a well-proportioned little boy, perhaps ten years old. He was fat as a cherub and he seemed deliriously happy. Young Tom kept both hands in his pockets but he could not stop glancing up at the three-masted ship and smirking.

"Here's the last of our crew, and just in time," boomed a hearty voice.

A husky slab of a man with shoulder-length red hair strutted down the gangplank. Glancing from side to side, he rolled aside the barrels.

"I'm Mr. Coil, first mate of the *Commerce*. Follow me aboard, lads."

As they stepped onto the deck, mariners hauled up the gangplank behind them. Above them Heathcliff saw men climbing like spiders into the spars and rigging. He saw the gate to the wet dock open. Ships began moving. Using long poles, men on the docks pushed the *Commerce* away. Heathcliff experienced the uneasy rocking sensation of a great ship floating free.

"Heads up, lads. Follow me."

The first mate led them across the deck to a slender man in a fine crimson frock coat. The man's long copper-coloured hair was clubbed back behind his head and tied with a black ribbon. On his head was the grandest hat Heathcliff had ever seen, a three-cornered beaver tricorne with a stylish white cockade.

"This is Captain Charles Collingwood, your captain and master of the *Commerce*," said Mr. Coil. "Captain Collingwood gives the orders, and we all obey 'em, hear? Aye-aye, sir?"

"Aye-aye, sir," the orphans mumbled.

Young Tom snapped to attention and managed an awkward salute.

HEATHCLIFF: THE LOST YEARS

"The little one will do for a cabin boy, Mr. Coil," said the captain. "Take him to Mr. Marconi."

"Aye, aye, captain," said Mr. Coil.

Captain Collingwood looked the three of them over. Heathcliff thought the captain's grey expressionless eyes the colour of cold rain.

"Get them fitted out right away, Mr. Coil," said the captain. "After dinner, bring up the pressed men."

"Aye-aye, sir," Mr. Coil said.

The first mate walked them to the bow of the ship. Ahead of them, connected to the bow with a long, taut rope, Heathcliff saw a longboat manned by ten oarsmen tugging the *Commerce* through the gate of the wet dock and into the pool.

Mr. Coil paused at the base of the bowsprit, rubbed his crotch, and winked at young Tom. "Here's the first thing a mariner must know."

Whipping out his penis, the first mate urinated over the bow. Heathcliff imagined yellow urine fluttering onto the outstretched wings and hands of Mercury before dripping down into the sea.

"This is the head," Mr. Coil explained, his long red hair blowing in the wind. "When a mariner must pee, he stands here, or he sits in that apparatus and he wipes himself afterward. Here's a bucket of sea water to clean your finger. Don't drink water from this bucket, do you understand?" Mr. Coil gruffly asked young Tom.

"Aye, aye, sir," said young Tom, managing a salute.

"And don't tumble into the sea," growled Mr. Coil, buttoning up his pants.

"Do mariners often tumble into the sea?" the lad asked, peeping down over the railing into the water.

"The oceans are littered with dead sailors, little lad," said Mr. Coil. "But enough of this. Let's get you to the slops."

Below deck, by the light of a lamp, the purser issued them all a rope-knife and sea clothes—shirts, pantaloons, short jackets, wool caps, weather gear, welted shoes, and a polka dot neckerchief.

"Thank you, Mr. Coil!" cried Young Tom, upon receiving his clothes.

"Hardly thank me, lad. This is charged against your pay. And a good deal more will be charged against your pay, too."

Mr. Coil led them into the forecastle, a large room beneath the bow of the ship. The low-ceilinged room was dark but two small open port-holes admitted air and light. Although Mr. Coil didn't seem to notice, there was a hammock hanging in the center of the room, with a person apparently hidden away inside.

"This is where you will sleep, before the mast," said Mr. Coil. "We shall issue you hammocks and lockers."

Against the far wall, Heathcliff made out a row of wooden lockers and a string of sea chests pushed against the bulkhead.

"I'll take this little man to meet our cook," Mr. Coil announced, clapping his hand on Tom's shoulder. "You two wait here."

"Aye-aye, sir," Peter said as they departed.

"He's the best of the Misters, our Mr. Coil is, but you'll despise all the others before this voyage ends, take my word for it," came a gruff voice.

The long pale face of a reddish blonde, green-eyed Irishman popped up over the edge of the hammock like the head of an exotic bird.

"Captain Collingwood thinks only of his profits and Mr. Bolt's a toady, but don't cross the bosun, Mr. Quayle," the Irishman said. "Quayle's a nasty dog with a wicked bite."

"Who are you?" Peter asked.

"I'm this ship's carpenter, and a seaman as well. My mother named me Barry Ryan but most call me Fiddler," he said. "Attend to this, lads. You must address Captain Collingwood always as captain. The mates you address as Mister or Sir. If you don't show respect and say aye-aye, you risk a flogging and by the way, I hear our new captain's quick with the cat."

"Aye-aye, sir," Peter said.

HEATHCLIFF: THE LOST YEARS

"Don't aye-aye *me*, lad," Fiddler growled. "I'm one of the hands."

When Mr. Coil returned, the Irishman retracted his head into the hammock like a turtle withdrawing into its shell. Mr. Coil ignored him.

"Follow me, lads," said the first mate. "Let's get you to work."

On deck, mariners hoisted the longboat up to its davits, pulling it from the sea like a great white fish weeping sea water. High above Heathcliff's head, sailors stepped perilously along the foot-lines and attended to the sails. Captain Collingwood stood on the quarterdeck, gesturing with his hat.

At the shriek of the bosun's whistle, mariners took up the halyards. Mr. Coil placed Heathcliff at the rear of one group, and Peter to the rear of another. Heathcliff began pulling rope with the others, and standing aside when they did.

As sails filled with wind, each produced a great thrilling *pop*. Sails snapped and billowed. The *Commerce* slowly began to move. Over Heathcliff's head, white sea-birds dipped and spun around the masts and sails, anxiously crying out.

Heathcliff glanced over his shoulder. All along the waterfront, plumes of black smoke coiled up from the shore.

Africa

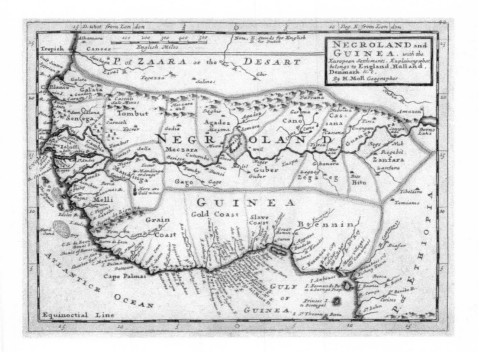

Chapter 23

Slowly, the *Commerce* glided out of the slate grey water of the pool, leaving the city behind. Beneath a billowing mass of sails, Heathcliff looked back at a double wake of white curls dissipating into the expanding vastness of the sea.

The first afternoon, Mr. Coil placed Heathcliff next to an old salt named Vito who was manning the helm. A short, big-shouldered man with the bloodshot eyes of a sad old sea dog, Vito knew his work. With one grizzled hand resting lightly on the wheel, Vito showed Heathcliff the 32-point mariner's compass, explained it, and handed Heathcliff an hourglass to keep ship's time. As Vito directed, Heathcliff turned over the glass every half-hour and rang a brass bell to mark ship's time. Eight bells signaled the end of a four-hour watch, Heathcliff learned, and also marked the end of his lesson.

That evening, mariners turned over a wooden tub called the kid in the middle of the forecastle. A one-eyed Italian cook named Marconi staggered in with a huge steaming slab of dripping salt meat between two large forks and dropped the wet, pink mass on top the tub.

"Eat the meat and don't complain," said the ship's cook, whose long greasy hair was piled and knotted on top of his head. "You'll get no better than this."

HEATHCLIFF: THE LOST YEARS

"This smells like horse meat," Fiddler said.

"What does a lubber like you know of *horses*?" Marconi scoffed as he left the room, wiping his hands on his apron.

Fiddler pulled out his rope knife and sliced off a chunk of wet, pink meat. He stuck it in his mouth, chewed it with some difficulty, and then opened his green eyes.

"It *is* bloody horse meat," he said. "They warned me this captain is a skinflint—he feeds us the cheapest meat he can buy."

Heathcliff unsheathed his rope-knife and reached for the meat but the Irishman caught his arm.

"Did you see our cook's new dentures? Our cook has wooden teeth. We believe his teeth fell out because he had to eat his own cooking," Fiddler said.

The Irishman laughed, slapping his knee. Others laughed, too.

Young Tom hurried in with in a canister of watered-down tea, and a handful of tin cannikins. The cook dragged in a sack of biscuits and scooped out a handful to lay onto the kid.

Fiddler snatched up a biscuit and rapped it on the kid. "Hard tack, already hard as a rock. I'd like to see the Misters eat this," he said to the departing cook.

"Eat the bread, complain of the flour," Marconi responded.

After dinner, Heathcliff walked past the galley. Marconi looked up from his cook-stove, blinking back smoke with his one good eye. When the cook smiled, Heathcliff noticed he had removed his wooden dentures.

"Eat the bwead, complain of the flwour," Marconi said.

Shortly after that, Heathcliff saw Mr. Coil escourt three motley-looking men up from the hold onto the deck. The three men, who were not yet in sea clothes, scowled at the crew.

"Those are our pressed men, for sure," Fiddler said. "Pressed for gambling debts I imagine. They do not look happy, those gamblers."

"Not at all," Heathcliff agreed.

"Pressed men make the worst of companions at sea. You must never turn your back on them," he said.

Near sundown, Heathcliff made his way to the prow of the ship. A stiff wind whipped through his hair. With one hand, Heathcliff shaded his eyes from the glare.

Far ahead of the ship, beneath a cowl of fat, orange-bellied clouds, a blood red sun burned on the horizon. The *Commerce* seemed to sail toward it atop an endless rolling sea of liquid gold.

Chapter 24

The following morning, three quick raps on the scuttle startled Heathcliff awake. As he slipped out of his hammock, he heard the eerie shriek of the bosun's whistle whistling up the crew.

"All hands to the quarterdeck! Tumble up, men!"

All over the forecastle, mariners rolled out of their hammocks. Heathcliff followed the men outside.

A couple of hands Heathcliff hadn't seen before were barefoot. Most of the crew was clean-shaven, with long hair tied behind their neck. A Negro sailor Heathcliff noticed for the first time had a shaved head. Many mariners sported brass hoop ear-rings and crude tattoos.

The older of the two orphans, Peter, moved next to Heathcliff. Shoving their way to the front of the group Heathcliff recognized the three pressed men, who now wore sea clothes.

Captain Collingwood briskly introduced his officers. Mr. Coil stood next to the second mate, Cornelius Bolt, a beanpole of a man who nervously smiled and blinked at the crew. The stout gentleman in a short grey periwig and spectacles the captain introduced as Jack Chum, the ship's surgeon. The short, heavily-tattooed man with long, ape-like arm was the boatswain, Danael Quayle.

Mr. Quayle slapped a rattan cane against his leg and glared at the crew as the captain spoke.

Captain Collingwood assigned every hand to a watch. The captain put Heathcliff on the port watch, under Mr. Coil. Peter was assigned the larboard watch under Mr. Bolt.

"Men of the *Commerce*," Captain Collingwood began. "Investors raised twelve thousand English pounds to outfit this ship. As captain, I promised our investors I would return to England with a handsome profit, and I mean to keep my word.

"As we depart for savage Africa, I want to impress upon you that we must pull together. You will follow my orders promptly, and any orders I give my officers. Any man who breaks discipline isn't worth powder and shot, as far as I'm concerned," the captain said, showing his small, even teeth and glaring at the crew.

Heathcliff noticed the cook prodding young Tom up the steps to the quarterdeck. The ship's new cabin boy wore a loose, ill-fitting jacket and on one shoulder he struggled to balance a tin tray containing a single bowl of steaming hot tea.

Captain Collingwood stopped young Tom with one hand. He picked up the tea, downed it in a single gulp, and grimly returned it to the tray.

With one hand on Tom's shoulder, the captain nodded to Mr. Quayle. The bosun extracted the cat o' nine tails from a baize bag. He held the whip over his head. From the whip handle hung nine strands of brown leather whipcord two feet long, studded with nine knots per string.

"I will take hide off any mariner who steals, lies, fights, lays off a watch, or disobeys my orders. Do you understand?"

"Aye-aye, captain," a few hands muttered, one after the other.

"Already he flaunts the captain's daughter," someone hissed.

Young Tom backed away from the whip but Captain Collingwood jerked him back. Thrown off balance, the orphan dropped his tray.

HEATHCLIFF: THE LOST YEARS

The captain's tea bowl smashed onto the deck. Loudly, the tin tray bounced and clattered away.

"You pushed me!" young Tom cried.

Mr. Quayle stepped forward and swung at the cabin boy with the cat. Surprised and frightened, the orphan put his arms over his head and received the lash again.

"I'm sorry! Aye-aye, captain!" Tom cried. "Aye-aye, sir!"

Mr. Quayle booted young Tom off the quarterdeck. When he hit the timbers, young Tom curled up into a ball. The pressed men slapped their knees and howled with delight.

"Clumsy little fucker!" one said.

The bosun blew his whistle. "All hands, disperse to your stations!"

Mariners hurried away as Heathcliff bent down to help young Tom. The cabin boy's head was bleeding.

"Come on, little man," Heathcliff said, offering his hand. "Let me take you to the surgeon."

The cabin boy shook his head no. He stood up, picked up his tray, and scurried back toward the galley.

Chapter 25

The next morning, Mr. Coil called Heathcliff and two of the pressed men aside, and issued them mops and buckets.

"Get to swabbing the deck, mates," said Mr. Coil. "You must swab the deck from stem to stern every morning before captain's inspection."

Heathcliff dutifully mopped his way down the deck. The pressed men dawdled behind, whispering to themselves.

"You there! Hipshit!" the smaller of the pressed men shouted. "Get to the ropes, man! Quickly, pass me the diamond!"

Holding onto the pen-rail with one hand, he pointed frantically at a group of dangling ropes not far away.

"Pass you which rope?" Heathcliff asked, confused.

"The *diamond*, lubber! Quick! Or you might sink the bloody ship!"

Heathcliff dropped his mop and hurried toward the dangling ropes. Now the second pressed man also gestured frantically.

"Pass him the diamond, man! Now! It's life or death!"

"I don't know which rope is the diamond!"

"He can't find the diamond!"

"I don't know which rope you want!" Heathcliff said.

"Well, aren't you a bloody fool." The taller pressed man elbowed his snickering companion. "Lubber can't find his diamond."

"His diamond!"

"There isn't any diamond!" the short one howled.

The pressed men laughed and slapped their knees. The smaller one howled like a dog. When they glimpsed Mr. Coil striding toward them, they quickly returned to mopping.

Heathcliff mopped his way down the deck, feeling like a fool. Vito called him to the helm.

"Don't listen to those beggars. You only take orders from captain or an officer. Understand?"

Heathcliff nodded. Humbly, he continued mopping.

After the captain's inspection, Mr. Coil waved him over. "This way, lad. You must learn to throw the log."

At the rear of the ship, Mr. Coil handed Heathcliff a knotted line wound onto a reel, with a pie-shaped board attached to the end of the line. He had Heathcliff fling the log over the stern and allow the line to drift away for two turns of the 30-second hour-glass he held in his hands.

"Sixty seconds, lad. Reel in your line," said Mr. Coil, looking over the stern. "As you pull in your line, count knots; one knot marks one nautical knot of speed."

"Three knots," Heathcliff announced, after he reeled in the log.

"Three knots is our speed. You must mark it down. To plot our course, our navigator must know the speed of our ship," he explained.

Mr. Coil walked Heathcliff to the traverse-board, a round wooden board painted like a compass containing holes to mark the ship's speed and direction. The first mate gave Heathcliff a wooden peg and pointed to a hole on the traverse-board.

"Mark the ship's speed, three knots, remember?" Mr. Coil pointed. "Place your peg here, for three knots."

"Yes." Heathcliff inserted the peg.

"Something else we shall call on you to do," said Mr. Coil, clapping him manfully on the shoulder. "If you apply yourself diligently, the captain may have you manning the helm before this voyage is over."

Every morning, after Captain Collingwood inspected the deck, the morning watch began. Watches rotated every four hours. The crew swept the deck clean every evening. Two-hour dog watches provided time for dinner and after that, four-hour night watches began.

The constant changing of the watches threw off Heathcliff's sleep. For the first several days, he struggled to keep up with the crew. Many of Mr. Coil's commands he did not understand. He sometimes felt he stumbled through a dream peppered with confusing, unfamiliar words.

"Bear a hand!"

"Man the fore tack and sheet!"

"Sheet home!"

In a daze, Heathcliff mimicked the movements of others, who were quick to set him straight. He learned that aft was to the rear of the ship, fore was toward the front, port was left, starboard or larboard right, the bow the front end of the ship and the stern the rear, the mainmast the larger mast in the middle, the mizzenmast the rear mast, and so on. Every object and action aboard the ship had a different name and he struggled to remember the meaning of new words that seemed to multiply faster than he could learn them.

The lamp in the forecastle went out at eight o'clock. Some of the time, Heathcliff could sleep four hours before being called aloft for a night watch. After that, he returned to his hammock to try to sleep four more hours before being called to watch again.

"You must never nap on watch, even at night, as it infuriates the bosun," whispered the orphan Peter, showing Heathcliff his welts. "If Mr. Quayle finds you napping, he'll t-t-take a c-cane to your legs."

The morning the *Commerce* passed the island of Angsley. Heathcliff set down his mop for a moment to observe it. The bosun soon crept up behind him and whacked his calves three times. Heathcliff danced at the pain.

"Wake up, lubber," sneered Mr. Quayle. "Attend to your duties! No more napping."

The pressed men mopping along behind Heathcliff snickered. He clenched his mop; the searing pain in his calves infuriated him. He wanted to break the bosun's cane in half, but he only scowled, and returned to mopping.

"Aye-aye, sir," he said.

Heathcliff soon observed the *Commerce* was a miraculous contraption, cleverly constructed to harness the power of the wind. Ropes extending from the yards down to the deck allowed the crew to rotate, pull, and fasten all twelve billowing square canvas sails into position. Yards could be easily rotated on their masts, allowing the sails to draw wind from any direction. Triangular sails called spankers and jibs on the butt and bow of the vessel could be let out to draw forth even more of the wind's seemingly inexhaustible power.

Standing watch with Fiddler Ryan, Heathcliff marveled at mariners scrambling up the ratlines to unfurl sails. As he watched his shipmates work the yards, they seemed to be walking across the sky. Fiddler told him the tallest of the masts extended seventy-five feet above the deck. Heathcliff dreaded climbing that high.

"Fiddler! Heathcliff! Man the main royal, tack and sheet," barked Mr. Coil.

"Aye-aye, sir." Fiddler slapped Heathcliff's arm.

"What did he say?" Heathcliff whispered.

"We must release the topmost sail, laddie. Quickly now. You just follow me."

The Irishman leaped onto the ratlines and skittered up the jiggling diagonal tar-covered rope ladder. Heathcliff took a deep breath, followed him up, and paused not far from the top of the sail.

He had never climbed that high before. His gut knotted when he looked down and saw the small faces of his shipmates and Mr. Coil shading their eyes, all of them observing him. Heathcliff clung to the ratlines like a frightened monkey He suddenly became aware of the slow sickening rocking of the ship.

"Come on, lad," the Irishman shouted. "Get onto the crosstrees."

The Fiddler clutched the yard and stepped from the solid wooden pegs hammered into the mainmast to the foot-lines, ropes that hung three feet below the yard and extended out to the far end of the sail.

Clutching the mast with both arms, Heathcliff gingerly stepped onto the crosstrees. His stomach trembled. He heard the obnoxious voice of one of the pressed men, cawing out for him to jump.

"Don't listen to that! Watch me, lad! Do as I do."

As adroitly as a spider, holding onto the yard, Fiddler slid both feet along the foot-lines all the way out to the weather side of the yard. Holding the mast with one hand, he motioned for Heathcliff to move to the other side of the sail.

"Onto the foot-lines! Quickly now! Mr. Coil's watching!"

Clutching the yard to his chest, and determined not to show fear, Heathcliff placed one foot on the quivering rope. The outstretched foot-line gave a little as he stepped on it, but he forced himself to step out with his other foot and balance there. His stomach fluttered. Very cautiously Heathcliff worked his way along the yard, moving his hands and feet together, gritting his teeth, hair blowing, both feet balanced on what felt like a rope composed of thin air.

An eternity later, Heathcliff reached the bunt gasket, which bound the folded sail atop the yard. He glanced down again, greatly regretted it, then angrily looked out at the unforgiving vastness of the blue-grey sea.

"Release your bunts! Watch me!"

Teetering on a tightwire of rope far above the deck, Heathcliff's heart pounded as he unwound the bunts exactly as the Irishman did, picking away the slippery hitches with trembling fingers. He coiled and knotted his ropes to keep them away from the sail. Finally, as the Irishman waved him in, Heathcliff slipped back along the foot-lines to the safety of the mast.

Heathcliff stood on the crosstrees, hugging the gently-moving mast, panting and grimacing up at the pitiless sky. He felt grateful to have survived. It infuriated him to hear the pressed men again cawing for him to jump.

"Get down, man! Swing a leg to the ratlines!" Fiddler shouted.

Heathcliff carefully eased his way back to the ratlines, and climbed down. At last, he swung down onto the deck, feeling much lighter and immensely relieved. His feet stung for a few steps but he took up a halyard between the two pressed men.

"Why didn't you jump, lubber?" the tall one hissed. "We gave you your orders."

"If I jumped, I feared I couldn't kill the both of you at the same time," Heathcliff replied.

Mr. Coil, not far away, overheard this and laughed heartily.

"To lose these good men would make captain frantic," Mr. Coil said. "Heathcliff, I thank the Lord you didn't kill them."

The pressed men grumbled away while other hands set the braces and sheeted the sail.

Heathcliff paused to watch the main royal draw wind high above his head. He felt a flicker of pride when the Irishman dropped to the deck and gave him a manly clap on the back, and they moved on to other work.

Chapter 26

Sails popped smartly in the wind as the *Commerce* sailed south down the Channel of St. George. One after-noon, under a bank of high grey clouds, Heathcliff watched Vito guide the ship into the cool rough waters of the Atlantic. The *Commerce* skimmed over the waves like a sea-bird flying just above the water.

At the end of each day, Heathcliff discovered, the forecastle became a place of pipe-smoking, boasting, story-telling, and gossip. Mariners mended their clothes. Others played checkers or cards for money. Old salts sometimes spoke of the curiosities and horrors encountered on their other voyages; a few opened their sea-chests to show off shrunken heads, strangely-coloured ears of corn, peculiar necklaces, carved rocks, and other exotic souvenirs of far-off lands.

Captain Collingwood was the subject of a great deal of speculation by the crew. Since it was captain's first Guinea voyage, some hands worried the captain was naïve and untested in the wilds of Africa, and might put them all at risk. Other hands thought the captain would be very well advised by the trustworthy and more experienced Mr. Coil.

"The first leg of the triangle trade is an easy slog, but we may well have trouble when we make landfall on the Gold Coast," an old salt predicted.

HEATHCLIFF: THE LOST YEARS

"Africa is a land of poisonous snakes, crocodiles, superstitions, sickness, and thievery," he added. "You would not believe the cheating, treachery, and double-crossery I've witnessed in the buying and selling of black flesh."

"The middle passage is more dangerous," Vito said. "With two hundred quashees packed into the hold, and a crew outnumbered, the run to the islands can become a voyage of horrors."

"African savages possess a powerful magic called *juju*, " said another. "Those that possess it cast terrible spells. Entire ships have disappeared. After a *juju* curse, captains have committed suicide in frightful ways, or been driven mad."

Standing watch one evening after dinner, the sweet, unfamiliar sounds of a fiddle broke the silence. Walking about the deck, Heathcliff found Fiddler Ryan sitting down on the deck, half-hidden from sight, with his back against the binnacle.

The Irishman played a handsome little fiddle Heathcliff had not seen before. With both eyes closed, Fiddler stroked out a strangely haunting lover's lament.

A few hands gathered about to listen. As the orange sun sunk into the horizon, the plaintive notes of the Irishman's fiddle, like the sounds of sadness itself, created a strange melancholy resonance on the wild, windblown sea.

Chapter 27

One evening, Heathcliff noticed the cook furtively roll a heavy wooden barrel out of the galley. Looking from side to side, Marconi attached a rope to the barrel and fastened the other end to the ship, then tossed it over the stern. He left the barrel bobbing along behind the ship, and slunk away.

At breakfast, Heathcliff questioned young Tom about what he had seen. The cabin boy told Heathcliff the barrel was full of salted meat. The cook dragged his barrels through the ocean to allow seawater to soften the meat. When Marconi boiled it, young Tom said, the cook skimmed off pots of grease to use as slush for the masts.

"The officers eat much differently than us," young Tom blurted.

Several hands grunted. Breakfast was oatmeal gruel with slivers of hard cheese and hard tack, the same breakfast Marconi had served the crew every day. Young Tom dipped his hard tack into the oatmeal, cocked his head, and gnawed off a piece.

"It's unfair the cabin eats so well, and we eat so very poorly," said young Tom, chewing at his biscuit. "I have never had enough food to eat, never in my entire life. Sometimes I fear I shall die hungry. When I see the food the officers eat, I stand by praying they'll leave a bit for me, but they rarely ever do."

HEATHCLIFF: THE LOST YEARS

"I've no remedy for that, Tom," Heathcliff said.

"You should see what Mr. Marconi fixes captain for breakfast. Eggs! Fresh biscuits! *Marmalade!*" blurted young Tom with a far-off look in his eyes. "I'd *love* a taste of marmalade!"

The cook shuffled into the forecastle, blinking and wiping his hands on his greasy apron. Marconi rapped his knuckles on the wall.

"Up Tom," he said. "Time to serve the cabin."

The cabin boy jumped up, stuffed the remains of his biscuit in his pants pocket, and followed the cook away.

Heathcliff often saw Tom hurrying about the ship. The cabin boy cared for the chickens and pigs aboard, cleaned up after the cook, served the cabin, and ran errands for the captain and officers. Tom seemed to be always running, but he ate his meals in the forecastle with the hands, when he was given time to eat.

Chapter 28

Disagreements between men sometimes occurred after dinner, following a sharp remark, an accidental bump on the arm, or an allegation of cheating at cards. In the close-packed atmosphere of the forecastle, disagreements between men could become violent. His second week aboard ship, Heathcliff watched one of the pressed men threaten to break the Irishman's fiddle. After some sharp words, the Fiddler bounded up and bloodied his opponent's nose.

When a fight began, a mariner hurried to the doorway to keep watch for the bosun, who sometimes strutted in unannounced. If Mr. Quayle discovered two hands fighting, they all knew, each combatant would receive five lashes.

But fights broke the routine. Mariners gathered round to watch the sweating, slapping, biting combatants until one man triumphed, or the other surrendered and began swabbing up the blood.

The pressed men instigated a great many fights, Heathcliff noticed, and the three of them complained constantly about every aspect of the ship. They had nothing good to say about Captain Collingwood, the ship's officers, the surgeon, or any individual member of the crew. Heathcliff disliked the three of them. The two pressed men on his watch impressed him as stupid, lazy braggarts.

HEATHCLIFF: THE LOST YEARS

The worst of the three was an obnoxious, big-nosed knave named Billy Gilding who was missing a good bit of his right ear. The remains of his ear protruded from the right side of his head like a tiny horn. A tall oak tree of a man, Gilding took advantage of his size to push the younger mariners about and snatch away their rations of grog. The other pressed men called him "the crazy one."

One evening in the forecastle, Gilding told the hands a story. He said a savage Indian chief in the American colony of Virginia chewed off most of his ear in a brutal grappling fight, after which he was left for dead. For revenge, Billy Gilding said, he personally stabbed the entire tribe to death with his rope-knife. Despite the disbelieving hoots of the other pressed men, Gilding swore that he cut the throat of every single savage in the tribe, including the ferocious chief, and then had his way the chief's pretty young daughter. After that, according to him, he singlehandedly robbed the savages of a king's ransom in gold.

"But where's the gold, Billy?" another pressed man asked. "You're poor as a church mouse."

"Lost it gambling," said Billy Gilding. "Lost it in Liverpool."

"Sure you did. And I'm the King of England," the taller of the two laughed.

Billy Gilding turned to Heathcliff and fingered the prong of his bad ear.

"You'd never stick a knife into an Indian chief and give a good fuck to his little daughter, now would you, pretty boy?" Billy Gilding asked.

"No, I doubt I would," Heathcliff replied. "And I do not believe you did, either."

The sailors hooted. Billy Gilding unsheathed his rope knife, waved it at Heathcliff's face, and turned away.

Darkness brought out the ship's rats. Lying in his hammock at night, Heathcliff heard them scratching and gnawing at the timbers. He hated rats; their odious gnawing kept him awake.

When the rats roamed about, a few of the hands made a game of trying to kill them with their rope knives. The first sailor to see a rat would hurl his knife across the forecastle, and occasionally kill one of the nasty creatures. Occasionally, a mariner got lucky and bragged about his prowess, holding up the rat to show the crew.

One evening, Heathcliff woke up with a dead rat on his face. He sputtered awake, shouted, jumped, grabbed the bloody lifeless creature in one hand, and hurled it across the forecastle.

Two of the pressed men stood the doorway, laughing. One-eared Billy Gilding, who Heathcliff suspected threw the rat, pretended to snore in his hammock not far away.

Chapter 29

A muscular, dark-skinned Negro named Oidah Blue worked on Heathcliff's watch. The bald, fierce-looking Negro did his work diligently, spoke only when spoken to, and mingled very little with the other hands. The Negro's ferocious demeanor kept most of the crew at bay. But when Heathcliff got to know the man, he realized the big Negro was shy, and probably the gentlest and most decent man on the ship.

Oidah never told Heathcliff how he went to sea. But he did tell Heathcliff he shaved his head every few days, because he was ashamed of his coarse, nappy hair.

"You always wear a hoop earring," Heathcliff observed.

"Protect me from drowning," Oidah said, fingering his large brass earring. "Protect me from evil spirits in the sea."

"Spirits? Oidah, you are superstitious."

"I tell you some things," Oidah Blue began.

In broken English, Oidah told Heathcliff that all mariners revered and respected the wind. The wind was a good spirit that watched over them and kept away demons that lurked in the deep. Bad spirits lurked beneath the surface of the water, he said. These included deceptively beautiful creatures called mermaids that were part woman and part fish. Mermaids did not have souls, Oidah said; they could draw an entire ship onto treacherous rocks merely by rising from the sea during a storm and singing.

Killing a sea gull or albatross would rouse the spirits of drowned sailors and cause them to haunt a ship, Oidah Blue believed. While a dolphin alongside the ship always portended good luck, sharks that followed a vessel were omens of death.

Even bathing at sea brought bad luck, Oidah said, and like the other hands Oidah never attempted to swim in the ocean of water around them. He told Heathcliff none of the crew was likely to bathe until they reached landfall in Africa.

At the end of his watch, Heathcliff walked into the forecastle and saw Billy Gilding strutting between the hammocks, brandishing the huge knife almost two feet long he claimed he won in a card game.

"Slaves cut sugar cane with this, but I'll use me new *machete* to protect all what's oughts to be mine," Gilding said.

"Please be quiet," said young Tom, who was trying to sleep.

"Bloke trifles with me, I trifle right back with me *machete*." Gilding poked young Tom's hammock with the point of his knife. "Fear me big knife, cabin boy? You should greatly fear it."

"I'll not have this!" shouted young Tom, sitting up in his hammock.

"Leave the little lad to sleep, Billy," Heathcliff said. "Be off to your watch. Leave young Tom alone."

Gilding strutted up to face Heathcliff, and jutted out his chin.

"I do as I please, pretty boy," he said. "I do what I please with me things."

Heathcliff stared Billy Gilding down. But before Gilding left the forecastle, Heathcliff noticed him open a sea-chest and drop the big *machete* into what sounded to be a rather large collection of knives.

Chapter 30

Heathcliff **awoke with a start** at the shriek of the bosun's whistle. He heard the voice of Mr. Quayle shouting to the crew.

"All hands lay aft to witness punishment!"

Heathcliff rolled from his hammock and followed the crew to the mainmast, curious to see what was transpiring. Young Tom slipped into place beside him. Heathcliff hoisted Tom onto his shoulders so he could see.

"Let me down." Tom soon pulled at his hair. "I'll not watch this."

When Heathcliff set Tom down, the orphan grabbed Heathcliff's hand and tried to pull him away.

"Mustn't leave, Tommy," Vito whispered, bending down to speak to the boy. "If you don't bear witness, you'll get a flogging, too."

Captain Collingwood stood frowning before the mainmast, flanked by his officers. Peter stood next to the captain with his back turned to the crew. The homely orphan grimaced while the captain turned him forward to face the crew. Peter blinked rapidly.

Captain Collingwood clapped one hand on Peter's shoulder. The orphan made an effort to stand erect, but Heathcliff thought Peter looked as if he might faint.

"One of our crew crept into the galley and stole Mr. Marconi's best cutting knife. Mr. Quayle found this in the forecastle, in young Peter's hammock," cried the captain, holding up the knife. "You broke the Eighth Commandment, Peter! What do you have to say for yourself?"

"I am n-not a t-t-thief!" said the orphan, his deep voice quivering. "I did not t-t-take that knife!"

"Mr. Quayle!" snapped the captain. "Where did you find this knife?"

"In 'is sleeping sack, sir. Another hand led me to it."

"Another hand p-placed it there!" Peter cried.

"You must not steal *and* lie, Peter. It's additional punishment. Quickly now—confess your deed."

Peter shook his head no. He swallowed and looked plaintively at the crew, his face white as freshly-fallen snow.

Mr. Quayle stripped the orphan's shirt from his shoulders. He led him to the grating over the hatch, pushed Peter's legs apart, and tied him to the grate. When Peter was tied down, Dr. Chum slipped a leather strap between his teeth.

Suddenly, Peter thrashed like a fish against the grating, breathing quickly. Heathcliff felt young Tom squeezing his hand, trying to pull him away. Heathcliff wanted to help Peter but knew he could not.

"Twenty lashes is the punishment for stealing, Mr. Quayle," said the captain. "All hands witness how we discipline a thief."

Mr. Quayle crouched low, the knotted tendrils of the cat hanging down between his legs. Blinking rapidly, the bosun approached Peter from behind, creeping forward like a cat stalking a bird.

Tom pulled Heathcliff's arms over his eyes before the bosun rocked back onto his heels and struck, leaving pink stripes dotted with small red marbles of blood all down Peter's back. The whip came down again, and again. Peter's blood spattered. Peter spit out the strap.

"I did not steal that knife!" Peter cried.

Mr. Quayle bared his teeth, breathing hard, his shirt stuck to his back with sweat. The bosun paused to pick bits of skin from the cords of the cat. He looked to the captain.

"Get on with it, Mr. Quayle," said the captain.

The bosun drew back his arm, and continued. Every time Peter was hit, he cried out. The orphan's punishment seemed to take quite a long time. Heathcliff grimaced and felt each blow. Young Tom threw his arms around Heathcliff and began sobbing.

Heathcliff hugged the trembling boy and looked out over the wide blue sea. When he looked back, he saw Billy Gilding leaning gleefully forward, a pearl of drool hanging from his lip.

"Do you admit your guilt and ask the Lord's forgiveness, Peter? As a Christian, you must ask the Lord's forgiveness," said the captain.

With tears in his eyes, the orphan weakly shook his head yes. "Yes," he whispered.

"Discipline administered," snapped the captain. "Hands return to your stations."

The mariners walked away. Heathcliff put his arm around young Tom and hugged the weeping boy.

He watched Mr. Bolt unbind Peter's hands and feet. Peter turned, moaned, sat down, and spit out what might have been a chunk of his tongue.

Dr. Chum trotted forward with a bucket of vinegar and salt water. He set the bucket down next to Peter, and extracted a rag.

"Back to your duties, gentlemen," he told Heathcliff. "I shall fix the lad up."

Chapter 31

Heathcliff swayed above the billowing sails, sitting lookout on the round wooden platform high atop the mainmast. An endless plane of flat blue ocean lay all around him. Suddenly, far to the left, he thought he saw land. He shaded his eyes, squinted, and looked again. Very clearly, he saw a thin line of grey volcanic mountains on the southern horizon.

"Land ho!" Heathcliff cried.

"Where does she lie, seaman?" came the voice of Mr. Coil.

"Four compass points to portside."

"That will be the Canaries, mate. On the other side of those islands lies Africa herself."

That they were drawing near the Dark Continent gave Heathcliff a moment of dread, and also thrilled him. That same day, he saw a group of gigantic sea turtles swimming like great proud dogs through the sea.

Heathcliff sometimes marveled at the vast expanse of water that surrounded the ship. The sea was an immense womb that teemed with strange and peculiar creatures. If England was a place of boundaries and laws where men grabbed and claimed every piece of land, the sea constrained no living creature's freedom. The ocean seemed generous and maternal enough to nurture them all.

HEATHCLIFF: THE LOST YEARS

Standing watch under an evening sky of twinkling diamonds, Heathcliff sometimes felt himself in the arms of a mystic feminine presence. He understood why mariners marveled at the sea, and feared and respected her. Doomed only to skim her surface or drown, men would forever remain trespassers here.

Quite early one morning, Heathcliff saw an enormous creature rise from the ocean fifty yards from the ship. As the sea parted, the head and back of a slick grey creature broke the surface of the water and turned back down, filling him with horror. At first he thought it a giant sea snake, coiling over in the water.

"Leviathan!" cried Mr. Coil, when he saw the whale.

Several hands moved to the bulwark as a second grey creature rose to the surface. The two great swimming creatures moved like grace itself alongside the Commerce, effortlessly keeping pace with the ship. Hands and officers gathered to watch until the gigantic creatures dove back into the deep blue water with a fine kick of their splayed tails, and were not seen again.

An old salt informed them all that whales alongside the ship brought good luck, and this put the crew in good humor.

Two days later, Heathcliff saw what appeared to be a bubble of silver rise from the sea far ahead of the ship. As the ship sailed forward, the bubble expanded to a vibrating cloud, flashing points of silver and growing larger.

"Summon the cook, Heathcliff," said Mr. Coil. "Go quickly."

By the time Heathcliff returned, flying fish crisscrossed the deck like birds in the air. Leaning over the bulwark, Heathcliff watched the fish fling themselves up from the sea like ducks flapping and flying off a pond.

Flying fish struck the masts and sails and fell to the deck, gasping, flapping their long stiff wings.

Marconi and young Tom hopped about the deck, catching fish and stuffing them into empty biscuit-sacks. Several hands helped them catch fish. Tom waved a stick in the air, trying to knock fish down.

That night, Marconi cooked a meal of fresh fish that for once seemed to please the entire crew.

Chapter 32

One Sunday morning after the captain's inspection, Mr. Bolt lifted his small, round head. The second mate hopped dramatically to the quarterdeck, wrinkled his nose, and whipped off his hat.

"I smell Africa!" he cried.

Mr. Coil moved to his side, sniffed the air, and nodded his assent.

"It's Africa, all right," the first mate turned to Heathcliff. "Africa can be smelled before she's seen. Can you smell her, lad?"

"I smell her!" Peter replied. "It's a b-beautiful s-s-smell!"

Hands filed out of the forecastle to sniff the bewitching aroma of Africa. Heathcliff tried his best to discern it, but he was not sure he smelled the Dark Continent at all.

The next day, the *Commerce* sailed beneath a bank of high thin red clouds that old hands called "the smokes." Mr. Coil told Heathcliff that wind lifted dust off the Sahara Desert and blew it far out to sea. On the third day, a cloud of clay-coloured dust descended on the *Commerce* and turned the crew's heads and shoulders the colour of blood.

The air warmed. Like most of the others, Heathcliff now stood day watches without shirts and shoes. His skin darkened in the sun and the ends of his hair turned so light it seemed tipped with gold.

Heathcliff had developed callouses; he no longer blistered his palms sliding down the backstays, or broke off fingernails handling sails and rigging. It had been days since he lay awake in his hammock at night with his hands on fire from pulling at the ropes.

Like the rest of the crew, Heathcliff looked forward to the ration of grog every hand received after the middle and morning watch. The watered-down rum seemed to make work and sleeping easier.

Marconi's meals did not improve. For variety, the cook gave them a dollop of cold sauerkraut or foul dry anchovies to accompany the salt meat. More often, the cook tossed a few potatoes or onions into a cauldron to make a notorious soup. The day Heathcliff received his first pannikin of soup, he puzzled at the old hands straining the soup through their neckerchiefs. When he found a cockroach at the bottom of his pannikin, Heathcliff immediately removed his neckerchief and began to do the same.

Weevils multiplied in the biscuits. Although young Tom told them the cabin ate better than ever, everything the hapless cook brought into the forecastle inspired a volley of complaints from the crew.

"Eat the bread, complain of the flour," was Marconi's automatic response.

One evening, Heathcliff lay in his hammock, nearly asleep. He felt someone tugging at his shoes. He opened his eyes to the bulbous nose and squinting eyes of Billy Gilding.

"I'm taking your shoes, pretty boy," Billy Gilding growled. "Mine are worn out."

"Go to the slops," Heathcliff kicked at Gilding from the hammock. "You can't take my shoes."

Gilding pulled a dirk from his waistband.

"You'll shut your mouth, pretty boy. Trifle with me and I'll lop off your eggs."

With a short kick, Heathcliff rolled off the opposite side of his hammock. He landed on his feet and backed up a step, still a little groggy with sleep.

HEATHCLIFF: THE LOST YEARS

Gilding lunged across the hammock, dagger in hand, slashing at Heathcliff's face as he lunged.

Heathcliff grabbed the wrist that held the blade. He pulled Gilding over the hammock and twisted him backwards onto the floor. Gilding dropped the knife. The dirk skitted and spun away.

They wrestled for the knife. Grappling and grunting, they rolled into the sea chests, knocking some awry.

The heads of other sailors popped up from their hammocks. Some jumped to the floor. Peter picked up the knife; he hurried into the doorway to stand watch for Mr. Quayle.

"You've found another knife, Billy?" Peter called out. "Did you steal this one, too?"

"I'll have those shoes," Gilding growled, rising to his feet.

Heathcliff ducked his head and rushed forward. He caught Billy Gilding in the chest with the crown of his head and pushed him across the forecastle and back over the sea chests, leaving him gasping against the bulkhead. When Gilding tried to stand, Heathcliff caught his right arm and yanked it up behind his back.

"Bosun aft!" Peter hissed. He skittered across the room and dropped the dirk into Billy Gilding's hammock.

"The shoes are *mine*," Heathcliff hissed, twisting Gilding's arm. "Say it! Mine!"

"Your shoes," Gilding finally gasped.

Heathcliff released his arm as Mr. Quayle sauntered into the room, looking suspiciously about and swinging his rattan cane.

"Knife in Billy Gilding's hammock," came a deep voice. "Go look and s-s-see."

Chapter 33

One starry night, Heathcliff discovered the captain crouching over the bulwark near the stern of the ship. The captain braced his elbows against the railing and peered into the eyepiece of an odd-looking, triangular brass instrument which he held between his hands. With the fingers of one hand, he turned a small brass dial. Heathcliff froze, curious and hesitant to pass.

"Sighting Polaris," said the captain, without looking up.

"Sir?"

"I am sighting Polaris. This is a sextant. With this instrument, I am fixing our ship's position with the North Star."

Captain Collingwood handed Heathcliff the instrument and jotted something down in a small leather notebook. The sky above them teemed with a thousand stars.

"Which is the North Star, captain?" Heathcliff asked.

Captain Collingwood pointed over the stern. With some help from the captain Heathcliff saw it at last, a glimmering point of light at the tail end of the Little Dipper. The North Star sat low on the horizon. It gleamed like a pale white diamond over the dark blue sea.

"Is the North Star truly north?" Heathcliff asked.

HEATHCLIFF: THE LOST YEARS

"The star sits directly above the Northern Pole. However, it's a bit tricky to sight this close to the equator." The captain took the sextant from Heathcliff's hands. "Tell me, Heathcliff, have you an interest in navigation?"

"I would hope to learn more," he said.

"If you like, I'll show you a bit. If you have a minute now, come to my cabin," said the captain.

Heathcliff had not set foot in the captain's cabin which lay directly beneath the stern of the ship. Captain Collingwood adjusted a whale-oil lantern suspended from the ceiling and bade Heathcliff sit down at the captain's table.

He unrolled a large nautical map. He showed Heathcliff Liverpool at the top of the map, and ran his finger down a string of reckoning points to the hump of Africa.

"At this moment, I reckon our vessel *here*," Captain Collingwood announced, moving his finger. "We must avoid shoals here and, God willing, swing around the hump of Western Africa, here, dipping south and east, here, to arrive at the Guinea Coast, which is *here*," he concluded. "This is where we shall purchase black ivory."

This excited Heathcliff's curiosity and he asked more questions. Combining information from the traverse board, the sextant, and his nautical books, Captain Collingwood explained, he determined the position of the *Commerce* each day and assigned it a reckoning point. This he used to set the ship's course for the next day.

The ringing of two bells roused the captain from his lecture. With a wave of the hand, the captain brusquely dismissed him.

Twice more Heathcliff happened upon the captain and his sextant. Once the captain invited him to his cabin and showed Heathcliff his brass Rittenhouse compass, which was fastened upside down onto the ceiling of his cabin. With a compass in his cabin, the captain said, he always knew in which direction the ship moved.

The next visit, captain showed Heathcliff his nautical books and let Heathcliff look over his charts. The captain broke out some rum and spoke of the difficulties in calculating latitude. When all the difficulties were considered, the captain told Heathcliff over his second cannikin of rum, it often involved a bit of luck and guesswork, this traversing of the sea.

Heathcliff saw no more of the captain's cabin after the *Commerce* rounded the hump of Africa. But he had developed an admiration for the man.

In the forecastle, mariners continued gossiping. Several noticed that Captain Collingwood was becoming irritable. They wondered if the captain worried about the business of buying and handling African slaves, something at which he had little experience. In this, they said, captain would surely be dependent on the more experienced Mr. Coil.

As the air warmed, Heathcliff felt a sluggish sense of dread descend upon the ship. Two mariners received a flogging on the same day, one for insubordination and another for daring to speak out in the other's defense. As the *Commerce* drew close to the Guinea Coast, Mr. Quayle became unusually active with his cane.

Chapter 34

Mr. Quayle's shrill whistle sounded again while Heathcliff lay in the forecastle.

"All hands on deck!" came the call of the bosun. "All hands aft to witness punishment!"

Heathcliff joined the crew beside the mainmast. Overhead, the mottled African sky threatened rain.

Next to the captain stood the cook, blinking and holding young Tom by the elbows. Heathcliff's heart dropped when he saw Tom. The cabin boy bared his teeth at the crew as they gathered, shaking his head no.

Billy Gilding pushed his way to the fore of the group, and the other pressed men followed.

Peter moved over next to Heathcliff, his thick lips trembling with emotion. Taking off his beaver hat, Captain Collingwood addressed the crew.

"Bear witness, men!" he said. "Little Tom here, our ship's cabin boy, got into something that didn't belong to him, a thing reserved for the officers of this ship. Tom stole and then lied about it!"

"A bit of marmalade!" blurted Young Tom.

The orphan tried to squirm away but Marconi held him fast and grimaced, showing his wooden teeth. Mr. Quayle poked Tom with his cane.

"Our little Tommy complains he gets no dinner!" the captain cawed. "But hungry or not, Tommy mustn't steal from the cabin."

"A very tiny bit of *marmalade!*" Tom cried.

Mr. Quayle slapped Tom's calves.

"Tom knew what was in that little cabinet he pried open! A jar of marmalade set aside for the officers of this ship. Our cook caught Tom with his face in the cabinet and this guilty little thumb in his mouth!"

The captain grabbed the thumb of Tom's right hand and pulled it up over Tom's head to show the offending digit to the crew.

Dr. Chum trotted forward, bearing the thumbscrew. The surgeon knelt before young Tom. He nonchalantly loosened the metal plates of the device, which fell open like the mouth of an obedient lizard.

"Put your thumb in the pilliwinks, Tom," said the captain. "Your little thumb broke a Commandment. We can't let that little thumb go unpunished."

"I'll not have this!" Tom shouted, again trying to pull away.

Marconi held the squirming, kicking youth tight against his chest while the surgeon pried open the fingers of Tom's small, moist hand. The wild-eyed orphan bared his teeth and looked at the crew.

"Do help me!" Tom cried.

"All hands witness punishment!" Captain Collingwood announced, putting on his beaver and staring defiantly into the faces of his crew.

Heathcliff winced as Dr. Chum clamped Tom's thumb between the jaws of the device. At the first turn of the screw, the orphan's eyes widened. Tom puffed for air. He tried to pull his arm away as the surgeon again tightened the screws.

"They torture the little lad," Peter hissed, blinking back tears. "They torture him."

"No!" Tom shook his arm up and down but he could not shake off the thumbscrew. "I'll not have this!"

Dr. Chum glanced at the captain, who nodded again.

At the third turn of the screw, Tom screamed. It was an eerie high-pitched scream, the cry of a tiny bird lost in the drizzling rain. The cabin boy released his bowels. A thin stream of mucus dripped from his nose and mingled with his tears.

"Please!" Tom fell to his knees. "I'm sorry, captain! I'll not steal again!"

"One last turn for the lie," said the captain.

The tip of Tom's thumb popped open; his split thumbnail dripped blood onto the deck. The cabin boy fainted and fell down with his thumb still clamped in the jaws of the pilliwinks, and his arm weirdly askew.

"Discipline administered! All hands return to your stations."

As the bosun's whistle sounded, the surgeon bent down to remove the device. A few drops of rain spattered onto the deck while the crew disbanded.

Peter chewed on Heathcliff's shoulder. Heathcliff slapped his back. Dr. Chum picked up the cabin boy and carried him away.

"To torture the tiny little lad! For a wretched spot of jelly?" Peter sobbed. "I hate this wretched ship! There is no Christian forgiveness here."

Chapter 35

Sun rose like a disc of burning flame over the bow. The Guinea coast materialized into a long deep green ribbon along the port horizon. A sticky equatorial breeze shuddered out from the African shore, smelling of moist earth and vegetation. When the ship passed by the mouth of a wide brown river, the current lifted the *Commerce* like a stick of wood and gently shifted her farther away from the shore.

All morning, the *Commerce* skimmed past desolate rock-strewn beaches flanked with walls of dark green vegetation. On his second watch, Heathcliff glimpsed the points of distant mountains protruding through a bank of low, grey clouds.

Heathcliff was not the first of the hands to hear African voices but he was the first to see their canoes. Mr. Coil ordered the crew to ease off the sails sent Heathcliff to fetch the captain.

Captain Collingwood stood on the the upper deck as the ship glided abreast of three long thin dugout canoes, each rowed by several nearly naked Negro oarsmen. With their faces painted yellow and tall knots of hair massed atop their heads, the black-skinned canoe men were unlike any creatures Heathcliff had ever seen.

The ship's officers gathered around the captain on the quarterdeck, examining their unexpected visitors through brass telescopes.

"Ahoy!" came a voice from the canoes. "Are you an English vessel?"

In the closest canoe, a pink-skinned oarsman stood up. He waved both arms and cupped his hands around his mouth. The man wore the loincloth of a savage, but he communicated in what sounded like the King's English.

"Are you an English vessel?" the man shouted again.

"This is Charles Collingwood, captain of the *Commerce*," said the captain, utilizing a speaking-trumpet. "My ship sails under the banner and blessing of King George III, the sovereign monarch of England and all the colonial lands."

As the oarsmen kept pace alongside the ship, the half-naked man cupped both hands around his mouth.

"Be you then a slaver?" the man shouted. "We have flesh to trade."

The captain spoke with Mr. Coil before responding.

"You have no safe harbor for our ship," replied the captain. "Your coast is treacherous."

"Drop anchor, man! We will take you ashore. We have good black ivory to trade!"

The captain conferred with Mr. Coil. The surgeon stood at the weather rail with Heathcliff and several of the hands, gawking at the canoes which rather easily kept pace with the ship.

"For God's sakes, Captain Collingwood," shouted the pale-skinned man. "You can trust me. I am an Englishman, a bloody Englishman!"

"Mr. Coil, you may go ashore," said the captain. "See what they have."

"I will not venture ashore alone, captain."

"Then take a man with you."

"I would have our surgeon," said Mr. Coil.

"Doctor Chum will remain with me," the captain replied.

"Take Heathcliff there. He's a good enough hand. You might show him what we're about."

The *Commerce* maneuvered closer to shore and dropped anchor at twenty fathoms. With some trepidation, Heathcliff followed Mr. Coil down the sea-ladder and squeezed into the first canoe between the pale-skinned man and Mr. Coil.

The man swiveled around and smiled wickedly, his face painted bright yellow. He had knotted his hair atop his head in the African manner but he had the bright blue eyes of an Englishman. The man turned away, shouted something in an African tongue, and all three canoes turned away from the ship.

Mr. Coil leaned forward to clutch Heathcliff's shoulder.

"Our captain fears a trick. If anyone dies upon this God-forsaken shore, Captain Collingwood does not wish it to be him."

Mr. Coil patted Heathcliff's shoulder.

"Hold tight, lad," he said.

The black-skinned oarsmen rowed toward the shore, their long dugout canoes skimming across the slowly shifting sea. As they drew closer, a haze of spindrift fizzled over the canoes. Heathcliff blinked, trying to see.

Directly ahead, the shoulders of long green waves rose from the sea like winged sea creatures, then broke savagely upon the shore. Large sharp boulders lay scattered across the narrow beach. Others protruded from the water, shattering apart the waves.

The Africans sang and chanted. As they approached the rising shoulders of the waves, the canoe men chanted louder.

"Hold on, laddie," came the voice of Mr. Coil.

Heathcliff spread his arms and gripped both sides of the canoe. Large rocks rose from the sea directly ahead.

With a shout from their leader, all three canoes darted up onto the spine of a rising wave and a burst of speed lifted them onto the crest. Paddling furiously, they rode the ocean's mad, thundering energy down between the rocks to a narrow fizzling rock-strewn beach.

HEATHCLIFF: THE LOST YEARS

Jumping into the ocean, the savages pulled their boats ashore. The yellow-faced man helped Heathcliff and Mr. Coil roll out of the canoe. He pulled them through the foaming surf onto dry land and led them sloshing up a trail to a cluster of huts not visible from the sea.

The pale-skinned man sat down on a rock before one of the huts, his skin reddened by the sun. He gestured for Heathcliff and Mr. Coil to sit; he clapped his hands. Two very old women hurried out of a hut and placed a basket of fruit before them.

"Eat, eat. We are guests here," he said. "It's rude to refuse a gift of food."

Relieved to have survived his journey through the waves, Heathcliff savored the taste of fresh sweet fruit. Mr. Coil ate with one eye on the canoe-men. They all squatted on their haunches behind the pale-skinned man, swatting away sand flies and awaiting permission to eat.

At a signal from the Englishman, the canoe-men jumped on the food, and began raking it into their mouths with their fingers.

"You must show us your flesh," said Mr. Coil.

The Englishman nodded and clapped his hands. Four canoe-men hurried into the woods. They returned with five big males pinioned awkwardly together, their necks clamped between two notched and lashed-together logs.

"These are Mandinka warriors, captured in battle," said the yellow-faced man. "The Mandinka live only to fight and fuck in the infernal heat. The Kumasi want them killed or sold away."

"The bulls appear to be in good health, but our ship's surgeon must inspect them," said Mr. Coil. "We must take them back to the ship."

The English-speaking man fingered his necklace and squinted at the sun.

"It is dangerous now. Night is coming. The Kumasi cannot return to shore before dark, so they will not leave now. Kumasi believe evil spirits live in the evening sea."

"Surely the *Commerce* will not leave us," Heathcliff blurted to Mr. Coil.

"This captain will not lift anchor without me," said the first mate. "The truth is, Captain Collingwood depends on me to teach him the finer points of this abysmal trade."

After the sun went down, the yellow-faced man stirred a small fire in the center of the hut where they were to sleep. An old woman brought him a gourd filled with bitter drink, and he shared the drink with his guests.

"Africa may yet kill me, sir," the pale-faced man told Mr. Coil, as he stirred the fire and sparks rose up. "I have seen too much of its savagery and the powerful magic they call *juju*. And you will not believe me, sir, but these pitiful savages believe the worst treachery of all is to be found among civilized men."

Chapter 36

The next morning, on the deck of the *Commerce*, the five muscular Mandinka stood roped together at the neck. They seemed docile as sheep. Dr. Chum removed his wig and cleaned his spectacles. Then he poked and prodded the five big Negro males before nodding his approval to the captain.

"These five are quite acceptable," Captain Collingwood told the English-speaking man, who had removed most of the yellow paint from his face that morning. "We wish to trade for all five."

"More flesh is on the way from the interior, I am sure of that. But I am in a compromised situation here, Captain Collingwood. I wish to make you a proposition."

"Sir?" asked the captain.

"These five Mandinka are my personal property; I own them," said the pale-skinned man. "But I am an Englishman in my soul. As an Englishman, I am weary of Africa. I propose to give you these slaves of mine, on one condition."

"On what condition, sir?" asked Mr. Coil.

"Take me aboard your ship. I dream every day I might return to England. I have remained too long in this savage land."

"And your tribesmen here?" asked Mr. Coil, gesturing to the canoes floating alongside the ship.

"These savages will obey me," the Englishman stated. "I have made a secret bargain with the Kumasi. I will tell them your ship will return to buy more black ivory."

The Englishman leaned over the weather rail. He shouted out words in an African tongue. One of the canoe-men shouted back; he pointed to shore. There was additional shouting and pointing and Heathcliff understood none of it at all.

"If you toss them a cask of rum, they will return to the village," said the Englishman, addressing the captain. "You heard me promise them I will return."

"This is quite peculiar, captain," said Mr. Coil.

"I will most certainly trade a cask of rum for five strong bulls, of course I shall," blurted the captain, who seemed giddy at the bargain he had struck.

The captain sent Heathcliff and Peter below to fetch a barrel of rum and had them toss it into the ocean. Heathcliff watched the canoe-men deftly hook the floating barrel with an oar and pull it up into a canoe before turning back to shore.

"You must shackle the quashees immediately, captain," said Mr. Coil. "They should be chained to the racks right away."

"Fetch our leg irons, Mr. Quayle," the captain said.

Heathcliff helped clamp the five muscular Mandinka into leg irons. Although the captives were shackled two and three together, he thought the Negroes amazingly docile. Heathcliff noticed the savages glancing at the Englishman, as if he was their protector.

"You will have no trouble with the Mandinka," the Englishman told the captain. "They are my slaves. With my help, you will easily control them."

As Mr. Quayle and the crew took the quashees below, Captain Collingwood heartily shook hands with the Englishman.

HEATHCLIFF: THE LOST YEARS

"Welcome aboard the *Commerce*, sir," said the captain. "But please, do tell me your name."

"I was called Ebenezer Bugg," he said, shaking his head as if in disbelief. "I must admit my English name has a curious sound in my ears after these many years. If you don't mind, Captain Collingwood, it would greatly please me for the moment if you would merely call me an Englishman."

Chapter 37

That very evening, young Tom lay in his hammock, describing the feast he carried to the cabin in great detail. Ebenezer Bugg dined with the officers at the captain's table. According to the cabin boy, the Englishman's lurid tales created a rapt and respectful silence amongst all the ship's officers.

"The Englishman eats with his fingers," the cabin boy giggled. "He eats like an African but captain seems fond of him."

Sitting at the tub, Heathcliff ate and nodded.

"The Englishman told captain of a great castle a few days sail ahead," young Tom said. "A terrible war between the African tribes is just now over, and the castle is in English hands. The Englishman told our captain he might fill the hold quickly, and be off for America."

"The man speaks of Gold Coast Castle," remarked an old salt. "My last sail to Guinea, the savages were fighting all over it. Their butchery was said to be terrible. My captain refused to stop there."

The next day, Ebenezer Bugg strutted freely about the deck, as if inspecting the ship. That night, in the forecastle, he told the hands his strange African tale.

"I signed out of Bristol on a Portuguese vessel called the *Black Joke*," he said. "As the only Englishman aboard, I was often abused. When we arrived in Africa, the first mate accused me of planning a mutiny. My captain—the man never warmed to me—put me ashore in a jolly boat and left me. The savages found me and dragged me to their village. Men, I feared for my life."

"Did you have a good fight then?" asked Billy Gilding, who seemed quite fascinated by the Englishman.

"They pitted me against the strongest warrior in the tribe, a huge black beast named Tu-Pik, who stood seven feet tall. I fought that big savage to a draw, and I wounded him. When Tu-Pik died in his sleep that very night, the savages believed I had taken his *juju,*" said the Englishman.

"I married an African princess and we had little ones. When other tribes attacked, I led warriors to battle. These scars attest to that. I have one scar on my face for every man I killed."

Heathcliff leaned forward to count the thin white horizontal scars under the Englishman's eyes. He counted four scars on each side.

"You killed eight men?" Heathcliff asked.

"While I was on a hunting expedition, the Mandinka raided our village. Three days later I returned. The savages impaled the heads of my wives and children on wooden staves outside my hut. After that terrible savagery, I fell to my knees and swore to God I would return to mother England, if ever I had a chance."

At that moment, young Tom hurried into the forecastle to call the Englishman to the captain's table.

L ater that evening, Heathcliff heard the Mandinka shouting and slapping their chains against the racks. The noise could be heard by everyone aboard the ship. The bosun's whistle sounded. Captain Collingwood hurried to the deck and drew his sword. He had several of the men take pistols, or pull out their rope knives, and handed Heathcliff a lantern.

"Lead us to the racks, Heathcliff," he said.

The Englishman appeared and accompanied them to the lower hold. Ebenezer Bugg had only to shout a few words in an African tongue to silence the Mandinka.

"They will be silent now," the Englishman announced.

"Good work, Ebenezer," said the captain.

"You may always count on my assistance," he replied.

At the Englishman's suggestion, the captain permitted Mr. Coil to bring up the Mandinka to the deck the next morning for a morning meal. While Dr. Chum looked on, the Englishman walked the Negroes back and forth across the deck in their chains, two and three at a time. After the exercise, Mr. Coil and the Englishman took them below and chained the Mandinka back onto the racks.

Ebenezer Bugg did sleep in the forecastle with the hands, but the captain chose not to assign him a watch. Captain Collingwood asked nothing of the Englishman but to help look after the Mandinka and to dine with the cabin, which the pale-skinned gentleman seemed more than willing to do.

Chapter 38

The Gold Coast of Africa drifted past the ship like a slowly sweltering dream. The thick green vegetation shimmered in the heat while the smell of roots and mud wafted out from the shore. All morning long, a sluggish wind moved the *Commerce* fitfully up the Guinea Coast.

Ebenezer Bugg frequently spoke with the captain. The Englishman seemed to know all the tribes by name and he seemed quite eager to share his knowledge of the savage tribes that inhabited the shore. The Guinea tribes all communicated with drums, Heathcliff overheard the Englishman tell the captain. He swore the drums moved news up and down the Gold Coast faster than any ship could sail.

The Englishman sometimes entertained the crew with tales of the exotic charms of Negro women, the great power of African magic, and the foul trickery involved in the extremely lucrative business of buying and selling slaves.

Although Captain Collingwood seemed quite taken with the man, Heathcliff felt there was something unknowable in the Englishman, perhaps because of the many years he lived among the savages.

One evening, Mr. Coil sent Heathcliff below deck to check on the Mandinka who had become unusually quiet. Heathcliff found the Englishman sitting on the rack, conversing with the Mandinka in their tongue. The Englishman had apparently slipped down the man-hole to speak to the Mandinka during the changing of the watch.

Heathcliff lifted the lantern. "Did captain send you to quiet the Mandinka?" he asked, puzzled.

Leg irons rattled. The little Englishman bounced to his feet up and thrust out his chin.

"The Mandinka think all you white men with red faces are going to eat them," he said. "I assure the Mandinka it is not so."

Five large black-skinned males, chained to the racks, stared up into the lantern. The whites of their eyes and their teeth gleamed in the lamplight. Quite outnumbered, Heathcliff felt a prickle of fear.

"Are you frightened of these big bulls, lad? Captain Collingwood tells me it's your first Guinea voyage," he said. "You might well say thank you to Ebenezer Bugg. I tell falsehoods for your captain. I tell the Mandinka they must behave, you good white men won't harm them. That's a falsehood I tell for you, now isn't it?"

The leg irons of the Mandinka rattled again. Heathcliff hardly knew how to reply.

"Go away, lad! You frighten these savages. Because of you, I must now calm them again," hissed the Englishman, waving Heathcliff away. "Leave me to my work. I shall be up top before long."

When Heathcliff told Mr. Coil what transpired, the first mate merely shook his head.

"The Englishman is a queer one," Mr. Coil observed. "It's a wonder our captain gives him run of the ship."

The next afternoon, six long dugout canoes rowed out to meet the *Commerce*. These Negroes wore conical straw hats, and they had not painted their faces. The canoe-men waved and hooted as they kept pace with the ship, several of them holding up what looked like cut yams. Heathcliff thought he saw burlap bags of yams inside the canoes.

"I believe they wish to sell us yams," Mr. Coil told Heathcliff.

Captain Collingwood and the Englishman walked to the rail.

HEATHCLIFF: THE LOST YEARS

Ebenezer Bugg squinted over the bulwark. The canoe-men shouted something in an African tongue, pointing at their burlap bags. The Englishman shouted something in return which seemed to upset them.

"I believe they've yams to sell," said Mr. Coil to the cook, who had come to the bulwark.

"I would welcome their yams," Marconi said.

"Captain Collingwood, I smell a trick," hissed the Englishman, whirling to face the captain. "I know this tribe. They are deceitful. You must not let them aboard your ship. Sail on, sir. I beg of you to trust me."

"Captain, I do not know this tribe," Mr. Coil admitted.

The Englishman leaned far over the rail. He shook his fist at the canoes, shouting in an African tongue Heathcliff did not understand. The savages shouted back at the Englishman. One of them threw yams at the ship as the *Commerce* sailed away.

Chapter 39

As the ship passed the mouth of a small river the Englishman cried, "Gold Coast Castle's at hand, captain! That way! Maneuver your ship into the harbour."

Captain Collingwood took the helm, with Mr. Bugg at his side pointing the way. Using only her topsails, the *Commerce* sailed through the entrance to a small natural harbour partially hidden behind a long spit of tree-covered land.

"Gold Coast Castle! Just as I told you, captain!" the Englishman said, loudly enough for Heathcliff to overhear.

"I see," Captain Collingwood replied.

"You'll be the only ship in this harbour! You've got the best of this, man, thanks to me. You shall get all the best flesh for yourself."

"To pack this vessel and depart quickly is my fondest wish," said Captain Collingwood. "I pray it comes to pass."

"It shall come to pass," said the Englishman.

In the fading light of the afternoon, Gold Coast Castle floated into sight like an image from a feverish Arabian dream. The sprawling white fortification sat high atop a rock cliff. An iron cross atop the tallest of the castle's four turrets reflected the last rays of the afternoon sun.

HEATHCLIFF: THE LOST YEARS

"She flies English colours, captain," announced Mr. Coil, lowering his brass telescope.

"The castle was built by Portuguese slavers, captain, years ago," the Englishman said. "Fortunately, we English drove them away."

Beyond the castle Heathcliff saw what appeared to be a single house built in the Tudor style, and a small circle of mud huts at the edge of the jungle not far away.

"Lower the anchor," called out the captain.

Heathcliff hurried to the capstan. They winched down the anchor and it struck bottom at ten fathoms. Gold Coast Castle faded away into the darkness of the night, with only a single light visible on its lower floor.

"You must fire your cannons, captain," said the Englishman. "Blast out your intent to trade, so that all in the castle may prepare."

"That's not the custom in any slave port I've set foot in," said Mr. Coil. "I've been up this coast a few times."

"It is the custom here," the Englishman retorted. "In this part of Africa, you must show force. The slavers respect only power."

"No harm in a bit of cannon," said the captain.

The captain ordered the crew to the starboard cannons. Before long, eight loud reports rang out over the water. Heathcliff noticed the single light inside the castle suddenly go out. The sulfurous odor of black gunpowder lingered in the humid air.

The Dark Continent

Chapter 40

First thing in the morning, Captain Collingwood had the crew kedge the ship closer to a long pier that lay at the base of the cliff. Before their landing party departed, Captain Collingwood strapped on his cutlass and issued each member of the landing party a Blunderbuss pistol or a musket. Climbing down the ladder, holding onto his three-cornered hat with one hand, Heathcliff thought the captain appeared worried and anxious.

"Their pier is barely serviceable," sniffed the captain, as the jolly-boat approached the base of the cliffs. "Whole planks are rotted away."

"It's Africa, captain," Mr. Coil replied.

Heathcliff helped tie up the jolly-boat. Mr. Coil led the landing party off the dock and up a well-worn stairway chiseled into the cliff. At the top of the steps, the air became sunny, hot, and humid. Guinea hens pecked at the bare earth.

Before them stood a tall empty chair on long wooden stilts, an observation platform with legs thirty feet long. Guinea hens skittered away as the landing party approached the castle entrance. Heathcliff noticed a human skull nailed onto each of its large double doors.

Heathcliff heard a scraping of metal as cannons slid into place through loopholes above them. Looking up, he saw a row of cannon barrels aimed down at the landing party. Heathcliff glimpsed black faces behind the cannons but quick as lizards the faces darted away.

One wooden door swung open. A short, stout black woman led six African men outside to face them. The door closed behind them.

Two of the blacks held rusty muskets while four brandished long, metal-tipped spears. The woman wore a long piece of white cloth wrapped around her body that ended in a turban atop her head. The men wore long dangling loincloths.

Captain Collingwood unsheathed his sword. Heathcliff pulled the Blunderbuss from his belt.

The stout little Negro defiantly lifted her chin. She raised one arm.

"Why fire cannon in the night?" the woman demanded, in English and Spanish. "Why fire cannon at Gold Coast Castle?"

"She is a gold-taker, captain, a translator," said Mr. Coil. "You can speak to her in English."

"I am Charles Collingwood, captain of the *Commerce,* an English merchant ship sailing under the flag of our English sovereign, King George III," the captain began. "We discharged our cannon into the sea, not at your castle. I understand it is the custom, to announce our intent to trade for black ivory."

"Custom? You want to buy *slave?*" The gold-taker began to laugh. "You scaring Mr. Ferrett. Mr. Ferrett he don't understand your custom. He think you pirates. Last night we loaded our cannons and he lock us all inside."

At a calming gesture from the gold-taker, the Negroes lowered their weapons. Heathcliff exhaled, suddenly aware he had been holding his breath for a long time. A small window swung open some distance to the right of the castle doors. A thin male voice cried, "Let the English gentlemen enter."

Chapter 41

Barnaby Ferrett waited quietly, quill pen in hand. An English flag hung limp on a wooden staff next to the trading company representative's ornate desk. As the landing party entered his office, the small, rather composed gentleman set aside his pen. Heathcliff noticed fly-specked oil paintings on the walls, and large, moth-eaten rugs spread out across the dirt floor. Horseflies buzzed lazily about the room.

Barnaby Ferrett wore a fine mulberry coat with gold embroidery and a shoulder-length, heavily-powdered wig of human hair. He tugged at the ruffled sleeves of his white cotton shirt, and officiously nodded. His office smelled of dusting powder, tea, tobacco, and perfume.

"Do sit down, English gentlemen. My name is Barnaby Ferrett. On behalf of the West Africa Company, I welcome you to Gold Coast Castle."

"I have a letter of introduction from my investors in Liverpool." Captain Collingwood placed an envelope on Barnaby Ferrett's desk before he sat down. "I am Captain Charles Collingwood, master of the *Commerce*. I presume you know what we're about."

"You are so fortunate as to the time of your arrival, gentlemen," sniffed the little man, turning over the letter in his long-fingered hands.

HEATHCLIFF: THE LOST YEARS

"Our dungeons have never held so much flesh. We have not seen a slaver since the little rebellion began two years ago. The native tribes butchered one another without mercy. Fortunately, neither had quarrel with me."

Barnaby Ferrett plucked up a small Oriental fan from the top of his desk and began fanning himself.

"In accordance with our most recent arrangements, the West Africa Company levies only two small duties—the first on goods you bring ashore to trade, which must pass through my office, and the second on the black cattle you purchase here," he said.

"This is a curious arrangement," said Mr. Coil.

"I could negotiate nothing better," he snapped, fanning himself rapidly. "Until I get the military support from the crown that I have been requesting, those are the arrangements. At this time, you must trade directly with the king."

"I beg your pardon," said the captain.

"The Ashante Akan tribe controls the castle and its dungeon. King Big Tucker Ashante Akan murdered his last rival not two weeks ago, upstairs in the castle. I understand he actually ate the man's face. The king has filled the dungeons with everyone who opposed him, and their wives and children, and he intends to sell them all," sniffed Mr. Ferrett. "So as I mentioned, you are fortunate as to the timing of your arrival."

Barnaby Ferrett rapped his inkwell on top of his desk. An African boy crawled out from beneath the desk, smiling broadly.

"This is one of our royal princes, you might say. He is the seventh of King Big Tucker's many sons. The boy speaks no English and he is here to spy on me. However, he can lead you directly to the king," Barnaby Ferrett said, fanning himself rapidly.

The tiny prince stood up and looked around the room, smiling unashamedly. He was quite entirely naked. At a sign from Barnaby Ferrett, the young man pulled open a door and darted into the castle.

Chapter 42

Heathcliff hurried down a dimly-lit hallway of hard-packed earth after the line of briskly-walking men, brushing away spider webs as he walked. Flames quivered in lamps as they passed. The Negro prince bounded up a winding stone staircase to the top of a turret. At a door at the top of the stairs, a large, bare-chested Negro turned away the boy and led them all into the dark, musky lair of the African king.

On the far side of the dimly-lit room a man sat on a wooden throne partially covered with animal skins. The man sat with his eyes closed. Two Negroes held a black umbrella over the man's head and others flanked the throne, armed with spears.

On the wall behind the throne were long shelves lined with what looked like human skulls interspersed with a patchwork of human and animal bones.

On the throne, a heavy-set mulatto with a scarred, diamond-shaped face opened his eyes. He wore a loose robe of colourful fabric and metal bracelets on his arms and wrists. A head-dress of bird feathers quivered when he blinked, and leaned forward.

"This King Big Tucker Ashante Akan, king of Gold Coast Castle," announced the gold-taker. "King speak a little English."

HEATHCLIFF: THE LOST YEARS

"Tell his highness I am Captain Charles Collingwood, captain of the *Commerce,* an English merchant ship. We bring English goods to trade for flesh."

As the gold-taker translated, Heathcliff studied the African king's wide, somewhat reptilian face. The king had small suspicious eyes, a large flat nose, and an odd crosswork of pale scars on his forehead, cheeks and neck. His right hand clasped a wooden staff topped by a large clear stone. When the gold-taker stopped talking, the king bared his teeth to speak.

Heathcliff shuddered. The king's front teeth were filed into sharp points and resembled the teeth of a dog. Heathcliff had never seen such menacing teeth.

"Dash," said the king. He tapped his staff three times.

"King want present now," said the gold-taker.

Mr. Coil removed a fat leather purse looped over his belt. He gave the purse to the captain, who presented it to the gold-taker. She bowed and carried it to the king.

King Big Tucker Ashante Akan peered into the purse. He lifted it several times to feel its weight, grunted, and sniffed the contents. He licked one finger, thrust it into the sack, and examined the gold dust clinging to his finger.

"I need two hundred five black cattle to sell in Jamaica. I will buy predominantly healthy able-bodied males, but I will take a few healthy females and young ones," said Captain Collingwood. "Great king, I shall bargain directly with you."

The gold-taker translated for the king. The king nodded, tapped his staff, and looked to one side. Several Negroes glided out of the corners of the room and hurried out the door.

"This bodes well, captain," said Mr. Coil.

A particularly loud horsefly buzzed crazily around the room. The fly settled on the king's neck. With a quick grunt, the monarch squashed the fly with one hand and examined its remains.

THE DARK CONTINENT

The king's men pushed three Negro males into the room, all roped together at the neck. With them came the fetid aroma of the dungeon, a sad mixture of human excrement, mold, urine, and sweat.

"Some of these will likely do, captain," said Mr. Coil.

"Tell your king our surgeon wishes to inspect all the flesh he has in the dungeon," Captain Collingwood told the gold-taker. "We will take the best of what you have. We will begin inspecting to-morrow."

The gold-taker translated for the king, who responded at length in Akan.

"King say no, no, he make feast for you to-night. King happy to trade. First he make party to welcome your ship," the gold-taker said.

The captain glanced at Mr. Coil, who nodded his approval.

Chapter 43

At dusk, **Heathcliff and Peter stumbled** into the circle of mud huts. Directly before them, orange flames leaped into the air. The smoke that drifted off the fire smelled of grease, sizzling fish, cooked chicken, and baking yams. When the wind shifted, Heathcliff noticed several old women squatting next to the bonfire, turning meat on hot stones. Negroes who apparently lived in the huts milled aimlessly about the fire.

Heathcliff sat down on a smooth upended rock not far from the fire, in the area set aside for the crew.

"Why was I given this necklace?" Peter asked Heathcliff. Dr. Chum, also the ship's purser, insisted on slipping a glass necklace around all their necks and mumbling a few words when they left the ship.

"You get a woman with it," growled the Englishman, sitting nearby and eating with his fingers. "When I eat my fill, I'll show you how it's done."

Barefoot black-skinned girls moved past the mariners with wooden platters of seared fish, guinea hen, yams, and fruit. Naked boys trailed after them with buckets of rum from which mariners could refill their cannikins.

One small boy absent-mindedly urinated while he walked. Billy Gilding encouraged the boy to pee on Young Tom, who had already fallen asleep.

On the far side of the clearing, African men began beating drums. As the drums beat faster and louder, Heathcliff noticed a large black umbrella floating above the crowd the other side of the fire. Beneath the umbrella, King Big Tucker Ashante Akan came into view, seated on a large, chintz-covered chair carried by four husky men.

The Africans placed the king's chair next to the chair of Captain Collingwood, who smiled thoughtfully into the fire. The captain wore his best clothes and his beaver hat. The king sported an embroidered cotton loincloth, a long beaded vest, and a leather headband inlaid with coloured stones and crocodile teeth. The captain nodded politely to the king, then smiled laconically as children carrying food and drink ran forward to serve them.

King Big Tucker soon rose from his throne, swaying to the beat of the drums. He began opening and closing his long, beaded vest. Heathcliff saw a bare-breasted woman rise to dance before the fire, and more women joining the dance.

King Big Tucker pulled Captain Collingwood to his feet. Captain Collingwood appeared to be sweating profusely.

Drummers slapped out a steady, haunting rhythm while bare-chested women with bright fabric knotted around their waists formed a moving, clapping line that weaved around the fire. The women stamped the earth together, lifted their hands, and turned in unison to beckon to the king.

"Look at the niggers! Drinking and dancing!" said the Englishman, elbowing Heathcliff. "The bastards love to entertain the English. Hey!" he slapped Peter's shoulder. "Here's what these women love."

The Englishman stood up and spun his glass necklace over his head. A Negro woman approached him, and reached up for the necklace.

The Englishman put the necklace around the woman's neck, threw one arm over her shoulder, and walked her toward the huts.

HEATHCLIFF: THE LOST YEARS

King Big Tucker danced toward the fire, clapping his hands over his head as he stepped toward the line of dancers. Women and children joined the line, clapping with the king. Two or three drunken sailors stood up, staggered toward the fire, and tried their best to dance.

Heathcliff dipped his cannikin into a bucket of rum. He had never seen such a riot of undulating hips and breasts, and such nakedly erotic dancing. A pretty young black-skinned woman grasped his hand and pulled him up into the dance as a hypnotic call and response began.

"All-lee, all-lee," chanted the drummers.

"All-lee, all-lee," the dancers responded.

Together the dancers turned in slow circles around the fire, arms upraised, moving gracefully as wind across grass.

King Big Tucker strutted toward the fire. The king stepped quickly in and out of the coals, making a complete circle around the fire. The fire seemed not to burn his bare feet as he clapped his hands over his head, laughed, and rejoined the line.

The king motioned to Captain Collingwood. The captain looked anxiously about, like a mouse caught in a trap.

The king gestured again. The drums intensified. The king motioned so insistently that Captain Collingwood finally slipped into the line of dancers next to Heathcliff, his face set in a curious grimace.

The captain tried his best to keep time as the king danced forward, nose to nose with the captain, smiling and shaking his hips.

"Which one you?" King Tucker shouted at the captain, with a sweep of his arm at the dancing females.

"I have a beautiful wife waiting for me in England, thank you very much," Captain Collingwood shouted, all the while gamely attempting to match the movements of the dancers.

The king snagged the arm of a bare-breasted young girl and pulled her between them, turning her to face the captain. He reached over the girl's shoulders and took the girl's ample breasts in his hands.

"You take," said the king. "She Africa wife."

Heathcliff looked away, dancing. He fell into a sort of trance, his body in rhythm with the drums. He danced next to the black-skinned girl, mimicking her movements, his hips against her undulating body, her body brushing slowly against his.

The girl's dark eyes danced with delight. She flashed her perfect white teeth, watching him and laughing. And Heathcliff continued dancing, lost in the drunken primitive pounding rhythm of it all.

When he tired, Heathcliff staggered away from the dancers and sat down on a stone, his head spinning. He stared dumbly at the roaring fire. He held out his cannikin for more rum.

The African girl tugged at his arm until he stood up. She walked him toward a hut near the edge of the clearing. She stopped at the open doorway of the hut and touched her chest.

"Kee-Sha," she said. "Kee-Sha."

"Heathcliff," he tapped his chest.

Kee-Sha lifted the glass necklace from around his neck. She put it on, giggled, took his hand, and pulled him inside.

The hut smelled of sex and sweat. In the flickering light, Heathcliff discerned the moving forms of love-starved sailors taking their pleasure with dark-skinned women, and the uninhibited grunts and moans and sighs of love.

Kee-Sha pushed him down onto a pile of animal skins. In the dim light she bent down to tug off his shoes, and then his pantaloons.

He grabbed her bare foot. "Kee-Sha?" he asked as she removed his pants. He could barely see her. She laughed. With her bare foot, she pushed him down onto his back. Breasts jiggling, she pulled the cloth from her waist while he removed his shirt.

Kee-Sha lay down gracefully as a cat. She pressed the length of her body against him, licking his face and nipping his ear. He caressed her, suddenly desired her. When his hand slipped between her legs, she made a sound deep in her throat and squeezed his hand between her legs; she tugged at his arm. He spread her legs apart. mounted her, and she rose up to him like a wave rising to embrace the shore.

HEATHCLIFF: THE LOST YEARS

Kee-Sha clung to him. Their bodies rocked together. Fingernails dug into his back. He squeezed her, pulling her close as she clung to him, moaning a little.

For a moment she soared over him, mouth open, small breasts and nipples trembling, her hands pressing his chest. He pulled her closer, he pulled her down, he rolled her onto her back and clasped her flesh with both hands. He pulled her into him and rose up like a thunderstorm to release lightning and rain.

When Heathcliff finally pulled away, he heard men and women groaning, and African drums pounding in the night.

Chapter 44

Falling asleep in Kee-Sha's arms, Heathcliff dreamed of Catherine Earnshaw. In his dream, his young friend ran away from him, up an unfamiliar rocky path through the hills. He followed her up the path as he did when they were children, quick on her heels, but he could not see her face or catch up to her. There seemed no end to the steeply winding path until he finally stumbled, then reached out.

"Cathy! Wait for me!" he cried.

Heathcliff bolted awake in the sluggish, early-morning African heat. He shook his head in the dim light as the details of his dream frittered away.

His head throbbed. He sat up surrounded by a netherworld of sleeping, half-naked people. Some of the crew slept with their arms and legs draped over sleeping African women, as if to pin them to the earth, but Kee-Sha was already gone.

A mosquito buzzed in his ear. Heathcliff swatted it. His arms itched. When he scratched his forearms, his arms itched and burned like fire. His entire naked body itched. When he picked up his shirt, it was crawling with red ants. He carefully shook the ants out of his garments, dressed himself, pulled on his boots, and stood up on the dirt floor.

HEATHCLIFF: THE LOST YEARS

Heathcliff staggered toward the light, scratching his crotch. He leaned against the open doorway, feeling nauseous.

Outside the hut, droplets of dew sparkled on the tree leaves and atop the tramped-down vegetation between the huts. When he glanced up at the sun, the light hurt his eyes.

Beyond the smoldering remains of the bonfire, a terribly skinny bare-breasted woman stood over a large wooden mortar and pestle, stoically pounding grain.

"Heathcliff!"

He recognized the voice of Mr. Coil.

Heathcliff stepped out of the hut and looked about. Waving one hand, the first mate hurried toward him.

Chapter 45

Captain Collingwood greeted them when they boarded the *Commerce*. The captain still wore his formal clothes, and he looked lost and anxious. All around him, mariners polished brass and swept the deck.

"You must prepare the cabin, Mr. Coil," said the captain. "I believe you know how all that should be arranged."

"Aye-aye, sir. I'll have Heathcliff to assist me."

Heathcliff followed the first mate below to the captain's quarters. The two of them draped the captain's table with bolts of Manchester cotton. Heathcliff helped Mr. Coil pack goods in a chest and prepare a makeshift throne just before the entrance of the king.

King Big Tucker Ashante Akan strutted into the cabin trailed by a half dozen wives and the gold-taker. After a formal welcome by the captain, Mr. Coil showed the king to his special chair. The king sat down; the gold-taker moved to his side. The king's dark-skinned queens squatted obediently at his feet.

"We shall fetch your samples, captain," said Mr. Coil.

Heathcliff helped Mr. Coil lug in the large, brightly-painted red and black chest and set it down on the captain's table.

Captain Collingwood unlocked the chest. With great fanfare, he began to lay out their goods before the king.

"Tell the king this is what we bring to trade," Captain Collingwood told the gold-taker. "Bolts of the best Manchester fabric. Mirrors of English silver. China plates, serving bowls. Silver eating-utensils. Iron ingots. Bars of copper to make tools. A proper English greatcoat for the king and necklaces for his all his beautiful queens."

As the gold-taker translated, Captain Collingwood plunged his hand into the chest and picked up a handful of sparkling necklaces. Necklaces of red, yellow, and green glass beads spilled from the captain's hand as he dangled them before the tittering queens.

"I shall fetch a musket," said Mr. Coil.

Mr. Coil returned to the cabin bearing a long object wrapped in coarse white linen and lay it on the table. The king's eyes widened as the captain unwrapped a very handsome British military issue Brown Bess. The .75-caliber British flintlock smelled pleasantly of gunner's oil, and its stock had been brilliantly polished.

"British infantry issue, the finest smoothbore flintlock in the world, with a generous supply of shot and powder. Our investors petitioned these from King George III himself," said the captain.

As the gold-taker translated for the king, Captain Collingwood loaded the weapon. He ripped open a paper cartridge, poured black powder into the flash pan, set the frissen, and poured the remaining powder down the muzzle. He ramrodded paper and ball down the 42-inch barrel and elegantly replaced the ramrod. The king watched like a fascinated, hungry child.

"With one of these in your hands, your enemies will run before you like sheep," the captain told the king, and pulled back the hammer. "With enough of these, you could rule the entire Gold Coast."

King Big Tucker leaped to his feet, snatched the loaded musket, and accidentally discharged it.

The loud report startled everyone in the cabin and left it smelling of black powder. The king dropped the gun.

Captain Collingwood smiled. He nervously laughed. He glanced at Mr. Coil, laughed again, picked up the rifle, attached an 18-inch steel bayonet, and allowed the king to touch the bayonet's sharp point.

King Big Tucker snatched the musket. He turned to the gold-taker and poked at her shoulder with the tip of the bayonet. The little Negress squealed and indignantly pulled away, clutching her bleeding wound.

Captain Collingwood reached for the musket. King Big Tucker clasped it to his chest and would not return it.

"Our monarch is greedy, captain," said Mr. Coil. "You might let him keep the gun. Tell the gold-taker it is a special gift for him. The minute he owns one musket, he will crave more."

Chapter 46

Behind Gold Coast Castle, a wooden door opened. Four naked African males blinked into the light, followed by two of the king's men prodding them forward with spears. King Big Tucker watched from a window atop the nearest turret.

The males cowered before Captain Collingwood with their heads down, glancing nervously over their shoulders at the guards while the captain made a quick note in his small leather-bound notebook.

"Heathcliff, these four bulls must go to Dr. Chum," the captain said. "Help take them in."

The gold-taker barked at the Negroes in an African tongue.

Heathcliff led the group into a room inside the dungeon where the surgeon waited on a three-legged wooden stool. The king's men prodded the naked males into a corner and slouched against the wall without bothering to close the door. Heathcliff stood in the doorway, watching.

After cleaning his spectacles, Dr. Chum turned and gestured for the first of the males, who was prodded forward.

The surgeon examined the male's hands and fingers. He jerked his head from side to side, peered up his nostrils, and opened his mouth to examine his tongue. He pinched and slapped his flanks, turned the male around, spread his buttocks, and fingered his anus. Turning the male around again, Dr. Chum clasped his scrotum. Finally, he stood up and licked the Negro's chin.

"We'll take this one. Bring me another," he said, gesturing for them to bring him another male.

"Why do you lick him, sir?" young Tom asked.

"I can taste disease, Tom," said the doctor. "I can taste it when I drink a bit of their urine, too."

As the surgeon examined the last of the group, Peter led another five males past Heathcliff and into the room.

In the confusion, a male twisted away from the doctor. He scurried toward Heathcliff like a frightened cockroach. Waving his arms and shouting loudly, the Negro sunk his teeth into Heathcliff's shoulder and shoved him to the floor in a desperate, spastic scramble to get out the door.

The king's men ran him down just outside the dungeon. One pinned him to the ground and put a spear in his mouth while others kicked at his legs and groin.

"Don't kill him!" Dr. Chum called out. "He wants finishing but he's strong and he'll fetch a good price."

Heathcliff struggled to his feet, holding his upper arm. He felt faint. He staggered forward while the Negroes stared at him. He felt warm sticky blood oozing from his wound. He stopped before the surgeon, frightened and breathing quickly.

"You have been bitten, lad. Take off your shirt."

As the Negroes stared, Heathcliff suddenly feared them all. The savage who bit away flesh from his shoulder probably wanted to kill him. They were monsters. While the surgeon swabbed his wound with vinegar, he thought any of the black-skinned beasts who stared at him would have ripped out his throat had they been alone. He gritted his teeth and told himself he must be wary of them all.

Dr. Chum bandaged Heathcliff's shoulder with cotton gauze and pressed on the wound with the heel of his hand.

HEATHCLIFF: THE LOST YEARS

"You will be fine, Heathcliff," said the surgeon. "You and Peter go assist the bosun. Help him mark the bulls."

Chapter 47

Mr. Quayle squatted before the coals of a small fire. He bent low and blew on the coals, lifted a wooden-handled branding iron from the fire, and stared at the iron as Heathcliff and Peter walked into the room.

"Bring me the first of the bunch," he said.

Heathcliff and Peter pulled a small Negro male from the group but the male was profusely sweating; he slipped away from them and ran into a corner of the room. The bosun had Peter call in Fiddler and Vito to help. With a great effort, the four of them pulled the first squirming, slippery male next to the fire, and struggled to hold him fast.

The bosun dipped a branding iron into a pot of palm oil and pressed its bright orange tip to the Negro's chest, just above his heart.

When the Negro struggled, Heathcliff saw the pink blistering brand of the *Commerce*, the letter C inside a four-sided diamond, as the quashee howled and backed away.

Heathcliff helped hold the squirming, gasping Negro until he calmed down. Breathing hard, he watched Fiddler and Vito maneuver the male into the next room and lock him in before returning.

"We do the Devil's work," Peter gasped.

HEATHCLIFF: THE LOST YEARS

"Give a big kiss to the Devil." Mr. Quayle poked at Peter's face with the tip of the iron. The frightened orphan jumped back, horrified.

"Another word from you and I'll sear those blubbering lips shut. You two fetch me another bull. We've work to do."

When pulled toward the fire, the males fought like ferocious beasts. One bull elbowed Peter in the face, breaking and bloodying his nose. Another scratched off Heathcliff's bandage and re-opened his wound as they pushed him toward the fire. At the touch of the hot iron, one male did not stop howling and jumping until all four of them wrestled him down, dragged him into the next room, and left him kicking and screaming on the dirt floor.

Heathcliff had no stomach for the work. The sight and smell of burning flesh nauseated him. As he went about his duties, he longed to escape the brutality and horror all around him. He told himself he must endure it; he must put iron in his heart. He realized he had cast his lot with hard, pitiless men who would give him no quarter in a hot, savage land.

They branded Negro females on the back, and with smaller irons. The females took it more stoically than the men, but several broke into tears and wailed at the sight of Mr. Quayle jiggling his branding irons in the fire.

The squeals and cries of the black-skinned children upset Heathcliff the most. Their cries tore at his heart and he was not alone.

Before the branding of a young female about young Tom's age, the cabin boy dared stand up and kick dirt into the bosun's fire. Young Tom actually attacked the much larger Mr. Quayle with his fists. The bosun put down his iron, grabbed the cabin boy by the hair, and beat his head against a post before returning to his work.

Chapter 48

Day after day, the African sun burned its slow arc across the pitiless sky. Heathcliff saw no end to the hot days and the interminable work. He felt no relief from the hellish heat when the sun set and he and the hands trudged from the dungeon to the huts in the twilight at the end of another long, sweat-drenched day. The screaming of the Negroes clung to his ears in a nightmare of sound that seemed never to end.

Every evening, young Tom told him, Captain Collingwood and the officers dined with Mr. Ferrett. The East Africa Trading Company's representative maintained a house behind the castle. Although he had several Negro servants, Mr. Ferrett often requested young Tom's assistance in setting a proper table for his English guests. Ebenezer Bugg remained on the *Commerce* much of the time now, attending to the Mandinka still imprisoned in the hold. When Tom caught sight of the Englishman on shore, he said, the man was usually in the company of Billy Gilding or another of the other pressed men.

Like most of the crew, Heathcliff slept in the small crowded mud hut assigned them by the king. After the day's toil, sweating shirt-less men sat around a small cooking fire, eating what food they were brought and complaining about the incessant heat.

HEATHCLIFF: THE LOST YEARS

Every evening, the same few village women came around to bargain with men for their favors. Darkness brought an influx of mosquitos and other small biting creatures to join the rats, spiders, and lizards that skittered freely about the hut.

Every Guinea rooster in the village crowed them awake at dawn. As mariners dressed for the day, curious village children peered at them through the entrance to the hut, which had no door.

One dismal morning, one of the pressed men shook Heathcliff awake and pulled him outside to watch a crocodile devour a live dog next to the latrine. When Heathcliff realized what he was seeing, he wondered if he would ever escape the nightmare that was Africa.

One overcast morning, after they finished up in the dungeon, the king led them to his barracoons. The crude wooden cages of upright logs lashed together lay in the jungle a distance behind the huts. The captain told Heathcliff that King Big Tucker kept the youngest and strongest of his captives there.

In the narrow cages, pitiful young males stood barefoot, staring at them, stepping about in their own excrement. A gentle rain fell as the king's men pulled boys from cages one at a time. Some had terrible sores on their feet, Heathcliff noticed, and runaway skin rashes. As Dr. Chum finished his inspections, the pattering rain became a rainstorm.

Heathcliff helped run the young males through the mud and rain into the dungeon for branding. The older Negroes still frightened him, but in the branding room Heathcliff pitied the young males. Some reminded him of boys at the work-house.

Hurrying back to the hut in the rain, Heathcliff wanted to throw open the doors to the dungeon and let all the young males run away into the jungle, but in Africa he knew he could never do it.

Rain drummed on the roof of the hut as Heathcliff changed into dry clothes. Around the cooking fire, mariners grumbled about the rain.

Again, Heathcliff stank of the dungeon. He could not escape the smell. The stink clung to his nostrils. The only thing that ever killed the stink was rum. Heathcliff drank all that remained of his bottle, blew his nose into the dirt, and stared at the fire. All around him, men slept and groaned in the dim light.

Before he went to sleep, Heathcliff noticed the anxious chatter of distant drums, their sound partially muffled by the rain.

Chapter 49

That night, Heathcliff dreamed he staggered back into the Fairy Cave. Pretty young Catherine Earnshaw sat waiting for him. Cathy held out her arms. In the dim light, Heathcliff and his friend hugged and kissed one another with the uninhibited innocence of youth.

Cathy broke away from him and crawled to the entrance of the cave. When she gestured for Heathcliff to crawl forward, he noticed a flash of bright light outside.

"Look," Cathy said.

Heathcliff peered out.

Below him, in the longest room in the castle dungeon, Negro males in leg irons shuffled past the entrance of the cave. Walking single file, the long line of Negroes wound across the room toward a distant fire. When he heard the clink of the branding irons, Heathcliff ducked back inside.

"I have seen too much of this," he said.

"Come back, Heathcliff. Everything is changing."

Cautiously he looked out. To his horror, every one of the shackled Negroes resembled him. Every dark-skinned male shuffling past the cave had his face and body.

Before a blazing fire some distance away, a man who resembled him blew on a white-hot branding iron.

Heathcliff recoiled from what he saw. He crawled back into the cave, desperately looking and feeling around for Catherine. But his best friend had surged away in the darkness, like the tide rolling back to sea.

Chapter 50

On the deck of the *Commerce,* Captain Collingwood closed his notebook and looked out onto the exhausted faces of his crew.

"We have purchased one hundred eighty-two slaves, and even counting the five from Ebenezer we have only one hundred eighty-seven. We need more flesh to guarantee the returns I promised our investors. Gold Coast Castle has nothing more to offer us. To-day, we shall make ready to depart."

"Captain—I've a notion," the Englishman began.

"Not now, Ebenezer," the captain snapped. "Mr. Bolt, bring up the goods marked for delivery to Mr. Ferrett. Take them in on the boats. Mr. Coil, have your watch prepare the lower hold."

"Aye-aye, sir."

"Aye-aye, sir."

In the lower hold, as the Mandinka watched, Heathcliff lay squares of white cloth at short intervals all along the racks.

"The bulls must have a cloth to cover themselves," Mr. Coil told Heathcliff. "They'll be naked when we bring them aboard and captain believes in tight packing. We position them front to back like spoons, heads facing the aisle to prevent them kicking the crew."

THE DARK CONTINENT

Heathcliff helped prepare a separate, much smaller compartment for the females. Their door would never be locked, Mr. Coil said, as Negro females were known to be docile and compliant at sea. The young males would be placed in the root cellar, where they were to sleep on top of the cook's yams piled three feet deep.

Mr. Coil instructed Heathcliff to place empty buckets about the sleeping areas, and chain and lock each bucket into place. Then he sent Heathcliff to the galley to assist the cook.

Heathcliff and young Tom dumped buckets overboard containing dead fish and chicken, spoiled vegetables, rotten fruit, fetid water, and even the dead rats Marconi cleaned up from under his cook-stove. The Irishman sauntered forward as Heathcliff and Tom dumped a bucket of rotten horse meat overboard into the bay. The Irishman shook his head.

"Our cook is a fool," Fiddler told Heathcliff. "Rotten food attracts sharks to the ship. If sharks attach themselves to our vessel they will follow us all the way across the sea."

"Look!" said young Tom. "A canoe."

A long canoe approached the ship, rowed by several of the king's men. Barnaby Ferrett grimaced in the bow of the boat, bundled up in a long cloak. The East Africa Company representative dutifully climbed up the sea-ladder, took off his tricorne, and immediately asked to speak with the captain.

"I bring a message from the king," he said. "You must not leave Gold Coast Castle. King Big Tucker wishes to bargain with you for more muskets."

"We've looked over the entire dungeon and his barracoons," said the captain. "He has nothing more to offer."

"The king has more black cattle he wishes to trade."

"Really? Well, then let's have a look," said the captain. "Heathcliff, fetch the surgeon."

Heathcliff helped row the jolly-boat ashore.

HEATHCLIFF: THE LOST YEARS

Barnaby Ferrett led them into his office, where they found King Big Tucker sitting at the trading company representative's desk, flanked by the gold-taker.

"King say trade more slave," the gold-taker said.

A small group of sickly-looking Negroes was brought into the room. Almost immediately, Dr. Chum recognized a skin disorder on one of the young boys he had examined in the barracoons, and exposed the ruse.

"We've seen these quashees before, captain, I recognize all of them now," said the surgeon to the captain. "This king has nothing new to offer us."

"King want more musket," said the gold-taker.

"We can return to my old village, captain," said the Englishman. "Perhaps more flesh awaits us there."

"I more slave!" shouted King Big Tucker, angrily tapping his staff.

"Does the king take me for a fool?" the captain asked the gold-taker. "To-day, I will send his goods through Mr. Ferrett. To-morrow, we shall take our black cattle from the dungeon, and depart."

The gold-taker translated. The king growled, scowled, scratched himself vigorously, looked from side to side, and tapped his staff on the dirt floor.

King Big Tucker glared at Barnaby Ferrett, and showed his teeth. The trading company representative nervously looked away. The king spoke heatedly to the gold-taker.

"King send canoes up river to-morrow," said the gold-taker. "He say he fill your ship with slave."

"Tell your king I shall tolerate no more deception," hissed Captain Collingwood. "We'll bring his goods ashore this afternoon. I am quite ready to depart."

"To-morrow, more slave," grunted King Big Tucker Ashante Akan. He glared at the gold-taker, and tapped his staff again.

Chapter 51

Captain Collingwood tasked Heathcliff with keeping an eye on the king's expedition. That morning, he found himself carrying one end of a long dugout canoe down a narrow path through the jungle that paralleled the ocean. After he followed them sloshing through a thicket of mangroves along the bank of the South Pongo River, all six flat-bottomed canoes hit the water. Heathcliff stepped into the last of the canoes, sweating ferociously and quite uncertain as to what he might expect ahead.

An eel slithered along the surface of the wide brown river. Much farther upstream, the river narrowed and the canoes glided through cloud after cloud of stinging gnats that whirled and twisted over the water. He swatted them away and scratched his arms. Small quick birds skimmed the surface of the mud-coloured water, feasting on insects. Trees formed a canopy over their heads that blotted out the sun and monkeys screeched as the canoes rounded a bend in the river.

The sun returned. A small group of mud huts lay on a clearing near the edge of the river. Smoke rose from a cooking fire in front of the huts. Several naked black-skinned boys dabbled in the yellow mud as the king's men jumped into the river and pulled their canoes onto the riverbank.

HEATHCLIFF: THE LOST YEARS

Heathcliff remained in the canoe. He heard a woman shout. He noticed a very skinny boy warily rise to his feet in the mud.

A slender white-haired Negro stepped from the huts, wearing only a loincloth, perhaps an elder of the village. The king's men shouted something Heathcliff couldn't understand and the older man walked forward, palms out, responding in a soft, firm voice.

Two of them attacked the old man with cudgels and knocked him down. The raiding party pushed their way into the huts and began pulling men, women, and children outside.

A young boy grabbed a smoldering stick from the cooking fire and stabbed it into the leg of one of the king's men. Big Tucker's man screamed. He grabbed the boy's head, slammed his face into the mud again and again, then dragged him by the hair toward the canoes.

A bare-breasted woman screamed out of a hut, clutching a baby. One of the raiding party pulled the infant from her arms, stomped it into the mud, and dragged her toward Heathcliff's canoe. When she tried to scratch the man, he hit her in the face with an oar and threw her into the boat.

Heathcliff's canoe pushed off last and headed back down the river. In the canoes ahead of him, the king's men silenced their captives with shouts and slaps before turning to their oars. When the muddy-faced boy turned to look at him, Heathcliff noticed his teeth bleeding.

As the canoes glided beneath a large flowering tree, a shower of red flower petals dropped into the water.

The air stank of rotting vegetation. Heathcliff could hardly look at the captives. They sat in the canoes with their heads bowed, beaten and pathetic.

In the twilight, Heathcliff heard distress in the cries of the jungle birds, and helpless anger in the accusatory chatter of the monkeys. The entire forest seemed to sing with pain.

Chapter 52

Captain Collingwood ordered Heathcliff on two more human hunting expeditions up the tributaries of the South Pongo. Each expedition lasted longer and was much less productive than the last. Captain Collingwood, Mr. Coil, and the Englishman met the third expedition at the mouth of the river. The Englishman waved a lantern over Heathcliff's canoe.

"No quashees, captain," cawed the Englishman. "I told you they were finished. All the bloody canoes are empty."

Heathcliff stepped out of his canoe and joined the men.

"Blast the luck!" exclaimed Captain Collingwood. "I need so few more black cattle to fully pack my ship. I wish to leave this treacherous land."

"We have enough cattle to depart for the islands now, captain," said Mr. Coil. "If I count correctly, we've altogether two hundred."

"I intend to pack this ship to the gills, Mr. Coil," the captain said. "I told you, my investors expect a great deal of me."

"Then return to my village," said Ebenezer Bugg, clutching at the captain's arm. "My village lies only a short distance back up the coast. It is closer than any slave port, and with me you will have your pick of the cattle. You may pack your ship as tightly as you wish, and depart."

"How do you know more black cattle can be had in your village?" the captain demanded.

"Last night the drums brought word of a great Kumasi victory. They have brought home more captives, captain, I am sure of it. With me to help bargain for you, all the quashees you want can be had for a special price."

"It would be prudent to depart for Jamaica now, captain," said Mr. Coil. "More Negroes will be more difficult to manage. With more aboard, there will be more losses."

Ebenezer Bugg heartily shook the captain's arm. His eyes gleamed in the lamplight.

"Sail back to my village, Captain Collingwood. I give you my word as an Englishman, you shall have all the flesh you desire."

Chapter 53

The African sky darkened as the male Negro captives made their way from the castle down the stone steps to the pier, where small boats waited. A few fitful drops of rain fell from black clouds massing over their heads. An occasional rumble of tropical thunder over the jungle added a note of foreboding to the departure of the slaves.

Captain Collingwood hired the gold-taker to accompany the ship to Jamaica. She stood next to Heathcliff on the pier, speaking sharply to the males as they picked their way down the stairway to the boats, shackled and roped together.

That morning, while Heathcliff was shaving the captives' heads, he heard rumors of treachery at the dungeon. The king's men apparently had moved seven sickly males into a holding cell, branded them, and tried to pass them off as slaves destined for the *Commerce*.

The bosun spotted the counterfeit brands and alerted Captain Collingwood to the trickery. The captain took the hapless Mr. Ferrett by the ear, Heathcliff was told, and insisted the trading company representative speak on his behalf to the king.

"This king is a bandit," the captain told Heathcliff, when he came to the pier. "He actually hid some of our cattle from us. I had to give him my last case of muskets to get him to release them. It disturbs me to deal with the unscrupulous blackguard. I swear I shall never return to this infernal castle again."

Heathcliff waited on the pier for the last of the Negro females to pick their way down the stone steps. Ebenezer Bugg joined the captain and stood next to him, looking over the females. The Negro females had only a piece of dirty cloth around their waists; their shaved heads and bare breasts were dotted with small clear droplets of rain.

"I would take that little one to my cabin if I were captain," said the Englishman, pointing out a short, big-breasted woman passing before them. "Look at the dugs! She's been suckling a baby! She'll warm your bed and give you warm milk, too."

"I shall stick to my rum," the captain replied.

Ebenezer Bugg slapped him on the back and laughed heartily.

Heathcliff recognized the last female to step onto the pier. It was Kee-Sha, the village girl. Heathcliff had not seen her since the night of the feast.

"That one does not belong here, captain!" Heathcliff blurted, and pointed her out. "Her name is Kee-Sha. She lives in the huts outside the castle."

"She is a slave, bought and paid for, Heathcliff!" retorted Captain Collingwood. "Look for yourself—she bears our mark."

When Kee-Sha passed him, Heathcliff noticed a fresh pink blister seared onto the girl's back.

"But she is not of the dungeons, captain," Heathcliff protested. "She is one of the tribe that lives in the huts. To take her aboard is surely a mistake."

"You address *Captain Collingwood* in this manner?" snorted the Englishman. "You are impertinent, young man. If I were your captain, I would have you flogged."

"I intend no disrespect; the captain surely knows. But Captain Collingwood, hear me. I believe you make a mistake. You should not take this girl."

"I do not make mistakes, Heathcliff," the captain wearily replied. "All morning long I have engaged in a tedious argument with King Big Tucker. Only with difficulty have I righted our accounts, and with almost no help from Mr. Ferrett. Now take up your oars. I am eager to depart."

As Heathcliff climbed into the jolly-boat, he could not bear to look at Kee-Sha. Some of the Negro females were already crying. When the gold-taker stepped into the boat, Heathcliff took up his oars and rowed toward the *Commerce* in the sprinkling tropical rain.

Chapter 54

The first night at sea, the captain entered the forecastle and informed the crew he intended to make a show of force to strike fear into every captive's heart. Mr. Coil passed out muskets, swords, and cudgels. Every hand had a weapon. The captain gave Heathcliff the lantern, drew his cutlass, and had Heathcliff lead the group below.

With a great clanking of boots and a ringing of irons and chains, the captain's party blustered loudly into the lower hold.

The air in the lower hold was sour with the smell of tightly-packed, frightened human beings. The upper and lower racks were fully packed with African males.

The Negroes became deathly silent at the gleam of the lantern. Two rows of eyes blinked at them from racks on both sides of the hold. A few Negroes looked into the light, but most looked away.

"Tell them the first bull who gives us any trouble will be beat to within an inch of his life," said Captain Collingwood, addressing the gold-taker. "The quashees must do everything we tell them to do. I don't fear the lash. Tell them I will enforce strict punishment for any small disobedience."

"And tell them if they don't mind, we'll cut off their testicles and throw them to the sharks. Savages fear the sharks," the Englishman added. "Have the little bitch tell them that."

The gold-taker indignantly stared at the Englishman.

"Tell them," said the captain.

The gold-taker addressed the captives for some time, speaking in what to Heathcliff sounded like three different African languages. The sound of her voice was followed by a ringing silence.

"Enough," said the captain.

As Heathcliff held high the swinging lantern and led them away, the crew stomped out of the hold like a breath of ill wind.

The Middle Passage

Chapter 55

Fat grey bulbous clouds straggled across sea and sky as the *Commerce* crept back down the Guinea Coast. It was slower going to return to Ebenezer Bugg's old village; the ship beat slowly against the wind. After the first morning's inspection, Captain Collingwood stood on the quarterdeck, wearing his cutlass.

"From here on out, the quashees shall do exactly what we order them to do. Alert Mr. Quayle to any hint of resistance. We don't want to kill any of them, but we'll whip them to within an inch of their lives," he said.

"What captain says to-day could save your life," Mr. Coil added.

Captain Collingwood moved to a wooden arms cabinet on the quarterdeck and slapped it with his hand.

"We have muskets, pistols, and broadswords under lock and key. We shall keep men stationed at the swivel guns all day. Guns remain loaded from here on," he said. "Dr. Chum."

The surgeon stepped forward.

"Beginning to-day, we will bring the black cattle up for feeding and exercise, then move them onto their assigned areas on the deck," said the surgeon. "Exercise and sunlight will help keep the creatures alive. The routine we establish to-day will help us control them."

HEATHCLIFF: THE LOST YEARS

"Do you understand?" Captain Collingwood asked.

"Aye-aye, captain."

"Aye-aye, sir."

A few minutes later, Marconi and young Tom carried a very large steaming cauldron out of the galley and set it down on the deck. As the crew looked on, the gold-taker led the females up to the deck for their first meal. The females stood quietly in line while young Tom gave them pannikins and Marconi ladled out the soup. Heathcliff looked for Kee-Sha but didn't see her before Mr. Coil called him away.

Chapter 56

Heathcliff helped stretch and tighten the hemp canvas over the wooden exercise platform the Fiddler built near the waist of the ship. As Captain Collingwood and Mr. Coil inspected the work, the Englishman approached the captain.

"Bring up the Mandinka first, captain," the Englishman said. "When the Mandinka comply, all the others fall in line. Trust me; I know the ways of these savages."

"It makes little difference who we bring up first, captain," Mr. Coil observed. "The blacks will fall into line."

"If it makes no difference, why not try it Ebenezer's way, Mr. Coil?" said the captain. "Heathcliff, you and Oidah bring up two Mandinka from the end of the rack, the two shackled together."

By the time Heathcliff and Oidah returned, Young Tom had taken his place next to the platform, tin pot and hickory stick in hand. The Irishman sat on the surgeon's three-legged stool beside the cabin boy, holding his fiddle and ready to play.

Oidah directed the two Mandinka across the deck and up onto the platform, the chains of their leg irons clattering as they walked.

The two big Mandinka blinked in the sun. They looked warily about the deck.

HEATHCLIFF: THE LOST YEARS

Mr. Quayle stood at the ready, holding the cat. Several of the crew gathered about, brandishing weapons. On the quarterdeck, Vito trained a swivel-gun loaded with grapeshot on the muscular, nearly-naked Negroes.

Ebenezer Bugg jumped to the platform and unlocked the shackles from the largest captive. When the gold-taker stepped up onto the platform, the Englishman jumped down onto the deck and hissed an African word.

"Why you say that?" the gold-taker demanded.

"I have lived among these savages!" said the Englishman. "I know how to talk to Mandinka. That one is a warrior!"

"He not warrior. He slave," snapped the gold-taker.

"Your black-skinned bitch is worthless." The Englishman told the captain. "She cannot make the Mandinka obey."

"You are white snake. You have two faces!" hissed the gold-taker, trembling with anger. "Why you say that?"

"You don't know the Mandinka, because you are stupid," taunted the Englishman. "If you don't respect me, I will have the captain sell you for a slave in Jamaica."

"Be silent, Ebenezer!" said the captain. "Step back. Let her show them what Dr. Chum would have them do."

The Englishman turned his back to the platform.

The captain nodded. The Irishman struck up a tune. Raising his hickory-stick, Young Tom tapped along on his cook pot.

Glaring at the Mandinka, the gold-taker lifted her robe to reveal her ankles and bare feet. She demonstrated a quick stomping dance step, then hissed out a command.

The Mandinka stared straight ahead. The gold-taker repeated the command, and demonstrated the step a second time. The Mandinka stared at her, as if in a trance.

The gold-taker pointed at the Englishman, who turned to face her. "He stop them. White snake say them something."

"The Mandinka dance before battle," the Englishman hissed. "You must approach them as a warrior."

"He not warrior. He slave!" hissed the gold-taker.

The Englishman turned to the captain. "Get her away from the Mandinka, captain. I will show you."

Ebenezer Bugg removed his shoes. He pushed the gold-taker aside and glared at the captives. He stamped his bare foot on the planks. The Mandinka looked up, and snarled.

The Englishman took three steps back and glanced at the captain. Hopping forward on one leg and then the other, staring intently, the Englishman moved toward the Mandinka like a predator stalking its prey. He slashed the air with one hand. He touched the Mandinka's forehead with his free hand, and spat out an African word.

"What that word?" the gold-taker asked. "What you say?"

"He is my slave," hissed the Englishman.

Keeping his eyes on the Mandinka, he stomped forward again, spat on the platform, and slapped the big Mandinka's face. They locked eyes for some time.

Captain Collingwood seemed entranced. Fiddler Ryan suddenly began to play, and Young Tom chimed in, tapping.

The Englishman began stamping his bare feet, one after the other, in time with the music. The Mandinka mimicked him, lifting one foot and putting it down, then lifting one foot and putting tit down.

"Extraordinary," said the captain.

"Stop!" the Englishman shouted.

He held up one hand and jumped from the platform.

"Let the little bitch show the others," he said. "The bulls will dance for her now."

The gold-taker glared at the Englishman. "White snake," she hissed.

"Black bitch," he replied.

Chapter 57

The second day at sea, Heathcliff watched a group of females stream up from the hold, chattering and upset. The gold-taker walked among them, carrying a limp corpse in her arms. A young Negro female had died during the night. The gold-taker lay the corpse on the deck with tears in her eyes. She signaled Mr. Coil, then obediently lined up the females for their first meal.

"Fetch the surgeon, Heathcliff," Mr. Coil said.

Heathcliff hurried below and woke up the surgeon. Dr. Chum bent down and took a quick look at the corpse.

"Toss her over the side right away," he said. "This one very likely bears disease."

No far away, the Negro females stood in line for their first meal of the day. They watched Heathcliff and Fiddler pick up the girl's hands and feet and unceremoniously toss her small stiff body over the stern.

The females shrieked. They surged toward the rear of the ship as fluidly as running water and crowded around the bulwark. The gold-taker hurried after them, calling them back and waving her arms, but the Negro women would not leave. The females clutched each other and watched the little girl's dead body float away from the ship, face down in the water.

Heathcliff saw the flash of a dorsal fin. Something he could not see tugged at the foot of the floating corpse and pulled it down into the deep.

The Negro women shrieked and held each other, jumping up and down and chattering at the rail. With some difficulty, the gold-taker herded all the females back into line to receive their morning meal.

"Sharks have followed our ship, and our idiot surgeon feeds them flesh," the Fiddler observed. "Mark my words, lad. This does not bode well."

Chapter 58

None of the crew wished to handle the large metal pails they called "poo-poo pots" scattered around the lower hold. The captain ordered the first watch to bring the pails to the deck first thing in the morning, empty them into the ocean, rinse them out with salt water, and return them below.

It was a distasteful task. Many Negroes were seasick. A pungent aroma of human feces, vomit, and sweat permeated the lower hold. Males chained to the racks could with only with difficulty climb over each other and get off the racks to reach the pots, which were chained to the lower rack and locked in place. The crew found many pots knocked over.

On the morning of the third day, to Heathcliff's surprise, Ebenezer Bugg volunteered for the odious task.

"Let me take on the pots, captain. I don't mind working below deck for a bit in the morning," said the Englishman.

"Are you sure?"

"I will handle it, captain."

"Very well, Ebenezer," said the captain, pleasantly surprised. "If you want it, the task is entirely yours. Come to my cabin and let me give you a better set of keys."

To Heathcliff's astonishment, the same Englishman who had never lifted a finger to help the crew diligently emptied and rinsed every one of the pails before the end of the first watch. Not only that, he seemed to enjoy the task.

That afternoon, when Heathcliff checked the lower hold, he came upon Ebenezer Bugg sitting on the racks with the Mandinka. The man bolted to his feet in the lantern light, startling Heathcliff.

"Who goes there?" demanded the Englishman. "Who comes at me with the lantern?"

"It is I, Heathcliff." Heathcliff lifted the lamp so that his face could be seen. "Have you not yet completed your work?"

"You mock me, sir," said the Englishman.

"*Ta mansa*," said a Negro, nodding his head.

"*Mansa*," said another. "*Mansa*."

"Do they call you master?" Heathcliff asked. "*Mansa*? Is that an African word?"

"*Mansa* is not *master*." The Englishman unlocked the chain around an empty pail and snatched it up.

"Mansa means I want to go home, sir," hissed the Englishman. "The Mandinka are homesick. I tell falsehoods for you, you know. I tell the Mandinka they are going home, but I am lying. Do you understand? Remove yourself from my path, sir, unless you wish to handle this filthy bucket yourself."

Heathcliff stepped aside to let the glaring Englishman pass.

Heathcliff told Mr. Coil about his encounter with the Englishman, but the first mate merely shrugged his shoulders. Although Heathcliff couldn't explain it, he felt something amiss.

When the females waited in line for their food the next morning. Heathcliff asked the gold-taker the meaning of the African word.

"*Mansa*?" the gold-taker asked. "Mandinka?"

"I believe so."

"To Mandinka, *mansa* is king," the little African laughed. "On this ship, Captain Collingwood *mansa*."

"Captain Collingwood?" Heathcliff asked. This puzzled him.

"Captain Collingwood *mansa*," laughed the gold-taker. "*Mansa* not you, *mansa* not me. *Mansa* is like king."

"Does it mean they want to go home?" Heathcliff asked.

At that moment, Marconi and Young Tom staggered out of the galley carrying a large iron cauldron of hot soup between them. The cauldron was unusually full and young Tom had trouble holding up his end, even using both hands.

"Heathcliff, help me," the cabin boy cried. "I fear I may spill the soup."

Chapter 59

Later that morning, Mr. Coil sent Heathcliff to slush the mizzenmast. High above the mainsail, with a tin pot of slush hooked over one arm, he smeared grease onto the weather-beaten mast, making the wood darken and shine. Directly below, Captain Collingwood chatted with Mr. Coil. The Negro females and young ones were just being moved beneath the canvas shades but the males remained below.

"Smoke ahoy!" cried the lookout.

"Where does it lie, seaman?" came the voice of Mr. Coil.

"Dead ahead, sir."

Heathcliff looked up to see a thick column of black smoke erupting from the sea directly ahead of the ship.

"Heave to, boys," came the voice of Mr. Coil. "Let's slow her down."

Heathcliff felt the *Commerce* change course and slow down as a two-masted brig came into view. Clouds of thick black smoke billowed up from her waist. All the brig's sails blew loose in the breeze and she listed to one side like a wounded animal.

Mr. Coil raised his looking-glass. "She is flying English colours, captain. Something foul burns on her deck."

Ebenezer Bugg joined the officers huddling around the captain.

HEATHCLIFF: THE LOST YEARS

"An English ship!" he cried. "We must help her!"

"*C-h-i-s-t-e N-e-g-r-o,*" Mr. Coil spelled out the name. "Spanish, is it, and a slaver?"

"Approach her cautiously, captain," Dr. Chum advised. "Entire ships have fallen prey to the flux."

"We must help the English vessel!" said the Englishman, tugging on the captain's sleeve.

On the deck of the brig, Heathcliff saw several men sprawled around a large metal cauldron on the deck. The cauldron belched a huge amount of smoke but the mariners appeared to be dead.

The *Commerce* slowed as it approached the brig. The captain lifted his speaking-trumpet. Behind him, Heathcliff noticed Ebenezer Bugg hurry down into the hatch.

"Ahoy *Christi Negro*! This is Charles Collingwood, captain of the *Commerce*, an English merchant. Call your captain to the deck. Let us know how we can assist you."

Captain Collingwood's words rang across the water, unanswered. The captain set down his speaking-trumpet and lifted his telescope again.

"Perhaps you are right, Chum. Perhaps the vessel has been ravaged by disease," said the captain.

Ebenezer Bugg vaulted up from the hatch with a Blunderbuss in each hand. All five Mandinka followed the Englishman, brandishing knives. Trailing after them was Billy Gilding, whirling a long *machete* over his head.

"Captain!" Heathcliff cried.

The Englishman fired a pistol in the air. "The *Commerce* is mine!" he cried.

"*Mansa!*" The Mandinka fanned out behind him. "*Mansa!*"

Oidah Blue snatched up the scuttle-butt and threw the half-full barrel of water into the mutineers, knocking one Mandinka down.

From behind the burning ship, Heathcliff saw three dugout canoes stop below the sea ladder. Yellow-faced Negroes and pirates jumped into the canoes and rowed toward the *Commerce,* which was not far away.

"Canoes to portside!" shouted the lookout.

"Mr. Bolt, man the cannons!" cried the captain, drawing his cutlass.

Ebenezer Bugg stood on the quarterdeck. He aimed a Blunderbuss at the captain who stood just behind Mr. Coil.

"Captain Collingwood! Throw down your sword!"

Mr. Coil leaped at the mutineer. Ebenezer Bugg fired. The first mate caught the Englishman's face in one big hand and pulled him backwards onto the ground.

"Traitor!" rasped Mr. Coil, his chest bleeding.

Heathcliff hurried down the ratlines. Below him, the crew fought mutineers with knives, knuckles, feet, and bare hands.

Emerging from the group of women, the gold-taker angrily pulled off her turban.

"Stop fighting!" She shouted in English and Mandinka, wading into the fray and holding up both arms. "Stop fighting!"

Billy Gilding slashed at the bosun with his machete. Mr. Quayle managed to duck the knife and, with both hands on his cane, rammed it up through the surprised mutineer's abdomen and punctured his heart.

A grapnel thudded onto the deck. Heathcliff saw Marconi pick it up and throw it overboard before snatching up a boarding axe, ready to meet the pirates.

Captain Collingwood slashed his way to the arms cabinet. Backed against it, slashing away at the Mandinka with his cutlass, he held off two mutineers who were trying to stab him with knives

As he descended the ratlines, Heathcliff saw Ebenezer Bugg bent over Peter, beating the orphan's head with the butt of his pistol.

HEATHCLIFF: THE LOST YEARS

Heathcliff leaped. He landed on Ebenezer Bugg and clung to his back as the man stood up. Heathcliff squeezed one arm around the neck of the spinning Englishman and pulled him to the deck as his Blunderbuss clattered away.

Peter snatched up the pistol. Holding the pistol in both hands, Peter stalked forward aiming to shoot the Englishman in the chest but the Blunderbuss had not been reloaded and it would not fire.

"*Mansa!*"

A Mandinka jumped Heathcliff from behind, wrapping one arm around his face while slashing at Peter with a knife. Heathcliff threw the savage over one shoulder, but the Mandinka stabbed his leg as he went down. The Englishman grabbed Heathcliff by the knees and pulled him to the deck as a cannon fired.

Oidah Blue threw his arms around the Englishman, holding him to his chest while Heathcliff fumbled for his rope knife. Heathcliff lifted the point of his knife to the mutineer's throat and pressed it in.

"Surrender!" cried Ebenezer Bugg. "I surrender!"

The gold-taker shouted out in Mandinka. The Mandinka dropped their knives. Heathcliff heard another cannon erupt, followed by two other cannons in rapid succession.

"The pirates run away!" came the voice of young Tom as another cannon fired.

"Clap those bulls in double irons and take them below!" cried the captain. "Mr. Quayle—chain this English mutineer to the mast."

Heathcliff felt faint. His thigh bled through the slash in his pants. He stared dumbly at the corpse of the dead Mandinka, which lay not far from Billy Gilding's *machete* and his dead, curled-up body.

"Heathcliff," said Dr. Chum. "Come here and assist me."

Mr. Coil writhed on the timbers below the quarterdeck, holding his chest. The surgeon crouched over him.

The two of them carried Mr. Coil below deck to the infirmary. Heathcliff held the first mate down while the surgeon inserted a probe and extracted the shot with a pair of slender brass forceps.

After they finished the operation, Captain Collingwood hurried into the infirmary still holding his cutlass.

"I am alive because of this good man," said the captain. "Treat our first mate with your best medicine, Dr. Chum. As soon as you can, move him to his cabin. He will be pleased to hear have set sail for the islands."

That night, Heathcliff lay in his hammock, his aching leg securely bandaged, and unable to sleep. Peter blundered into the forecastle, eager to talk. Peter had just helped the bosun dispose of the dead mutineers, a task he found disgusting.

"Mr. Quayle pulled out Billy Gilding's eyeballs and made me carry them to the c-cook, with my bare hands," Peter shuddered. "Then he d-d-dismembered the bodies with a boarding-axe. I had to fling their bloody arms and legs into the s-sea."

Chapter 60

The next morning, the sun rose brightly over the sea. Surrounded by the crew, Captain Collingwood confronted the mutinous Englishman who had remained chained to the mainmast all night but seemed in good spirits.

"You are a loathsome traitor, Ebenezer Bugg. And I believed you my friend," Captain Collingwood hissed. "What have you to say for yourself?"

"I regret that I failed to take the *Commerce*," the Englishman smiled. "The ship carries rich cargo."

"You tried to kill me, sir."

"I would never kill you, captain. We are friends. You must set a course for this ship. You would have gotten this vessel to Virginia. When we made landfall in the Americas, I planned to give helf the profits to you."

"You are a liar. You would slay us all."

"But you must keep me aboard, captain. The Mandinka obey me, you have seen it with your eyes, all the blacks aboard will obey me," he said. "Remove my chains right now and I will assist you."

Mr. Quayle sauntered forward and kicked the mutineer in the groin, then left him squirming against the mast. While the Englishman gasped in pain, two mariners strapped a leather harness around his chest and shoulders and unchained him. Meanwhile, Heathcliff noticed two of the crew pull a thick rope under the bow and begin working it back beneath the ship.

"You are a treacherous sinner, Ebenezer Bugg! My first mate lies in his cabin nearly dead, wounded by you! You would steal my ship, lie to me, take my cargo, and slay us all besides," Captain Collingwood hissed. "I have prepared fit punishment for you."

Ebenezer Bugg clutched at the harness fastened around his torso. His eyes widened when the bosun snapped his harness to the thick, tar-covered rope that had been maneuvered all the way under the hull to the waist at the middle of the ship.

"You can't keelhaul me, captain!—I'm a bloody white man! Clamp me in irons! Give me fifty lashes! I will help you!"

While the Englishman kicked at the crew, they pulled off his shoes and pants, leaving him naked from the waist down. The Englishman bolted to his feet, half-naked, eyes flashing.

"Collingwood, stop this! Don't force me to employ *juju*. African magic will destroy you! If I curse your ship, my curse will sink this vessel to the bottom of the sea!"

At a signal from the captain, a line of mariners on the opposite side of the deck yanked hard on the rope. This jerked Ebenezer Bugg off his feet and pulled him flush against the bulwark. Then Oidah Blue singlehandedly picked up the kicking Englishman by the harness and threw him overboard as if he were a small dog.

"Charles Collingwood, I curse you! I curse you!" the Englishman screamed, bobbing and shaking his fist. "Pull me back now or I swear by the blackest gods in Africa you *die* before you reach the islands!"

The mariners jerked Ebenezer Bugg down into the sea. Pulling from the opposite side of the ship, they tugged hard on the rope. They dragged the Englishman underwater, pulling him under the sharp-edged, barnacle-encrusted keel of the *Commerce,* and finally hoisted his body up on the other side.

HEATHCLIFF: THE LOST YEARS

Miraculously, the Englishman was alive. He gasped and flailed his bloody limbs like a man raked by a thousand claws.

Blood dribbled into the water as mariners hoisted his body up from the sea, arms and bare legs dripping blood. The Englishman flailed and kicked in the harness, screaming for his life.

Captain Collingwood crossed his arms as the crew worked one end of the rope over a yardarm, and swung the Englishman out over the sea like a piece of dripping bait on the end of a long string. They jiggled the mutineer up and down, bouncing him over the sea while a few others taunted him and poked at him with long poles.

Sharks roiled up beneath the dangling man. Flesh-eating predators rolled over in the water, excited by the drizzle of red blood that dripped into the sea.

"Give our mutineer a good long swim!" the captain called out.

Ebenezer Bugg kicked one leg, lustily screaming out for help as the hands lowered him into the churning water.

When mariners again lifted up the mutineer, he remained only half alive. Sharks had ripped his legs and genitals away and his intestines dangled from his trunk like pink spaghetti. His mouth moved as his torso spun like a dismembered doll on the end of the line.

"I believe you know what to do, Mr. Quayle," said the captain.

"Aye-aye, sir," the bosun nodded.

Captain Collingwood smiled grimly and retired to his cabin.

Chapter 61

That afternoon the captain ordered all the quashees brought to the deck to observe punishment of the Mandinka mutineers.

"The rebellious bulls are too valuable to kill, but I intend to break them so thoroughly no man will ever need punish them again," the captain announced to the crew.

The first two Mandinka males, shackled and manacled together at the arms and legs, looked warily about as Mr. Quayle prodded them onto the dancing platform with his rattan cane.

Mr. Quayle pushed the two mutineers to their knees and unlocked the manacles that bound their hands together. The gold-taker set down a pail before them in which four human eyeballs rolled around in a pool of brown goo. When Heathcliff noticed what was inside the pail, he felt himself gag.

"Tell this one to pick up an eye and eat it," said the captain.

As the gold-taker translated, the Mandinka hesitantly picked up an eyeball. He quickly dropped it back into the pail, and muttered a few words to the gold-taker.

"He think bad spirit looking at him," the gold-taker said to the captain. "He not eat."

HEATHCLIFF: THE LOST YEARS

"It does contain an evil spirit. It is the spirit of Ebenezer Bugg," said the captain. "The bull must eat it here and now, before us all. If he doesn't eat it, tell him I'll castrate him in front of the women and throw his testicles to the sharks."

The gold-taker bent over the pail to translate the captain's words. Standing behind her, as if to emphasize the point, Mr. Quayle pulled out his knife.

The big Mandinka shoved the gold-taker backwards onto the knife. The gold-taker screamed. She threw out her arms and fell against both Mr. Bolt and the captain.

In the confusion, the two Mandinka rose like the wind. Still chained together at the ankle, they glided and hopped toward the knot of wide-eyed Negro females. The shrieking women parted as the Mandinka hobbled rapidly across the deck in a clumsy, ferocious clatter of swinging chains and leg irons.

"Stop them!" shouted the captain.

The smaller Mandinka jumped the bulwark but the chain of his leg-iron bound him to the second captive already pinned against the bulwark by Oidah Blue. The littler mutineer dangled over the side of the ship, suspended upside down by his leg iron over the water.

When the crew hauled him up, the Mandinka kicked at the men desperately and wildly with his free leg but the crew subdued him.

"Tie them both to the grate," said the captain. "We must give them a very long taste of the cat, Mr. Quayle."

Heathcliff helped tie the struggling Mandinka onto the grating. Under the shades, the other captives stared silently, or looked away.

Swinging the cat, the bosun moved relentlessly from one mutineer to another, shredding their backs and bodies. When the bosun paused to rest, dripping with sweat, Heathcliff heard both Mandinka gasping for air. Their backs and thighs gleamed with blood.

"Give the big one his dinner," said the captain.

Mr. Quayle unfastened the exhausted captive, lay him on his back, and opened his teeth with the point of his knife. He pushed an eyeball

+ [198] +

between the Mandinka's teeth with the palm of his hand and held it there. When the Negro choked, the men held him down while the bosun forced the eyeball down his throat with the handle of the cat. After the Mandinka vomited, the captain ordered Mr. Quayle to take a hammer to one of his hands.

Heathcliff helped carry the broken, moaning mutineers below, and chain them to the rack. Back on the deck, in the fresh air, he leaned against the forward mast, sickened by the brutality he had witnessed. He did not understand why the Mandinka tried to escape which made their dreadful punishment even worse.

"Why did the Mandinka try to jump into the sea?" Heathcliff asked the gold-taker. "They could not possibly escape."

"Mandinka only want to go home," the gold-taker explained. "They homesick. Mandinka believe their spirits return to their home village after they die."

Chapter 62

Clouds drifted lazily above the trade winds. Captain Collingwood told Heathcliff the northeast breezes were as perfect as could be desired, and the captain thanked God for his good luck and prayed his luck would hold. The captain's luck held steady for the next two weeks of the voyage.

As Mr. Coil had not yet recovered, Captain Collingwood and the other officers assumed his duties. The captain seemed quite concerned about his ailing first mate, and visited Mr. Coil often in his cabin to see him and ask his advice.

From his own visits, Heathcliff knew Mr. Coil remained feverish. The surgery to remove the shot had been successful, but the wound was festering and so far, there was little improvement. The first mate remained weak and got no better despite several bloodlettings.

The crew fell into their routine. Every morning they brought the Negroes to the deck, fed and exercised them, and herded the males and females beneath shades on opposite sides of the deck. Before dusk, the captives received a second meal and a final ration of water before being looked over by Dr. Chum and herded below for the night.

Three times a week, the crew bathed the captives with vinegar. The Negroes were now so cooperative it was not necessary for Mr. Quayle to cane the legs of the males to hurry them up into the tubs, and on and off the dancing-platform, but the bosun continued to do so and sometimes seemed to enjoy it.

Some mariners went for the females at night. Those who did pushed their way into the women's quarters under the ship and took their pleasure with the Negro women, something which Heathcliff was often warned to ignore.

Early on, the officers had picked out females and took them to their cabins. Consorts of the officers sometimes joined the captive females on deck during the day, and these women were known to be off-limits to members of the crew.

After the mutiny, Heathcliff discovered Captain Collingwood had taken Kee-Sha to his cabin. When he saw her on deck, she no longer met his eyes. It pained him that she had been taken aboard and he often worried about her. He thought her pretty face considerably aged.

Quite by chance, Heathcliff encountered Kee-Sha in a passage-way below deck one afternoon. He clutched her shoulders, hoping she might understand the words that sprang to his lips.

"Kee-Sha, it is wrong that you are taken captive here. I regret I can do nothing to help you. I am sorry."

Kee-Sha looked him in the eyes for a moment; then she turned away.

For some time, Heathcliff regarded the black-skinned males as wild, dangerous animals. Although the males were compliant, he kept a wary distance from them. Around them, he watched his back and kept a hand on his rope knife. He did not forget the savage who bit him and ripped open his flesh in the dungeon, which left him with an unsightly scar. Indeed, he saw the same man's black, wary face every day.

Heathcliff slowly became accustomed to the sight of so much black skin and nearly naked black bodies. One day, Heathcliff realized the males were frightened of him, too. He began to recognize individual faces, to see differences between them, and to wonder if any had a heart and soul like his own in their dark-skinned bodies.

HEATHCLIFF: THE LOST YEARS

Heathcliff sometimes sensed a terrible sadness among the African males. He felt their sadness when they shaded their eyes to squint back over the flat blue ocean, as if in search of lost Africa.

Chapter 63

North of the equator, in the middle of the night, Heathcliff actually felt the wind die. An unnatural stillness came over the ocean in the middle of his watch, he sensed, and the stillness seemed to settle in.

A pitiless sun beat down on the floating ship all the next morning when he mopped the deck. He felt no whisper of wind during Captain Collingwood's inspection. All that day, the sails hung limp on their yards. The captain's lucky wind had apparently disappeared, the crew began whispering. The *Commerce* lay mired in the doldrums.

Each hot and cloudless morning, before the captain's inspection, mariners wet the decks to cool the ship, producing a moment of relief followed by a cloud of warm, slowly-rising steam. With no wind in the sails, the watches were reduced to days of slushing masts, mending canvas and lines, and polishing and re-polishing fittings.

Every day the mariners brought up the Negroes, fed and exercised them, held them under their shades, and took them below.

The lower hold, now unmercifully warm, stank of excrement, sweat, and human suffering. An increasingly foul odor penetrated every nook and cranny in the ship.

HEATHCLIFF: THE LOST YEARS

The captain ordered the crew to pull the grates off the hatches to allow as much heat as possible to escape from the hold but the air below deck remained foul, still and painfully hot even at night.

The ship's officers went to sleep in their cabins with portholes, passageways, and cabin doors propped open. Heathcliff and several other hands abandoned the forecastle to sleep on deck under the stars. Every morning, while Heathcliff swabbed the neck, he waited for a breath of air that never came.

Chapter 64

S **tanding his night watch,** Heathcliff heard a fearful screaming below. The captain heard it, too. Captain hurried to the deck and called together several of the crew.

"Fiddler, fetch the gold-taker and the surgeon," the captain said, drawing his cutlass. "Heathcliff, get the lantern and lead us down. Something disturbs the bulls. We must put a stop to it."

As they dropped into the lower hold, Heathcliff made out a group of males shouting and waving their arms at one end of the bottom rack.

The gold-taker shouted out for quiet. She led them forward to the stiff body of a dead Negro sprawled out on the lower rack, his body still shackled to the leg of a frightened, living male.

Lifting the lantern, Heathcliff recognized the dead Negro's face. It was the black man who bit his shoulder in the dungeon of Gold Coast Castle and scrambled so desperately to get away.

Dr. Chum bent over the corpse and rubbed its lips with his fingers.

"The lips are shrunken with dehydration. Heathcliff, do bring the lantern closer."

The surgeon got down on his hands and knees to examine a dark pool of blood and excrement beneath the rack that held the corpse. Dr. Chum put a finger in the pool, smelled his finger, and touched it to his tongue. He groaned and stood up in the pitiless heat, perspiring, his spectacles fogged. He took off his spectacles to clean them on his shirt.

"Fling this poor devil over the side," he said.

"Heathcliff," said the captain. "Oidah."

Heathcliff and Oidah unchained the corpse and picked up the body. Its limbs were loose and moist. With Oidah leading the way, and both of them sweating profusely, they muscled the limp dead body up through the manhole and finally onto the deck, where the air felt considerably cooler.

"Let us rest just a moment," Heathcliff gasped.

He and Oidah lay the body onto the deck. The dead Negro's mouth immediately fell open. The corpse's teeth shone like a string of lurid pearls beneath the white Equatorial moon.

Chapter 65

Doctor Chum addressed the crew the following morning. Captain Collingwood looked on grimly, dabbing at his forehead with a handkerchief.

"We've had a touch of the hot flux, men. The hot flux is a powerful contagious disease, and it kills. A bull died of it last night and more will likely soon suffer and die," said the surgeon. "Keep an eye out for fever, nausea, diarrhea. When you see fresh blood under the racks or in the buckets, notify me right away. We must quarantine the sick, and keep them below."

"Will I fall sick, too, sir?" asked young Tom.

"I have medicinal Ipecac, Tom, and I have my blue pills. What medicine I have is often helpful but I cannot ever guarantee beneficial results."

"And if I happen upon a dead one?" Fiddler Ryan asked.

"Fetch me; I must have a look. After that, dispose of the bodies quickly. After you handle a corpse, rinse your hands in vinegar. Keep your eyes open, men, and hope for the best."

As the surgeon predicted, more Negroes came down with the hot flux. The disease terrified the sick captives, who were kept below and chained together.

As more captives began to fall sick, the crew struggled to maintain a semblance of order.

During the first week of the epidemic, Heathcliff helped throw three bodies over the side. Since the ship remained in the doldrums, the corpses did not float far away from the ship. Some of the crew so feared the floating, bloated bodies that they hurled them away from the ship as far as they could and pushed them farther away with long poles. But the bodies floated eerily back. Eventually, sharks took them, or the horribly bloated bodies sank into the sea.

As mariners fell sick, Heathcliff and the others took on additional work. Daily exercises were suspended. Dr. Chum appointed hands to carry soup and biscuits to the sick quashees below.

When Heathcliff visited Mr. Coil, he saw the first mate was rapidly losing weight. The much slimmer and much weaker Mr. Coil remained feverish and when he talked he was increasingly pessimistic about his prospects for recovery.

"Some nights I feel the Angel of Death hovering over my body, and it cries out for me," Mr. Coil said. "I weep when I think of that pretty lass I left behind in England who I may never see again."

"You are strong, Mr. Coil," Heathcliff said. "Dr. Chum believes you will soon recover."

"The surgeon does nothing but stick me like a pig and bleed me," Mr. Coil sighed. "But do attend to your duties, Heathcliff. Always do your best for your captain and your ship."

Mired in the doldrums, the *Commerce* became a floating prison of disease. Before it was over, half the captives and crew were ill. As exhausted as he was, when Heathcliff looked into the faces of the sick quashees, he saw only fear, resignation, and despair.

Chapter 66

When Heathcliff came down with the hot flux, Dr. Chum placed him under a canvas awning near the waist with several other sick members of the crew. The surgeon gave Heathcliff three blue pills and a dipper of water and left him there.

Heathcliff's face and limbs burned with dry fever. As he lay on the deck, he watched sick mariners crawl to the bulwark and vomit over the side and he sometimes did the same.

In a fever, he noticed the sun set, and rise again. He could not drink enough liquid to slake his burning thirst. Half awake, he heard the voice of the captain, dolefully announce a rationing of water.

The gold-taker brought an African female with a broad, tired face to help care for him. The woman sponged his brow and chest with a moist rag one afternoon, humming a strange melody as she worked.

The next morning, the African woman and the gold-taker brought Heathcliff a cannikin of bitter-smelling brown liquid. The gold-taker pulled him into a sitting position.

"You drink soup. She make this help you. Soup make sick fly away like bird."

HEATHCLIFF: THE LOST YEARS

Heathcliff swallowed as much as he could of the warm, foul-tasting liquid, then lay back and tried to catch his breath. In the distance, the sun hovered over the horizon like a luminous pearl. The expanse of still water beneath it seemed coated with silver foil. Finally, he slipped into delirium like a small boat pushed onto a lake of still, dark water.

"Heathcliff!"

The ghostly voice of Catherine Earnshaw called for him across the wide moonlit sea. He recognized her voice immediately. Heathcliff felt her spirit reverberate in the darkness, and reach out for him.

Heathcliff sat up on the deck in the moonlight. Every atom of his body yearned for his lost and only love. For a moment, if he willed it, he knew he would find her again.

"Cathy!" he shouted.

Heathcliff surged to his feet, and grew wings. He stepped onto the bulwark, spread his arms, and dove from the ship in the moonlight. He took flight like a bird, determined to unite with Catherine, and soared high above the moonlit motionless sea until he felt himself very slowly tumbling down.

Heathcliff bolted awake, dripping with sweat, his fever broken. He shook his head. He stood up. His legs felt weak. Unsteadily, he walked to the rail, then collapsed.

The kindly face of the African female appeared above him. She placed a wet cloth on his forehead and touched his cheek as lovingly as she might have touched the cheek of her own child.

She whispered something he could not understand, smiled, and left him alone in the moonlight. She had cured him, Heathcliff thought, and he did not even know her name.

Chapter 67

As quickly as possible, Heathcliff resumed his duties. The tropical sun burned across the deathly quiet ocean. The Fiddler told him all the sea-birds which followed the ship out of Africa had vanished from the air.

The timbers of the *Commerce* shrank in the sun. Every morning now, Heathcliff and the others dropped to their knees on the deck and pounded oakum into the cracks with carpenter's mallets, then covered the oakum with hot pitch and wet down the deck before bringing up the captives.

"I believe Mr. Coil may have seen the worst of it," the surgeon told Heathcliff, more than once. "I see signs of recovery every day."

When only a few Negroes remained sick, they were all brought back up on deck. Heathcliff helped swab the lower hold with vinegar and lye; he and Oidah burned pitch and gunpowder below.

Captain Collingwood paced about the ship, clutching his tricorne as if ready to depart. The captain avoided the flux, but he had dark bags under his eyes. Heathcliff thought the captain looked haunted.

Every morning, right after inspection, the captain began opening his Bible. He read the crew a few verses, and instructed the hands to all get on their knees and pray for a bit of wind.

HEATHCLIFF: THE LOST YEARS

One hot morning, after the prayers, the captain suddenly put on his beaver hat and grimaced up at the pitiless sun. Young Tom tugged on his sleeve. The cabin boy looked frightened.

"If our prayers are not answered, captain, will we all die?"

Captain Collingwood's face turned bright red. The captain hurled his tricorne to the deck. As he stomped on his hat, the captain cursed the doldrums, he cursed Ebenezer Bugg, he cursed King Big Tucker, he cursed Africa, he cursed the quashees, he cursed the sharks, he cursed the hot flux, he cursed the crew, and he cursed his horrible bad luck.

When his fit of temper subsided, Captain Collingwood glowered at the wide-eyed cabin boy.

"Of course we won't perish at sea, Tom. Not while I am captain of this ship," he snarled between his teeth. "Get to the galley. I shall think of something."

Captain Collingwood bent down to pick up his tricorne, slapped it twice against his legs, and re-shaped it with his hands. The captain stared at his hat for a moment before looking up at Heathcliff with an odd look on his face.

"Fetch the gold-taker," he snapped. "Bring her to my cabin."

When he went for the gold-taker, Heathcliff saw she had not fully recovered from the hot flux. The little Negro looked quite weak, but she dutifully followed him to the captain's cabin. Captain Collingwood shut the door behind them and began talking immediately.

"Ebenezer Bugg put a curse on my ship," the captain told her, his eyes burning feverishly. "African magic can break the spell."

The gold-taker shook her head no, sniffling.

"*Juju* bring bad spirits," said the gold-taker. "Wind is good spirit. We must pray for wind."

"Woman, I cannot pray anymore!" cried the captain, trembling with emotion. "My heart is sick! I ration water! I refuse to let us die in the middle of this god-forsaken sea!"

"Wind good spirit," the gold-taker said.

"A wretched African curse can be broken by Africans! Some of your women must know something more of *juju*. I command you to find one immediately, to help me break this cursed spell!"

The gold-taker sniffled. She glanced at Heathcliff. She shook her head. She started to speak, apparently thought better of it, and sniffled out the door.

Chapter 68

Heathcliff watched the gold-taker glide beneath the canvas shade, moving from female to female. She jabbed at the air with her finger as she talked. Several females shrank away. Finally, Heathcliff saw her approach the captain, who waited impatiently on the quarterdeck not far away.

"To-night, an Igboo woman try to draw up spirit," the gold-taker said. "All women must sit on deck, here, to take power from moon."

"I will instruct the crew to leave you alone," said the captain. "Just have the Igboo break the curse."

The gold-taker shook her head. "Try," she said.

"Do not *try*. Blast it, *break the curse!*" the captain shouted, his grey eyes flashing. "I am depending on you to remove the spell that holds this ship fast in the water."

After dinner, Captain Collingwood and Mr. Quayle visited the forecastle and warned the crew not to disturb the women. By the time Heathcliff came on watch, the Negro females had arranged themselves in a double circle, Kee-Sha and the gold-taker sitting among them.

The indigo sky was dusted with white stars. A full moon appeared over the coal black sea. In the silvery moonlight, the Negro females began chanting.

As the women chanted, they raised bare arms in the moonlight, bending one way and then another, like a field of wheat blowing in the wind.

When Heathcliff climbed into his hammock, he heard the Negro females continue their chanting, a sound that resembled the humming of industrious bees.

When he returned for his early morning watch, the females had not stopped chanting. At six bells, he saw a slender Negress rise gracefully as a black flower in the center of the double circle and slowly lift both arms in the near-darkness.

The women around her chanted louder, clapping their hands in unison. The Igboo began speaking in what sounded like an old man's thin, high-pitched voice.

With a loud shout, the Negress bared her teeth and flung both arms up, as if to embrace the fading moon. With flailing arms, she fell face down, and slapped both arms hard onto the deck.

The females suddenly went silent. At seven bells, Heathcliff saw a burst of grey light on the eastern horizon.

The gold-taker rose from the circle and staggered toward Heathcliff and Oidah Blue. In a small voice, she asked Oidah to help her take the females below.

When Oidah returned from the hold, the big man looked angry.

"Captain *wrong*," Oidah hissed. "*Juju* call up devil. Evil spirit will haunt our ship."

Chapter 69

Standing watch late that night, Heathcliff heard males screaming in the lower hold. The captain sent him to fetch the gold-taker but despite his knocking the little woman would not open her cabin door.

The lower hold was pandemonium. Every male on the racks seemed to be waving his arms and shouting in the infernal heat. Oidah Blue grabbed Heathcliff's lantern, held it over his head, and shouted two words in an African tongue. After a sudden silence, only a whimpering, high-pitched wail remained. Returning the lantern, Oidah led them toward the sound.

The wailing came from a medium-sized Negro on the lower rack. The Negro held his hand over a bleeding neck wound; his fingers gleamed with blood. The Negro stopped wailing and looked up when Heathcliff stood over him with the lantern.

Shackled to the wounded man, a large Negro banged the back of his head onto the bulkhead behind them. When Heathcliff moved the lantern, he noticed the back of the man's head spotted with blood.

"He devil," said Oidah Blue.

The bull continued to bang his head. Negroes all around him pulled at their chains to try to move away.

"The bull is mad," said Dr. Chum. "Look, he bit this one on the neck. Now he harms himself. We can't allow it. Heathcliff, go fetch blankets and rope."

"Sir?" Heathcliff didn't understand.

"Bring me a good wool blanket and a coil of rope. We must get this lunatic out of here. He terrifies the others."

Before Heathcliff returned, Dr. Chum had managed to unchain the wounded Negro and move him away from the madman.

In Heathcliff's absence, the madman had suddenly become rigid. He lay with his right leg shackled and the loose chain and empty cuff dangling out over the edge of the rack. He lay as if frozen on his back, both hands clutching his chest, eyes closed, his bloody teeth set into a grimace.

"The bull has fallen into a stupor," said the surgeon, taking the lantern. "Oidah, pick up his feet. Pull him from the rack. Heathcliff, ready the blanket and rope."

The madman hit the blanket flat on his back, like a slab of heavy meat. The big Negro didn't move at all as they maneuvered the blanket around him and began wrapping him in rope.

"Be careful now," said the surgeon, sweating and holding up the lantern. "Secure the ropes before you lift him up. He could bite you."

Heathcliff and Oidah helped muscle the awkward bundle through the manhole, up the steps, and finally onto the deck as the Negro's loose chain and shackle bumped along the timbers behind them.

They lay the Negro down on the moonlit deck. Wrapped in the blanket, the bull remained still, with his hands locked into position on his chest.

"He will likely remain in a stupor for some time," said the surgeon, who followed them up.

He set down the lantern and loosened the ropes. He peeled the blanket from the Negro's face and trunk. Although the madman's mouth was ringed with blood, he looked like an innocently sleeping baby, with both eyes closed and his hands limply folded over his chest.

HEATHCLIFF: THE LOST YEARS

Heathcliff recognized the black face. The madman rarely spoke to the other captives, and was extemely obedient. He had always rushed to comply with orders given by the crew.

"Devil not move." Oidah poked him with one finger.

"Perhaps his fit has passed," said the surgeon. "We will chain him to the mast and keep him up here for the night. Perhaps the still air and quiet will calm him."

"So here's the screaming savage that interrupted my sleep," said Captain Collingwood, strutting across the deck with Mr. Quayle on his heels. "Heathcliff, Oidah, die the devil to the grate."

"It's not flogging this one needs, captain," said Dr. Chum. "The bull has gone mad. The poor creature's mind is gone."

"I will enforce discipline on this ship, Chum. This bull must learn he cannot get away with upsetting my entire ship."

"But look at the pathetic creature, captain. He's fallen into a stupor. The poor creature cannot move at all."

The captain took up the lantern and bent down over the Negro. He waved the lantern over the madman's face.

The bull's eyes popped open. He poked his fingers into the captain's eyes and mouth, and screamed.

Captain Collingwood backed up, shrieking with pain. The lantern shattered on the deck, producing a moment of darkness.

The madman scuffled to his feet, high-stepped out of the blanket and ropes, and spun away from them all like a phantom made of air.

"Stop him!" shouted the captain, who had fallen to the deck.

The lunatic spun and danced to the railing, the iron chain and empty shackle clattering behind him on the deck. Before anyone could stop him, he vaulted onto the bulwark, rolled over the safety net, and tumbled into the motionless sea.

Heathcliff and Oidah hurried to the rail. Beneath the light of the moon, the madman thrashed and bobbed in a sea of black ink, and then went down.

Chapter 70

Shortly before noon, a zephyr of wind shook the canvas shades. Standing watch, Heathcliff looked up and around, amazed. He felt a steady wind roll in from the east, with a cool, driving edge to it. On the horizon, Heathcliff saw the first clouds he had seen in weeks.

"Man the fore. Tack and sheet," came the captain's voice.

Mariners fell into position on the deck and scurried up the ratlines. Sailors released the bunts and tugged at the downhauls. In a flurry of activity, the hands unfurled sail after sail and squared them against the wind. Beneath the shades, Negroes backed out of the crew's way.

As the trade winds resumed, the *Commerce* suddenly began to move, her ropes and timbers creaking and groaning.

When the crew unfurled the jib and spanker, Captain Collingwood ordered an immediate extra ration of grog for all the hands.

Laughing a little too loudly, the captain waved his beaver hat high in the air.

When he personally took over the helm, he let the *Commerce* run with the wind.

Chapter 71

The next morning, Heathcliff knocked on the door to Mr. Coil's cabin. The first mate didn't answer. When Heathcliff stepped inside, he discovered the first mate's dead body. The cabin smelled of death. Heathcliff ran for the surgeon. Dr. Chum sent him to fetch the captain, who held the dead man's hands for a long time before turning away.

"Have Fiddler build Mr. Coil a good sound coffin," the captain said. "Keep the quashees below deck this morning. We must give our first mate a proper burial at sea."

"Aye-aye, sir," responded the second mate, who had joined them in the dead man's cabin.

Heathcliff helped the surgeon wrap the first mate's emaciated body in his hammock and place the body inside the wooden coffin with his sea chest and personal effects. The Irishman nailed the coffin shut. Clouds rushed by overhead as they brought Mr. Coil's wooden coffin up to the deck.

"Take care with that," said the captain.

"He weighs very little," Fiddler said. "His coffin may not sink."

"Open it up. Place cannonballs on both sides of the body," said the captain. "His casket must sink into the sea."

After prying open the coffin and carefully placing several twelve-pound cannonballs on each side of the body, the Irishman quickly nailed Mr. Coil's coffin shut.

Mr. Bolt pointed out thunderheads massing on the horizon behind the ship.

"Some bad weather coming, captain," said Mr. Bolt. "Could be on us before long."

"It is my duty as captain of this vessel to assure our first mate a proper burial at sea, Mr. Bolt. I will go with the longboat. You stay here and attend to the ship. I must personally conduct the burial."

"Aye-aye, sir," said Mr. Bolt.

Wind blew hard from the north as they placed Mr. Coil's coffin onto the longboat and carefully lowered the boat into the sea. With his Bible between his teeth, the captain descended the sea-ladder and took his place at the steering oar.

As Heathcliff began to row, the Atlantic became choppy. Dark clouds raced past overhead. A few scattered drops of rain began to fall. The ocean swells seemed to grow larger.

A good distance from the ship, Captain Collingwood stood up. Shouting into the wind, he opened the Bible with some difficulty and read a verse and then stopped, apparently disabled by emotion.

A steady rain began. With Mr. Coil's casket across it, the longboat rode low in the water.

"Good, loyal Mr. Coil, your wise counsel helped me on my voyage to African climes," said Captain Collingwood, passing his Bible over the coffin. "Your counsel will be missed by me, and every man aboard the *Commerce*. Good Mr. Coil, helpful and wise Mr. Coil, as master of the *Commerce*, I hereby commit your body to the deep."

With a wave of his hand, the captain closed his Bible, crouched down, and made his way back to the stern.

Some distance away, a bolt of yellow lightning snaked to the water. The longboat tilted to larboard as mariners struggled to lift and push the coffin over the side.

HEATHCLIFF: THE LOST YEARS

With a deathly rumble of rolling cannonballs, mariners shoved off the coffin. To Heathcliff's surprise, the coffin stood up erect in the sea, weighted down by the cannonballs at one end. Half buried in the waves, it bobbed like a ghastly bottle before their eyes.

"Good God!" said the captain.

Slowly, Mr. Coil's coffin rolled over backwards into the sea. In the blowing rain, Heathcliff thought the longboat was drifting farther away from the ship.

"Captain," he said, pointing at the ship.

"Give way, lads!" the captain shouted. "Put your backs to the oars!"

Heathcliff clenched his teeth and pulled at his oar, then glanced over his shoulder. Ahead of the longboat, a ring of lightning bolts electrified the sea around the ship, producing a blast of light brighter than daylight and bone-banging thunder.

For a moment, the upper tips of the masts and yards glowed with violet light, like three ghostly crosses hovering above the ship. The sea around the *Commerce* turned luminous as liquid silver. The entire ocean seemed strewn with glistening diamonds.

"Damn St. Elmo's Fire! Keep to your oars!" shouted the captain.

Mr. Coil's coffin popped to the surface on Heathcliff's side of the longboat, its lid apparently loosened in the rough sea. The first mate's pale hand had worked itself out from beneath the coffin lid, as if the corpse was seeking to escape its watery grave.

Peter stood up from the thwart, pointing frantically at the coffin.

"C-captain!" he shrieked.

"Sit down and row, Peter, all of you" screamed the captain. "Pick up your stroke! The *Commerce* drifts away!"

Fear put desperate strength in Heathcliff's arms. In the hammering rain, the longboat strode toward the ship through the madly galloping sea.

Chapter 72

Heathcliff climbed up the sea ladder, exhausted, blinking back rain. He made out several hands aloft, reefing the main sails. Oidah Blue manned the helm.

"Lower the sea anchor! Fiddler, secure the screw-pump!" Captain Collingwood shouted, squinting into the rain. "Heathcliff! Peter! Go triple reef the main royal right away!"

Heathcliff followed Peter up the ratlines toward the highest sail on the mainmast. The rope ladder dripped with cold rain. Peter moved adroitly out to his side of the mast. Balanced on the foot-lines and blinking back rain, Heathcliff clung to the wet yard, folding and tying reef-points as quickly as he could with cold, stiff fingers. Peter finished up first and hurried back to the mast.

Heathcliff's stomach rose as he felt a great wave smack into the side of the ship. While the *Commerce* listed to the left, he clung to the wet shuddering spar, fearing he would slip to his death. When he reached the crosstrees, the bowsprit plunged down into the sea before them, and a great fan of foaming water sprayed up over the bow.

Lightning flashed, followed by timber-rattling thunder. Heathcliff swung onto the ratlines in a blinding wall of rain.

"Lash the wheel! All hands below!"

HEATHCLIFF: THE LOST YEARS

Heathcliff barely heard the captain's cry as he made his way down the ratlines and slipped onto the wet deck.

A huge wave slowly moved toward the stern. He saw Oidah Blue struggling to lash down the wheel.

"Oidah!" Heathcliff shouted. "Get below!"

Heathcliff grabbed a hanging rope and climbed for his life. He saw Oidah slip along the wet timbers toward the hatch. The Negro crouched before the hatch, but could not pull the hatch open.

Heathcliff wrapped his wrists in the life-line as a shuddering surge of water smacked into the stern and swept over the weather deck. Rushing water pulled at his dangling legs. He saw Oidah caught in the swirl below him, swept over the side of the ship like a gnat into the pitiless sea.

"Help! *Help!*"

It was Peter's voice, crying out. Heathcliff dropped to the wet deck. He found the orphan dangling under the bowsprit, one hand caught in the nets, trying to balance on the figurehead. Heathcliff grabbed Peter's wrists and pulled him to the deck. He cut the net with his rope-knife. Standing up, sliding and slipping, he pulled Peter to the cover of the hatch. As the deck tilted sideways in the punishing rain, Heathcliff pounded his fist on the hatch. Locked. He pounded again.

Mr. Bolt cracked the hatch cover and quickly lifted it a bit. He helped Peter down; they both tumbled into the safety of the hold. Mr. Bolt fastened the hatch as Heathcliff felt another wave smash against the side of the ship.

"We must help Oidah!" Heathcliff gasped. "A wave swept him overboard."

"He won't survive in this sea," the captain said.

"The grumete is gone," intoned Mr. Bolt. "No power on earth could save him now."

Seawater dripped onto them through the overhead timbers. As Heathcliff looked into his officers' tired faces, a thunderclap humbled them all.

Chapter 73

The next morning, Heathcliff stepped out onto a sunlit deck still wet with rain. A morning breeze blew cool and fresh. A few plump grey clouds drifted lazily across the sky.

The captain sent Heathcliff and Fiddler below to bring up the first of the males. The lower hold was ankle-deep in seawater and stank of vomit, shit, and bilge water. They quickly unchained the first of the Negro males from the racks and walked them to the deck.

In the brisk air, eating their meal, many Negroes stared up at the blue sky. Heathcliff felt they were all grateful, every one of them aboard, to have survived the terrible storm.

The next few days were uneventful. There was no end to the work but the wind held steady and the *Commerce* raced toward the islands.

The days became balmy. Every few days, it seemed, the surgeon woke them to pitch another limp, dark-skinned body over the side. Most nights, Heathcliff slept on deck under the stars.

"Someday I would like a turn at the helm, captain," Heathcliff said one evening, while on watch.

"You've not yet handled the tiller?" Captain Collingwood asked.

"Never, sir. But I'd like very much to learn."

HEATHCLIFF: THE LOST YEARS

"I'll give you a bit of it tonight. Come with me."

Vito manned the helm as the captain led Heathcliff to the binnacle, an enclosed cabinet ahead of the wheel. A whale oil lamp burned in the binnacle, illuminating the two compasses inside, one of which could always be seen through the spokes of the wheel.

"Our course is north northwest, as is here on the compass," the captain said. "If the ship veers off course, you must turn the wheel to correct the course. You must pay attention, but you'll soon get the hang of it. Do you understand?"

"Aye-aye, captain."

"Vito, look after Heathcliff for the duration of the watch," said the captain. "Make sure he stays the course. If you need me, I shall be in my cabin."

"Aye, sir."

Vito quietly turned over the great eight-spoked wooden wheel to Heathcliff. Amazingly, Heathcliff felt the ship move in his hands.

The sad-eyed Italian dutifully watched over Heathcliff, correcting his moves here and there. Only a little movement of the wheel was needed to hold the course, Heathcliff learned, and he soon got the feel of it. It exhilarated him to steer the great vessel through the darkness, blown through the night beneath a cowl of twinkling tropical stars.

To Heathcliff's surprise, the captain gave him the helm several nights in a row. The Irishman teased him, and announced to the crew that he'd become the captain's favorite.

Gentle tropical storms came and went. The deep blue Atlantic turned a lighter shade of green.

One morning Heathcliff saw a flock of white birds soaring all around the sails, like a handful of angels tossed down from heaven. Captain Collingwood said the sea-birds came from land which could not yet be seen, but was not far away.

One afternoon, the captain told Heathcliff they were entering the waters of the West Indies.

The *Commerce* would soon pass the isle of Hispaniola, he said, which would likely be visible from portside. In a very few days, he predicted, the *Commerce* would make landfall on Jamaica, the most important of Britain's colonies for the slave trade.

Chapter 74

The Commerce glided past the long rocky tombolo of land called the *palisadoes* and east to Kingston Harbour. Powered only by her spanker, the Commerce slipped into place among several dozen close-anchored merchant ships whose masts resembled a forest of tall naked pine trees. Beyond the skyline of Jamaica's capital city, the dull green points of the Blue Mountains broke through a line of low summer clouds. After the crew set the anchors, Captain Collingwood summoned them to the quarterdeck.

"We are in Kingston! I take off my hat to my officers and crew!" said the captain, whipping off his beaver. "Every man aboard will have a double ration of grog to-night. If all goes well for us here, every man among you shall have a handsome bonus before we return to England!"

"Huzzah! Huzzah!" Cheers rang out among the crew as Marconi and young Tom rolled a cask of grog onto the deck.

Cordoned off from the crew, Negroes responded to the ebullient tone of the captain's voice. Heathcliff felt a whisper of happiness spread among them, like a rolling breath of fresh air. The Negro females hugged each other. Several males stood at the bulwark, placidly looking toward the shore.

"We will let the black cattle mingle this afternoon," said the captain to the gold-taker. "Tell them that all will be well after we prepare them to go ashore to-morrow."

At the surgeon's direction, Heathcliff helped carry a wooden tub to the deck and fill it with vinegar and fresh water. The gold-taker had the females and children line up and bathe. After the females bathed, the males were released from their shackles, two at a time, and cleaned themselves, too.

It was a deceptively happy moment. The Negro males and females mingled and talked. Black-skinned children danced and slipped across the wet deck. Marconi rolled out a cask of a drink he had prepared for the Negroes.

"Dolly!" he cried. "Line up."

Young Tom passed out cannikins. The captives lined up before the cask as Marconi ladled out the dolly.

"Mr. Marconi makes this from the dregs of our rum, and then adds water and cooking spices," young Tom told Heathcliff. "Dr. Chum adds his minerals, too."

"A concoction to help fatten them up for market," said Dr. Chum, as he was passing by.

Heathcliff noticed the poor devils drinking their fill of dolly, of which the cook seemed to have an endless supply. The captives looked relaxed that night, and many actually seemed happy.

The captain encouraged the crew to bring out their old shirts and give them to the Negro males, who had been given only a loincloth to cover themselves all during the long voyage.

After this, as was also customary, the officers brought out their old garments and linens, and presented them to the Negro females. Some of the women immediately tore the fabric into strips, and fastened the strips of cloth around their loins, as they had done in Africa.

As the captives were taken below for the night, the Irishman played a merry little song on his fiddle.

HEATHCLIFF: THE LOST YEARS

That night, as Heathcliff spread his blanket on the deck, he glanced at the string of golden lights along the waterfront. Pale blue signaling-lanterns hung from the sterns of the ships around them. A tropical breeze skitted over Kingston harbor and a pale sliver of moon climbed up into the indigo sky.

Jamaica

Chapter 75

Heathcliff awoke to the sound of squawking. A pandemonium of parrots whirled low over the ship. As he made his way toward the head, two small single-masted fishing boats sailed by on their way out to sea.

Dr. Chum put Heathcliff shaving the heads of the young males, to make them appear stronger and older. Others of the crew rubbed black soot from the galley stove into the hair of the older men to disguise their grey. The surgeon personally worked warm black tar into the scars of the males who had been severely flogged while others rubbed the dark skin of the captives with a mixture of lemon juice, gunpowder, red pepper, and palm oil to give their skin a deceptively healthy luster.

Captain Collingwood went ashore first. As he left, the captain bade Heathcliff come in with the first boat.

Around noon, Mr. Bolt and the bosun began loading the captives. When the first boat had its quota of males, Heathcliff took up oars and helped row toward the shore.

The city of Kingston seemed lazy and innocent in the afternoon light. Beyond the brick buildings that lined the waterfront, Heathcliff saw wisps of smoke rising between the tops of palm trees.

HEATHCLIFF: THE LOST YEARS

As their boat approached the pier, Heathcliff pitied the captives. It was difficult to look at the hope he saw on some of their faces.

Standing atop a section of the finger pier, Captain Collingwood waved in the launch. A group of grizzled white men helped tie up the boat. Several of the men held long, sharply-pointed sticks and some had pistols in their belts. The captain had a few of them pull Negroes onto the pier while the others warily held the males at bay.

"Heathcliff, you must be my eyes and ears to-day," the captain said. "Go with these gentlemen. Make sure the quashees stay together. I need for you to assure me that all our black cattle are secure in their quarters."

Heathcliff followed behind as the men prodded the group of males off the pier and herded them along Harbour Street, poking at them with sticks and shouting.

They herded the group along a sand-packed street for ten blocks, then turned them left down a narrow alley. They stopped the group at the rear of a windowless brick building where a man with a ragged black beard met them and unlocked a thick wooden door.

They prodded and whistled the males inside like so many cattle. The bearded man shut the door and locked them inside.

"Bring me all you have," he told Heathcliff.

Horses and wagons scurried past on Harbour Street, kicking up clumps of manure and sand before a line of warehouses and shops. When more captives were brought onto the pier, the captain dispatched Heathcliff to look after them.

Late that afternoon, the last boatload of females arrived at the dock, with Kee-Sha among them. The men made lewd comments and poked at the females all the way to the brick building. When the bearded man unlocked the door, Heathcliff heard loud hoots and whistles as the women walked inside.

A young female darted away. Three men ran to chase her down and the bearded man drew a pistol. Heathcliff stepped past the bearded man and looked inside.

Hundreds of black-skinned men, women, and children huddled together in a dark, high-ceilinged room. It was a human stable. Beneath a hanging lantern was a trough of drinking water. The room smelled of feces, sweat, and straw. When the little female who tried to escape was pushed inside, someone yanked Heathcliff out and closed the door.

"Heathcliff!"

Captain Collingwood jauntily pulled him toward the front of the building. Most of the crew loitered before the trim, red brick façade of *Negrille & Sloan, Merchants*. Heathcliff noticed a placard in the front window announcing an auction of African slaves.

Captain Collingwood vaulted onto the low wooden porch, tricorne in one hand. He again congratulated the crew on a successful voyage.

"We nourish the lifeblood of this mercantile island—the island cannot survive without us. The land-owners of Jamaica need black cattle to harvest cane. When our slaves are purchased, I promise every one of you shall have a good bonus—"

A carriage pulled up a short distance away. A well-dressed man in a cream-coloured suit got out and walked toward the group, leaving his Negro coachman to attend to the horses.

"My good friend Angelique Devine has joined us, I believe," said the captain, gesturing at the man with a sweep of his hat. Angelique Devine lifted a wan hand, and waved.

"All hands are at liberty to enjoy this city. Dr. Chum will distribute an advance on your pay. Do enjoy yourselves!" cried the captain with a wave of his beaver hat and white cockade.

"Huzzah for our captain!"

"Huzzah! Hooray!"

Donning his tricorne with a flourish, Captain Collingwood stepped off the porch and linked arms with Angelique Devine. Arm in arm, the two gentlemen strutted to the waiting coach. They stepped inside and Devine's Negro coachman obediently bowed and closed the door. Heathcliff thought both gentlemen looked quite impressive inside the carriage as it pulled away, drawn by six rather spirited grey horses.

HEATHCLIFF: THE LOST YEARS

A warm breeze blew toward the sea as Dr. Chum distributed brass coins to each of the crew.

"You give us peculiar coin, doctor!" said the Fiddler, who was first in line. "This is not English money."

"These are Jamaican *reales*, minted in Cuba. You can very easily spend them here on the island," Dr. Chum replied.

"These coins would not be accepted in England," said the Fiddler, pocketing his coins and turning to the crew. "But gather around, boys. Let's go try and spend the captain's money."

The Fiddler led them into Kingston, a city of many black faces. Wagons containing downcast-looking Negroes rumbled by on the street. Black-skinned females swept porches while Negro men watched horses. Heathcliff noticed a long line of barefoot Negro men traipse around a corner with wooden casks on their backs, followed by a bored-looking mulatto overseer on horseback.

At a bakery, the crew purchased the first fresh bread they'd seen in months. They tore at the loaves with their hands and ate chunks of it. The Irishman found a vendor of fried fish and hot cross buns, then led them all into a tavern, where he ordered a plate of sausages and helped them wash his sausages down with beer.

Fiddler led the crew out of the tavern at dusk. In the gloaming, Kingston had become a city of shadows. Wrought iron balconies drooped down over narrow streets. The silhouettes of palm trees stood out in black against the lavender sky. Swallows soared and dipped over their heads, feasting on mosquitos.

Heathcliff heard snatches of music, clapping, and a bit of distant singing. The Irishman flagged down a pair of mariners, plied them with questions, and returned with a smirk to the crew.

"Every man among us shall have a woman to-night," the Irishman announced.

"I got to find me a church," said young Tom. "During that big storm, I promised God if he saved me from drowning, I'd go to church the minute I stepped on land."

Fiddler mussed the little cherub's blonde hair with his hand.

"No churching to-night, young Tommy. A little pip like you will have ample time for churching to-morrow. To-night, you must enjoy yourself like a man."

Chapter 76

The street was dark when Fiddler Ryan stopped the group before a two-story, wood-frame house whose veranda was festooned with festive red paper lanterns.

On the veranda, Heathcliff made out several Negro women in rocking chairs, all fanning their grey, powdered faces with Oriental fans. The women wore fine dresses and high, pale grey wigs which were also heavily powdered. The woman closest to Heathcliff tugged up the hem of her gown to display a pretty pair of ankles and bare feet. When she caught Heathcliff's eye, she wiggled her toes, and smiled.

The front door opened, releasing a gust of musky perfume into the humid night air.

"*Buenas tardes, Bonne soiree*, Good evening," cooed a female voice, greeting them in three languages. "I am Madam Marie Cortez DuBois, proprietor of this establishment. My door is open to you."

A stately-looking, light-skinned Negress stepped onto the veranda, cradling a tiny white hairless dog in one hand.

"Come in, English gentlemen," trilled the lady, stepping aside and tucking the dog under her left arm. "We entertain Englishmen here. You may all come in."

Fiddler led them past Madam Marie DeBois, the first mulatto woman Heathcliff had ever seen. Madam DeBois looked older than the other women, but her skin was the colour of chocolate and her green eyes twinkled. She playfully stroked Heathcliff's crotch as he walked past, and did the same for the others.

"Inside, inside, English gentlemen. Men of the sea find pleasure behind these doors."

Madam DuBois led them into a large, dimly-lit parlor. A few men and women sat on couches or at tables beneath a chandelier, talking and drinking.

Heathcliff sat down at a table. Through a doorway next to the stairs, he saw a grey-haired black man bent over a cook-stove. The easy breeze that moved through the parlor brought the smells of frying fish and burning wood.

Two or three women glided down the stairs. Others drifted in from the porch. They moved as lightly as feathers among the sailors, some bringing glasses of Jamaican rum or plates of cooked fish, papaya, and jackfruit.

A Negress moved from table to table, kissing all the men, but Heathcliff brushed her away. She reminded him of Kee-Sha, locked away for the night. When the girl abandoned his table, he observed a sailor he didn't know staggering down the stairs and slinking out of the parlor without bidding anyone good-bye.

Suddenly, he heard a cacophony of bells. Bells rang from belfries of churches, in civic buildings, and even on ships in the harbour. Madam DuBois picked up a small brass hand bell and dutifully joined in the ringing, her little dog barking along.

"Six bells, *monsieurs*," chirped Madam DuBois, when the bells fell silent. "Your government forbids us to serve spirits to you after six o'clock. Every business establishment in Kingston must ring a bell to alert you. But don't worry. If an inspector calls, my ladies will drink up your rum."

HEATHCLIFF: THE LOST YEARS

Young Tom sat alone at the end of a great sofa, staring at a glass of rum he had not touched.

"Hello, Tom." Heathcliff sat down. "You don't care to drink?"

The orphan stared glumly ahead. "I'll not have this," he replied.

As Heathcliff watched two of the crew take women up the stairs, Madam DuBois quietly glided up to where they sat, still carrying her tiny dog in one hand.

"And who is this handsome little *garcon*?" she cooed, bending down to clutch Tom's fingers. The cabin boy jerked away his hand and looked away.

"Tom's our ship's cabin boy," Heathcliff said. "If I'm not mistaken, this evening he wishes to be left alone."

Madam DuBois moved on, but Fiddler Ryan staggered to the sofa with a glass of rum in one hand. He flopped himself down between Tom and Heathcliff. He slapped Tom's knee. He was obviously drunk. His green eyes twinkled. He leaned toward Heathcliff.

"I say we get little Tommy a girl," he said. "Young Tom ain't had a girl yet but to-night's the night for that, right, little Tommy?"

"I don't want no girl," the cabin boy said.

"Yes ye do, Tommy. Ye do want female companionship this very evening, though ye may not know it just yet," said the Irishman. "Every sailor must have a lass when he's in port. Now. Look at that wee little girl over in the corner. I believe she has her eye on you."

"I don't want no girl," young Tom said.

Fiddler again slapped Tom's knee. He bolted to his feet, caught the arm of Madam DuBois, and whispered something in her ear. He pointed at Tom, and then pointed to the young dark-skinned girl who looked about Tom's age. To Heathcliff, the girl appeared to be nearly as reticent as young Tom.

"I've made all the arrangements," the Irishman told Heathcliff. "Your girl is the grand-daughter of Madam DuBois, Tommy. She's never had herself a man. You will be her first. It's an honor for you. Now quick, drink up and begone."

Tom shook his head no. The girl approached him in the dim light. With her head down, she tugged at his sleeve. Heathcliff thought he could see the cabin boy blushing.

Madam DuBois motioned to the girl. She picked up a saucer on which sat a lit candle, and began climbing the stairs alone. When Tom didn't move, the Irishman picked up him by the belt and carried him kicking and protesting up the stairs after her.

"Be gentle, young Englishman!" cried Madam DuBois, watching and stroking her dog.

Heathcliff brooded quietly on the sofa, lost in his own black thoughts. When more rum was brought, he drank it down. He watched the crew take women upstairs but felt little desire to join them.

Before long, Tom rejoined Heathcliff on the sofa. Young Tom looked crestfallen. Heathcliff slapped the cabin boy's shoulder when he sat down. Tom picked up his rum and emptied the glass. He soon curled up on the sofa and fell asleep.

Heathcliff brushed away the women who approached him, but he drank their rum. He drank to forget all he had seen of disease and death, and the callousness and cruelty that seemed to come so easily to other men. It took several glasses of Jamaican rum to blot these memories away.

Late in the evening, a pretty mulatto woman in a lightly-powdered wig very cautiously approached him. She sat down beside him. She folded her hands in her lap. She did not touch him at all. Heathcliff waved her away but the woman looked modestly at her hands, and remained seated.

When he stood up, the Negress stood up beside him and lightly took his arm.

Her touch reminded Heathcliff of Catherine Earnshaw. She had once taken his arm in that way. Savoring his memory, Heathcliff yearned only to see Catherine, to kiss her lips again.

The Negress seemed to understand. She held his arm for some time, then took his hand and looked cautiously into his eyes.

HEATHCLIFF: THE LOST YEARS

She bent down and picked up a candle without letting go of his arm. Heathcliff followed her upstairs into a small room with a bedsheet for a door.

The Negress took off her wig and opened her bedroom window to the moon. A warm breeze swirled through the room.

Heathcliff reclined on her small narrow bed. With a little groan, the Negress broke away her dress. She blew out the candle and lay down next to him in a pool of yellow moonlight.

He drank her like a glass of cool fresh water.

Chapter 77

Heathcliff and young Tom walked to Negrille & Sloan under a cloud-laden tropical sky. A bedeviling breeze frittered in from the sea. Heathcliff noticed a great many horses, wagons, and carriages tied up along the street. On the porch of the auction house, a red and black wooden sign propped up on an easel announced "Slave Auction To-day," in English and Spanish.

A group of men loitered on the porch and around the front door, most smoking cigars. Several who were perhaps the owners of the great plantations wore pale, loose suits favored by white slaveowners in the tropics. The less polished men that Heathcliff took to be overseers wore plain cotton work clothes, high-topped leather boots and flat-brimmed hats; most carried coiled whips, and a pistol in their belts.

Bright-eyed little Mr. Sloan popped open his front door at exactly eight o'clock, strutted to the porch, and showed his teeth. He rung a large brass hand-bell eight times to attract attention. Heathcliff and young Tom followed the crowd inside.

The long, narrow room smelled of sawdust, sweat, and tobacco. Above them on one side of the roof was a long bank of high, fly-specked windows propped open with sticks to admit fresh air.

"Heathcliff! Good morning!"

HEATHCLIFF: THE LOST YEARS

Captain Collingwood stood with Dr. Chum, watching buyers crowd into the room. Leaning closer, he showed Heathcliff a small leather-bound notebook.

"I shall record the high bid received for each of our quashees. This notebook allows me to double-check the price before I transfer ownership. I tell you, no islander will cheat my investors out of one penny," the captain said.

"One hundred and sixty-seven black cattle, every one put to market to-day," the surgeon added, raising his eyebrows and puffing on his cigar. "The number includes one that is my privilege."

"And three are mine," added the captain. "Our reward for a job well done."

Behind a raised podium on the left side of the room, a well-dressed, pock-marked young auctioneer brought down a gavel three times. A door behind him opened. Sloan's men pushed eight half-clothed Negro slaves into the room and up onto a low platform, with the males shackled at the ankles.

"Eight Guinea Negroes to be inspected for sale," he announced.

Slave buyers swarmed forward. With Cuban cigars between their teeth, men pinched and twisted arms and legs. They pulled open mouths to look at teeth. One or two shouted into the ears of slaves to startle them, which assured buyers they were not deaf. Some buyers made each slave jump, and jump again, to assess their stamina. One buyer slapped each slave in the face, to test their temperaments. When the man slapped one of the females, the Negress broke down before him in tears.

"I'll not watch this," Tom said to Heathcliff, and he departed from the room.

As the auction began, each Negro received a numbered plaque to hold before them.

Sloan's men prodded them onto the auction block one at a time. The auctioneer described each humbled creature in very general terms, rapped his gavel, and called for bids.

Heathcliff recognized two males from the *Commerce*. Waiting glumly in line at the auction block, both looked exhausted, anxious, and terribly afraid. Heathcliff realized that every Negro who survived the terrible voyage would be sold at auction like a pig or a cow. He had not quite understood this horrible degradation before.

"What damnable business!" Heathcliff blurted, without thinking.

"I feel damned good about this particular business, Heathcliff," said Captain Collingwood, glancing up from his notebook.

"We do God's work, Heathcliff," said Dr. Chum. "Black ivory is purchased. Our commercial responsibilities are fulfilled."

"Even with our difficulties, I believe our losses are within reason," said the captain. "We shall likely be rewarded for our good work. From what I see, the black cattle may fetch a higher price than the investors anticipated."

"Your investors will all sing your praises," said Dr. Chum, puffing happily at his cigar.

"I am told no investor is ever completely happy with the returns from a Guinea voyage, even returns as handsome as these may prove to be," Captain Collingwood replied. "Investors have great expectations. But mark my words, Heathcliff—every investor who makes a bit of money will hurry out to invest again. This business runs on greed and gain, and it runs spectacularly well."

At another rap of the gavel, four Negro females stepped onto the platform. Heathcliff recognized them immediately. One of these was the African woman who nursed him back to health on the ship, whose name he never learned. Next to her stood Kee-Sha. All four females looked frightened by the crowd. Men hooted when the buyers were called forward to inspect them.

The jacket Captain Collingwood gave Kee-Sha was soiled with mud and excrement, Heathcliff noticed. Stepping on the auction block, she clasped her arms over her breasts but after some shouts and whistles from the crowd the auctioneer pulled her arms aside with his cane. The older Negress kept her head down. For that warm-hearted woman, so cruelly robbed of her natural dignity, Heathcliff felt a great pitying rush of guilt, sadness, and shame.

The bidding began. As the captain scribbled in his notebook. Heathcliff felt a helpless anger rise up in his throat. He could not bear to watch the women being sold. It shamed him to watch and not help them. All around him, he felt, greedy white men shoved and slapped at each other in the lusty, unstoppable pursuit of gain.

Heathcliff stepped outside, his head reeling. Dr. Chum joined him on the porch, smelling of rum. With a light-hearted glimmer in his eye and sporting what looked to be a freshly-powdered wig, the surgeon lit himself a fresh cigar and smiled mischievously.

"That last black cow on the block was my privilege, Heathcliff," gloated the doctor, puffing away. "She fetched a decent price. Note net profit for Chum, seventy pounds."

"That's terribly good for you, I'm sure."

"Seventy pounds is *quite* good, Heathcliff," sniffed the surgeon. "Seventy pounds is the point of this entire undertaking, you know. And Collingwood will make more money than I."

"Congratulations, I suppose."

"I gratefully thank you, sir," smiled Dr. Chum, performing a mock elaborate bow with the lit cigar clenched between his teeth. "I accept your congratulatory words with considerable delight."

The surgeon turned back toward the door in a cloud of smoke but he paused. Reaching into his pocket, he grandly offered Heathcliff a big black cigar.

"The captain tells me you may join us for dinner," the surgeon winked, before opening the door. "Make sure you do not stray far."

Heathcliff walked the streets of Kingston, looking for young Tom. Low black clouds raced past overhead. Heathcliff noticed a biting edge to the breeze; his chest trembled from the cold.

The church bells of Kingston rang twelve noon. Heathcliff walked the streets and looked in vain for young Tom. His mood remained gloomy and dark as a winter's day.

Chapter 78

Later that afternoon, **Heathcliff returned** to Negrille & Sloan beneath dark, overcast sky. Wind rolled over the rooftops of Kingston and sent loose sand skittering along the streets. Heathcliff felt a wicked chill in the air as he watched little Mr. Sloan bar the front door of his auction house, jump onto a handsome horse, and hurry away.

Behind Negrille & Sloan, overseers pulled groups of slaves out the back door, chained two or three together. They crowded male and female slaves into the beds of horse-drawn wagons and pulled away. Heathcliff looked for Kee-Sha but did not see her.

When Angelique Devine's carriage pulled up not far away, Captain Collingwood opened a carriage door, and called out.

"Heathcliff," said Captain Collingwood. "Come with me. To-night we shall dine at Sugar Hill."

Heathcliff got into the coach next to Dr. Chum, who stared out the window with a dead, half-smoked cigar between his teeth. Outside the coach, Angelique Devine flagged down an empty wagon apparently driven by his overseer and directed the wagon to the rear door.

"Angelique has purchased a good many of our quashees, including the three that were my privilege," Captain Collingwood said. "I have stationed Mr. Bolt and Mr. Quayle on the *Commerce* to-night but Mrs. Devine invited two of my officers for dinner. We'll see how Heathcliff handles himself in good company."

"Captain Collingwood— "

"Be silent, Heathcliff. You must not thank me yet."

Peering out the coach window, Heathcliff noticed a black-skinned night watchman walking the street, ringing a large hand-bell.

"All seek shelter!" he cried. "Big storm coming!"

Angelique Devine grunted into the carriage. His coachman closed the door behind him and the carriage pulled away.

"I do despise the look of this weather," said Angelique Devine. "But within the hour, we shall be safe at Sugar Hill."

Wind howled over the island. The carriage made its way out of Kingston along a road of blowing sand, beneath a fitful sprinkling of tropical rain.

Chapter 79

Taking a deep breath, Heathcliff joined a number of gentlemen and ladies in Angelique Devine's large parlor. He wore clothes loaned to him by the captain and the clothes felt a bit too snug. Surrounded by well-dressed ladies and gentlemen, Heathcliff felt suddenly self-conscious and out of place at Sugar Hill.

"My wife asked me to give you all a tour of our home to-night," Angelique Devine announced, with a half-empty glass in one hand. "Dinner is almost ready and I must say my wife spent a goodly sum to bring over all this new furniture from England."

The ebullient and witty gentleman gave his guests a tour of the plantation he had inherited fifteen years before, and apparently much improved. Heathcliff thought every room in the large Spanish-style mansion contained beautiful things. Sugar Hill had so many rooms with polished wood floors and new furniture that tagging along behind the pack of guests, Heathcliff lost track of exactly how many rooms there were.

Angelique Devine's impromptu tour ended back in the parlor, where uniformed Negro servants waited with trays of sweet *falernum* cocktails. Lifting high his glass, Angelique Devine graciously proposed a toast to the officers of the *Commerce* and several other distinguished guests at Sugar Hill.

HEATHCLIFF: THE LOST YEARS

They adjourned to the dining room. At a long, elegantly-set table, a serious-looking old Negro servant seated Heathcliff before the most elaborate array of gold-rimmed plates, glasses, and silver eating utensils he had ever seen.

"I fear we may have more wind tonight," said Angelique Devine, after taking his seat at the head of the table. "There are storm warnings out. The winds nearly toppled our carriage on the road."

"A ship will drag anchor in winds like this if she is not properly secured," said Captain Collingwood, with a nod to the ladies.

"Is your ship in danger to-night, captain?" a lady asked.

"I left two good officers with my vessel. Even in fairly strong winds, I think the *Commerce* entirely secure."

"I doubt you have storms of this ilk in Liverpool," said Angelique Devine. "A good storm will likely breach the sea-wall."

"During the last big storm, a bolt of lightning struck the belfry of the Church of St. Thomas the Apostle," said the full-figured, elegantly-coiffed Mrs. Devine, who gracefully interrupted. "Lightning knocked our great bell out of its belfry and onto King Street. More than a year later, our belfry still remains under repair."

"Captain Collingwood," said a pretty lady on Heathcliff's right, whose melodic voice silenced the table. "Do tell us of your exciting ocean voyage."

As rain slapped the dining room windows, Captain Collingwood recounted his experiences. The ladies' eyes grew wide at his tale of the Englishman's treachery, which the captain suspected all along, as well as his heroism in single-handedly taking a cutlass to the mutineers. The captain spoke somewhat modestly of his struggles during the storm that threatened to take down his vessel, but he pulled it through.

"You are a hero, Captain Collingwood," the pretty lady said.

"Hardly a hero," he replied. "As captain, it is my primary duty to protect my ship, and of course I must look after my cargo, and my crew."

"He is a hero," the woman told the guests.

The captain bloomed under the pretty woman's flattery. He began to recount his many difficulties at Gold Coast Castle, and his difficult and heroic triumph against the savage pagan king. As he listened to the captain, Heathcliff wished only to forget it all.

Courses of food and cocktails came and went. Heathcliff struggled to pick through his many eating utensils. He nodded at everything said by the dour gentlemen to his left who owned a small plantation and disliked all his slaves. With some fanfare, Negro servants brought in a silver dish of sweet whipped dessert, and bowls of dark island coffee.

Shutters banged loudly against the house. A uniformed Negro whispered something to Angelique Devine. The master of Sugar Hill rose to his feet and tapped his crystal wine glass with a silver spoon.

"The tropical winds are up considerably, and may well continue for some time. My house-servants tell me we have terrible winds already, and hard rain. I fear the storm is unlikely to subside anytime soon. In fact, it will likely get worse. I daresay I shall not let any of you venture onto the roads this evening. We shall put you all up here," Angelique Devine told the guests.

"I've ordered my slaves to secure your carriages and horses in our stables. When you finish dessert, I will ask that you all follow me downstairs to our storm cellar. I apologize for the inconvenience. From the looks of it, this may be a rather long night."

The guests rose to their feet. Negro servants began extinguishing candles around the dining room.

Clutching a silver candelabrum, a uniformed Negro led them down a flight of narrow stone steps to a rather sizeable storm cellar below the mansion.

Dark-skinned maids scurried up and down the stairs with candles and pallets and bedding and chamber pots. Black men immediately strung up a velvet curtain across the middle of the cellar for the privacy of the ladies, and the well-dressed ladies and gentlemen prepared to bed down.

"Does this not remind you of our lower hold, in the *Commerce?*" Heathcliff impishly whispered to the captain. "So many bodies here, and crowded so close together."

"This looks *nothing* like the hold of our ship," the captain snapped. "Take care you don't ever repeat that, Heathcliff. Remember, you are in good company here."

Heathcliff lay down and closed his eyes. He heard muted claps of thunder, and the sound of wind knocking down trees.

Chapter 80

The hurricane raged for two days. Heathcliff and Captain Collingwood were the first of the guests to leave Sugar Hill. The captain told Devine he needed to check the condition of his ship. Angelique Devine offered a horse and wagon. As they left the great plantation, Heathcliff noticed trees partially blown down, and buildings deroofed and damaged in the storm.

Palm fronds littered the streets of Kingston. Many buildings were damaged, or completely knocked down. Waves breaching the sea-wall had left curious patterns of sand in the streets.

Horses and wagons picked their way around piles of debris. Near the waterfront, vendors with push-carts sold cannikins of rum and pies before damaged shop-buildings. As Heathcliff looked out onto the ghoulish tableau, the sea breeze brought him the smell of dead fish, excrement, and cooking fires.

Not far from the severely-damaged pier, Heathcliff saw the corpse of a young Negro half-buried in sand. Dead fish and birds with halos of flies littered the shore like lurid gifts washed in from the sea.

The captain found a boat to take them to the ship.

"She slipped her moorings. The *Commerce* rides much too low in the water," the captain observed as they approached.

An ashen Mr. Bolt met them on the deck.

"She drifted sideways into another vessel during the storm, captain. Slipped both anchors and sustained a good bit of damage but she's afloat," Mr. Bolt reported. "I have not seen the likes of that storm."

"Where is Mr. Quayle?"

"He took the jolly-boat ashore on the first evening of the storm, captain, to fetch additional chain for the anchor. I advised him not to go. The man didn't return. I pray he's alive."

All around them, Heathcliff noticed yards snapped, masts cracked, and a great deal of torn canvas and rigging down. Below deck, the ship stunk of bilge water and the captain found two cracked ribs in the hull.

"We may all be in Jamaica for a good while," the captain said.

Chapter 81

Angelique Devine's large carriage waited for them at the end of the dock. Next to the carriage, a glum-looking Angelique Devine flagged them over.

"All our new slaves escaped," Angelique Devine announced. "My overseer locked them in our old barn, but this morning he found the barn door broken off its hinges. All the slaves I purchased from you are gone."

"The three were my privilege," snipped the captain. "Certainly, I do wish to be paid."

"Unfortunately, I've no insurance to cover that," said Angelique Devine. "Old Sloan tells me slaves often slip into Kingston. He sent men out looking. I do hope my slaves can be found and retrieved."

"My crew will help," said the captain. "Heathcliff, search out the men. Have them walk every street in Kingston. You know the faces of our quashees. When you catch them, bring them to Negrille & Sloan."

"Mr. Sloan has promised to hold them here for me," Angelique Devine explained.

Heathcliff set out to round up the crew. He found most of them in an inn not far from the house of Madam DuBois. He divided the men into three groups and they set out to search the port city.

HEATHCLIFF: THE LOST YEARS

The first afternoon of walking the rubble-strewn streets yielded nothing. When Heathcliff returned to Negrille & Sloan, the captain ordered him to have the men continue looking.

The morning of the fourth day, Heathcliff met with the captain inside Sloan's office. Sloan's bounty hunters had turned up nothing, he said. The lost slaves seemed to have vanished into thin air.

"If our bounty hunters can't find them, they've run into the hills," said the little auctioneer, scratching his nose as he stepped into the room. "For my money, it's Three-Fingered Jack."

"Who is Three-Fingered Jack?" asked the captain.

"A damned *maroon*," said Mr. Sloan. "A renegade. A black devil that's the curse of this entire island."

"Years ago, an overseer took off two of Jack's fingers to punish him for eating cane. Jack snatched the man's *machete*, cut his throat, and ran away," said Angelique Devine. "Jack's been up in the hills ever since."

"The Spaniards should never have freed their slaves when they gave up the island," snarled the auctioneer, bending over to make use of a spittoon. "Now we've got thievin' black-hearted nigger revolutionaries! They go wild in the hills but Jack's the only one with enough brass to come down and snatch up slaves from right under our noses."

"In that last big storm, Three-Fingered Jack grabbed four slaves right off the Burlington plantation," Angelique Devine said. "Two years ago, he snatched up two of mine."

"The niggers think Jack's got magic powers," Sloan told the captain. "The niggers don't think a white man can kill him."

Angelique Devine crossed his arms and stared out the window.

"Two years ago, Jack snatched two of my house niggers but one old slave found his way back to the house. I don't remember what all happened now, but I say let's talk to him. He might just know where to find Three-Fingered Jack."

"Mr. Devine," said Mr. Sloan. "That is a capital idea."

Chapter 82

The old Negro servant crept into the parlor at Sugar Hill, looking from side to side. Heathcliff didn't know the Negro's name, but he recognized him as the man who seated him for dinner several days before. Angelique Devine told the Negro to stand before them in the center of the room while he made his way to an overstuffed chair.

Heathcliff sat on a sofa between Sloan and Captain Collingwood. He thought the Negro perhaps fifty or sixty years old. The man had a precarious dignity but his livery seemed a bit too tight for his frame and his short wiry hair was beginning to turn white on both sides.

"Gentlemen, this is Black Tom, one of my good old house niggers," said Angelique Devine. "We call him black Tom because he has the blackest skin of any servant in the house. Tom, you must help us."

"Yessir."

"You were up in the Blue Mountains a few years ago, Tom, held against your will, isn't that right?" cooed Angelique Devine. "Up there in the mountains, with Three-Fingered Jack?"

Black Tom winced. He plucked a handkerchief from the top pocket of his uniform. He dabbed his forehead, folded up the handkerchief, and put it back in his pocket.

HEATHCLIFF: THE LOST YEARS

"Three-Fingered Jack pull me out my shack in the rain, yessir. Took me way back in the hills, yessir, but after just a few days I run back. Master Devine—you know I run right back soon as I could."

"We think Jack broke into the barn during the storm, Tom. I lost six new slaves, including three I purchased from Captain Collingwood, this good man here. Do you think Three-Fingered Jack might have snatched my slaves?"

"Storm come in, Jack slipping down the hill, yes sir," nodded Black Tom. "That's the way he do you. Maybe took 'em away like he took 'em me."

"That's exactly what I think, Tom. Now. Tom. I want you to help find those slaves. Captain Collingwood and Mr. Sloan brought some men to help us bring them home."

"I didn't survive a mutiny at sea to be robbed of what's mine in Jamaica," blurted Captain Collingwood, who was visibly upset.

"But I can't go back up those mountains, no sir, no sir, I can't. Three-Fingered Jack *juju*. He be *spelling* me!" Black Tom unfolded his handkerchief to dab his forehead again.

"Listen up, Tom," said Angelique Devine. "Three-Fingered Jack grabbed you and that little girl bakes bread in the kitchen. Where did Jack take you?"

"Took us up through the mud, back and forth up there, all in the rain and in the night," Tom said. "When the lightning flashing, we go past three little trees. Turn this way, turn that way. When Jack go out to hunt *coney*, me and that little girl run. We kept running, down this way, down that way we got here, but that a long, long time ago, sir. A long time ago."

"Two years isn't that long ago, Tom," cooed Angelique Devine. "I happen to know you're a very smart nigger. My wife says you remember every order she gives you. I bet you could lead us right to that camp. In fact, I'm counting on you to show us the way."

"Master Devine, sir, if you excuse me, sir, I may just not remember all that."

"Your bull is impertinent," Captain Collingwood snapped. "I'd take the hide off any bull who talked to me like that."

Black Tom stepped back as if slapped in the face. He clutched his handkerchief. He lowered his head.

"But that's not the way we do things here at Sugar Hill, Captain Collingwood," cooed Angelique Devine. "You catch more flies with honey than you do with vinegar."

The master of Sugar Hill whistled. Black Tom raised his head. Then Angelique Devine pointed right at the servant's chest.

"Get to your shack, Tom. Meet us at the boiling house first thing in the morning," said Angelique Devine.

"Sir—" Black Tom began.

"Yes, sir," said Angelique Devine.

"Yessir." Tom looked at his feet.

"Get to your shanty, Tom," said Angelique Devine, with a glance at the captain. "We'll all see you first thing in the morning."

Black Tom straightened up. He lifted his head and tried to smile. "Yessir," he said.

Angelique Devine waved him away.

Chapter 83

The next morning, Heathcliff found himself on a horse near the end of a single-file line of mounted men. A half dozen barefoot field hands from Sugar Hill walked behind the caravan, carrying hoes and shovels and bringing up the rear.

To the right of the dirt road, a crew of shirtless, sweating Negro slaves methodically chopped through a field of tall, green sugar cane. An unshaven white man in a wide-brimmed hat watched them from horseback, lazily cradling a musket.

At the end of the road, the caravan plodded up a narrow trail into the foothills of the Blue Mountains. Droplets of water fell from the trees. Blue and yellow butterflies glided over patches of glistening ferns.

Some distance ahead, riding alongside Angelique Devine, Captain Collingwood had donned his beaver hat and long cockade. Ahead of them rode Devine's mulatto overseer. Leading the procession, astride a swaybacked mule, Black Tom led the search party into the hills.

At every fork in the trail, Black Tom got off the mule, scratched his head, and after some prodding reluctantly pointed the way.

Heathcliff thought the old Negro looked haunted. The whites of the old servant's eyes were yellow and bloodshot and he jumped at the slightest noise.

When a pandemonium of parrots wheeled over the caravan in a whirl of green and yellow wings, Tom jumped off his mule before the birds screeched and chattered away.

From time to time, Angelique Devine summoned his field hands to move a broken tree or tree limb off the trail. The search party got off their horses and waited. Men perspired in the tropical heat. Horses drank from puddles of still water that had pooled up along the trail.

That afternoon, a field hand noticed smoke not too far away. The Negro shouted and sprinted to the head of the procession to inform Angelique Devine.

Devine led the horses down a rocky slope dotted with trees, and pulled up partway down. Directly below them was a crude lean-to. In front of the lean-to, three Negro women stirred an iron pot over a cooking fire. The smell of their cooking wafted up the hill.

"You best go quickety down, Master Devine," Black Tom said. "They fixing to eat when Jack get back."

White men on horses thundered down the slope, followed by Devine's field hands running behind them through the trees.

"Grab them! Get every one of them!" Angelique Devine shouted, reining in his horse.

Negroes surged out of the lean-to. Men dismounted. They grabbed women and wrestled them to the ground. Two young boys burst out of the hut and tried to run through the horses.

Heathcliff saw a Negro slip from the rear of the lean-to. He kicked his horse and gave pursuit. The runner wore only a flour sack, but ran quickly, dodging between trees. Heathcliff kept his eyes on the flour sack as he pursued the runner and his horse gained ground.

The flour sack jumped a rocky stream, spreading both arms and splashing and staggering barefoot over jutting rocks. Heathcliff leaped off his horse and pursued the flour sack on foot through a thick stand of trees and dense vegetation. Making a huge effort, he leaped up a slope and with a desperate lunge, pulled the flour sack down.

"Kee-Sha!" he gasped.

HEATHCLIFF: THE LOST YEARS

The Negress bared her teeth. She scratched at his face. He grabbed her hands and pinned her to the ground. She spat in his face and squirmed beneath him.

"Be silent!" he hissed.

Heathcliff glanced over his shoulder. He saw no one. He heard only the sound of a running stream.

On an impulse, Heathcliff released Kee-Sha's hands. He rolled onto his back. Kee-Sha scrambled to her feet and picked up a stone.

"Go," he said, waving his hand. "Run away."

He heard her scamper away through the ferns. Soon he heard only the soothing sound of quietly running water.

Captain Collingwood met him back at the lean-to. The captain looked upset.

"We recovered only two of my privilege. Blast it, one has gotten away," he hissed. "Angelique says we must return before dark. Keep a sharp eye out."

The caravan made its way back down the hills. The captured slaves walked just ahead of Heathcliff, roped together at the neck like a string of pack horses.

"Yaa-ya-ya!" came an eerie cry. "I spellin' you!"

Heathcliff pulled up his horse. A ragged figure stood atop a great limestone shard of rock, legs apart, looking down at their procession. He knew immediately it was Three-Fingered Jack.

The infamous renegade lifted an old musket and fired. Heathcliff flinched at the report. From the corner of his eye, he saw Black Tom pitch sideways off the mule, clutching his neck and hemorrhaging blood.

"Let go my people! Let my people go!" shouted Three-Fingered Jack.

Angelique Devine and his men pulled their muskets from saddle holsters, took aim, and fired at the renegade.

Three-Fingered Jack crossed his arms and braved the fire. Musket balls kicked up bits of rock around him, but the rebellious slave did not move until they stopped firing.

This show of bravery astounded Heathcliff. The shooters all cursed the rebel, and got off their horses to reload their muskets. Three-Fingered Jack faded away like a phantom into the wilderness of ferns and hardwood trees.

Chapter 84

Early the next morning, Heathcliff and Captain Collingwood sat in one of Mrs. Devine's pink little carriages as it bounced back down the muddy road to Kingston. The Negro coachman cracked his whip. Captain Collingwood brooded. He stared out the window of the satin-covered coach and did not speak as they entered the damaged city. Unable to sleep, Heathcliff had thought about Black Tom for much of the night.

"The old servant," Heathcliff began. "To die like that."

"Dead and gone," the captain snapped.

"I think the man knew he was going to die."

"You waste my time talking nonsense, Heathcliff. An old bull is dead. Angelique Devine is a sentimental fool to take his body back to Sugar Hill for burial. Had we been at sea, I'd have you pitch the corpse overboard, and think no more about it."

The captain turned to face Heathcliff, and scowled.

"I have been thinking of my lost privilege," the captain said. "Sixty hard-earned English pounds have slipped through my fingers, unless I can conjure some way to make it up."

At Negrille & Sloan, the carriage stopped. When Heathcliff stepped out, Captain Collingwood remained in the coach.

"I've business to attend to to-day, Heathcliff. Be a good man. Tell the other hands we must all remain on the island a bit longer. Wait until Friday, then gather the crew and bring them all to the ship."

"Aye-aye, captain," Heathcliff replied, proud to shoulder this new responsibility.

Three days later, the Irishman led Heathcliff, Peter, young Tom, and several other members of the crew up the sea-ladder. The *Commerce* still rode low in the water. Heathcliff thought nothing aboard the ship had been touched or repaired.

"Where is our captain?" Young Tom asked.

"Likely he's waiting in his cabin, Tommy," Fiddler said. "I'll be off to the forecastle to fetch me fiddle. I'll meet you below."

As Heathcliff led the mariners into the cabin, Dr. Chum sat at the captain's table, flanked by two rather large, rough-looking men from Negrille & Sloan. The surgeon took off his wig, set it aside, and greeted them with a businesslike nod of the head. Heathcliff noticed an open bottle of rum, a few dram glasses, and several short stacks of coins on the table next to Captain Collingwood's leather notebook.

"Line up, men, and make it quick," the surgeon said. "I'm here to settle with all of you."

"Where is captain?" asked young Tom. "He's to meet us here."

"Captain Collingwood departed for England two days ago, Tom, and Mr. Bolt along with him. Captain's work is finished here."

"Captain abandoned us on this terrible island?" cried young Tom.

"He's returned to England, Tom," said Dr. Chum. "But cheer up—he left me to settle accounts. Here's a glass of rum for you."

The surgeon pushed a glass of rum across the desk. When the cabin boy shook his head no, Dr. Chum downed the rum in a single gulp. With his free hand, he pushed a short stack of Spanish *reales* across the table toward the cabin boy.

"Take your pay, Tom," he said. "Quickly. Move out of the way."

HEATHCLIFF: THE LOST YEARS

"Why did captain leave us?" the cabin boy asked.

"Captain Collingwood felt it his duty to return the proceeds of the sale to his investors as quickly as possible," he sniffed. "Investors want their profits, Tom. I'm to oversee repair of the *Commerce,* but if I find a buyer, I may sell her off right away and begone."

Fiddler Ryan strutted into the cabin, holding his instrument in one hand. Dr. Chum pushed a stack of *reales* across the table toward him.

"You've retrieved your instrument, Fiddler. Now take your pay."

"What in God's name is *this,* doctor?" cried the Irishman, picking up a coin. "More *island* money? These coins are worthless in England! Give us English money, man."

"You can spend *reales* anywhere on this island, Fiddler, as you well know. You've flung many away, blowing and strutting pompously about the brothels."

"This is not right, sir," said the Irishman, setting down the coins.

"Captain C-C-Collingwood promised me a bonus, doctor!" said Peter, his lower lip trembling.

Dr. Chum pushed a small stack of coins toward Peter.

"This is what captain's notebook says you're due, Peter. I see no note of a bonus for you. When I return to England, I'll inquire."

"Now what good will *that* do, doctor, with Captain Collingwood departed?" Heathcliff demanded. "All of us were promised a bonus by the captain, and promised a bonus several times."

"Fancy Hat Collingwood abandons his ship, abandons his crew, and then *cheats* us?" Fiddler snorted. "You would give us *island* money, doctor, and not enough of it, after all you put us through?"

The Irishman carefully handed young Tom his fiddle. Then he lunged across the table and caught the surgeon by the lapels of his shirt.

The men from Negrille & Sloan drew their cudgels, jumped in, and beat the Irishman back from the table.

"Don't hit my hands!" Fiddler backed toward the door. "You're a bloody liar, Chum! And you cheat us!"

"I follow orders, Mr. Ryan! This not England! You are now in the colonies. Throw this man out!"

With a scuffling of feet, Sloan's men backed the struggling Irishman out of the cabin and closed the door.

Dr. Chum poured himself another glass of rum. He cleaned his spectacles on his shirt. Sloane's men returned to their places beside him.

"Take your pay, gentlemen," said the surgeon.

The Irishman pushed open the door, panting wildly.

"God damn Captain Collingwood! May Neptune carry that lying two-faced devil to the bottom of the sea! With his fancy hat, too! He's not man enough to face any of us!" the Irishman roared.

One of Sloan's men stalked out after the Fiddler, leaving open the door. The surgeon stood up, walked around the table, and plucked the fiddle from Tom's hands before returning to his desk.

"Hey!" Tom protested.

"Our carpenter will take his *reales* and thank me or I'll have these men smash his bloody fiddle and throw it overboard after him," the surgeon growled.

Dr. Chum waved Heathcliff forward and pushed him a short stack of coins. Heathcliff's stomach trembled when he realized how little money the captain left for him.

"This is not ten percent of what I was promised. I signed articles in Liverpool. I will show them to you," Heathcliff said.

"This is exactly what the captain's ledger allots you, Heathcliff. Here is captain's notebook. You have items from the purser, two advances and a bit of long credit."

"I should have very little credited to me," Heathcliff said.

"The captain deducted the price of three slaves who died on your watch from your wages," Dr. Chum added.

"I had nothing to do with their dying, any more than you did. The Negroes died of the hot flux, doctor, as you well know. At your orders, I helped throw them overboard."

HEATHCLIFF: THE LOST YEARS

"Captain Collingwood's notebook assigned the loss of those three slaves to you, Heathcliff. Remember our poor captain suffered financial losses. He had to make his losses up somehow, you mustn't forget."

"You cheat me, sir."

"I cheat you of nothing. You listen up, lad—here's the truth. I've just this morning sold this ship. When I leave here to-day, I shall not return. Take your money. You earned it."

Heathcliff felt his stomach tighten into a knot as he scooped up the coins.

"I am due a great deal more than this, sir, we all are," he said. "I swear to you, I will find a way to collect what I am due."

"I hope you do," the surgeon said, gesturing about the room. "You're mariners, lads. When you've had your fill of the islands, sign onto another ship. Unless you wish to remain here, there's nothing else you can do."

Chapter 85

That afternoon, Heathcliff sat in a tavern drinking with a few of the hands. Fiddler Ryan was spending several of his *reales,* buying the crew drinks.

"But why did our captain leave?" moaned young Tom, who still didn't seem to understand.

"He cheated us out of our money and left us, Tom. That's plain enough, isn't it?" Heathcliff said. "Men deceive each other for gain, and take advantage. I fear that's the way of the world."

"But to abandon us all on this terrible island!" the orphan wailed.

"Stop your whimpering, Tommy," said the Fiddler. "We have all survived worse than this together."

"We are able-bodied men, Tom," Heathcliff said. "We shall find something."

Early the next morning, the entire crew strolled to the waterfront. The finger pier remained in shambles, but slaves overseen by white men worked to repair it. Other mariners loitering about the docks told them the storm damaged a great many ships. A good many mariners roamed the waterfront, looking for new vessels. That morning, the news everywhere was disappointing.

HEATHCLIFF: THE LOST YEARS

That afternoon, on the way back to the inn, a distraught-looking gentleman jumped from a carriage and waved Heathcliff over.

"Can you lads help a man in desperate need?"

"What do you need, sir?" Heathcliff asked.

The gentleman pointed to what had once been a two-story wood-frame house. The house had collapsed during the storm, leaving only two walls and the brick chimney standing amidst a heap of rubble.

"My wife and I got out in time, but a little child may still be alive under there. I can't find men to help me. I cannot even rent slaves. Help search through that rubble and I will pay you well," he said.

As the owner watched from his carriage, Heathcliff and several hands began pulling splintered boards and timbers off the stack of rubble and flinging them aside. Near dusk, Heathcliff lifted a thick wooden door covered with dust and debris. Holding up the door with both hands, Heathcliff saw something wrapped in a pink blanket that seemed to move.

"Pick that up, Peter, there, in the blanket," Heathcliff said.

Peter bent down and scooped up a tiny, white-skinned baby. The infant moved its arms, but it could not cry.

"It's a little girl," Peter blinked. "S-s-she's alive."

A woman shrieked. The door to the carriage burst open. A pale lady in a long dress and bonnet hurried toward them. She snatched up the infant, cradled the child to her chest, and burst into tears. Her husband followed after her, looking grateful and relieved.

"Thank God for you lads," he said. "You saved our child. Take all the money I have in my purse. Here! Thank you!"

He pressed some bank-notes into Heathcliff's hands. On the way back to the inn, Heathcliff divided the money between the men.

At the docks the next morning, Fiddler buttonholed a young American officer, explained their situation, and asked for help. The man led them to a stately waterfront inn six blocks from the wharf, a neatly-painted pale blue building with lace curtains in every window.

"A good many officers frequent this establishment while ashore," the American told them. "You might try your luck here."

Heathcliff and several of the hands joined a group of mariners waiting outside the inn. As ships' officers walked out, seamen hailed them and clumsily introduced themselves. Within a week, Peter and Fiddler signed onto a vessel bound for Cuba and Mexico. Three hands caught a ship departing for the Carolinas, where a rebellion against the crown was in progress. Vito and most of the others signed onto a vessel sailing to Brazil.

Heathcliff and Tom held out for a ship returning to England. But for several days, the pair had no luck.

One sunny morning, a fit-looking, white-haired Englishman bounced down the steps of the inn. Perhaps fifty years of age, the man's quick step, frock coat, and cap marked him as an officer.

"Excuse me, sir," Heathcliff hailed the man, with Tom following behind. "May I have a word with you?"

"Perhaps you may."

The man stopped in his tracks. He had the thick white eyebrows and sharply-pointed nose of an exotic tropical bird.

"Might you be the captain of a ship sailing for England?" Heathcliff asked.

"My name is Henry Fowler. I am captain of the *Minerva*," he said, removing his cap. "The *Minerva* is bound for Liverpool and London."

"Might you need two capable hands?" Heathcliff asked.

"I am in need of only one man, to assist my navigator, Mr. Plum. Our Mr. Plum came down with the Yellow Jack and he remains weak from the effects of the disease. He cannot do all he must do just yet but I'm determined to find him an assistant so we may set sail."

"What manner of assistant might your navigator need?" Heathcliff asked.

Captain Fowler stared into Heathcliff's eyes. He raised and lowered his white eyebrows, as if giving him very careful scrutiny.

"Mr. Plum needs a man to handle the navigational instruments, throw the log, that sort of thing," Captain Fowler said.

"I've done a bit of that," said Heathcliff.

"Exactly what do you know of navigation, sir?"

"I know the sun-dial and compass combined with the sextant and formulas and charts from nautical books yield a very accurate latitude. Longitude is more difficult to calculate, particularly near the equator. However, if you have a timepiece set to Greenwich time—"

"Blast it, sir!" cried Henry Fowler, raising both hands to his ears. "This manner of talk gives me a headache. I know nothing of navigation, nor do I intend to learn."

"My last captain taught me a bit, sir."

"And where is your captain?" Henry Fowler crossed his arms and raised one eyebrow. "Why aren't you with your ship?"

"Captain Collingwood deserted us," blurted young Tom.

"An English captain abandoned his crew?"

"The storm damaged our ship," Heathcliff said. "Captain felt he had to take the profits from auctioning slaves and return to England."

"Slaving is bad business." Captain Henry Fowler carefully fitted his cap over his white hair. "Well, you may come to meet Mr. Plum."

Heathcliff caught his arm.

"Tom, here, my shipmate, must sign on with me. Tom was our ship's cabin boy—a very excellent cabin boy."

Captain Fowler placed his fists on his hips, bent over, and looked down his long nose at young Tom.

"This miniature little fellow?"

Undaunted, Tom leaned backwards, put his hands on his hips, and returned the captain's gaze.

"I attended the captain's table, sir. l cleaned officers' cabins. I started fires for the cook and put them out. I cared for our animals, I gathered eggs. I even helped Mr. Marconi make his soup," said Tom, stopping to take a breath.

"I mended captain's clothes, I mended sail, and when needed I helped haul the halyards."

"But you are only a wee slip of a lad," Captain Fowler said.

"We sail together, the two of us," said Heathcliff, squeezing Tom's shoulder. "I promised Tom we'd return to England together."

Captain Fowler frowned. He stared out over the harbor for some time, muttering to himself.

"Before we go any farther, sir, I daresay, you must come with me," he told Heathcliff. "Our Mr. Plum is quite particular."

Chapter 86

Heathcliff marveled at the condition of Captain Fowler's ship. The *Minerva* was miraculously untouched by the storm. The little brig was superbly outfitted. Her masts and deck timbers shone. Every sail, rope, and fitting appeared brand new and her hold had already been loaded with sugar. After formally introducing Heathcliff to his white-jacketed young officers, Captain Fowler led Heathcliff below to the navigator's cabin.

A distinguished-looking old gentleman with pale yellow skin waved them in. Mr. Plum sat propped up with pillows, using a lap-desk. His cabin was quite warm, and Mr. Plum kept a grey wool blanket snug over his shoulders. Nautical instruments and books lay scattered about.

"I have found a young gentleman who may meet your demanding criteria, Mr. Plum," said Captain Fowler, in a hearty tone of voice. "Now interrogate the young man. Perhaps you will like this one."

Mr. Plum set aside his lap-desk and with some difficulty rose to shake hands. The old navigator's hands were cold but his blue eyes were kind and intelligent. Heathcliff easily answered his questions.

"I believe he may do, Henry," said Mr. Plum to the captain. "This one has a brain in his head. He is not such a blockhead as those others you brought to me before."

When the *Minerva* sailed out of Kingston Harbour, Heathcliff's realization that he was finally returning to England released a flood of memories. Catherine Earnshaw sprang immediately to mind. Heathcliff remembered his many idyllic days at Wuthering Heights, and the unbreakable bond he felt with Catherine when they were children. He remembered the time he dared kiss her, the way her body melted into his. He remembered feeling that the two of them would always be one person, with their spirits forever united as one.

All Heathcliff really knew of love was bound up with memories of Catherine Earnshaw. He so longed to see her again. He left her engaged to Edgar Linton but he suddenly thought it possible their engagement had faltered. The knowledge that he was neither rich nor gentleman enough to merit Catherine's hand continued to drive him mad, and he again vowed to himself that he would one day become wealthy enough to reclaim the part of himself he left behind at Wuthering Heights.

His shipmates on the *Minerva* included a good number of young English gentlemen from Liverpool and London out "to get a taste of the sea." The young gentlemen worked occasionally alongside the crew but there were so many aboard they all had a great deal of leisure time.

For the well-heeled young gentlemen men in crisp white outfits, the voyage to Jamaica was just another of their formative experiences, and something of a lark.

The fey young gentlemen gossiped a great deal. They spoke about coffee houses, theatres, and the most presentable young women in the cities, things of which Heathcliff knew nothing. It pleased him to tend to his work, overhear their conversations, and very occasionally join in. He spoke frequently with young Tom, who had been given a crisp white uniform of which he was quite proud. Tom seemed delighted to be aboard a ship which served everyone ample, excellent food.

As Heathcliff listened to the young gentlemen, he realized he would need quite a lot of money to dream of returning to Wuthering Heights. He could hardly call himself a gentleman but as far as he could observe, it was only money and manners which separated the rich from the rabble.

One lonely night, Heathcliff dreamed he had found his way back to Wuthering Heights. It was a cold spring day. Out of the house burst Catherine Earnshaw, in long white dress and lavender bonnet, as breathtakingly beautiful as a violet popping up through the snow.

Heathcliff clasped his hands to his chest. He felt his heart singing. He assumed Catherine came out to greet him but she did not seem to see him, or to realize he was there.

He heard hoofbeats, and the springs of a one-horse gig.

Edgar Linton pulled between them in a little carriage bedecked with white streamers and bells and stopped the coach. He wore a fine black suit and tall black hat. Linton doffed his top hat to Catherine, and silently held out his hand.

"Cathy!" Heathcliff cried. "Wait!"

Catherine stepped into the gig without looking his way. She and Linton jingled away, leaving him waving his arms and shouting and feeling like he wanted to die.

Heathcliff shuddered awake in his hammock, sweating profusely. All around him, pale white hammocks swayed with the rocking of the ship. A young gentleman on the far side of the forecastle was snoring.

F arther out to sea, Heathcliff dreamt himself transformed into a fine, well-dressed gentleman. Now he wore fine black clothes, and a diamond stickpin in his lapel. He looked out of a carriage drawn by four muscular black horses that hurried across the moor under a dark, foreboding sky.

Flying spirits told him of the marriage at Gimmerton Kirk. He was determined to prevent it.

Empty carriages and horses were tied up around the little country church. Heathcliff leapt from his coach and sprinted inside, fearing he was too late.

Bursting into the sanctuary, he moved slowly up the aisle. He felt he was wading through thick water. Indignant parishioners turned to stare. His strong clear voice rang out over the silence.

"Stop the wedding! Catherine must come with me!"

Under the astonished eyes of the minister, Heathcliff forced bride and groom apart. He turned to the congregation, and took Catherine's hand.

"I swear before God and man Catherine Earnshaw is mine!" he cried. "Catherine has always been mine, and I am hers! We shall never be separated!"

Heathcliff pulled Catherine down the aisle toward the door. She did not resist. They could have been floating as one person. Her body felt light and graceful as a zephyr over the moor.

Outside the church, Catherine's face glowed like a pearl under the gloomy sky. They had reunited. Heathcliff's entire being pulsed with love as he giddily helped her into his carriage.

Heathcliff sat down. They clasped hands. The coach pulled away.

To his horror, the beautiful creature beside him began dissolving into air. Her radiant face and shoulders fell away in pieces, like glowing chunks of broken clay. When he clutched Catherine's hands, his own hands began to break apart and dissolve.

Rising from the coach, they became two ghostly spirits, turning in the wind over the moor.

Young Tom shook Heathcliff's hammock, rousting him awake. Heathcliff opened his eyes to the worried face of the little cabin boy.

"You were shouting, sir," whispered young Tom. "Surely it is not true, what you cried out, that you wish to die?"

As the weeks passed, old Mr. Plum reclined in his cabin. Heathcliff continued sighting Polaris with the sextant, throwing the log, and gathering information every hour from the traverse board.

HEATHCLIFF: THE LOST YEARS

Heathcliff pulled down the nautical manuals, helped with the calculations, and ran messages back and forth between Mr. Plum and the captain which kept him busy much of the night and day.

The cool days on the North Atlantic seemed to pass quickly. After one particularly long day on rough seas, Heathcliff collapsed in his hammock and slipped into a dream.

He burst through a curtain of stars astride a strong black stallion. He urged the horse along a narrow road through the moor. Along the way to Wuthering Heights, his long black cloak fluttered behind him and above his head the night sky twinkled with diamonds.

Outside the old house, Heathcliff pulled up his horse.

"Ride on, sir!" growled the voice of Hindley Earnshaw from a high dark window. "You have no business here. You have no money and you are no gentleman. Ride on!"

Heathcliff's hatred of Hindley flared up. They had a score to settle. Once again, he wished to crush the man who pushed him down.

"I must see Catherine, and I must see her now!" Heathcliff cried, his heart pounding madly in his chest.

A shadowy figure opened the front door. It stepped onto the front porch, holding high a lantern. A smaller figure slipped up beside the first, a figure he thought he recognized.

Catherine Earnshaw stepped forward in the light of the lamp. She wore a long black dress. Her lips quivered like moth wings but she did not speak.

"Ride on, sir! You must not return!" came the thin voice of Edgar Linton.

Heathcliff saw a very small figure between them on the porch, a child, perhaps. The three phantasms stood flickering beneath the lamp for a long time in a tableau silent and permanent as death.

Finally, with his heart again breaking, Heathcliff reluctantly turned the stallion away.

"Heathcliff!"

JAMAICA

At the sound of Catherine's voice, Heathcliff desperately reached out for her.

He tumbled from his hammock. He woke up in the forecastle of the *Minerva* with his hands and face pressed against the floor.

Chapter 87

Heathcliff felt a thrum of anticipation when he noticed the deep green Irish Sea had turned slate grey. As the *Minerva* entered the pool, the smoke-filled skyline of Liverpool appeared in the cool air. The *Minerva* slipped into place at Salthouse Docks having made excellent time, and in good condition.

Heathcliff bid farewell to Mr. Plum, who was very nearly recovered. He put on his weather cloak and sea clothes, and gathered his things. At the top of the gangplank, Captain Fowler stood with young Tom at his side.

"You might come with us to London," Captain Fowler said. "We must unload our sugar and take on some other goods, but we'll be sailing around the island in two weeks."

"I must attend to some business here in Liverpool," Heathcliff said. "This business has been all I have thought of these last few days. Thank you, but I must now attend to that."

Captain Fowler lifted his white eyebrows, nodded, and shook Heathcliff's hand. Young Tom tugged at his arm.

"And here's young Tom, and more of him, too," said Heathcliff. Tom had grown taller since they departed, and gained several pounds. "Tom will be staying aboard the *Minerva*, I presume."

Heathcliff knew the orphan had found a home on the *Minerva*. But the little cabin boy struggled to maintain his composure when he extended his hand.

"You and I have been through much together, Tom," Heathcliff said.

"You helped me and defended me, sir. I will sorely miss you," said young Tom, his eyes suddenly filling with tears.

"Good-bye my friend." Heathcliff bent down and clasped Tom's hand. "I believe you have a bright future on the sea. In fact, right now I feel certain of it."

Walking away from the *Minerva,* Heathcliff took a deep breath. The odor of the seaport was everywhere. Over his head, a cloud of seagulls awked and drifted lazily over the masts of tall ships.

Heathcliff felt considerably older than when he departed. On the sidewalks of Liverpool, as he watched well-fed gentlemen in frock coats and silver-buckled shoes come and go from their shops, Heathcliff felt out of place in his sea clothes. To settle his affairs with a merchant, he thought, he must dress as smartly as the merchants did.

Heathcliff stepped into a tailor's shop, and purchased new clothes.

As he made his way toward the inn on Duck Lane, Heathcliff was astonished to find Nathanael Jones, begging. Nathanael squatted on his hams before a butcher's shop next to a pile of entrails, dressed in rags and holding out his hand.

"Nathanael Jones?" Heathcliff said.

Heathcliff immediately recognized the man. Nathanael blinked for a moment when their eyes met; quickly he turned his dirty face away.

"I am a ruined man," Nathanael said.

"I cannot believe my eyes," Heathcliff said. He bent down and clasped Nathanael's hands.

"I remember you well, Nathanael. You helped me. You are a strong capable man, with a good family and a future."

"My family found work in a factory here, but the owner often cheated us on our pay. I gathered the workers together, and we asked the owner to make it right. Instead, he turned the lot of us out. Now no business in Liverpool will employ me and I haven't money to leave," Nathanel said.

"My Meg became ill and died in an almshouse. Little Robert was jailed for stealing food. My two girls ran away. The city turned me into a beggar, lad."

"That's terrible. I cannot believe it," Heathcliff said.

"Surrounded by wealth and nothing to eat!" said Nathanael Jones, gesturing around him. "No hint of Christian charity, and no neighbor or family to help us. I was not man enough to hold my little family together, lad. This city crushed me like a snail."

"You were kind to me, Nathanael. Let me help you."

Heathcliff impulsively pulled out the bank-notes he received from Captain Fowler and thrust most of them into Nathanael's hand. The beaten-down cottager balked, but took the bank notes. He thanked Heathcliff not with words, for he said nothing, but with the tears that formed in his eyes as he gritted his teeth, stood up, and limped away.

To see such a good man cruelly beaten down by the city unsettled Heathcliff. He had seen precious little justice in the world.

At the inn on Duck Lane, Heathcliff secured a room. Opening his window late that afternoon, he watched tendrils of fog creep through the streets of Liverpool.

From the pocket of his new coat, he took out the articles he signed with Joshua Bullin. In his satchel were the *reales* he received in Jamaica. The next morning, Heathcliff planned to pay a call on the merchant who sent him flying off to sea.

Chapter 88

Much of the morning fog had lifted by the time Heathcliff put on his new clothes and finished breakfast. Outside the inn, under a ponderously low grey sky, horse-drawn carriages and wagons clattered across the cobblestones.

At Number 55 Paradise Street, Heathcliff lifted the polished brass door-knocker and rapped on Joshua Bullin's front door.

The Negro servant Pompey opened the door, resplendent in canary yellow velvet livery. A heavily-powdered goat's hair wig covered the Negro's natural hair.

"Hello, Pompey, is it?" said Heathcliff.

The little Negro pursed his lips. He showed no sign of recognition.

"I wish to speak with Mr. Bullin," Heathcliff said.

"You may leave your calling card with me, sir."

The Negro extended a small silver tray.

"I have no calling card but I wish to discuss this document, signed by Mr. Bullin himself, in this very house." Heathcliff thrust his articles into the Negro's hand. "Is he here?"

Pompey haplessly looked over the papers. Heathcliff experienced a flush of sympathy. He realized the Negro probably could not read. The perfumed and bewigged creature squinting at the document before him was very likely forced aboard a foul slave ship and ripped from his native land as a young boy.

"Wait, sir." Taking the document, Pompey closed the door.

After many months away from England, Heathcliff had returned to paradise. Beyond the merchant's marble porch, an idyllic footpath meandered through the yard between banks of blooming flowers. The air smelled sweetly of roses. He heard a songbird trilling from deep inside the foliage of a tall, handsome tree.

After a considerable wait, Pompey cracked open the door.

"Take your matter to Mr. Bullin's place of business to-morrow, after five o'clock. I bid you good day, sir."

Heathcliff placed the tip of his new silver-buckled shoe between the door and the frame to stop Pompey from closing the door in his face.

"You have not returned my articles," Heathcliff said.

"Sir?"

"I shewed you a document. Give me my papers back."

"Sir! You block the door!"

"Get me my bloody document," Heathcliff hissed. "I'll not leave here without it!"

"Sir, sir, sir!" Pompey tried several times to close the door.

"Fetch my bloody *articles*, Pompey!" Heathcliff hissed. "Get them now or you will regret you ever left Africa."

Pompey disappeared. After a short while, the Negro returned and flung the articles down on the porch.

When Heathcliff stooped down to retrieve his papers, Pompey closed and bolted the door.

Chapter 89

Darkness arrived early that afternoon. All along Bank Street, tired-looking merchants locked up their shops with their heads down. As he approached the warehouse, Heathcliff heard the heels of his new silver-buckled shoes tapping smartly against the wooden sidewalk and fancied himself a gentleman.

Outside the warehouse, young men unloaded a dray. Heathcliff recognized Henry Willits in the doorway to the warehouse, scowling at the crew with folded arms. The foreman made no sign of recognition when Heathcliff extended his hand.

"I believe I know you, sir. Your name is Henry Willits. Many months ago, I worked here for you."

"We have no work. Move along, you."

"I came to speak with Mr. Joshua Bullin."

"And who, pray tell, might you be?"

"My name is Heathcliff. I have business to discuss with Mr. Bullin. When I went to his home, I was told to call here after five o'clock."

Henry Willits stared back into the warehouse. He unfolded his arms, looked at his pocket-watch, and spat on the ground.

"Wait here," he said.

HEATHCLIFF: THE LOST YEARS

Henry Willits sauntered into the warehouse. Heathcliff saw him mount the flight of steep wooden stairs that ran up the far wall. He stopped at the landing on the second floor, knocked on the door, then disappeared inside. Not long afterwards, the big man descended the stairs.

"Mr. Bullin's busy in the counting-house. You'll have to wait."

"I don't mind."

"Step outside, you. You're in my way."

Heathcliff moved next to a lantern by the door. He leaned back against the building and crossed his arms over his chest, shivering a bit at the cool damp air that blew in from the sea.

It was pitch dark when the crew left the warehouse. Henry walked outside with a man Heathcliff had never seen before, looked around, and gestured.

"You, this way," Willits said.

Heathcliff followed Willits and the other man up the stairway and into Joshua Bullin's counting-house. It was a large, plain room with no windows. Heathcliff noticed a metal safe nestled against the rear wall and two or three empty wooden chairs lined up to face the merchant's desk.

Joshua Bullin copied sums into a ledger that lay open before him. He did not acknowledge Heathcliff's presence for some time. Finally, the merchant lifted his watery eyes and squinted. His thin lips parted.

"Your business?"

"Mr. Bullin, sir, I must speak with you."

"Speak quickly," he said.

Heathcliff stepped forward. Henry Willits and the other man slouched against the wall behind him, watching the proceedings with their arms crossed.

"May we speak privately, sir?"

"My men remain exactly where they are. They have business with me," said the merchant.

The merchant showed Heathcliff a chair. When he sat down, Heathcliff unfolded his copy of the articles he had been given months before. He smoothed them out the best he could, handed them to Joshua Bullin, leaned back, and quietly awaited a response.

The two men slouching against the wall behind him did not make Heathcliff comfortable. He heard Henry Willits whispering. It shocked him when Joshua Bullin tossed the articles back into his lap with a thin-lipped smile.

"Why do you bother me with this?" the merchant demanded.

"Because I received less than ten percent of what I was promised for the voyage, sir. I was paid in money I cannot spend. In addition, three improper deductions were made against my pay. I am here to ask for a fair settlement of this from you," Heathcliff replied, feeling his breath quicken. "I believe additional money is due me."

"I owe you nothing, sir," Joshua Bullin said.

"I beg your pardon." Heathcliff's throat constricted. He took a deep breath before he was able to pick up his articles and continue speaking.

"In this very document, which is signed by your hand, sir, a definite sum of money was promised me. I sailed to Guinea on the strength of your written promise."

"You were paid everything you were owed, sir, if indeed you sailed on the *Commerce* or any one of my ships. I do not remember you at all."

"Of course I sailed on the *Commerce*. You cannot deny that. And witness the amount, your signature, and the date inscribed," Heathcliff said. "Did you not assure me that your word is your bond?"

"My word certainly is my bond. You did not complete the Guinea voyage as you agreed to do." Joshua Bullin managed a cold smile.

"Your document is worthless. Captain Collingwood returned to Liverpool and settled accounts with me more than a month ago."

"Captain Collingwood abandoned the ship! He left Kingston and did not take his crew!"

HEATHCLIFF: THE LOST YEARS

"And what of it?" the merchant snorted. "You were paid all you were worth in Jamaica. I warn you, young man—I am schooled in the law. My paperwork is quite in order."

Clapping his hands together once, Joshua Bullin rose to his feet. With a condescending smile, he gestured toward the counting-house door.

"So, you returned to Liverpool for nothing. Good night, sir."

Heathcliff stood up to face the merchant, clutching his document.

"I tell you I have not been fairly paid, sir. By heaven, I ask you to pay me a fair amount of English money for the voyage I undertook for you."

The two men grabbed Heathcliff's arms and pulled him backwards, tripping him and knocking over his chair.

"Show this arrogant young scoundrel the door," said the merchant. "And teach him his manners on the way out."

Heathcliff struggled to free his arms as the two men dragged him to the counting house door. Willits kicked the door open. The other man pushed Heathcliff sideways through the doorway and onto the landing.

Willits stepped out, jerked up Heathcliff's arm, spun him around, and pushed him backwards down the stairs. Heathcliff tumbled end over end, both arms flailing.

He came to at the bottom of the stairway, shaking his head. His ears rang. He heard the slap of work-boots descending the wooden stairs. He struggled to pull himself up by the bannister, using both hands.

Henry Willits' boot-heel struck Heathcliff in the face and knocked him backwards against the wall. Before he could stand, they both set upon him with their feet and fists. On the floor of the warehouse, as he tried to crawl away, they kicked him and stomped him until in one painful flash of light, his world went black.

Many hours later, Heathcliff opened his eyes. It was first light. He lay sprawled out on the bank of a brine pit outside the salt works. A fine grey rain fizzled down from the low, grey sky.

His head throbbed. Every muscle in his bruised, beat-up body sang with pain. Each inhalation felt like a knife thrust into his chest. With difficulty, Heathcliff slowly pulled himself into a sitting position.

His new clothes were ripped and torn in several places. Around the torn fabric, clumps of dried blood softened in the rain. His face felt swollen and hurt when he touched it. When he felt his mouth, his lips were completely numb but he still had all his teeth. Warily he looked around.

Through an open door not far away, Heathcliff saw a man wearing a dirty canvas apron shovelling coal into a furnace. Plumes of smoke rose from smokestacks that towered over the kilns. The air over his head was alive with the shrieks of invisible gulls.

Chapter 90

Painfully, pulling himself forward like a snail, stopping to lean against buildings, Heathcliff made his way back to the inn on Duck Street through dim, drizzling rain. He locked his door, stripped off his garments, cleaned himself as best he could, and collapsed onto his wool mattress, dead to the world.

Heathcliff slept all day and night, rising only to painfully relieve himself in the chamber-pot. When he staggered into the dining room the following evening, the innkeeper took one look at him, waved him away, and sent a servant-girl to his room with food and drink. But after a few days, the swelling and the terrible soreness in his body began to subside.

Heathcliff crept warily back onto the streets of Liverpool, wearing his weather cloak and sea clothes. He began to monitor the movements of Joshua Bullin, always from a discreet distance and always taking care to remain out of sight of the merchant himself.

This is what he learned:

1. At ten minutes before seven o'clock every morning, a coach pulled up beneath the *porte-cochère* at No. 55 Paradise Street.

2. At exactly seven o'clock, Joshua Bullin stepped into the coach and rode to his warehouse on Bank Street.

3. When he arrived at the warehouse, Henry Willits met him at the door.

4. After speaking with Willits, Joshua Bullin disappeared into the counting-house and remained there all day.

5. At six o'clock, a few minutes after his crew was dismissed, the merchant personally locked up his warehouse. He lit a clay pipe and strolled onto the docks with the air of a medieval king looking over his kingdom. If he had a ship at port, he boarded her and conferred with the captain.

6. His business complete, Joshua Bullin walked home alone.

The merchant didn't open the warehouse on Sunday. He patronized none of Liverpool's new banks. He apparently conducted his financial dealings in the counting-house and he paid his crews on Friday, in cash.

When Heathcliff determined Joshua Bullin's habits, he seized upon a plan.

At a pawn shop, he bargained with a Jew for a Blunderbuss of Spanish manufacture, a wide-barreled flintlock capable of blowing off a man's head at close range. The pistol's smoothly-polished wooden handle fit neatly into the palm of his hand.

As the church bells of Liverpool sounded six o'clock, a slow wind off the Irish Sea drew a veil of damp thick fog over the city. In the cold early darkness, Heathcliff filled his pockets with *reales* and set out to execute his plan.

Heathcliff followed Joshua Bullin as far as the docks, and then waited in a doorway along the merchant's usual route home. By the time the merchant headed home in the fog, the streets of Liverpool were deserted. The street-lamps along Bank Street could hardly be seen through the thick fog.

Heathcliff stepped out of a doorway, blocking the merchant's path. Joshua Bullin stopped, looked up, surprised.

Heathcliff grabbed the merchant's left arm and pulled him into the doorway, pressing the Blunderbuss to his head.

HEATHCLIFF: THE LOST YEARS

"Take my purse!" the merchant growled, his watery eyes focused on the barrel of the pistol. "Begone! Let me be!"

"Let you *be?*" Heathcliff grabbed the merchant's hair and slammed his head into the casement of the door. The merchant froze like a man hypnotized, both arms dangling at his sides.

"Take my purse!" Bullin blinked. "Don't kill me!"

"I don't want your purse. Turn around."

With the pistol concealed beneath his cloak, Heathcliff shoved the barrel of the gun into Bullin's ribs. He pushed the merchant back down the sidewalk through the fog.

Joshua Bullin tottered forward, stumbling, blinking, glancing over his shoulder, his exhalations trailing after him like small clouds.

At the warehouse, Heathcliff pulled the street-lantern from its hook next to the door.

"Unlock the door. Be quick about it."

By the light of the lantern, Heathcliff prodded Joshua Bullin through the deserted warehouse and up the stairway to his counting-house on the second floor.

"Open the safe. I wish to see your money."

Fumbling with his ring of keys, shaking his head no, the merchant opened the cast iron safe. He pulled out his iron money-box. He placed the box onto his desk, his watery blue eyes blinking.

"You must not kill me, sir," the merchant said. "You'll be put in the stocks and hanged. They'll draw and quarter you."

Heathcliff set the lantern on the desk and handed Joshua Bullin his articles.

"You will pay me exactly what you promised me in writing, sir. I'll have only that but I should take it all after the beating I received."

Joshua Bullin stared dumbly at the articles, his mouth opening and closing. Heathcliff poked him in the ribs with the barrel of the gun.

"Move quickly, sir. Don't make me treat you like I was forced to treat your wretched Negro slaves," Heathcliff hissed.

With trembling fingers, the merchant opened his money-box.

"Do you know how many black-skinned children perished aboard the *Commerce*? Do you know how many dead Negroes I heaved into the sea, with these hands! Can you imagine the fate of the women you ripped from their homes, who are everyone the better of you?"

Joshua Bullin counted out bank-notes on the desk. He counted the bank-notes a second time, and pushed the stack to Heathcliff.

"Count your money and make sure it's correct, sir," said Joshua Bullin. "It's sound business practice."

Heathcliff thumbed through the bank-notes, folded them in half, and stuffed them in his breeches. The merchant stared at the Blunderbuss. His watery eyes blinked rapidly. He nearly smiled.

"You're ruthless, lad. Come work for me. In a few years, you can make a hundred times more money than this buying and selling slaves."

Heathcliff took the *reales* out of his pocket and dropped the coins on the merchant's desk.

"What is this?" asked the merchant.

"I will have exactly what you promised me in writing, and not a penny more, sir. Your island money I leave for you."

Joshua Bullin slumped down into the chair behind his desk. With his head down, he scooped the *reales* into his money-box and closed it. Then he clutched the money box to his chest. He glanced up at Heathcliff, nervously blinking.

Heathcliff left the merchant behind his desk in the darkness. He paused on the landing to lock the counting-house door.

As he left the warehouse, he locked the main door, hung up the lantern, and tossed away the keys before hurrying away in the fog.

What he dared accomplish now frightened him. His thoughts came and went quickly as breath.

He could not remain in Liverpool. The merchant would send men to reclaim his money. This time, he thought, they would try to hunt him down and kill him.

London

Chapter 91

Heathcliff arrived at the port of London with money in his pockets. He was prepared to seek his fortune but he was not prepared for the overwhelming sprawl of almost a million men, women, and children that awaited him up the River Thames, on the other side of London Bridge.

Captain Fowler insisted Heathcliff accompany him to his hotel, where he believed Heathcliff might find suitable quarters during his stay in the city. Beyond the windows of their coach, the rooftops of the great metropolis stretched out for miles.

According to Captain Fowler, east of the Thames lay the enormous beehive of British manufacturing. There lay block after block of factory buildings, with men, women, and children in from the country toiling from daylight to dusk for extremely modest wages. This migration fed the growing ooze and creep of the slums. Every day, flimsy structures filled past overflowing collapsed, and shoddy new buildings sprang up on their foundations like mushrooms after a spring rain.

West of the Thames lay the sumptuous palaces and courtyards of London's wealthy aristocrats and the city's aspiring commercial elite. The most magnificent of these, Buckingham Palace, the captain said, was recently renovated for Queen Charlotte by her indulgent husband, King George III, the monarch who reigned over it all.

HEATHCLIFF: THE LOST YEARS

London was a city of clattering carts and carriage horses, the captain observed, home to gentlemen, scoundrels, soldiers, beggars, guildsmen, vendors, gypsies, shopkeepers, gamblers, matrons of leisure, foreigners, factory owners, sailors, prostitutes, night soil men and knaves.

"London attracts people from all over the world, many seeking to make their fortunes," Captain Fowler observed as the coach drew up before the Metropole. "You may meet a few honest people here, but I myself greatly prefer the sea."

The Metropole Hotel was in Covent Gardens on the edge of Drury Lane. The best of London had long ago abandoned the elegant old neighborhood, according to Captain Fowler, but he thought the Metropole perfectly situated for his brief stays in the city.

The three-story Georgian town-house retained the elegant façade of a great mansion, Heathcliff noticed, with a large handsome portico and window-frames of pink stone.

"Our establishment attracts many patrons who do appreciate good value," sniffed the carbuncular young proprietor as he registered. "The neighborhood isn't what it was but our monthly rates are reasonable and we do include a decent dinner."

Heathcliff rented a room for a month. After Captain Fowler retired to his quarters, Heathcliff ventured outside to stroll down Drury Lane at dusk.

Lamp-lighters lit streetlamp after streetlamp. Small boys hawked newspapers. Carriages clattered past. Vendors with push-carts sold tarts and meat pies. A rivulet of raw sewage dribbled down one side of the street, but beneath the streetlamps the sewage shone like a tiny river of molten gold.

Over Heathcliff's head, on sturdy metal poles extending far out over the street, banners advertised the names of shops below. Twin torches flared at the entrance to a Turkish Bath. Gentlemen walked the street, some with ladies on their arm.

Heathcliff marveled at the imposing facades of the Drury Lane entertainment palaces, and the uniformed coachmen waiting outside.

LONDON

As he returned to the Metropole, women he thought prostitutes smiled at him on the street, or beckoned from doorways.

Suddenly, an urchin in ragged clothing leaped out of an alley, boldly thrust one hand into his pocket, and tugged at his pocketbook. When Heathcliff realized what the boy was about, he caught the young thief's hand, twisted back his arm, and flung him to the cobblestones.

"Thief!" he said. "Criminal!"

The dirty little creature scrambled to its feet, spat at Heathcliff, and skittered away before Heathcliff realized it was a girl.

Just as Heathcliff returned to the Metropole, a black four-wheeled carriage stopped before the portico. A uniformed coachman jumped from the box and pulled open the door to the coach.

A dainty woman in a pale blue satin dress and matching hat stepped to the ground. Clutching a satchel, the lady lowered her head, walked up the stairs, and hurried through the front door without looking back.

Heathcliff thought the lady extremely fetching. When he stepped into the lobby of the old hotel, a hint of her exotic perfume lingered in the air.

Chapter 92

Residents crowded about the long dining room table for the Metropole's modestly festive dinners. At one end of the long grey-green dining room was a swinging door to the kitchen. Shortly before six o'clock, two harried-looking servant girls burst through the door carrying heavy platters of food and placed them along the table for the guests.

The day Captain Fowler returned to his ship, Heathcliff sat down next to a stocky gentleman he had not noticed before. The gentleman's yellowish-green embroidered waistcoat was peppered with food-stains; he held an upturned knife in one hand and an upturned serving-fork in the other.

The gentleman glanced up from beneath his periwig and looked Heathcliff in the eye. But when a serving-girl set down a platter of sliced beef before the man, his attention immediately shifted to the beef.

"Good evening, sir," sniffed the gentleman in the green waistcoat, who carved slices of beef to heap upon his plate. He put aside his knife for a moment and limply shook Heathcliff's hand.

"My name is Peter Pincher. I am the owner of a business and a long-time resident here."

"I am pleased to meet you," Heathcliff said.

"Of course you are. Surely you arrive bearing a name."

"My name is Heathcliff."

As a second servant girl swept past, the man suddenly threw up one arm and leaned back in his chair to pluck a fat warm roll from atop the moving platter.

"And what brings you to our fair city, may I inquire?" Peter Pincher continued, splitting the roll with a flick of the knife.

Before Heathcliff could respond, every head in the room turned to witness the entrance of the woman Heathcliff saw step from the coach a few days before. The woman entered the dining room lightly as a spring breeze. She wore a fashionable yellow gown and matching hat. Without acknowledging the gentlemen, the well-turned lady removed the hat from her mass of gleaming auburn hair, placed it on a hat-rack, and sat down next to a rather plain woman at the far end of the table. The woman in question ate quickly, Heathcliff noticed, with downcast eyes. She took her food in small rapid birdlike bites.

The woman glanced up. Her wide-set hazel eyes caught Heathcliff staring. The ghost of a smile flickered across her lips before she looked down and returned to her food.

Heathcliff thought the woman's large hazel eyes an enchanting complement to her heart-shaped face and her small, full-lipped mouth.

"*Bonne soiree*, Mademoiselle Sorel," trilled Peter Pincher, from their end of the table. "It is a pleasure for all we gentlemen to see you."

The Frenchwoman glanced up, forced a polite smile, and did not reply. She quickly finished her meal. She dabbed at the corner of her mouth with a cloth napkin, plucked up her hat, and flew out the door.

"That is our Mademoiselle Sorel," said Mr. Pincher. "The little Frenchwoman is not always so unfriendly."

"I have seen her before. She is quite lovely," Heathcliff said.

"Oh yes," Peter Pincher replied. "Unless I am mistaken, the lady has a great many admirers."

Chapter 93

The last day of every month, the cooks at the Metropole roasted a pig for dinner. The succulent roast pork was a special treat, Peter Pincher confided to Heathcliff, and one greatly anticipated by a good many of the residents.

Peter Pincher arrived first at the table and awaited the arrival of the pig with carving knife in hand. Heathcliff took a seat not far away.

At six o'clock the kitchen door burst open and two small struggling house-servants appeared with a great wooden platter balanced between them on their shoulders. Atop the platter was the treat of the evening, a small roasted brown-skinned sow with a baked red apple in its mouth.

Peter Pincher immediately pushed back his chair, forcing the girls to stop and set down the great platter on the table next to him.

"Thank you," he said.

Other guests hurried in to take their places around the table. Agnes Sorel seated herself in an empty chair next to Heathcliff. She wore a simple grey linen dress which clung to her trim figure. Her auburn hair hung in a cascade of ringlets around her shoulders.

"Good evening, gentlemen," she said, in French-accented English.

"*Bonne soiree*, Mademoiselle Sorel," grunted the factory owner, who immediately turned his attention to the pig.

Bringing down his carving knife with an animal snort, he attacked the flanks of the unfortunate animal without looking up.

"You have perhaps met our neighbor, Mr. Heathcliff?"

"Hello," Heathcliff extended his hand. "I have seen you two times before. It is a great pleasure to meet you."

"Is it?" she asked.

Without taking his hand, the Frenchwoman stared into his eyes for what seemed much too long a time. His ears burned. But before he could withdraw his hand, Agnes clasped it in her own, and smiled.

"Good evening," she said. "My name is Agnes Sorel."

Several guests began grumbling for Mr. Pincher to relinquish his control of the pig. The factory owner hurriedly gestured for Heathcliff's plate and heaped it with slices of roast pork. Other plates flew round the table toward him.

"Our war in the colonies does not go well," Peter Pincher began. "Additional soldiers are needed, Mr. Heathcliff. The crown pays a twenty-pound bonus merely to enlist in the army. Recruiting stations are up all over the East End."

"I for one am not so frightened of this General Washington as you English pretend to be," said the Frenchwoman. "It is said France may support the American rebels."

"France supports a rebellion in our colonies at great peril," Peter Pincher replied, taking a bite of pork and deftly passing along the plate. "As usual, the French sovereign is misguided."

"War does nothing but increase the profits of armament makers like yourself, Mr. Pincher," said the Frenchwoman. "Tell me—have not your sales of gunpowder greatly increased?"

The factory owner paused, plate in hand, blinking. Silence fell over the dining room while Peter Pincher chewed and swallowed a large mouthful of pork, which took a bit of time.

"*Touché*, mademoiselle," the factory owner replied. "Perhaps you are the wisest of us all."

HEATHCLIFF: THE LOST YEARS

"Have you a yearning for military adventure, Mr. Heathcliff?" Peter Pincher asked. "The crown offers a handsome bonus. A few young men have even slipped away with bonus in hand, as I understand, and some avoided military service altogether."

"I've had my fill of fighting," said Heathcliff. "I hope to better myself here in the city."

"One day you must visit my business, Mr. Heathcliff," he said. "It may behoove you to see what I do. In times of war, fortunes can be made and lost as quickly as lives."

As the factory owner spoke, he stacked slices of pork in the centre of a linen napkin. When he had accumulated a mound of meat six inches high, he folded the corners of the napkin over the meat and managed to tuck it all into a pocket of his waistcoat. The armaments maker rose to his feet with one hand still in his pocket, and rather grandly surveyed the dinner table.

"Do you see the pig in my pocket, mademoiselle?" he whispered, with sly wink at the Frenchwoman.

Mme. Sorel nodded without looking up.

"Mr. Heathcliff," Peter Pincher announced. "Since you are recently arrived in our city, here is a bit of advice. Never trust a Frenchman, or a French woman, with your fortune or your life. *C'est vrai, Mademoiselle Sorel?*"

The Frenchwoman smiled without looking up.

"Go drink your *absinthe*," she said. "Your little bottle cries for you."

Moving out along the length of the table, passing gas as his belly bumped against the backs of dining room chairs, Peter Pincher made his way as discreetly as he could manage from the dining room.

He paused at the door with one hand still in his waistcoat pocket and looked over the room. He waved at Heathcliff with his free hand, and marched away.

"Tell me, Mr. Heathcliff," said Agnes Sorel. "Have you business in London?"

"I hope to make my fortune here. I have some small funds, which I hope to increase."

"London offers many opportunities to the nimble," smiled the Frenchwoman. "All that the world can offer is to be found here. I find greater opportunities here than even Paris."

"Really?"

Agnes Sorel looked into his eyes. For a moment, the Frenchwoman reminded him of Catherine Earnshaw. When she pleasured him with her fetching smile, Heathcliff's heart dropped and he smiled as boldly as he could in return.

"To-morrow I shall attend a hanging, perhaps the most spectacular hanging of the year," the Frenchwoman said. "I have need of an escort. If you are free, Mr. Heathcliff, you might accompany me."

"Did you say to-morrow?" Heathcliff coughed. He had been knocked off-balance by the sudden invitation. "Of course. Yes. Yes, yes, I am free. I would like that. A great deal."

"My coach arrives at ten," she said. "We can go together."

"I will be delighted to accompany you," Heathcliff smiled as he regained some of his composure. "I am very quite delighted, indeed."

Agnes Sorel looked into his eyes with an enigmatic smile. The Frenchwoman touched the corners of her lips with a napkin, stood up, and daintily excused herself.

At last, Heathcliff turned his attention to his dinner. Two thick pieces of pork grew cold on his plate. He ate ravenously, more heartily than usual, and was the last guest to leave the table.

Strolling down the hallway toward his room, Heathcliff noticed a partially-open door. As he passed, he absent-mindedly glanced inside.

Agnes Sorel stood naked to the waist before a long mirror. He stopped walking, embarrassed but unable to take his eyes from the Frenchwoman's lithe, cream-coloured body.

Agnes Sorel looked up into her mirror and glimpsed his face. The Frenchwoman gasped. Covering her bare breasts with one arm, she strode to the door and slammed it in his face.

HEATHCLIFF: THE LOST YEARS

"I said ten o'clock in the *morning*, sir," came the lady's voice. "And I give you fair warning now. If you wish to accompany me to-morrow, you must agree to behave like a proper gentleman."

Chapter 94

Heathcliff took a deep breath and climbed into the waiting coach. He sat down next to the magnificently attired Frenchwoman, exhilarated by the look and smell of her but slightly ashamed of his own garments, which seemed perfectly fine the day before.

Agnes Sorel wore a long black dress with décolleté neckline, topped by a stylish black hat and veil. In her lap, she clutched a prim grey satchel trimmed in red. She could have been the most aristocratic lady in London. The coach was alive with the smell of her exotic perfume as the coach pulled away under an overcast sky.

"*Bon jour,*" Agnes smiled politely. "Do you know Tyburn, Mr. Heathcliff, and what awaits us there?"

Heathcliff reluctantly admitted he did not.

"We will attend a most spectacular hanging. A French aristocrat will be put to the gallows."

"An aristocrat? Is that not unusual?"

"The Duchess of Burgundy stole a diamond necklace from Queen Charlotte, your king's beloved wife. The necklace was composed of very rare diamonds of a pale blue cast and greatly valued by your queen."

"How did the Duchess steal a necklace from the queen?"

HEATHCLIFF: THE LOST YEARS

"Queen Charlotte entertained a group of aristocratic ladies from the continent at Buckingham Palace. The following day, a maidservant noticed the necklace missing, and alerted the queen. That very evening, the Duchess foolishly attended the Opera Royale wearing the queen's necklace. But several ladies at the theatre saw it on her."

Heathcliff nodded. He noticed how the Frenchwoman relished the telling of this story.

"When confronted by the king's ministers, the Duchess denied she stole anything at all. King George threatened to have her thrown in jail. French diplomats rushed to London. King Louie XVI petitioned for her release, but the French court is unpopular here. To defend Queen Charlotte's honor, King George III swore the Duchess would swing from the gallows unless she immediately returned the necklace, and soon had her arrested. Perhaps she thought it beautiful enough to die for."

The Frenchwoman's eyes shone as she concluded her story.

"Everyone in London thinks the Duchess will deny her guilt all the way to the gallows," Agnes added. "But at the last minute, a few believe she might confess her crime."

Agnes said the French aristocrat would ride to the gallows in a fine black mourning coach commissioned for the day, with her black coffin strapped atop the coach. The coach would move west out of the City of London, through the crowds along Holborn, St Giles, and then up Tyburn Road to the gallows at Hyde Park.

The ill-fated procession would be led by the City Marshal and the Under Sheriffs of London astride their very finest horses, she said, to part the crowds. Londoners who dared rush the coach would be beat back by marshal-men, javelin-men on horseback, and constables armed with staves.

Heathcliff helped Agnes out of the coach under a dark cold sky. They pushed their way through a chaos of vendors hawking food and souvenirs into the enormous, milling crowd.

A deafening shout went up. "A black coach! She's coming!"

Over the heads of the crowd, Heathcliff glimpsed an elegant black coffin strapped onto the top of a coach rocking around a corner nearly a block away.

The Frenchwoman pushed Heathcliff forward when the Under Sheriffs trotted past. Heathcliff glimpsed four large, muscular horses draped in black silk, pulling the coach through the crowded streets. Just ahead of the horses, men swung long wooden staves to keep back the crowds. All manner of people cheered and whistled as the coach drew near, many shouting for a word from the Duchess.

In a fine black hat and veil, a sickly-looking lady opened the coach window and leaned out to address the crowd.

"I swear I am innocent!" she cried in English. "I swear before Christ I am pure as falling snow!"

A roar rose up from the crowd, as from the belly of a great beast. A boy heaved a live dog against the coffin. The Duchess retreated into the coach. Rotten vegetables and eggs splashed against the carriage and coachman as he whipped the four sweating, heaving horses forward into the crowd.

"Thief!" cried an old crone. "French thief!

"Hang her! Draw and quarter the bitch."

Heathcliff and Agnes moved with the flow of people hurrying to St. Sepulchre's Church, opposite Old Bailey. Someone tossed a white pigeon from the church belfry to signal the approach of the coach. Heathcliff watched the pigeon suddenly take flight above the crowd.

St. Sepulchre's great bronze bell began to toll. It rang continuously until the coach halted before the church.

Through the double doors came the archdeacon in a white alb, dalmatic and cincture, and a long, embroidered cope. Three pale-faced young boys in purple robes hurried after him, holding sticks topped with ornamental wooden crosses painted gold.

The archdeacon slowly approached the coach.

The great crowd surged toward him like sharks in the water, but they fell silent when he raised one arm in the air.

HEATHCLIFF: THE LOST YEARS

"You that are condemned to die, although not of English blood, repent with lamentable tears; ask mercy of the Lord for the salvation of your soul," cried the archdeacon.

As the crowd roared, the three boys stepped forward to touch the coffin with the tip of their crosses. Two little girls in white dresses burst from the church and tossed flowers into the coach. Heathcliff glimpsed the woman inside the coach, her face buried in a floral bouquet.

"All good people pray unto God for this poor sinner who now goes to her death, a sinner for whom the Almighty bells of Heaven toll," the archdeacon cried, backing away and lifting both arms to the sky.

The great bells rang and rang and rang as the black coach began to slowly move away through the crowd.

"This way!" Agnes shouted.

Taking his hand, Agnes pulled Heathcliff past the grandstands of Mother Proctor's Pews opposite the gallows, which were already filled to capacity.

Vendors prowled back and forth before the stands. A man with twenty hats stacked atop his head sold hats. Boys hawked listening and looking-devices. An old woman offered oranges from a wheelbarrow while one-legged girl sold cordial glasses of gin.

Agnes clutched Heathcliff's arm. "The coach will go to Mason's Arms. The Duchess will receive her last drink. We must move quickly."

Agnes pulled him toward a large three-story building across the street from the gallows. It was owned by the Sheriffs of London and the Under Sheriffs of Middlesex, she told him, and they had invited a thousand guests. The iron balconies of the building, already packed with spectators, hung out precariously over the milling crowd.

The Frenchwoman led him around the house to a back door. A stern-faced man with a Blunderbuss tucked into his belt stepped into their path. Agnes took Heathcliff's arm.

"We are the invited guests of Lord Martingale, whom we are to meet inside," Agnes explained, lifting her veil with one hand to peer at the man.

"I am Lady Diver. I am accompanied by Baron Fischer, a second cousin of Lord Martingale's."

The man bowed his head and stepped aside. They passed quickly up the stairs and into the insanely crowded house. Heathcliff stopped Agnes at the foot of the stairs.

"Are you Lady Diver, then?" Heathcliff whispered.

"You don't believe the Sheriffs of London would invite me into their house?" Agnes said. "When you address to me to-day, address me as Lady Diver. If I call you anything, I will address you as baron, or Mr. Fisher."

In several very crowded rooms, a fire crackled in the hearth, with chairs and sofas around the fire. Other rooms contained tables heaped high with food. Uniformed servants bumped through the guests with trays containing sampler glasses of wine and beer, and cups and pots of coffee and tea.

Heathcliff had seen nothing like it. Heavily-powdered aristocratic ladies accompanied by gentleman in periwigs drifted happily about. In the corners of many rooms, big-chested Sheriffs held forth about the details of the hanging.

Agnes moved with great confidence from room to stuffy room. The Frenchwoman nodded briskly at the ladies. She paused occasionally to smile and banter with one or another of the portly gentlemen, then quickly moved on.

Heathcliff felt intimidated and exhilarated by it all. He felt himself blush and smile as ladies and gentlemen jostled and bumped him from either side. He was still blushing when Agnes pulled him up a crowded stairway and onto a wrought-iron balcony on the third story of the house, where the air blew cold and fresh.

Below them, a shifting, pushing mob swirled around the mourning coach like a whirlpool made of human beings. Here and there, hawkers lifted up food and souvenirs over the heads of the crowd.

The coach had stopped less than a hundred yards from the gallows. Marshal-men tugged at a small boy holding fast to a hand-rail of the coffin. A group of drunken men tried to pull open the coach door. Others rocked the coach from side to side while javelin-men poked and clubbed the surging crowds away.

"The coach cannot move," said the Frenchwoman. "The crowd is eager for blood. Come, let's go back inside and spread the news."

In a room on the second floor, Agnes advised Heathcliff to help himself to the feast spread out upon the table, and disappeared. He picked at the food with a tiny fork, watching well-dressed ladies and gentlemen move like brightly-coloured fish to and from the table, plucking up food with their fingers as they came and went.

"Are these fine ladies and gentlemen your friends?" he whispered when Agnes re-joined him. Having had two glasses of beer, Heathcliff had begun to rather enjoy himself.

"When you eat your fill, meet me on the lower balcony," Agnes replied. "I fear we must leave shortly."

Heathcliff made his way onto the second-story balcony in time to see the hangman ease down from his perch atop the gallows. The black coach stopped below the sturdy triangle of death. From three wooden timbers joined at the top dangled the rope and noose.

A roar arose from the crowd as the woman in black stepped from the coach and tripped down an aisle of javelin-men. She stepped onto the gallows and bowed her head before the hangman. The roar grew louder as the hangman turned her to face the crowd and pinioned her elbows behind her, leaving her hands free to pray.

In the deafening roar, the doomed aristocrat showed her teeth and defiantly shook out her hair. She shouted at the crowd as the hangman placed the noose around her neck but Heathcliff could not hear her last words. He watched the hangman pull a white cloth cap over her head, and she folded her hands in penitential prayer.

"We must go." Agnes tugged at his sleeve.

Agnes led Heathcliff downstairs and out the back door of the house. They hurried through a small rose garden, out the rear gate, and walked down an alley to meet the coach.

Heathcliff could hear the crowds behind them, roaring.

Neither of them saw the trap door beneath the gallows swing open. They did not see the woman plummet eight feet down to her death, her neck snapped in the sudden jerk of the noose. Heathcliff heard only the crowd's loud, approving roar as the coach hurried away and a few sad flakes of snow began to fall.

Newspapers would report the Duchess swung before the crowds for a full hour until the hangman pulled down her corpse. Her fine black dress would be stripped from her body, of course, as property of the hangman who also placed her body in the coffin. The rope that snapped her aristocratic neck would be cut into lengths and sold for souvenirs. Before they arrived back at the Metropole, Agnes told him the print shops of London were already printing copies of the Duchess of Burgundy's last words.

Out the coach window, Heathcliff watched snowflakes fall onto London. He turned to stare at Agnes Sorel, who clutched her satchel to her chest and looked wistfully out the other window.

The bold, mysterious Frenchwoman enchanted him. She seemed a character sprung to life from a fairy tale, a fairy tale which had enlarged to include his life.

To accompany the lovely Frenchwoman to such a grand event and to brazenly mingle with the finest gentlemen and women in London stoked the fires of ambition smoldering within the young man. At that particular moment, Heathcliff believed Agnes Sorel might possess the keys to all he desired in the world.

Chapter 95

Heathcliff **walked the Frenchwoman** to her door. When she unlocked it, she turned to him in the doorway. She squeezed his hands and looked up into his eyes. Quite naturally, Heathcliff slipped his arms around her waist and kissed her.

Into her room they danced, through the door she kicked shut with her small foot, groaning past her mirror into the wall, arms entwined, gasping, the two of them locked together. With one hand, Agnes tossed her satchel into the closet. Her mouth opened, her tongue snaked into his mouth and he fought to possess her, all of her, pulling her waist and hips against his body as if to split her in half.

Agnes playfully pushed him down onto her bed. To his delight, she began to remove her clothes.

"Do take off your shoes, Mr. Heathcliff," she said.

Heathcliff undressed. Agnes slipped out of her dress as gracefully as if rising from a bath. She hung her dress on a brass hook in a fastidious dainty way that touched him, then carefully hung her hat beside the dress and removed her stockings, her undergarments, and her stays.

She joined him in bed, both of them naked. He encircled her body with his arms. He longingly kissed her with his hands and mouth, his mouth on her nipples, lusting to hold and possess her, to join and capture her. When his lips moved down her smooth white belly and he kissed her navel, Agnes spread her legs and guided his head into the moisture between her legs. In a haze of perfume and sweat, her body rose up to greet him, as wet and salty as the sea.

When she tugged at his arms, he slithered up between her legs, over her, and slid easily into her wetness. At last, rearing up like a great thundering wave, he released everything he had inside her.

The next morning, Heathcliff opened his eyes to the sight of the Frenchwoman's beautiful face, and her hand shaking him awake. He noticed a pleasant smell in the room.

"And did you enjoy our hanging, sir?" Agnes asked.

"Yes, I did," he replied. He rose from her bed on one elbow, took her hand, and kissed it. "And I loved every sweet delicious moment that followed."

The Frenchwoman offered him a small gift in a paper bag—two warm croissants and a chunk of white cheese purchased that morning at a *patisserie*. When he opened the bag, the crisp smell of the bakery enlivened the room.

Agnes placed two newspapers containing vivid accounts of the hanging on his pillow and flung open her bedroom window to the cold. Heathcliff rose to his feet and put his arms around her. Below them lay the spectacle of London's cobblestone streets and rooftops dusted with snow.

"We must go to the East End," Agnes said, "I wish to see Mr. Pincher's military recruiters. Would you accompany me, good sir?"

"Agnes, I will accompany you anywhere," Heathcliff said, kissing her neck. "But look there—the entire city is covered with snow. We'll have time for that to-morrow, or the day after, or the day after that."

Agnes giggled a little and turned round to face him, keeping her body encircled in his arms. Before long they were in bed again.

HEATHCLIFF: THE LOST YEARS

That morning, and again that evening, Heathcliff discovered the beautiful Frenchwoman knew ten thousand delightful ways of kissing him, and even more ways of gleefully and passionately making love.

Chapter 96

Several days later, Agnes led Heathcliff to a hackney stop not far away. A yellow Flying Coach trimmed in red and black carried them to the East End. They arrived at dusk. Heathcliff stepped out into the cold; he noticed his breath making clouds in the air.

"Link boy!" Agnes cried.

A ragged boy of about ten years old shuffled forward. "Here, ma'am."

"Show us to the military recruiters. I believe they are quite close by."

"They're out on the square, ma'am. Follow me." The link boy blew on the end of his torch, which burst into flame, and led them away.

They followed him to a huge bonfire crackling in the middle of a public square. Ragged men, women, and children streaming out from surrounding factories stopped by the bonfire to warm their hands. Not far from the fire, a red-coated recruiter motioned them to his small table, handing all that wanted a drink cannikins of gin.

Heathcliff and Agnes moved behind a group of shabbily-dressed young factory workers who were grouped around a raised platform, seemingly entranced by the speaker.

HEATHCLIFF: THE LOST YEARS

On the platform, standing next to an easel, a red-coated English army recruiter flashed a great handful of bank-notes.

"I've a twenty-pound bonus for any of you lads to claim tonight!" cried the recruiter, holding high the banknotes. "Where's the good brave lad who will fight for our King?"

The recruiter turned to his easel. He unrolled a poster containing a caricature of General George Washington. The cartoon general wore a motley uniform; red horns protruded from his wig and he held a small black pitchfork in one hand.

"The Devil's jumped up in our colonies! We need some English boys to give the traitor a good thrashing! Where's the brave young lad will help King George?" cried the recruiter, flamboyantly waving the banknotes over his head. "Enlistment bonus! Big bonus to-night, lads! Twenty English pounds!"

A pale young factory worker who looked to be about thirteen years old raised his hand and staggered forward through the crowd.

"I'll fight for my King! I'm not afraid!" cried the boy, turning to scowl at his companions in the crowd.

"Step over to our recruiting table, lad," said the recruiter, who pointed out the table. "Our good bursar has twenty pounds for you to-night!"

"I have to tell me Mum," said the boy.

"Go home and get your Mum. Bring Mum back to-night and we'll give your *Mum* twenty pounds!" the recruiter said. "That's a good boy."

A red-coated drummer boy standing behind the bursar rolled his snare drum as the boy hurried away.

"Twenty English pounds!" cried the recruiter. "Where's our next brave lad?"

Agnes clutched Heathcliff's arm, her eyes twinkling. Another young man approached the recruiter, pulling a reluctant, sniffling young woman behind him.

"I'll gladly fight for the king—but I'm married, sir," said the young man. "What might you do to make my poor wife happy?"

+ [318] +

"A married man! We've *forty* pounds for the two of you, sir!" crowed the recruiter, pointing at the young man while addressing the crowd. "This brave young lad will leave a pretty wife at home to fight for the king! Ladies and gentlemen, witness a good, brave English patriot standing before you!"

The recruiter leaped from the platform. He put his arm around the young man and his wife, then turned them to face the crowd. As the bonfire popped, he pressed some banknotes into the young wife's hand.

"I shall give twenty pounds from King George to your lovely wife. This advance is all hers this very night, and may it comfort her!"

A cheer went up. The recruiter pointed to the red-coated bursar, who nodded and waved from his table. The snare drum rolled again.

"Go speak with our bursar, lad. Go home with your little woman to-night and give her a good long kiss goodbye!" he told the boy. "Bring her back to-morrow with your certificate of marriage and we'll give your little wife an additional signing bonus of twenty more pounds to keep her safe while you're away! God bless you, lad! And God Save the King!"

"God Save the King!" cried the crowd.

"I'll bring him back to you to-morrow night, sir, I promise," cried his wife, as her husband pulled her toward the bursar's table.

After a vigorous roll of the drum, members of the crowd began drifting away in the cold. The recruiter leaped from the platform to the bonfire, grabbed a burning faggot, and set fire to the poster of George Washington. The paper Devil undulated in flames as it burned.

"Come back to-morrow! Bring the lads! King George III offers a handsome bonus to good English fighting men!"

Agnes signaled the link boy, who loitered at the edge of the crowd. The lad saw her and blew on his torch. Holding high the sputtering torch, he led Heathcliff and Agnes away.

At the hackney stop, Agnes gave the link boy two pennies. Then they waited for the Flying Coach home.

HEATHCLIFF: THE LOST YEARS

"Forty pounds for a married man!" Agnes exclaimed, her breath forming small clouds. "Twenty pounds in advance!"

The Frenchwoman's eyes twinkled. She playfully pinched Heathcliff's buttocks, looked away, and quietly giggled. They rubbed their hands together to keep them warm.

Chapter 97

Over the next few weeks, Heathcliff spent more time with Agnes Sorel. The first time they walked into the dining room of the Metropole together, Heathcliff drew envious glances and snorts from many of the men, including Peter Pincher. Several gentlemen stopped speaking to him, but the armaments maker maintained his ebullient friendliness, entertaining them with polite chatter about the progress of the war.

Agnes sometimes went away in a coach alone. On other occasions, she requested Heathcliff's company.

Heathcliff did not think to ask Agnes where she went, or how she paid for her enchanted life. She seemed like a magical creature to him, able to sustain herself by merely breathing air. Agnes did advise him to spend time in particular coffee houses, learning what he could and listening for opportunities. Since he had a good sum of money left, he followed her rather pleasant advice.

As their lives entwined, Heathcliff spent more time in her living quarters, and she in his. One night, Agnes showed him a handsome amount of cash she kept in a cloth bag pinned to the back of a drawer in her room. A few days later, Heathcliff showed Agnes the stash of English banknotes he kept in a pocket-book clipped to the bottom of his rope bed.

HEATHCLIFF: THE LOST YEARS

Agnes did not ask Heathcliff how he acquired his money, and he did not ask how she acquired hers. It hardly seemed to matter. He loved her childlike talk of squirreling away money, and her obvious pleasure at securing a good bargain on hats and pretty clothes.

"I shall take you to the theatre," Agnes announced one morning, as if she had awakened with the idea in her head.

"I should like that."

"Your garments are unsuitable. If you wish to accompany me to the theatre, you must dress like a gentleman," she said. "This week, we shall find you some proper clothes."

Agnes took him around to the tailor shops. Very discreetly, she asked about castaway gentleman's clothes. Garments commissioned by aristocratic gentlemen but never picked up and paid for, Heathcliff learned, could be had for a modest price.

Heathcliff found a handsome greatcoat, an embroidered wool suit, a stylish long waistcoat and matching breeches; a tailor happily took them in to fit him. At another shop, Heathcliff purchased a cream-coloured linen shirt with ruffled sleeves, a cream-coloured silk cravat, and silk stockings to go with his new shoes. At still another shop he purchased a pair of soft kid gloves, with Agnes helping him negotiate a surprisingly reasonable price.

At the Frenchwoman's urging, he tried on several periwigs, but found nothing that pleased her. Heathcliff thought it odd to have a woman leading him all over London and making bargains for him, but the close attention secretly flattered him.

A private coach took them to the King's Theatre, Haymarket. They arrived in Westminister before dark.

Well-dressed gentlemen and ladies stepped grandly from their coaches before the triple arches of the King's Theatre's brick façade. Agnes pointed out the theatre's impressive frontispiece, commissioned from the famous painter Thomas Gainsborough for quite a handsome fee.

They found seats in the first balcony beneath an ornately-painted ceiling festooned by hanging crystal chandeliers. Below the balcony, Heathcliff watched a crowd of well-dressed gentlemen and ladies move to their seats. At the far end of the room a red velvet curtain concealed the great arch of the stage.

The theatre smelled of new fabric, tobacco, beeswax, and a mixture of exotic perfumes. As the air warmed, Agnes extracted an ornamental fan from her satchel and began languidly fanning herself.

"I feel I have been brought to an enormous palace built to entertain a very great, great king," Heathcliff said, looking innocently around. "In fact, I fancy I might easily pass for an aristocrat myself."

"In your new clothes, a few might mistake you for a gentleman, Heathcliff, but you are not. You must keep your mouth shut. You gawk and talk like a bumpkin from the country," Agnes snapped behind her fan.

"English gentlemen come here often and are they are not at all so impressed. To be bored with the best of London is all the manner. Look at the gentlemen below and take note of what you see."

Heathcliff was already blushing. Beneath the balcony, he observed well-dressed gentlemen sauntering down the aisles. All the gentlemen did look vaguely bored. A few actually yawned. Well-dressed ladies quietly vied for their attention as gentlemen languidly strolled past their seats but most of the gentlemen appeared supremely disinterested and did not bother to respond.

A bell rang. A bustle rippled through the crowd. The curtain parted to reveal what appeared to be a dark forest on a moonlit night.

A large black cauldron steamed before the foot-lamps, churned by three hideously ugly crones. A handsome soldier entered with a friend, fresh from the wars. In riddling verse, the witches predicted the soldier would become King of Scotland. The prophecy perplexed both men.

HEATHCLIFF: THE LOST YEARS

The soldier's wife confronted him in the bedroom of their castle, wearing a peaked red cap and scarlet gown. Her eyes flashed angrily as she spoke, beating her breast and speaking of what he must now do to become king.

The wife's passionate plea thrilled Heathcliff, who marveled at the soldier's indecision.

The curtains closed for intermission, to whistling applause.

"Accompany me outside. They will be talking of Mrs. Siddens," Agnes said, rising to her feet with the others.

Outside the theatre, groups of well-dressed gentlemen stood about, many of them smoking. A gentleman in a brown cape relieved himself against a wall, staring listlessly over one shoulder. Gentlemen nodded politely at the ladies as they passed although many ignored them.

Twice the Frenchwoman clumsily stumbled, accidentally pushing Heathcliff into a startled, well-heeled gentleman. Each time, the man pushed Heathcliff away with an indignant look. Heathcliff backed up and stammered out an apology while Agnes flitted between them, her small hands patting the indignant gentleman's chest, soothing him, smiling flirtatiously and cooing in French before moving away.

"Why do you speak French to them, Agnes? Englishmen may not understand you," Heathcliff said on the way back into the theatre.

Agnes smiled serenely, and did not reply.

After the play, they walked outside the theatre. Agnes stumbled. She pushed Heathcliff into a bewigged old gentleman standing with his elegantly-coiffed wife. The couple stood quietly awaiting their coach. Both the man and his wife looked indignantly down their noses at Heathcliff, like two figurines frozen in ice. Heathcliff lamely attempted an apology.

Agnes moved between them, cooing at the gentleman in French. She stroked the old gentleman's chest and arms, profusely apologizing in rapid-fire French, curtseying before them and almost breaking into tears before pulling Heathcliff away.

"Around the corner, to the coach," Agnes whispered, breaking from the crowd and walking briskly.

"Is it over?" he asked.

They jumped into her coach and sped away. Heathcliff thought the theatre quite exciting.

"But why did you push me into those gentlemen?" Heathcliff asked. "I felt like a fool."

"When a man mingles with the very wealthy, Heathcliff, he must always anticipate whatever duplicities which might occur," Agnes sniffed.

She gave him a sweet, condescending smile.

Heathcliff did not really understand what she said. He suspected Agnes thought the incidents were his fault. He felt too embarrassed to ask the Frenchwoman to explain.

Chapter 98

Heathcliff sometimes felt Agnes was preparing him for something grand. He did not speak to her of his feeling, and he did not yet understand what the grand thing might be, but the Frenchwoman dropped what he took as tantalizing hints as she introduced him to the pleasures of the city. These thoughts curried his ambition. As the days passed, he trusted her more each day.

One morning in April, Agnes rose at first light. Heathcliff heard her moving about the room in the near darkness, but he went back to sleep in her warm bed. He awoke to the aroma of the *patisserie* and Agnes tearing off tiny bits of bread and cheese and placing them into his mouth as if he were a pampered child.

"This morning, my darling, you must do a little favour for me."

"Of course," Heathcliff replied.

From her closet, Agnes took out a plain canvas sack closed with a drawstring.

"Take this to London Bridge and toss it into the Thames," she said.

He looked at the sack, puzzled. "What is it?"

"It contains several old things which I do not want—gifts from old admirers which mean nothing at all to me now." She smiled wearily. "It would tire me to explain them all. Will you help me?"

"Agnes, I will do anything for you."

She broke off a small piece of cheese, placed it in his mouth, and then kissed him.

After Heathcliff put on his clothes, he picked up the sack. It weighed very little. He flung the sack over his shoulder and walked out the door on a gloomy winter's day.

He heard the bells of St. Paul's ring ten o'clock as he walked through the city toward the Thames. A woman flung the contents of a chamber pot from a third-story window and urine fluttered into the street.

"Hey!"

Heathcliff jumped into a doorway. He cautiously looked overhead, but saw no one at the window. A horse and wagon splashed down the street through a rivulet of sewage and he again backed up against the door.

As the wagon passed, he idly opened the bag and looked inside. At the bottom of the bag were pigskin and leather pocket-books, wallets, and a several embroidered coin-purses. Heathcliff fished one out and looked inside. The coin-purse was completely empty. Several others were empty, likely they all were. As he stepped into the street, this puzzled him.

The crowds began to thicken as he approached London Bridge, the sack slung over his shoulder. He waded through a small flock of sheep. He pushed his way onto the bridge past people, horses, and push-carts. Part-way across, he elbowed his way to the lower side of the bridge.

Holding the sack to his chest, Heathcliff waited for a barge to pass below, then dropped it into the broad, grey-green, slowly-flowing river. The bag floated away astride the water like a bubble half-full of air.

On the way back to the Metropole, the bells of St. Paul's rang twelve noon. Heathcliff puzzled over the mystery of the empty coin-purses all the way home. Agnes' face dropped when he stepped into her room.

"You have discovered my secret, as I hoped that you would not do," she said.

"Agnes, I don't understand."

"You looked into my sack."

"Yes."

"Then you know that I am a pickpocket," she said.

"No. I do not know that."

"You think the worst of me now," she said, her voice trembling. "Even as I share your bed I am nothing to you."

"Dear Agnes," he moved toward her, his voice thick with emotion. "Please, don't say that. I adore you."

Agnes backed away, trembling.

"An unmarried woman in London! How would you have me live?" Agnes cried. "Your factories turn little girls into crones! Women sell their bodies in alleyways, for two shillings. Would you have my name in *The Whoremonger's Guide*? Would you have me sell my body, which I give now only to you?"

"What you say is ridiculous."

Heathcliff tried to understand but a surge of anger overcame him. He lunged for the door, overwhelmed by all she said.

"You are angry," she said.

Heathcliff stopped at the door and whirled to face her.

"You used me, Agnes! You used me to distract those gentlemen while you stole their purses. You used me at the theatre! You used me at the hanging! I believed you an honourable woman, but you are a thief!"

"And where did you get *your* money, sir?" she demanded. "All that money you hide away in your room? And you dare to call yourself a gentleman?"

Before Heathcliff could reply, Agnes stepped forward and slapped him in the face.

"I am exactly what you want me to be!" Agnes shouted. "I give you the gift of my body! You break my heart! You cannot condemn me until you know all the struggles of my life!"

Heathcliff pulled open the door to leave. Agnes stepped forward and blocked his departure with her own body.

"Heathcliff, control yourself!" Agnes hissed. "Your terrible anger turns you into a fool! If you cannot control your anger you will lose everything you desire in the world!"

Her words struck home. Heathcliff closed the door. He wished to flee but he could not leave the room. He felt short of breath. He leaned back against the door.

Agnes slipped forward and took his arm. She placed an index finger on his lips.

"Until you know all I have endured, Heathcliff, you must never question me again."

Agnes opened her mouth to kiss him. With a rush of feeling, he pressed her tightly into his arms.

Chapter 99

At dinner a few days later, Peter Pincher invited Heathcliff to visit his business on the East End. This time, Agnes encouraged him to go. Early the next morning, and somewhat dutifully, Heathcliff caught a hackney coach with Mr. Pincher and set out to see his factory.

"At last you shall see the workings of my enterprise," the factory owner said. He seemed delighted to have Heathcliff along.

Peter Pincher happily showed Heathcliff all around his rather large, dreary building. He explained his factory's operations in some detail, and with a great deal of pride. Heathcliff saw black powder being mixed, dried, and weighed out into barrels. Young boys with smudged faces and black hands pushed small carts to and fro across the factory floor.

"What do you think, sir?" asked the factory owner. "Does this manner of business interest you?"

"It is a curious enterprise," Heathcliff politely replied. "Honestly, I do not know exactly what to think of this. But I thank you for showing me around."

But when Heathcliff returned to the Metropole that afternoon, he found the door to his quarters ajar. He always locked his room.

He pushed on the open door. Someone had pulled out the drawers of his dressing-cabinet. His shirts and stockings lay scattered about the floor. Looking under his bed in a panic, Heathcliff discovered his stash of bank notes missing. With the exception of a few coins in his pocket, he had been robbed of all the money he had in the world.

He hurried to tell Agnes. He found the door to her room partially open. Glancing inside, he noticed her garments scattered about. Agnes had been robbed, too.

Heathcliff could not locate the proprietor anywhere. Impatiently, he waited for Agnes outside the building. He paced up and down the street until Agnes arrived on foot.

"Agnes, we have been robbed! My money is gone. I think you have been robbed, too."

"What?" she cried.

Agnes yanked out the drawer under which she hid her savings. When she looked beneath the drawer and saw her money gone, she dropped the drawer and collapsed back onto the bed.

"Robbed!" she said. "Ruined!"

"Who would steal from us, like that, from both of us?" Heathcliff asked. "Who would know?"

"There are thieves on every street-corner in London, Heathcliff. Our idiot proprietor leaves our front door unlocked and never changes out the keys."

"We must speak to him immediately," Heathcliff said.

"No! You will say nothing to that horrible man! He always makes problems for me with his nosey questions."

Agnes rose to her feet.

"Leave me alone, Heathcliff. I will think on this. You must trust me—I will think of something."

That evening, the Frenchwoman seemed quiet and subdued when she entered the dining room. But after dinner, when they went to her room, Agnes revealed her plan.

HEATHCLIFF: THE LOST YEARS

"To-morrow you will marry me, Heathcliff. We shall visit your military recruiters and then we shall have twenty pounds."

Chapter 100

Heathcliff's hasty marriage took place in a dusty old shop not far from Fleet Street Prison. The little shop smelled of gin. A drunken man in an off-centre goat's hair wig tottered out of the back room, his face partially shaven. He placed their hands together on a Bible and hurried them through the vows.

Agnes paid him a few shillings to forego the posting of the banns. Heathcliff signed a bond. The man entered their names into his book and presented them a marriage license.

Quick as it was, the marriage was quite sobering for Heathcliff. As he recited the endearing words of the vows, swearing to honour and obey until parted by death, Heathcliff felt a surge of great tenderness for Agnes. But the minute they left the shop, his new wife snatched their marriage license from his hands.

"To-night, this will fetch us twenty pounds!" she said.

They hurried across London in the twilight. When a wheel fell off the crowded hackney, they were forced to get out, wait, crowd aboard another Flying Coach, and pay a second time. The air was chilly and damp when they arrived and found their way to the military recruiters on the square where a new military recruiter harangued a somewhat smaller crowd.

HEATHCLIFF: THE LOST YEARS

"King George III needs five thousand good men with courage in their hearts and fire in their belly, and he'll have his five thousand men this year!" cried the recruiter, holding up banknotes in both hands. "I've twenty pounds for the first brave lad steps forward tonight!"

"That's me, sir," cried a very young man.

A diminutive youth hurried forward. The recruiter stopped him short. He measured the lad's height against a stick and then nodded his approval to the crowd.

"Five feet of good English fighting man off to the recruiting table," said the recruiter. "That way, lad. Our bursar has twenty pounds for you."

A snare drum pattered as the boy hurried to the table. The burser lifted one of the boy's hands and led the crowd in applause. Heathcliff took a deep breath and pulled Agnes forward through the crowd.

"I'm willing to fight for our king!" he shouted.

"But we're married, good sir," Agnes cried, clutching Heathcliff's hand. "We've no money at all and little children to feed!"

"I'll give you twenty pounds to help feed your wee ones to-night, good woman, and we'll have twenty more for you to-morrow," said the recruiter.

He jumped from the platform and clutched Heathcliff's shoulders, looking him up and down. "You'll make a fine soldier, lad. Go collect your twenty pounds! Accompany your little wife to the bursar."

To a smattering of applause, and a very loud drum roll, Heathcliff and Agnes hurried past the bonfire to the recruiting table which lay on the opposite side of the fire.

A hawk-nosed bursar sat erect at his recruiting table, flanked by two muscular British soldiers. The uniformed old soldier lifted his big nose and squinted at Heathcliff as they approached.

"You say you are married, lad?"

"I have my wife right here beside me," said Heathcliff.

Smiling sweetly, Agnes showed the man their marriage certificate.

"Married at the Fleet, and not so long ago!" clucked the bursar. "Very well, Mr. Heathcliff. Your little wife shall have twenty pounds to-night. Come back here to collect the balance to-morrow, after five o'clock."

Agnes opened her hands to receive the banknotes. Heathcliff signed a stack of documents that the bursar pushed his way.

"What time would you have me report for duty to-morrow?" Heathcliff asked the bursar. "I mean to be here promptly."

"To-morrow? Who is it told you to report to-morrow?"

Two soldiers stepped forward and took Heathcliff's arms. As Agnes watched, open-mouthed, the soldiers led Heathcliff away.

"I cannot report to-night!" Heathcliff protested, struggling to free his arms. "I must have one last night with my wife! I was promised that, gentleman."

From the corner of his eye, Heathcliff saw another poster of George Washington being set afire.

"This Devil will burn in Hell when our lads drive him from our colonies!" cried the recruiter. "Where's another brave young English lad will step up to-night and help King George?"

Soldiers threw Heathcliff into a military prison-wagon with several motley men, and locked the door. One of the pressed men lay on his back, smelling of gin, holding his both hands over his eyes and kicking away at the iron bars.

"Heathcliff!"

Heathcliff thought he saw his new wife run after the prison-wagon as it spirited away.

Chapter 101

After a long rough ride, Heathcliff and the other pressed men were pulled out of the prison-wagon in Woolwich, Kent, in the middle of the night. The lamps of the Royal Arsenal and Military Academy burned behind them.

"You don't dare run for it, lads—we'll shoot you as deserters," a uniformed soldier whispered.

Soldiers with bayonets fixed on their muskets marched the group to the end of a short, dark pier and loaded them into a boat at gunpoint.

Looming up before the launch was a great dark hulk, moored in the middle of the Thames. The abandoned ship retained only one of its masts; entirely stripped of its yards, sails, and rigging, the deck was covered in a tent made of net.

Heathcliff was the first of the pressed men to climb the sea-ladder and pull himself through an opening in the net.

"Stand back. Be silent," said an armed soldier who waited on deck with a lantern.

Heathcliff glanced about. A finely-woven rope net hung down from the top of the mainmast, fitted over the weather railing like a great grim spider web to prevent prisoners from escaping. The opening over the sea-ladder was the only break in the net he could see.

Behind them, on the southern shore, Heathcliff saw a light at the end of the dock and beyond that an orderly pattern of lanterns that marked the military installation. The north bank of the Thames lay in complete darkness. For an instant, twinkling through the nets, he glimpsed the North Star over the north shore.

"We'll all be taken over there, will we?" Heathcliff asked the soldier watching him, pointing to the dark side of the river.

"Nothing over there but grass and weeds," the soldier replied. "Stand back and be silent now."

When the last of the pressed men climbed aboard, an officer told the group they could expect to remain on the hulk for approximately three days while the army prepared their living quarters across the way. With a sort of laugh, the officer said the British Army would feed them well until they began military training.

Soldiers with bayonets marched the group below deck and into the forecastle. Given a military issue blanket, Heathcliff joined a group of about three dozen men locked in and trying to sleep on the rather crowded floor.

None of the pressed men had volunteered for the military training that awaited them. They were fed twice a day, and fed quite poorly. The atmosphere was volatile, with frequent arguments and fights.

The second day, Heathcliff sat down next to a red-headed Scotsman named Joseph who had dark bags under his eyes. Because of all the nits, he told Heathcliff, he refused to sleep on the floor in his fine clothes. Joseph had been trying to sleep standing up, with his back wedged into a corner. A week before, the Scotsman said, he had been pressed into service for gambling debts. He told Heathcliff he would do anything on earth except join the British Navy to get away.

"If you could get back up onto the deck, you might scramble over the side," Heathcliff said. "There is an opening in the net just over the sea-ladder."

"Eh?"

"You could part the net and jump into the river," Heathcliff said.

HEATHCLIFF: THE LOST YEARS

"The buggers would catch me and pull me from the river right away," said Joseph. "They'd shoot me as a deserter."

"At night they could hardly see you. If you make it to the far side of the river, there is no military there."

"Are you sure?"

"A soldier told me there was nothing there but weeds."

"Do you wish to run away then?" Joseph asked.

"I have a wife waiting for me, and I am no soldier."

"I've an idea how we might slip out of here, but I need another man to help me. Let me tell you what I think," Joseph said, drawing him closer.

The second and last meal of the day was served after dark. Four of the five guards were tasked with lugging heavy cast iron pots of soup into the forecastle and setting them down for the men amidst the usual grumbling. For a brief instant, Joseph had observed, only one soldier guarded the door. If they worked together, Joseph thought they might disarm the guard and get away.

The next evening, Heathcliff and Joseph loitered near the forecastle door. After the last of the steaming cauldrons was muscled in, Joseph moaned, clutched his stomach, and collapsed before the red-coated guard at the door. When the guard leaned over, Heathcliff pulled the musket from his hands and flung it away. At the same time, Joseph grabbed the guard's arms and pulled him to the floor.

"Hey!"

Heathcliff and Joseph scrambled out the door and up to the deck. Joseph turned about in the darkness, confused.

"I can't see," he whispered.

"This way," Heathcliff hissed, feeling his way toward what he thought was the location of the sea-ladder.

Three soldiers scrambled to the deck, one holding a lantern.

"Halt! Both of you! Halt right there!"

A wooden gate Heathcliff never saw before was closed and locked over the sea-ladder. Heathcliff kicked the little gate off its hinges and squeezed through the tangle of net feet first.

"Joseph! Over here!"

Heathcliff threw out his arms and leaped from the ship. He seemed to tumble down forever, into a maw of darkness. He smashed into the cold, foul stinging water and sank down into the depths. Paddling for his life, he struggled to the surface, gasping for breath.

Above him, a lantern moved along the deck of the hulk. Heathcliff thought he saw Joseph, captured. A soldier fired into the river.

Heathcliff kicked off his shoes and swam with the current. Past the end of the hulk he lost sight of the lantern. He became lost in the flowing expanse of ink-black water until he glimpsed Polaris.

Heathcliff paddled toward the North Star, fighting his way across the current and gasping for breath. For an eternity he swam, fearing he might die in the unforgiving river. The current was much stronger than he expected, but the fear of death energized him and he angrily willed himself toward the shore.

He swam like a dog, gasping and paddling quickly, both hands moving beneath him in the wet, eerily flowing darkness. His clothing restricted his movements, floating about him, and tugging at his limbs. Finally, at last, one hand touched mud.

His fingers clutched a clump of grass and he held on. With a great effort he pulled his exhausted body out of the moving river and onto his belly in the soft wet mud, still clutching the clump of grass, gasping like a fish flung out of the water.

Before he found the strength to rise, Heathcliff heard the plaintive bleating of a lamb, calling out for its mother in the darkness.

Chapter 102

Heathcliff made his way back into London, barefoot and exhausted. By midmorning, his mud-smeared clothing had dried on his back. He staggered through the front door of the Metropole very late that afternoon, the soles of his bare feet on fire. He carefully picked his way upstairs, wanting only to throw himself onto the bed he hadn't seen in four days.

He found the door to his room wide open. All his fine clothes were gone. His closet was completely empty except for the clothes he wore when he arrived in London. On the dresser lay a key to his room, marked with a snippet of red ribbon. It was the key he gave to Agnes. He limped to her door and knocked, but received no response.

Heathcliff sought out the proprietor, who barely glanced up when he approached.

"Where are my things, sir?" Heathcliff demanded. "Whoever has been in my room?"

Somewhat hastily, the proprietor pulled his spectacles from his pocket, unfolded them, and pulled them on.

"I am surprised you returned, Mr. Heathcliff. Your wife said you decided to join the King's army," he said.

"That is ridiculous, man! I am here!" Heathcliff hit his chest. "Can you not see me before you?"

"Your wife took away your things two days ago. She insisted that I refund the balance of your rent. She showed me your marriage license."

"Where is she?"

"A man came for her things early yesterday morning."

"Agnes is gone?"

"I am certain of that, sir."

"Where did she go?"

"The lady left no address with me."

Heathcliff turned away, devastated. He realized Agnes tricked him and cheated him. The Frenchwoman made off with his military bonus, and even took away his gentleman's clothes.

As Heathcliff trudged back to his room, it struck him that Agnes probably also stole the bank-notes he brought from Liverpool, since only she knew where he so carefully hid them. What she gave him was fakery and tears, a woman's ruse. He was truly a bumpkin from the country, as she once said. His city wife, if Agnes could even be called his wife, had disappeared with all he had in the world.

The realization crushed and humiliated him. And yet, as Heathcliff climbed into his bed ready to weep from sheer exhaustion, he wished he might hold the beautiful Frenchwoman in his arms again.

After a very lengthy nap, Heathcliff put on his old clothes and on aching feet descended to the dining room. He brooded darkly on the recent events of his life as he dined, still agog at the breadth of the Frenchwoman's deception.

"Mr. Heathcliff!" Peter Pincher clapped him on the back. "Top of the evening, sir!"

"Is it a good evening?" Heathcliff asked, without looking up.

"You look not well, sir, may I be so bold to observe," said Mr. Pincher. He plucked a fat leg of chicken from the platter passing by and lay it onto his plate before he sat down.

HEATHCLIFF: THE LOST YEARS

"I am not well to-night, Mr. Pincher," Heathcliff said.

"Whatever happened, sir?"

"Agnes has gone. She took all the money I had and left me with nothing."

Peter Pincher pursed his lips. He cut a thick slice of bread, buttered it with a bread knife, and dropped the buttered bread on Heathcliff's plate.

"Do not trust a Frenchwoman with your money or your life, sir," he sniffed, and turned his attention to the chicken.

"You gave me excellent advice."

Heathcliff watched the factory owner nip away the meat from his chicken leg. After he nipped it clean, Peter Pincher dropped the pale white bone onto his plate, plucked up a napkin to dry his lips, and met Heathcliff's eyes before he looked around for more chicken.

"Perhaps I have something to offer you, sir. I have experienced an unusual demand for black powder. I need someone to supervise my operations at night, a reliable man, someone I can trust," Peter Pincher said, fixing Heathcliff in his eyes.

"The pay will not be lavish at first, and it is hard work, but I offer you an opportunity. Might I interest you in this?"

Chapter 103

When **Heathcliff entered** the Serpentine Chemical Works for the second time, he counted more than one hundred and fifty young boys and girls hard at work.

The air inside the large, nondescript brick building had a grim heaviness borne of sulphur and smoke. The factory floor was crowded. Young employees laboured under a long row of high dirty windows by day and beneath the lamps at dark. The factory walls reverberated with the incessant sounds of metal mixers and hammers banging into pans.

With a war in the American colonies, and other wars likely to break out in other places, the Serpentine Chemical Works did enjoy a considerable demand. To capitalize on this opportunity, Peter Pincher told Heathcliff, the factory must produce gunpowder six days a week, twenty-four hours a day.

Wagonloads of saltpetre imported from British India arrived in the mornings, fresh from the docks. Tarpaulin-covered carts brought softwood willow charcoal. More wagons arrived late in the afternoon, heaped with bags of yellow sulphur. As wagons rolled into the loading dock, boys shoveled ingredients into large open bins in the rear of the factory, and other boys shoveled materials into wooden push-carts. Their push-carts heaped with ingredients, boys waited in a line before the factory's huge bronze vats and tubs.

HEATHCLIFF: THE LOST YEARS

Peter Pincher's secret wetting ingredient—a mixture of river water and cow's urine—he added to a mixture of 75 percent saltpetre, 15 percent charcoal, and 10 percent sulphur by weight. Boys spread the wet mixture onto metal pans, heated the pans over a coal fire, and pounded the resulting crust into granules, a process which required the hands of many boys and burned and crushed many little fingers.

Girls with sifting screens shook granules into pans containing three granule sizes; boys shoveled granules into wooden barrels while girls measured granules out into smaller tins. Barrels of black powder were stamped or labelled "Serpentine Chemical Company—Gunpowder" just above the company logo, the head of a skeleton ringed by a hooped black snake swallowing its tail.

The work was dirty and dangerous. The cooking and crushing made the air particularly foul.

Heathcliff soon learned that Peter Pincher paid the children very little. The factory owner's employees were young, he reasoned, and without children to support of their own. The boys were less reliable, he said, but good for heavier work, while little girls with nimble fingers could be relied upon to keep working through twelve and fourteen hour shifts whether they were sick or not.

Heathcliff noticed that one or another of the shovel boys, mixers, or crushers was forever breaking out into a fit of coughing, slipping away, or asking to be sent home. Some sustained frightful burns. Any child who complained of injuries, the factory owner instructed him, was to be immediately given a few pennies, fired, and sent home. A few children also slipped out the back door in the middle of the week and did not return, to Mr. Pincher's eternal dismay.

"You must keep constant watch on our little devils. It is important they work through the entire evening. Our materials are volatile and we have high standards to uphold," the factory owner said.

During the first few weeks, Heathcliff found himself bucking up tired little boys under the lanterns, or encouraging the little girls to keep working, and not to cry. Despite this, some children could hardly keep their eyes open.

Heathcliff forced himself to rouse and encourage any young worker he found asleep, although he himself felt drowsy in the early morning hours and was often in foul humour.

But barrel after barrel of gunpowder rolled out the door, almost all of it ordered by the British Army. Military wagons arrived early in the evening, just after dark. Uniformed soldiers supervised loading the barrels onto wagons, done by the larger boys under Heathcliff's direction. Afterwards, the military caravans pulled away into the night. Over time, Heathcliff became accustomed to supervising this process which occasionally dragged on for hours.

He and Peter Pincher soon settled into a routine. Six mornings a week, Peter Pincher arrived by hackney coach to supervise the factory's operations by day. At six o'clock, as the younger workers arrived, Heathcliff lit the lanterns over the shop floor and began his long night's work.

Heathcliff left the factory after Peter Pincher arrived. Sitting in a crowded hackney, his ears rang with the clatter and bang of the factory and the din of the crowded city springing to work around him. As time wore on, Heathcliff found himself longing for the smells and solitude of the countryside, or the comforting silence of the sea.

While London worked, Heathcliff slept with curtains drawn. Life became lonely and solitary. Sometimes he stopped to bargain with the sad young prostitutes who tugged at his sleeves on the street. When he took one to his room for a few moments of rough pleasure, he paid her as little as he possibly could, and soon showed her the door.

Sunday evenings, his day of rest, he dined with Peter Pincher at the Metropole.

The armaments maker seemed happy enough with their working arrangement. He gave Heathcliff considerable responsibility over the factory, and expressed pleasure at the production increases they achieved.

On several occasions, the factory owner hinted that he might make Heathcliff his partner in the business. However, he was also reluctant to raise Heathcliff's wages.

HEATHCLIFF: THE LOST YEARS

Peter Pincher granted Heathcliff an increase in salary only once, after Heathcliff had been employed for almost nine months and after he had asked for a raise several times.

Heathcliff **sometimes dreamed** of Catherine Earnshaw, whom he still loved with his fierce heart. To his surprise, his love for Catherine had grown stronger. At times he dreamed of returning to Wuthering Heights as a gentleman on a great horse, or in a fine expensive cabriolet.

But working in the factory, Heathcliff managed to put aside only a modest amount of money, and it was hardly enough to return. When he thought of how much money he would need to accomplish his dreams, his stomach tightened into a knot, and he put his back to his work.

More frequently now, unmarked wagons were arriving a few hours before the dawn. Coachmen in plain work clothes gave him documents signed in Peter Pincher's hand, and demanded their wagons be loaded at once so that they could be at the docks before daybreak.

A large fleet of unmarked wagons pulled up very late one night, driven by a group of rough, impatient men who had no patience with their teams. To Heathcliff's surprise, Peter Pincher showed up at the factory that night and waited to observe the loading.

"What are these strange wagons?" Heathcliff asked. "These are not British army transports."

"Your observation is correct," the factory owner admitted.

"I don't understand, sir."

"You are not required to understand this, Heathcliff," he snapped. "The details are none of your concern."

Peter Pincher spoke so harshly that Heathcliff turned away. But the factory owner thought better of it, and caught Heathcliff's arm.

"These wagons take black powder to the docks. The powder will be shipped to France, and from there to the American colonies."

"To the American colonies? Is that not against the law, sir?"

As they spoke, Heathcliff watched men fastening canvas tarpaulins over their wagons to conceal their contents.

"It may well be, but it's also good business," Peter Pincher said, with a twinkle in his eye.

"King George III pays me after the fact and makes me wait months for my money. The French pay in advance, they pay in full, and they always pay in gold."

At a sudden cracking of horsewhips, the loaded wagons rattled off into the night. When Heathcliff noticed sunlight hit the tallest factory windows, he wearily prepared to go home.

"Glorious things lie in store for you at the Serpentine Chemical Works, Mr. Heathcliff," said his benefactor, using exactly the same words Heathcliff had heard before. "We must make a bit more profit, of course. But if you work hard, I promise you one day I shall make you my partner."

Chapter 104

Before Heathcliff knew it, a full year of his life had passed. At the Serpentine Chemical Works, thrifty Peter Pincher continued to treat him much like a son. The man effusively praised his work, complimented his dedication, and rarely spoke to him harshly. The factory owner gave Heathcliff almost all the responsibility for managing his young labourers, but he did insist that Heathcliff come to work early every day and work deep into the night.

Although Heathcliff functioned much like a partner, he did not receive a partner's share of the pay. His modest salary forced him to live quite simply, and even then, he found it difficult to save. To his dismay, he realized he had less money tucked away than he had on the day he arrived in London. He was forever weary, and restless. When he realized he had been working for Peter Pincher for more than a year, he began to feel a kind of desperation about his plight.

One evening, two British military wagons arrived in the middle of the night. A uniformed soldier stepped from the lead wagon and Heathcliff immediately recognized him as Joseph, the Scotsman who helped him escape from the hulk. Heathcliff stepped back into the shadows and tried to avoid his eyes.

Joseph made no sign of recognition, but the sight of the him sent a prickle of fear coursing through Heathcliff's veins.

Stepping out of the hackney coach the next morning, Heathcliff noticed a woman in a formal dress run out the door of a fine brick town-house and hurry to the middle of the street. Her auburn ringlets flew about her shoulders and she clutched a small blue satchel. An agitated older gentleman followed the lady, barefoot and clad in only a long plaid flannel night-shirt. The rotund old gentleman waved one hand in the air.

"Mademoiselle!" he cried.

Heathcliff stared. Looking from side to side, the befuddled old gentleman seemed to suddenly realize he had come outside wearing only night-clothes. He slipped in a rivulet of sewage that ran beside the sidewalk. After nearly losing his balance, the man withdrew his bare feet and backed away.

The woman leaped before a hackney coach. Desperately waving her satchel, she stood firm as the coachman with some difficulty pulled up his team. Heathcliff recognized the woman. It was Agnes Sorel.

"Agnes!" Heathcliff cried.

The Frenchwoman scurried into the red and yellow Flying Coach, before it pulled away. Without thinking Heathcliff sprinted after the coach. He was nimble enough to jump onto a stair and hang onto the coach with one arm hooked through the open window.

The other passengers indignantly stared. Agnes looked away.

"Unscrupulous wench!" Heathcliff shouted. "You cheated me!"

Agnes ignored him. She looked straight ahead. Several passengers glared.

"Where is my money, Agnes?" Heathcliff demanded, slapping the coach door with his free hand.

As the hackney bounced along the cobblestones, an older gentleman poked Heathcliff's shoulder with the tip of his walking stick. "Do get off the coach, sir," he said. "Your behaviour will not do."

Agnes continued to ignore him as the coach rounded a corner and with some difficulty Heathcliff clung to the door.

HEATHCLIFF: THE LOST YEARS

At the next stop, Agnes slipped from the opposite side of the coach. Heathcliff watched her open the satchel, pay the coachman, and stuff some bank-notes into the bosom of her dress. By the time he reached her, the coach pulled away. Heathcliff caught Agnes by one arm.

"Agnes! Where is my *money*?" he demanded.

"That money was spent long ago, Heathcliff," the Frenchwoman said, handing him her empty satchel. "It's gone. I'm sorry. Goodbye."

"Agnes! You are my wife!"

"Our marriage license was not worth the paper it was written on, Heathcliff," she said. "Besides, I sold it long ago."

Heathcliff clung to her arm as Agnes hurried down the crowded street. The touch of her arm exhilarated him. He felt confused and angry, yet strangely delighted to see her again.

A wagon lumbered past. Heathcliff's fingers darted into the bosom of her dress. He plucked out the bank-notes hidden there.

Agnes slapped him. "Thief!" she hissed.

"This money is mine, and it's not even everything you took from me!" he shouted, shaking the bills in her face. "I suppose you have someone else now, another husband to sell off to the recruiters?"

"You may not believe me, but I married only you, Heathcliff," she said. "However, I do have a partner now."

"A partner?" he gasped.

"Must you be so naïve? John is a business acquaintance. Perhaps he could help you make some money, since you apparently have so very little."

Agnes danced aside and took Heathcliff's arm, her fingers light as feathers. The Frenchwoman smiled at him sweetly, melting him with her large hazel eyes.

Agnes had an extraordinarily beautiful mouth, he noticed again. He wanted nothing more than to hold her and kiss her again.

Heathcliff felt himself grow weak as she plucked the banknotes from his hand and tucked them back into the bosom of her dress.

He wanted her, but he did not trust her. But as he strolled down the street in the company of the beautiful Frenchwoman, feeling her hands on his arm, he did not want to lose her again.

He impulsively bought a bouquet of white roses from a vendor, and presented her with the bouquet. Agnes smelled the roses but returned them with a sad smile.

"Thank you for this small gesture, Heathcliff," she said. "It would turn the head of any English shop-girl. But I do have rather expensive tastes."

Hurt and surprised, Heathcliff placed the bouquet back into her hands. He looked into her eyes.

"Agnes, please. I work for Mr. Pincher. I have been his assistant for more than a year. Mr. Pincher has promised to make me a partner."

"Is he paying you with promises?"

"I am paid a salary," Heathcliff said, wincing a bit.

Agnes stopped to smell the bouquet. "A very large salary, befitting a partner?"

Heathcliff did not reply.

"Men of business don't give anything away, Heathcliff. They hold everything they have tight to their chests. You have to swindle their money away, or worse, try to charm them."

The Frenchwoman's words struck home. Agnes couldn't know that Peter Pincher refused to increase his wages several times, including the last time he asked just a week before. She couldn't possibly know that despite his frugality, he had accumulated precious little money.

Yet somehow, Heathcliff felt, Agnes already knew everything. Something akin to the old enchantment returned, the feeling that she was wiser than he in the ways of the world, and could teach him many things he did sorely need to know.

Pausing on the stoop of her new lodging, Agnes smiled sadly.

With a wistful sigh, and a note of finality, the Frenchwoman returned Heathcliff's bouquet and turned to unlock the door.

"I want to have expensive tastes, Agnes. I want to become a great gentleman worthy of you. I want to live in a grand house with you, and buy you all the beautiful things that you deserve, things grand enough to befit any gentleman's wife," Heathcliff blurted, also extending one hand to prevent her from opening the door.

"Damn it, Agnes," he added. "Don't leave me again. I have sorely missed you."

Impulsively he kissed her. When he pulled her small frame tight against his body, a pool of loneliness opened within him. Agnes clung to him for a moment, but she finally pulled back and broke off the kiss.

"Oh, blast it, Heathcliff," she said. "Come in."

Chapter 105

Heathcliff reunited with Agnes for a few delicious days of bliss, and long, sweet nights of delirious pleasure. Together they finished the bottle of gin Agnes kept by her bed, and went out for another. She awoke him in the morning with her light, airy voice, a matter-of-fact kiss, and sweetbreads from the *patisserie*. But Heathcliff did not feel so free and unrestrained with her as before. After he gave notice at the factory, he kept a careful watch on the Frenchwoman, and never left her alone with his wallet.

"I did miss you a little, Heathcliff," Agnes admitted only once. "But we must soon find a way to make some money."

One cold evening, Agnes put on some fine clothes and informed Heathcliff he must accompany her, but did not explain why. Their cab stopped on Mulberry Road, in a neighbourhood of grim three-story buildings Heathcliff had never seen before.

The light was dim under the street-lamps as they stepped from the cab into the cold night air. Agnes clutched his arm and led him away, their heels clicking against the cobblestones.

"My partner's name is John," Agnes explained. "John's rough as a cob. If he doesn't stick a knife into you, perhaps you'll get along."

HEATHCLIFF: THE LOST YEARS

Agnes led Heathcliff through a doorway and into a sumptuous gin palace. The high-ceilinged room smelled of juniper berries, tobacco, and perfume. A large crystal chandelier hung down from the ceiling and tapestries and mirrors adorned the walls of the candle-lit room. A few gentlemen loitered at small round tables scattered about the room, drinking and smoking.

At a table near the wall, a short, stocky man with thinning hair stood up and motioned them over. Before they sat down, the man scowled at the tall gentleman sitting at the next table. Heathcliff took a seat next to Agnes. A barmaid hurried toward the table with cordial glasses of gin.

"John, this is Heathcliff. The gentleman I mentioned before."

John Blighter chewed a small, half-smoked cigar. He fastened his small sharp eyes on Heathcliff, and eyed him suspiciously. Heathcliff extended his hand. Rather cautiously, John reached over the table and shook Heathcliff's hand with the tips of his fingers.

At the very next table, Heathcliff noticed a tall solitary man with a tricorne hat pushed far back on his head. The tall man held an empty cordial glass in both hands. He stared at his empty glass and rapped it against the table.

The sullen gentleman looked up with deep-set eyes. He stared at Heathcliff. He touched the butt of a flintlock pistol stuck in his belt, and his lips parted in a rictus smile. Heathcliff could not take his eyes off the man. Finally, the man lowered his gaze to again stare dumbly at his empty glass, and began rapping it on the table again.

Agnes lifted her glass of gin, and proposed a toast.

"To Heathcliff … King George's unknown soldier … and my dear, dear, dear husband."

John lifted his glass with a cynical smile.

"The little bitch give you the slip, did she?" he asked Heathcliff.

"She most certainly tried."

"I often say, where there's change in the world, there's opportunity," John said.

+ [354] +

"Yes," Heathcliff agreed. He thought for a moment of Peter Pincher and the job he left behind. "And when there's no change to be had, there's no opportunity at all."

"That's right," Agnes said.

"Some days, opportunities come knocking where you don't expect them," John said. "Some days, they follow you around like bloody debt collectors."

John smiled wickedly at Agnes. Agnes smiled at John in return.

Heathcliff forced a smile, but he felt left out. Agnes seemed to have some secret understanding with John; the cozy way they smiled at each other puzzled and annoyed him. Heathcliff began to suspect that Agnes was playing him for a fool. But Agnes reassuringly clutched his arm.

"Think about diamonds, *mon cheri*," she said.

"Have you any idea of the diamonds amassed by the aristocrats of France in the last fifty years?" John asked.

Heathcliff shook his head no.

"The French cannot get their fill of diamonds," John said. "They are quite greedy about them. I am told the daughters of French kings have diamonds sewn into the tips of their brassieres."

"When the gentlemen of the French court attempt to fondle a royal breast, they are often surprised by the precious stones they discover beneath their fingers," Agnes said.

John laughed heartily.

"The French are in love with beauty. The French made their finest diamonds into necklaces, but these were never enough. All the French aristocrats covet more," John added.

Agnes laughed. She and John looked into each other's eyes. John winked at Agnes.

Heathcliff's suspicions rose up again. He began to suspect he was being made the butt of some secret joke.

"It is possible you may find our association profitable, Mr. Heath-cliff," John said. "This little bitch and I are only two. We do need an

English gentleman of about your look and size, but the man must have nerves of steel."

"My nerves are steady enough, if it will yield a handsome profit for me," Heathcliff snapped, somewhat defensively.

"Mr. Heathcliff has sailed to Africa, and the Americas," Agnes said.

"A world traveler, you say?"

From the corner of his eye, Heathcliff saw the tall man at the next table jump to his feet. The man raised his arms and flew at Heathcliff like a dervish, knocking his own table aside.

With two large hands the surprisingly powerful gentleman lifted Heathcliff by his lapels and thrust him flopping like a fish against the mirror on the wall. Remembering the man's pistol, Heathcliff pulled it from his belt and pointed it at his head.

"If you don't shoot me, I shall kill you," the man hissed.

Heathcliff calmly pulled the trigger. He heard only a "click." The flintlock had not been loaded.

The tall gentleman glanced at John. He flashed his rictus smile and very gently set Heathcliff down.

The tall man plucked his pistol from Heathcliff's hand and tucked it into his belt. Picking up his tricorne, which had fallen onto their table, the gentleman nodded to John and turned on his heels. Quietly, he sauntered out of the gin palace.

Heathcliff's knees felt weak. He took a deep breath. His heart beat rapidly. He placed one fist on the table, and glanced nervously and suspiciously about.

"Now you have met our Mr. Worm," Agnes said.

John looked at Agnes. He nodded once.

"Your young gentleman passed our test," John said.

Heathcliff sat down, breathing deeply. He reached for his glass of gin and managed a wary smile.

Chapter 106

When the overture began, the King's Royal Theatre, Westminister, was packed to capacity. Before they took their seats in the balcony, Agnes told Heathcliff he would likely understand nothing of what transpired on stage, as the entire opera would be presented in Italian. Heathcliff looked down on the gentlemen strolling languidly before the front row of seats below, greeting the young ladies and moving like bees from flower to flower. But as the overture concluded, they all turned to face the stage.

A group of scantily-dressed sprites wearing white gossamer wings fluttered across the stage, looking behind them and singing perhaps of approaching danger.

To the sound of anxious violins, three *castrati* strutted to the centre of the stage in flowing Roman costumes, with golden laurel wreaths upon their heads. The three men sang with the odd high pure voices of very young boys, their voices weaving harmoniously together.

The larger of the three *castrati* stepped forward. As his companions quietly stepped back, he opened his arms and produced long lyrical bursts of sweet high song so sweet and tender he could have been a visiting angel. His solo elicited shouts and whistles from the audience, and considerable applause.

HEATHCLIFF: THE LOST YEARS

At a clash of cymbals, a red-coated king strutted onto the stage from behind a curtain, followed by a group of soldiers. At a word from the king, the soldiers grabbed the *castrato*, bound him in chains, and in a clash of cymbals and French horns sang him away.

At the first intermission, Agnes took Heathcliff to the lobby. Very discreetly, she pointed out a certain very relaxed gentleman who was dressed entirely in black.

A number of fey young gentlemen surrounded the man, many wearing oversized bouffant periwigs in the *macaroni* style. As the young men bantered and vied for his attention, the gentleman in black paid little heed.

The man leaned on a black walking-stick inlaid with diamonds. He seemed amused and comfortable in his skin. He was not old, but he had the deep-set, decadent eyes of a much older man. Heathcliff watched him light a fine little black cigar.

"That is Lord Score," Agnes whispered. "Observe him."

The handsome aristocrat was about Heathcliff's height, and he had a similar build. He had a fine, nearly Roman nose and his raven hair framed his face in artful curls. Heathcliff thought the man might have been Greek, with his dark skin, or from one of the Mediterranean countries, but his manners and finely-tailored garments shewed him to be quite a proper English gentleman.

Lord Score wore a very large diamond stickpin in his lapel. For an instant, when he moved beneath a chandelier, Heathcliff noticed the stickpin brighten to emit dazzling flashes of light.

"The gentleman is fond of diamonds," Heathcliff observed.

"Yes."

"He rather resembles me," Heathcliff added.

Agnes squeezed Heathcliff's arm. "Now you have it," she said. "Study the man. It is you who must become Lord Score."

The next day Agnes took Heathcliff to Savile Row, where a tailor fitted him with extraordinary new clothes. He purchased a fine wool frockcoat with death's head obsidian buttons, a black waistcoat and breeches, a fine white shirt to pull over his head, and a black silk scarf with matching gloves and silk stockings. The long black wool cape discreetly trimmed in red Agnes thought just right. At a cane-maker's shop, Agnes bought Heathcliff a fine new black walking-stick which she insisted he use on the way home.

Agnes soon led him to his sumptuous new quarters. As Heathcliff stood before a great mirror, Agnes showed him exactly how to hold himself like an aristocrat. He learned to lean lazily against his cane in the languid manner of Lord Score. Over the next few days, Agnes watched over him like a schoolmaster until he could enter and leave a room with studied elegance.

Agnes supplied him engraved calling cards on thick white paper. When he came to the door, Agnes shewed him how to pluck a slender silver carrying case from his breast pocket, take out his calling card just so, and place it onto a silver tray with practiced assurance.

Heathcliff met John three times a week for fencing lessons using both foil and heavy sabre. A crack swordsman, John taunted him all the while they fenced, which Heathcliff rather despised. Ignoring John's taunts, Heathcliff bore down and became ferocious. At last, Heathcliff became practiced enough to knock even the sabre from the older man's very skillful hands.

Once again, Agnes took Heathcliff to the King's Royal Theatre to observe the languid young aristocrat. At the second intermission, and pulling Heathcliff very close behind her, the Frenchwoman tripped and threw herself into the circle of gentleman and landed with both hands against the chest of a very surprised Lord Score.

Agnes let out a little squeal and threw up her hands, exclaiming rapidly in French. She slapped one of the bouffant young gentlemen and pulled Heathcliff outside and up the alley from the theatre, where a coach waited to spirit them away.

Their last night together, in Heathcliff's new quarters, the three of them again went over their plans. Heathcliff was to pose as Lord Score, a notorious fancier of diamonds. His task was to approach a secretive French jeweler and establish his serious intent.

HEATHCLIFF: THE LOST YEARS

The rest of the plan remained flexible, and dependent on a number of things. Heathcliff's role would require finesse, a bit of luck, daring, and rock-hard nerves.

Agnes longingly kissed him goodbye and left him alone. For some time, Heathcliff lay awake in his large bed, going over all he must do perfectly the next day.

When he fell asleep, he dreamed a coach pulled by six grey horses stopped before a line of tall, shape-shifting fir trees. In his fine black clothes, walking-stick in hand, Heathcliff hurried toward the coach. Suddenly his legs felt shackled, as if weighted down in heavy chains. Only with great effort did Heathcliff reach the black coach and pull open its door, which seemed to weigh a thousand pounds.

Agnes waited for him inside the coach, dressed entirely in black, her face covered in a long black veil. When Heathcliff plucked up the veil to kiss her, he met the hurt, haunted eyes of Catherine Earnshaw.

Chapter 107

Thick fog crept over the city. When Heathcliff climbed into the waiting coach, wearing his fine black clothes and cloak, he looked the equal of any aristocrat in London. He pulled his walking-stick against his leg as his coachman closed the door. Beneath the soft canvas top of the landau he removed his gloves, folded them as he had learned to do, and absent-mindedly fingered the large diamond stickpin in his lapel.

As the landau picked its way through Westminister, Heathcliff pulled his wool cloak around his shoulders. Outside, pedestrians moved like phantoms through the London fog.

The coach pulled up before No. 118 South Bank Lane, a brick building on the West End. A little too abruptly, the coachman pulled open the carriage door. Heathcliff took a deep breath, picked up his walking-stick, and stepped outside. Without glancing into the face of the coachman, he walked toward the entrance to the building.

The afternoon before, when they were alone, Heathcliff took Agnes into his arms for what felt like the last time, and softly caressed her.

"My beautiful wife," he said. "I shall miss your lovely breasts and every sweet intoxicating crevice of your body."

Agnes pushed him away. "Be a gentleman, Lord Score. You must remain a gentleman at all times."

"Agnes, I fear I will lose you."

"Are you *frightened?*" Agnes demanded, a note of fear in her voice. "Are you losing your nerve?"

Heathcliff smiled. He shook his head no. Agnes slipped her hands beneath his shirt and kissed his throat very tenderly, her lips moving to whisper into his ear.

"You are a perfect gentleman, Lord Score," Agnes whispered. "Your anger has put iron in your heart. If you are clever and bold, we shall have everything of which we dream."

Agnes pulled a large diamond stickpin from her satchel. Heathcliff recognized Lord Score's stickpin as she fastened it to his lapel.

At No. 118 South Bank Lane, Heathcliff lifted the door-knocker and tapped briskly. A squat, stooped-over servant opened the door and peered at him like a suspicious monkey.

"I wish to speak to Monsieur Finley," Heathcliff said.

"There is no such person here."

Heathcliff languidly pulled out his silver case and extracted a single calling card. Showing his teeth in a condescending smile, Heathcliff thrust his card into the hands of the stooped-over servant before him.

"I am Lord Score. I sent a letter before me. Monsieur Finley, if such a gentleman exists, might like to know of my presence right away since I do not enjoy standing in the cold and I shan't wait long."

The servant glanced out at the coach. He threw open the door and showed Heathcliff a chair. He picked up a small silver platter, placed the card upon the platter, and shuffled out of the room.

A short time later the man scurried back. Limping ahead, he led Heathcliff down a flight of stairs to a shop in the basement. The little shop smelled of cut metal, sawdust, and gunner's oil.

Under a hanging lamp, on the other side of a wooden workbench, Roland Finley wrinkled his small wide nose. He lifted one eye to meet the eyes of Heathcliff; in the other was his jeweler's *loupe*. Immediately the Frenchman released the *loupe* which tumbled to the end of a string tied around his neck.

Finley was a heavy-set Frenchman of medium height. He had a sensual mouth and cautious, deliberate eyes. A wooden case of rings lay open before him on the work-bench and loose stones and cutting tools were lying about.

"Lord Score," the jeweler flashed a grim French smile. "I would have known you in an instant. Your reputation precedes you. Permit me to introduce myself. I am Roland Finley."

"The pleasure is mine, sir. Let us dispose of formalities."

"Very well."

"I am hopelessly in love, sir. I have fallen in love with a Venetian countess who continues to taunt and bewitch me. I promised the lady a necklace of blue diamonds. The stones must be of the highest quality. The lady will have nothing else."

"Blue diamonds are extremely rare, Lord Score. Such diamonds are very small. As you may know, only a few have been set in necklaces. Blue diamonds are almost always found in rings."

"As I just told you, sir, I must have a necklace of fine blue diamonds, and I must have it quickly. I don't give a damn about the provenance, and I doubt that any Venetian will know or care, if you understand my meaning."

The jeweler slipped from behind his workbench. The Frenchman circled Heathcliff with a cautious, admiring glance. Heathcliff slouched against his walking-stick. Finley's eyes twinkled with curiosity as he reverently touched the diamond stickpin in Heathcliff's lapel. But he smiled a knowing smile, and shook his head.

"I am extremely honoured to make your acquaintance, Lord Score. But I am sorry. I do not believe I can help you to-day."

"The lady haunts my dreams, sir. For two weeks I have been unable to sleep peacefully. Frankly, it doesn't concern me how you find the necklace. I will pay your highest price," Heathcliff sniffed.

Finley smiled, but again shook his head no. Heathcliff took a step back.

"I know you only by reputation, Monsieur Finley, but I know your reputation," Heathcliff said. "You are shrewd, and you are discreet. I believe you might help me. Let me leave you with a small token of my sincerity."

Turning to the workbench, Heathcliff carefully moved aside the case of rings. He removed the diamond stickpin from his lapel and placed it in the centre of the wooden bench. He plucked up a mallet and drove the diamond into the wood with three short sharp slaps of the mallet.

The abruptness of this gesture left the jeweler holding his throat and unable to speak, like a great stammering frog.

"I have little time, sir," said Heathcliff. "I sail for Venice at the end of the month."

"What you ask is not customary, Lord Score," croaked the jeweler.

"These are not customary times."

With a grand sweep of his cape, Heathcliff turned to go.

"You have my card, Monsieur Finley," Heathcliff said. "I believe you know where you might find me."

Chapter 108

Heathcliff returned to his elegant suite of rooms on Westminster Road and awaited a response from Roland Finley. One day passed, and then another. His maid and private chef came and went. One afternoon, he opened the door to the sight of a diminutive young girl in a white dress, waiting quietly outside. The girl reached up and handed him a bouquet of crimson roses.

Tucked into the bouquet he found an envelope containing a note from Agnes Sorel.

My Dearest Husband,

I assume my part in our plan. You shall not know me when you see me again. May your heart remain hard as iron, and your courage burn like a great fire in your breast. I dearly miss you. Have patience, my darling husband, for we shall achieve all that we dream—

Your Loving Wife

The Frenchwoman's note touched his heart. Agnes had not often addressed him as her husband, nor had he ever heard Agnes call herself his wife.

HEATHCLIFF: THE LOST YEARS

The note on fine parchment, with its hint of Parisian perfume, rent open what felt like a fresh wound in his heart. The Frenchwoman's words placed a final stamp on all he determined to do.

Heathcliff tossed the note into the fireplace of his drawing-room and watched it burn. If the world was a place where men cheated and deceived one another for gain, as he now knew it to be, he intended to boldly step forward and claim his share of that world.

The next afternoon, a sealed note from Roland Finley requested the pleasure of Lord Score's company at ten o'clock the next day.

John Blighter waited by the carriage, clean-shaven and dressed in impeccable blue livery. When John opened the door to the coach, Heathcliff avoided his eyes and climbed inside. Heathcliff soon heard the hooves of the carriage-horses carrying him across the city.

Distant church bells rang out ten o'clock as the coach pulled up before No. 118 South Park Lane.

Roland Finley waited grimly outside the building, wrapped in a long brown wool cloak. The jeweler removed his hat, immediately waved away the coachman, and pulled open the coach door himself. He climbed inside and closed the door. The landau pulled away.

"I have found a necklace that may please your Venetian countess, Lord Score," the Frenchman sniffed. "I can guarantee the diamonds are the absolute finest that can be had, but the price is extremely high."

"I don't give a damn about price, sir."

"The owner will sell the necklace for fifty thousand pounds, and not a penny less. The seller must be paid in full, paid immediately, and paid entirely in gold. If you can meet the terms, we must proceed only in absolute secrecy."

"Why secrecy, sir?"

"The seller does not wish the sale to be known, Lord Score. It is a very delicate matter. You will certainly understand when you know the particulars."

"I don't give a damn about the particulars," Heathcliff said. "I have little time. Let me examine the necklace."

"The owner will not part with the necklace for a minute, Lord Score, not even for me."

"Then arrange for me to view it, sir. I will buy nothing I have not personally inspected."

"How much time would you need to amass the gold, Lord Score?" the Frenchman sniffed, looking out the window. "Fifty thousand pounds is a large amount."

"I need three days," Heathcliff said. "But quickly, sir, as I said, let us be on with it."

"Very well," sniffed the Frenchman. "You shall hear from me on Friday."

When the carriage stopped at No. 118 South Park Lane, Monsieur Roland Finley leaped out and waved away the coachman. Without looking back, he hurried into the building as the coach pulled away.

Chapter 109

Drizzling rain fell on the rooftops of London. Late Friday afternoon, Roland Finley again waited outside No. 118 South Park Lane, holding a large black umbrella. Waving away the coachman, Finley pulled open the door to the coach, and impatiently stuck his head inside.

"You did bring the gold, as I requested, Lord Score?" he snarled, without getting in.

Heathcliff lifted a fine leather satchel filled with bricks. He patted the satchel as if it were a thing of great value, and set it down again.

"I wish to see the gold," Finley said.

"First, I wish to see the necklace," Heathcliff replied.

Roland Finley reached up and handed John a piece of paper. "Take us to this address," he said.

Finley climbed inside, watched John close the door, and set aside his wet umbrella.

"We shall have no trouble to-day, I assure you," Finley said. He showed Heathcliff a French Cavalry pistol tucked inside his greatcoat.

At the snap of the coach-whip, their carriage clattered away through drizzling rain.

Sometime later, the coach slowed down before a mansion on the West End. The building's long impressive marble façade fronted an entire block. Heathcliff looked outside.

Blocking the entrance was a glowering English soldier, with one hand on the hilt of his sword. Heathcliff saw a large red cross painted on the front door and the sign, MILITARY HOSPITAL.

The coach stopped. The Frenchman handed Heathcliff a cloth medical mask and gestured for him to put it over his face.

"What the blazes is this, sir?" Heathcliff demanded.

"Put on your mask, Lord Score. I will speak for us both," Finley said. "Please, bring along your satchel."

Heathcliff caught Finley's arm. He glared at the jeweler.

"You bring me to a military hospital, sir?" Heathcliff hissed. "Why?"

"You must trust me, Lord Score," the jeweler whispered through his mask, and patted Heathcliff's arm. "Things are not as they seem."

Together they approached the entrance to the mansion where the glowering young sentry drew his sword and barred their way.

"You cannot enter, gentlemen. This is a military hospital. Upstairs, a gentleman is in quarantine."

Finley pulled down his mask and snarled.

"I am aware of this quarantine, soldier. I am Doctor Finley. You have seen me before. We are here to visit the patient upstairs, the Frenchman with smallpox. We will not be long. We wish to leave our coach here at the door."

The Frenchman betrayed no emotion as he stared down the soldier. The red-coated sentry reluctantly sheathed his weapon, stepped aside, and pulled open the front door.

The lower floor of the mansion smelled of wounded flesh. Sick and bandaged English officers lay in the parlour on cots. At the foot of the stairway, a second sentry barred the way but Finley again pulled down his mask and snarled out his intention to visit the French gentleman in quarantine upstairs. The soldier stepped aside to let them pass.

At the top of the stairs was a door marked "Quarantine." Finley pulled down his medical mask and knocked three times.

Agnes Sorel opened the door. She wore a black and white maid's uniform. She stared at Heathcliff without recognition. Agnes put her head down, and bowed a servile curtsey.

"*Bonjour,*" she said.

"Good day, mademoiselle," said the jeweler, speaking in French. "We have come to see the patient. The patient is surely not asleep?"

"The patient did not sleep well," Agnes replied in French. "To-day, I am permitted to admit no one."

"Please present my card. I await the patient's response," said the jeweler.

Finley tossed a calling card onto the silver tray. Heathcliff set down the satchel for a moment and placed his calling card next to Finley's. Heathcliff did not look at Agnes as she hurried away.

Agnes returned and said, "This way, sir."

They followed Agnes through several doorways and, after three gentle knocks on the door, entered an enormous bedroom that smelled of rosewater. Heathcliff glanced at the large casement window on the far wall which overlooked the street. The window was closed.

A middle-aged Frenchwoman lay on an embroidered canopy bed, propped up with a mountain of pillows. The Frenchwoman did not appear to be ill, but she seemed agitated. The Duchess of Burgundy placed the back of her hand on her brow and addressed the jeweler in French.

"Life is difficult for me in this horrible country, Roland," she said, in a high nasal voice.

"To elude the hangman was difficult, but to remain here day after day is the greatest trial of all. I feel I am in prison. I am forever hungry. I abhor the dreadful English cuisine. I must return home."

"I have found a way for the Duchess to acquire the gold she needs to return to France," Finley began.

Agnes came in bearing a platter of purple grapes and placed it on an end table next to the bed. The Duchess of Burgundy plucked off a grape, examined it critically, and dropped it into her mouth.

Roland Finley pulled Heathcliff down onto a rust-coloured damask love seat not far from the bed. Two beeswax candles burned atop a low table before them, which was inlaid with wood and ivory.

Agnes walked to the casement windows. Nonchalantly, she tried to pull the windows open, but could not.

"Someone has locked our windows," she said in English, without looking at Heathcliff.

"Luckily for this nation of dogs, I found a sick Frenchwoman who resembled me to send to the hangman. I promised to support her six miserable children, and provided for them with all the money I had," snarled the Duchess, who suddenly began speaking English. "But now the joke is on me, Roland. I have no gold to pay off the authorities, and of course they want gold."

"I bring good news for my beautiful Duchess. The Duchess may sell a particular necklace to-day and escape from this isle of dogs. You may have all the gold you need to facilitate your escape," said the jeweler.

"The necklace is cursed!" The Duchess vaulted from her bed in a long white silk chemise. "Queen Charlotte gave the necklace to me! Then she told the king I stole it! The necklace is all I have left!"

"The English queen was unfair. And for the Duchess to suffer the humiliation of the gallows, if even by proxy," Finley cooed, shaking his head and looking down as if with great sadness. "But as you admit, my dearest Duchess, your situation is perilous here. Fortunately, you can sell the necklace."

"Who is this man?" the Duchess suddenly demanded.

"A very discreet English nobleman, as I told you before. He seeks a necklace of fine blue diamonds, and he will have nothing else," Finley began.

"As I suggested, this gentleman wishes to purchase the necklace. I quoted him a price of fifty thousand pounds in gold, and he has brought it," Finley sniffed, nodding significantly at Heathcliff.

"I do not wish to sell my necklace to-day, or any other day," said the Duchess. "Never! I will not sell it."

Roland Finley leaned forward, sniffing earnestly.

"My dearest Duchess, do you not need gold to bribe your way out of England? Surely you do not think you can regain the good graces of Queen Charlotte? Or King George III, who callously sentenced you to the gallows? Do you believe you have unlimited time, in this precarious situation?"

"As I prepared to depart, the English appropriated this building for a military hospital!" she hissed, addressing Heathcliff. "Without warning, they seized everything! Only my French physician could keep them away, by declaring the upstairs in quarantine. But now I am a prisoner. My enemies prowl beneath me like wolves! How much longer can I endure this cruel parody of life? No, of course, Roland, you are right. I must return to France, and right away!"

The Duchess of Burgundy slipped into a pair of Arabian slippers next to the bed. She pulled on a long, embroidered Turkish robe over her chemise. She clapped her hands two times.

"Marie," she said in French. "Fetch the silver casket I keep in the *armoire*."

The Duchess sat down in a chair near the table. She lay the back of her right hand against her brow and leaned back with a plaintive sigh. Finley nodded and winked at Heathcliff.

Agnes Sorel hurried into the room carrying an artfully-engraved silver casket inlaid with rubies and pearls. The Duchess plucked the jewel case from her hands and placed it on the table between the two burning candles.

The Duchess paused for a moment. She took a deep breath and opened the jewel case.

When she lifted up the necklace, the string of pale blue diamonds lit up with tiny prisms sparkling in the candle-light.

"My poisoned gift," said the Duchess, cradling the necklace against her cheek with both hands. "It is so beautiful I still do not wish to part with it."

Heathcliff stood up and extended his hand.

"I must inspect the necklace, Mr. Finley."

Roland Finley tugged at his arm.

"Sit down. You must show the Duchess your gold, Lord Score."

Heathcliff bent down to pick up the satchel. He dropped it into Finley's lap.

Agnes plucked the necklace from the hands of the Duchess and passed it to Heathcliff, who stuffed it into his waistcoat.

"*Mon Dieu!*" the Duchess gasped.

"Lord Score!" cried the jeweler.

Heathcliff ran for the casement window.

"Heathcliff! A pistol!"

From the corner of his eye, Heathcliff saw Agnes run to embrace the jeweler. A shot rang out. Clutching her bosom, Agnes reeled away.

With his elbow before his face, Heathcliff leaped through the casement window in an explosion of wood and broken glass.

He tumbled onto the canvas roof of the waiting coach, which broke his fall. He rolled off the roof onto the cobblestones and bounced to his feet. The soldier at the door drew his sword.

"Lord Score!"

From the box of the coach, John tossed down a broadsword.

Heathcliff turned in time to parry a downward slash. He countered with a riposte.

While they fought, Agnes pushed open the front door, one hand on the doorknob, teetering and threatening to fall.

"The Duchess of Burgundy lives!" Agnes shouted behind her. "The enemy of your king is upstairs, in this very building!"

Pressing one hand to her chest, Agnes staggered out of the mansion into the drizzling rain. She tripped over the guard, who lay wheezing on the porch at Heathcliff's feet.

"Lord Score!" Agnes fell to the ground.

Heathcliff pulled Agnes to her feet. He picked her up and carried her to the coach. The coach-whip cracked as he got her inside and the carriage jerked away.

Hugging Agnes to his chest, Heathcliff heard the sounds of gunfire. His heart pounded like a mad African drum.

Chapter 110

The landau sped through the darkness. The wheels of the carriage clattered and bumped along the wet cobblestones and rain fizzled into the coach through broken windows.

Heathcliff sheltered Agnes from the rain with his cloak. With his monogrammed handkerchief, he wiped the rain from her face.

Agnes bared her teeth and groaned. She arched her back and clutched the front of her uniform with her right hand, as if to squeeze shut her bleeding heart. Heathcliff placed one hand over hers and felt warm blood stick to his fingers.

"Agnes! We must take you to a doctor!" he said.

Agnes shook her head no. She pulled away his handkerchief and squeezed it in one hand.

"There is no time. We must go to the carriage-house ... as we planned."

Agnes wiped her face with the handkerchief, and glanced up into Heathcliff's eyes. When she returned the handkerchief, it was streaked with blood.

"You are wounded—we must find you a doctor."

"Not yet," Agnes whispered.

HEATHCLIFF: THE LOST YEARS

Heathcliff crumpled the wet handkerchief in his fist. He feared his heart would burst. He desperately wished to help Agnes but she would not allow him to help her.

He kissed her fingers, which smelled faintly of rosewater. He saw creases of pain around her beautiful mouth. Her haunted hazel eyes met his own, conveying a sadness he had never seen in them before.

"Agnes! You cannot die! You are my wife! I love you!" he angrily whispered, seeking to will her injury away.

"Do you?" she asked.

Agnes shook her head and looked out the window into the street. "I have known too many," she whispered, and her voice trailed away.

His heart sank like a stone in his chest. "Agnes!" he said.

Agnes stared out the window. She would not meet his eyes. He felt his old anger storming up inside him, but he controlled it, as she taught him to do.

"There is a dagger in my heart. But I will bear it, I will bear the pain," she gasped, and closed her eyes.

A single tear trickled down her cheek. Agnes wiped away the tear with the back of her fist and managed a brave smile.

With great difficulty, from the top of her maid's uniform, Agnes extracted a bloody piece of paper and pressed it into Heathcliff's hand.

"This is where you rendezvous with Worm. Be wary of John. If necessary, go alone," she whispered, coughing and clutching her chest.

"Agnes—you must not die!" Heathcliff blurted, feeling tears spill from his eyes. "We shall find a doctor! We shall build a grand estate in the country, as we planned to do."

"I do not think I will see your grand estate," Agnes whispered.

At that moment, Heathcliff realized his beautiful wife was going to die.

"All I sought has eluded me," Agnes whispered. "The world has forced me to live only by my wits."

Her small blood-stained hand fell into her lap. Her head dropped loosely to one side.

The landau thundered into the carriage-house and John Blighter with some apparent difficulty pulled up their team.

Chapter 111

Heathcliff was clutching the Frenchwoman's body when John pulled open the door to the coach. John pushed Heathcliff roughly aside, took off his cap, and peered into the eyes of the corpse.

"The little bitch is dead." He pulled at Heathcliff's arm. "We must leave her."

"We cannot leave her here!" Heathcliff hissed, with fresh tears in his eyes.

"Get out!" Blighter pulled Heathcliff from the coach. "A man will come for the carriage. Everything is arranged."

Heathcliff grabbed the umbrella. John pulled a carriage-lamp from the front of the landau and led them from the empty coach-house out into the rain.

By the light of the lantern, Heathcliff noticed a bloody gash on his left hand where he was struck by the sabre. When he moved his fingers, and opened the umbrella, he felt prickles of pain.

"Did the little bitch give you the address?"

"I have it here."

"Where is the paper? The bitch kept it from me."

"Control your tongue," Heathcliff snapped. "Agnes was my wife."

"She was my wife too," John said. "You don't think we're the only ones, do you? She had a string of them."

Heathcliff pulled out the blood-stained piece of paper, carefully unfolded it, and read it aloud.

"That's just ahead," John said, snatching away the paper. "Follow me."

They walked together. They moved to the side while a horse and carriage splashed past, its wheels kicking up ribbons of dirty water. Heathcliff heard a distant bell tolling the hour, its peals softened by the rain.

John paused before an ornate three-story building. He lifted the lantern and double-checked the address.

The lower floor of the building was dark but lamps flickered on both sides of the front door. Heathcliff saw golden light in the second story windows.

"Give me the necklace. You wait here," John growled, holding out his hand.

"We go in together, as we planned," Heathcliff said.

"Give me the bloody necklace. Don't make me take it from you."

"Go to Hell," Heathcliff said.

As John threw down the lantern, his knife blade glinted in the light. Heathcliff brought down the umbrella between them, like a black axe. John's knife blade burst through the umbrella, missing Heathcliff's face.

As if using a foil, Heathcliff thrust the point of the umbrella in the direction of John's face. John cried out like an angry bull. Heathcliff caught his wrist and pulled his arm through the torn umbrella, his hand still clutching the knife.

They turned and grappled in the rain, whirling clumsily, with the remains of the umbrella flapping between them.

HEATHCLIFF: THE LOST YEARS

Heathcliff strained to twist away the knife as he fell back onto the cobblestones. John fell on top of him, his chest pierced with the blade of his upturned knife.

Heathcliff stood up. John writhed on the cobblestones. Blinking and gasping, John moaned but did not cry out.

"You tried to kill me," Heathcliff said.

Heathcliff staggered to the front door, breathing hard. A uniformed butler quietly opened the door, silver tray in hand. Heathcliff fumbled for a calling card, found one smudged with blood, and placed it upon the tray.

"We have been awaiting your arrival, Lord Score," the butler chirped, glancing approvingly at his card. "Do follow me."

Heathcliff followed the butler up a winding marble staircase and into an upstairs drawing-room. In a wing-backed chair facing the fire, a man he couldn't see sipped a glass of wine. On a satinwood tea-table next to the man's chair was a crystal decanter of red wine, and three empty wine glasses.

Mr. Worm leaned sideways in his chair. He looked back over his shoulder, and gave Heathcliff a wicked grin. Heathcliff recalled the rictus smile and the test of nerves that now seemed two lifetimes away. Without getting up, the tall man extended his hand.

"Lord Score, I presume," he smiled. He gestured for Heathcliff to sit down. "I see you came alone."

Mr. Worm poured another glass of red wine, set down the decanter, and graciously handed Heathcliff the glass. The butler quietly plucked up the two empty glasses and slipped from the room.

"You brought the necklace, of course," said Mr. Worm.

Heathcliff sipped the thick, rich burgundy. He took a deep breath and savoured the wine, trying to clear his mind. Too many things had happened too quickly. He could not quite process it all.

"You must give me the necklace, sir," said Mr. Worm, again.

Heathcliff set down his glass. He extracted the diamond necklace from his waistcoat and held up the necklace between them.

+ [380] +

The string of gems seemed to catch fire, filling the room with a hundred tiny rainbows of dazzling light. For the first time, Heathcliff appreciated the necklace's exquisite beauty. He thought it the most beautiful thing he had ever seen.

Mr. Worm plucked the necklace from his hands, and lay it down on the tea table between them. The tall man cradled his wineglass in his hands and stared for a moment into the fire.

"King George III and Queen Charlotte are immensely grateful to you, sir," said Mr. Worm.

"I beg your pardon?"

"Our sovereign is grateful for all you have done. He will never meet you or see you, sir, but be assured he is grateful. This affair was quite distressing to the queen. We could devise no better way to find the necklace, and to have it discreetly retrieved."

"This was not our agreement," Heathcliff said.

"The necklace was and is the property of the Queen of England," said Mr. Worm. "I do not have the authority to buy it. The necklace must be returned. However, since things turned out as I hoped, I do have something of value for you, Lord Score."

He placed the diamond stickpin in Heathcliff's hand.

"Lord Score has long since replaced this, of course, although this particular diamond is valuable. It is an extraordinary yellow diamond, you see, from the heart of Africa," said Mr. Worm. "Your wife plucked it from Lord Score's lapel."

"Yes," Heathcliff admitted. At the mention of Agnes, Heathcliff felt a great moaning stab of anger, longing, and regret.

Heathcliff gulped down the remainder of his wine and examined the diamond stickpin. A bitter aftertaste of wine remained in his mouth.

"The diamond is a personal gift to you, from us, sir. And along with this gift, I shall give you a bit of advice," said Mr. Worm.

Before he continued, he strode to the hearth and pulled on a sash to summon his man.

HEATHCLIFF: THE LOST YEARS

"You must sell the diamond quickly. You will then become the wealthy gentleman that you now only pretend to be. Take your money and get out of London. Go back from whence you came. Pursue the thing you desire most. A man can do no better than that."

Mr. Worm's butler walked up the stairs, followed by four uniformed soldiers. The soldiers escorted Heathcliff down the stairs and the butler respectfully showed him the door.

A single street-lamp flickered above the empty street. Wrapping his cloak about his shoulders, Heathcliff walked away in the drizzling rain.

He had been betrayed again, but his fortune was made. He knew his heart would harden over these fresh new wounds, as it had learned to do. For as long as he lived, he would keep iron in his heart.

He yearned to depart from London. The metropolis had nothing more to hold him.

In the profound loneliness that flooded over him like the sea, Heathcliff longed for his first love, whose memory had haunted him for years. His heart jumped into his throat at the thought of seeing Catherine. How he yearned for a glimpse of her face, the sound of her voice, or merely the touch of her hand. He might settle his old score with Hindley. He might book passage on a ship to Bristol, and then travel inland. Perhaps he would purchase a grand carriage, and ride triumphantly across England. An eternity ago, Heathcliff realized, he had left a great many things unfinished at Wuthering Heights.

THE END

ABOUT THE AUTHOR

David Drum is the author or co-author of seven nonfiction books, several artist's books, the novel *Introducing the Richest Family in America*, and *Facade*, a collection of poetry. The author of *Heathcliff: The Lost Years* has worked as a newspaper reporter, a Hollywood prop assistant, a ranch foreman, a craps dealer, an encyclopedia salesman, a funeral director, a hot tamale vendor, and an inner-city schoolteacher. He has been fascinated by *Wuthering Heights* and the character of Heathcliff for more than thirty years.

Mr. Drum received an MFA from the University of Iowa's Writers Workshop. He currently resides in Los Angeles.

www.daviddrumthewriter.com

ACKNOWLEDGEMENTS

The author wishes to thank a few special people for their help and assistance over the five years it took to complete this book. My good friend, the novelist Jane DeLynn, was kind enough to read earlier versions of this manuscript, and offer spot-on suggestions, one of which was incorporated into the book's title. My longtime coffee compadre and good friend, the biographer Jon Krampner, has been uniquely supportive of my efforts as a writer for many years. Lynnie Westafer, another writer, offered feedback on two earlier chapters. Charlie McElfresh provided a good bit of nautical advice. The author's first creative writing teacher, the poet Lewis Miles, stressed the importance of writing clear, clean sentences and I remain grateful for his encouragement. Most especially, the author extends his most heartfelt gratitude to Emily Bronte, whose short life produced the extraordinary masterpiece, *Wuthering Heights*, which inspired this book.

CPSIA information can be obtained
at www.ICGtesting.com
Printed in the USA
LVHW031122141019
634125LV00001B/86/P